All the Gates of Hell

Richard Parks

ISBN-13: 978-1492993261

ISBN-10: 1492993263

DEDICATION

This book is dedicated to the memory of author and friend K.D. Wentworth, who left us much too soon.

CONTENTS

ACKNOWLEDGMENTS

Sections of Chapter 5 were published as "The White Bone Fan" in **Japanese Dreams: Fantasies, Fictions & Fairytales**, edited by Sean Wallace. © Lethe Press, 2009.

CHAPTER 1

On the morning of Jin Lee Hannigan's apotheosis she sat in her cubicle looking over one more in a seemingly endless stack of client's eviction notices when her boss, Joyce Masters, peered out the window for the third time in as many minutes.

"Your stalker is back," she said.

Jin didn't even glance up from the forms. "You mean Teacher?"

Joyce gave her a look. "I don't mean Gandhi." She was a zaftig black woman with a military-looking buzz cut, forty-something, and not currently in the mood for nonsense. Then again, Jin couldn't remember a time Joyce had *ever* been in the mood for nonsense. The attitude tended to go hand in hand with Joyce's duties as director of the Pepper Street Legal Aid office.

Jin yawned and stretched. She brushed her hair out of her eyes and glanced toward the window. She saw Teacher Johnson standing on the corner by the florist shop. There was a young man in a leather jacket just beyond that, leaning in the entrance to an alley. "That's Teacher, Joyce. You know him," she said. "But who's that other guy looking this way?"

"What other guy?"

Jin looked, but the young man was gone. She shrugged. "Don't see him now. Anyway, we're talking about Teacher here. He's harmless. Been hanging around downtown for years. You know that."

"That's why I'm worried--I've noticed something different about him lately. He's *watching* you. He never did that before."

"Have you taken a good look at the poor guy? I could break him in half if he tried anything."

Joyce glanced toward heaven. "Oh, to be young and ignorant and have that 'never gonna die' feeling again. Just be careful, ok? I'd consider it a personal favor."

Jin smiled. "Yeth, Mommy."

"So. You going to see Jeff tonight?"

Jin sighed. "Not tonight or any other night. We broke up."

"Oh," said Joyce. "I'm sorry."

Jin just shrugged. "He wanted to sleep with me. I wanted him to not want that. Neither of our needs was being met."

Joyce just shook her head. "For someone who is both straight and as cute as a china doll, you got some strange attitudes about men. Or maybe you're just having a streak of bad luck. Jeff was...what? The third one this year?"

"Yes, and thanks so much for reminding me of the sorry state of my love life," Jin smiled wistfully as she turned her attention back to the eviction notices. Later that afternoon she checked her email to find this note from her mother:

SUBJECT: THE FORCES OF EVIL

Lotus Blossom:

I'm going to India for a week with my new boyfriend. Or maybe a year. We're going to stop the violence, or try to. And, by the way, you were too good for Jeff in the first place. Even if he was a cutie.

Love Ya,
XXOO Mom

At first Jin could only think, what new boyfriend? She finally sighed. There had never been much point in worrying about her mother, Kathleen Margaret Hannigan. Just because there was no point to worrying didn't mean Jin wouldn't, of course, but there really was no point -- her mom did what she was going to do, always had, and always would so long as she drew breath.

Joyce stopped by Jin's desk again. "Haven't seen your shadow all afternoon. I guess that's good."

Jin shrugged. "Maybe he had other plans," Jin said. "You know: 9AM stalk Jin Lee Hannigan, 10AM drown kittens, 2PM plot violent overthrow of orphanage, 4PM beat up puppy?"

Joyce started to say something, but finally just shook her head, looking mildly annoyed. The waiting room was full up today and there wasn't much time, apparently, for nagging. Jin was almost grateful, but not quite. She glanced at her inbox and sighed gustily. The mountain never seemed to get any smaller. When she looked up again Joyce was standing at her desk and it was almost half past six.

"Sorry we were so late today. I've got a meeting of my tenant association in fifteen minutes. Can you lock up?"

"Sure."

Just before she disappeared out the door, Joyce frowned. "He's still not there."

Jin didn't have to ask who she meant. She took a moment to glance out the door herself before she went to wash out her coffee cup and fetch her jacket. The curb by the florist's shop was empty, and the florist shop itself was already closed. This late in the day, most of Pepper street would already be shut down for the night.

Jin couldn't get the thought out of her mind -- Teacher Johnson was supposed to be on that corner from around four-thirty to seven o'clock. You could almost set your watch by it; he was always there when he was supposed to be there. Only now he wasn't. It was simply wrong; there was a rhythm, an ebb and flow to life on Pepper Street. Jin had come to think of the area downtown as home, and something in her home wasn't right. She had a sudden image of Teacher lying broken and bleeding in some dark place, and she shivered.

"It's nothing," she said aloud, and to no one in particular. The evening was getting chilly; fall was in the air. Jin shut the door of the Legal Aid office behind her and listened for the click of the lock. Then she stuck her hands in the pockets of her jacket and started up Pepper Street. Every now and then she heard a faint whisper, like the multitude of whispers she'd imagined hearing for the last few days. But this one was different.

"Help..."

Jin stopped. This sound wasn't just in her head; it was an actual sound and it came out of the alley by the florist. "Teacher, is that you?"

"I-I'm hurt bad. Please help me..."

Jin looked into the darkness of the alley. "In there? How stupid do you think I am?"

There was no answer. Jin reached for her cell phone before she remembered that it was at home, recharging in its cradle, right where she left it. She looked around. No one was about. The door to the Legal Aid office locked when she closed it, and Jin's key was on the same ring as her car keys, likewise at home because she didn't need them. The one pay phone was three blocks away and didn't work anyway.

The safe, smart and logical thing to do would be to head for home and call for help from there. Only doing the smart thing could mean that Teacher bled to death before anyone got there. Assuming, of course, that he was telling the truth. Jin groaned. "Ohhhh...how stupid am I?"

She went to the entrance to the alley and looked more closely, but still could see nothing. "Teacher, I swear if this is some trick I'll break your scrawny neck!"

"Help..."

Teacher's voice was weaker; she could barely hear him. Jin just shook her head. "I'm this stupid, obviously."

Jin entered the alley. The sun had already set and the buildings blocked most of what light remained. Jin waited a few moments for her eyes to adjust to the gloom before she went any farther.

"Where are you?"

"...here..."

Either Teacher was barely alive or he was further away than Jin thought at first. Fortunately there weren't any cubbyholes for an attacker to hide in. There was a side door to the florist's shop but it was padlocked and reinforced with steel; no one was hiding there. Jin slowly moved down the alley but, even after her eyes adjusted, there was little more than gloom for a while. Then ahead of her the passage began to lighten a bit. It was a strange, flickering sort of light, like torches. Jin stopped. Something was definitely wrong. She turned around and faced a stone wall.

What the hell...?

The alley going back to Pepper Street was totally blocked by a wall of large granite blocks, more appropriate to a moldering castle or ancient city wall than an alleyway. When Jin looked carefully to either side there was no brick visible, just more plain stone blocks, up to a height of about ten feet. Above that, spaced at regular intervals for the short distance she could see, there were niches carved into the stone. A figure was carved into each niche in bas relief. In the poor light Jin couldn't quite make out their features and, the harder she tried, the more she realized that, perhaps, she really didn't want to. She got an impression of weapons, distorted bodies, fangs and fire.

Jin knew she had seen something like it before, and it took her a few moments to realize that the carvings had at least a passing resemblance to a type she had seen carved into a Buddhist temple she had once visited with her mother, when Kathleen was going on one of her periodic "try this other religion for a while now" phases. Yet Jin was pretty sure there had been no temple down that alley when she'd passed it that morning. It simply wasn't possible that this place was here now. Yet here it was, and here she was and, apparently, wasn't leaving the way she came. She reached out and touched the stone. It felt cold and hard beneath her fingers, and very real.

"Well, Teacher, I can't go back. I guess I'll go on."

There was no answer, no more faint voice calling out to her. There was just cold stone, and darkness, with that one flickering promise of light ahead. Jin headed in that direction.

It occurred to Jin as she walked that she was taking the strangeness of the situation with remarkable calm. She wondered if this was a good thing, or a sign that she was simply numb with shock and the hysterics and collapse would soon follow. She shrugged. She didn't feel particularly hysterical, or wobbly in the knees, or anything that suggested a crash was imminent. Rather, there was a sense of *inevitability* about being trapped in a strange stone passage in what had appeared, in all the years she had known the place, simply a back alley off Pepper Street in the city of Medias, Mississippi. She couldn't explain the feeling, but she clung to it. For all she knew, this delusion was all that was keeping hysteria at bay.

The passage ended abruptly at a thick wooden door, now slightly ajar. Jin pushed it open and, in that moment, wondered if delusion would be enough.

Jin stood at the entrance to a vast cavern, so tall she could not see the ceiling, so wide that it was hard to see clearly from one end to the other. The air in the cavern was cool, and smelled of sandalwood and smoke. Flanking the doorway on either side were two massive stone figures. One was a demonic-looking creature holding a club, the other a fierce armored figure that was possibly intended to be human, but its features and posture were so distorted that it seemed like something out of nightmare. It wielded a sword at least twenty feet long. Amazing as these figures were, they were only able to hold her attention for a moment, for beyond them she saw something even more astonishing.

In the center of the cavern was a raised dais at least sixty feet across, and in the center of that were a group of three statues. The ones on either side of the main figure were easily ten feet high, one male and one female, but it was hard to tell much else about them. Between them stood a female figure taller even than the guardians at the entrance. She stood on what Jin recognized as an open lotus blossom, similar to the one tattooed on Jin's upper arm; she bore a vessel that looked like an old-fashioned sake' bottle cradled in her left arm, and her right hand was raised in a sign of blessing. All three of the statues shone like gold, and before them smoke rose from iron braziers.

"Holy...."

"Got it in one, Jin," someone shouted.

Teacher Johnson stood just in front of the dais between two smoking braziers taller than he was, grinning like a Cheshire cat, especially such a cat who has just eaten or is about to eat your favorite parakeet. Jin turned around only to confront a solidly closed door.

"You can't go back that way, Jin. Not yet."

"Where am I?"

"Now she asks. Did you seek to satisfy your curiosity first? No. Your first instinct was to run. I find that very interesting."

"I was lured into some sort of weird cave by an obvious deranged man! Of course I tried to run!"

Teacher sighed. "That's one way to spin it. Another is that you ran because you know exactly where you are, and who I am."

"Look, I don't know what game you're playing B "

Teacher's smile went away. "Oh, for... Are you still pretending you don't remember? Really, Jin, this is very annoying."

Jin's hands balled into fists. "You pretend to be sick or hurt and lure me into the middle of heaven knows what, and *you're* annoyed? Tell me where I am and what's going on right now or I'll show you what annoyed means, Teacher."

"Come over and we'll discuss it."

Teacher waited for her while Jin made her way down. There was a very slight incline toward the center of the cavern, which Jin hadn't noticed at first because the height of the statues made almost everything look "up." The ground was sand embedded with rocks and loose stones. She almost slipped once or twice but finally made it down to where Teacher stood between the braziers.

"Now then," Teacher said, "what's going on is a little complicated and you're obviously a little confused by that physical body you're wearing, so let's stick with the basics for now: You are at the Gateway of all the Hells."

Teacher had barely finished speaking when Jin took one step forward and struck him hard in the jaw. He staggered and fell back against the dais. There was a trickle of blood from his mouth and he wiped his jaw, slowly, but if he was angry he didn't show it. Rather he looked like a patient father who wasn't really sure how much longer his patience was going to last. Jin, for her part was a little stunned. When her fist had connected with Teacher's jaw and just for that instant she'd had a vision of a deep red boiling ocean. It looked like blood.

"Really, Jin," he said. "Is that any way for a goddess to behave?"

"Goddess!?" Jin took a deep breath. "Teacher, I've had just about enough of your bullshit. You will tell me where I am and what's going on right now or so help me I'll beat the living shit out of you!"

Teacher just sighed. "The answer is behind you, if you really want it."

Jin glanced behind her, intending to do no more than that as she kept most of her attention on Teacher. "No tricks...oh, crap."

She saw the vast circumference of the cavern, marked at intervals by doors identical to the once-open one she had come through. There were hundreds, possibly thousands.

"You asked where you were and I told you-- the Gateway to All the Hells."

Jin glared at him. "Stop it! How are you doing this, anyway? Are you some sort of magician?!"

He spat blood. "Don't be ridiculous, Jin -- of course I'm no magician. I'm the King of the First Hell."

Teacher stood up in one fluid motion, and in that instant he seemed to tower over Jin, despite the fact that he was only an inch or two taller than she was at best. He was surrounded by an aura of flames and, though Jin could not feel any heat, she still staggered back.

"You're the Devil...?"

He looked disgusted. "Oh, for pity's sake. Jin, if you could get your head out of this dualistic universe for a second you'd know very well that we don't have *a* devil. We have millions. And no, I'm not one. I'm the King of the First Hell, as I said. Now, are you going to stop pretending you don't know me or do you want to take another swing? Suit yourself, but I warn you--only the first poke is free."

Jin just stared at him, for many long moments. She finally relaxed her hands and let her arms drop down to her sides. She kept her eyes straight on Teacher. "Look. Just tell me what it is you want so I can get out of here."

Teacher's puzzled expression slowly gave way to a look of honest surprise. "You're not pretending, are you? You really don't know?"

"Listen to me very carefully, Teacher: I have no idea who the "King of the First Hell" is, I've never seen this *place* before, and I don't like it one bit. It's creepy and the smoke from that incense or whatever is making my eyes water. I want to go home."

"All right," Teacher said.

Jin blinked. "You're going to let me go?"

"I don't have a choice, Jin. No one can bar any door against you for very long, and that includes me. Even so, a part of you knows that I'm telling the truth, and sooner or later you will remember. Whether you do it here or back in Medias makes no difference to me."

"I'm no goddess! I'm Jin Lee Hannigan. I've lived in Medias most of my life and you've known me for years!"

"The one doesn't change the other. I wasn't sure at first, but when you smacked me with that hard little fist of yours you saw something, didn't you? So did I. Your contact with me generated a vision. That's an attribute of a bodhisatva."

Jin had a little more idea of what he was talking about now. She had heard of the bodhisattvas through her mother. She at least knew what spiritual corner of the cosmos Teacher was talking about.

"Dammit, how can I be a *bodhisattva*? I'm not even Buddhist!"

Teacher shrugged. "What has that to do with anything? You are what you are. You have a job to do. A job, I might point out, that you've been slacking on for the past couple of centuries."

"Job? I work at the Legal Aid office. You know that. And what's this 'centuries' nonsense? I'm only twenty!"

"Your fleshly incarnation may be twenty but the real you inside is a *lot* older than that. And I'm talking about your actual job. As the mortal incarnation of a goddess -- ok, technically a *bodhisattva* -- you have many attributes but only one real power. That power brings obligation."

Jin just glared at him. "What power? What obligation?"

"To bring those suffering in torment out of hell. You are the mortal incarnation of the Goddess of Mercy, Guan Shi Yin."

CHAPTER 2

Teacher walked past Jin back toward the two huge guardian statues she'd passed on her way in. Jin hesitated then fell into step behind him.

"I hope you appreciate your place in the scheme of things," he said over his shoulder. "The ability to fetch a person out of hell is quite a talent. I'm the anointed king of these regions but even I can't do that. I can only put them there."

"You do realize I don't believe a word of this," Jin said.

"Yes, and that's very strange. A Bodhisattva may choose to incarnate for any number of reasons, but normally they do so with their memories intact. It took me nearly a hundred years to track you to this plane and nearly another seventy to get a rough idea of your location! I hope you're wearing that physical body for a good reason."

"Why shouldn't I be wearing a physical body? I'm a living person."

He shrugged. "Granted, if there's a better way to patch into space and time I don't know what it might be, but incarnation does have its inconveniences. Pain, for one." Teacher felt the side of his face, gingerly. "For a moment I thought you'd broken my jaw."

"I did my best," Jin said grimly.

"You always do." Teacher stopped in front of the door that was flanked by the statues. "The guardians mark the way you came. If you really want to go back to Medias, this is the way."

Jin reached for the door, hesitated. "That's it? I walk out of this mad house and I'm done?"

"You most definitely are not 'done.' I said this is the way back to Medias and it is. There is a catch, of course."

Jin sighed. "Yes, I was expecting that. What is it?"

"Simply this: when you came down the passageway the first time, you thought it was deserted. Now you'll know better. Your third eye is opening, Jin -- " Jin gasped and reached for her forehead, but Teacher smiled and said, "Metaphysically speaking. It was already happening or I wouldn't have been able to find you. You're waking up, like it or not. Perhaps you'll remember more when you meet what's waiting for you in the passageway."

"What is it?"

"I can't tell you that. You'll deal with it or you won't, but it stands between you and Medias."

"Fine, so how do I open this door? It's locked."

"No door is locked or barred to you, Jin. Didn't I mention that? That's an attribute of Guan Yin, in case you were wondering. You'll discover the others in time."

Jin leaned close, examining the door. It looked solid enough. "It damn well *is* locked. Where's the key?"

"You're the key."

Jin felt a shove on her back and she stumbled forward. She stuck out her hands to block her fall against the door and felt a lurch in her stomach as her hands passed through the door with no more resistance than the surface of a pool of water. She flailed to regain her balance, failed, and landed hard on the cold stone floor of the passageway.

"Crap!"

It was several long moments before Jin could breathe normally again, and several more before she staggered to her feet, her hands pressed into the small of her back all the while. "Lousy old man... that hurt! Hey, Teacher! Where are you?"

No answer. Jin reached toward the door, hesitated, thought better of it. If he wasn't going to follow her now, that suited her fine. The sooner she was out and away from him, the better. Jin headed back down the passage at a brisk walk. Another moment and she was running. She ran until she was out of breath and had to stop; there was no end to the passageway in sight.

Jin told herself that this was some sort of trick. She could go back to her apartment, back to Pepper Street Legal Aid, back to her life. She wouldn't go down any more alleys or breathe anything Teacher Johnson set fire to. In time she could even forget that it happened, or chalk it up to a bad dream. She would be all right again, and if Teacher came anywhere near her she'd swear out a complaint and have him committed. She could do it; she knew the procedure. Teach the Teacher to mess with her...

"If I say it's not real, it's not real."

Jin started walking again for want of a better plan. She hadn't gone more than a few yards more along the passageway when she heard someone crying.

Fool me once... "I'm not listening, Teacher. Whatever stunt you're pulling, however you're doing it, I don't care! It's not going to work this time, you hear me?"

Jin took another step and the crying stopped. "There, that's better -- "

"Fix him."

Jin shivered. There was a rustle of movement ahead of her, but she could see very little. No matter, it was not what she had seen that startled her -- the voice had been enough. It sounded like some unnatural mixing of the cry of a lost child and a madman.

"Who's there?"

What approached her then was a living shadow. It was small, maybe three feet high. She couldn't see its eyes, there was nothing but a greater darkness coming toward her out of the gloom, a darkness in the shape of a child. It held what looked like a broken doll.

"Fix him!"

Jin's notion of running around or over or through whatever she met in the passageway died then and there. She stopped. "Stay back!" In that instant the creature's eyes became visible, as if it had only now opened them, only now truly knew that she was there.

"Please..."

Please?

It was several moments before the word registered, and the change in the voice, but even when it did there was no time to think about it just then. From one instant to the next Jin changed. The hands she held out to ward off the creature turned green, the nails became talons like those of some great cat. She towered over the shadow, impossibly large and, for an instant, she saw herself mirrored in the shadow's eyes. Not as Jin Hannigan, but a green-skinned horned demon, over eight feet tall. Jin recoiled in shock, but there were two screams in the dark passageway and only one belonged to Jin.

What's happened to me?

Jin stared at her hands in horror. She raised them slowly to her face, felt rough scaly skin, tusks. She felt a roaring in her ears and for a moment the world went dim, and for a moment Jin thought that the light would go out completely and she would never find it again, never find *herself* again. For an instant Jin hovered there, hesitating between insanity and sheer blind terror as if unable to decide which way to run.

The tears brought her back.

Not her own tears though she knew she must be crying; her face was wet. She ignored that. The small shadow shaped like a child was crying. It huddled on the cold stone floor of the passageway. Jin took a step toward it, and now she did not see a shadow at all. A little girl sobbed on the stones. She might have been five or six, but no more than that, with long auburn hair in ringlets and very pale skin. She held a doll with a broken head cradled in her arms.

"...won't let the monster get you, Matthew. Won't! But I'm so scared..."

Somewhere in Jin's brain she was still screaming, but for some reason she could not focus on her own fear, her own shock. That remained, but Jin could not take her eyes off the child.

That's all it was? A child?

Why hadn't she known that? How could she possibly have mistaken that little girl for some sort of monster?

"I won't hurt you," Jin said. "I'm not what I look like!"

It seemed a silly thing to say, even then. Of course she wasn't what she looked like. She was Jin Hannigan, not some demon. It suddenly occurred to her that this, too, might have been one of Teacher's tricks. Not real. She held onto that thought with all her strength, even as she held out her hand toward the child. "I won't hurt you," Jin said again. "It's all right."

Jin gasped. Her hand was back to normal. She reached up and touched her face. She was herself again; the demon was gone. Jin was almost giddy with relief, but she forced herself to concentrate on the child. "What are you doing here? Are you lost?"

The little girl finally opened her eyes and looked at Jin, blinking through her tears. Jin was doing the same, though in her case they were tears of relief.

"There was a mo'ster," the little girl said.

"Don't worry, it's gone now. What's your name?"

"Rebecca. This is my brother Matthew. He's broken. Can you fix him?"

Jin stared at the doll. It had a porcelain head that had cracks radiating out its crown; the body was of rotten and stained cloth. Jin didn't see how the thing managed to stay together. "I'm sorry, I can't fix your doll..."

"Not a doll!" the child shrieked. "He's Matthew! Please fix him!"

As the child screamed, Jin saw the shadow again. It flowed out from the body of the doll as if the thing was sweating ink, then crawled out to touch and flow over the little girl. In that moment her voice changed back to the one Jin first heard, the one that had made her blood turn to crystal shards of ice.

"Fix him!"

Jin did not flinch this time. Whatever was happening here, this was not some sort of monster. This was a little girl named Rebecca who needed help. Jin stared at the broken doll, at the darkness oozing out of it and, finally, realized that the thing was staring back at her. She didn't give herself time to think about it.

"It's you. You're causing this!"

The shadow actually recoiled from her, but in that instant Jin's hands shot out and she ripped the doll from the girl's fingers. There was a shriek that could have shattered stone, and in that instant Jin went away. She was in the passageway and yet she was not there at all. She was in a hundred places at once, a thousand, more. She was with Rebecca in the passageway. She was with a young man named Shiro in a garden made of stone. She was with an old woman named Pei in a temple where the incense was thick and choking and the sound of chanting never stopped. She was with a woman named Two Doves in a place of fire and choking ash. She was in all these places and more, and in every one she saw the shadow. She knew him, had known him for years past counting, and yet she could not see his face, hear his name. Then the motion she had begun at that one time and that one place came to an end and she flung the broken doll back down the passage in the direction she had come from.

"Matthew!"

Rebecca tried to scramble past her and Jin grabbed her arm. "That's not your brother! That's..." Jin stopped. She didn't know. She refused to know. Then the images started again, only this time they featured Rebecca, not the shadow at all. Jin held Rebecca and she saw the tragedy unfold, like watching a dream that she couldn't control: No fast forward. No pause. No way to make it stop.

In the vision Jin walked through a large old house lit with flickering gas lamps. That is, the house should have been old. The style was Victorian, as were the furnishings, and yet everything was new. She walked past a man and a woman seated at a formal dining table; their clothing was Victorian as well. The man wore a gray suit with waistcoat and the woman a high-necked blouse with puffed sleeves. He read a paper while she worked at needlepoint. A maid in a starched white cap brought tea. On a whim, Jin reached out toward one of the cups but of course her fingers passed through it. No one there could see her, as if she wasn't really there. Only she was, in some fashion that Jin didn't yet understand. She was there. And this was happening, had happened, was about to happen. Jin leaned close to the man's paper and checked the date: November 2nd, 1897.

"Where are the children?" the man asked. "I hear crying."

"In the nursery," the woman said. "Nanny's mother is ill, poor dear, so I let her have the afternoon off. I'll go up in a moment."

"One of you needs to go up *now*," Jin said, but of course they did not hear her. She barely heard herself; she sounded like someone whispering at the bottom of a well. Nor did she really think it would have made a difference if they had heard. Whatever was going to happen had already happened. It was just about to happen again, was all.

Jin found the stairway and headed up. The crying got louder, but that was to be expected. Jin knew where she was going, even if she had never been there before. The nursery was just off the landing on the second floor. The crying was coming from there.

Rebecca stood by the large ornate crib containing the crying baby. She was addressing him in her "big sister" voice. Jin knew she'd been practicing it ever since she'd learned that the new child was coming. Jin didn't know *how* she knew that, any more than she knew where the nursery was. It was as if she couldn't keep from knowing, and that included what was coming next.

"Don't pick up the baby," Jin said. She knew it wouldn't change anything. She still had to say it.

Rebecca lifted her baby brother out of the crib, though it obviously required some effort. Matthew was a large, healthy infant and Rebecca, even at her relatively advanced age, wasn't so much bigger than he was. "Don' cry, Matthew. We'll find Nanny."

Nanny's room was next to the nursery. The door was closed. Rebecca called out, but no one answered, nor could she turn the knob with Matthew in her arms. "Come on, Matthew," Rebecca said. "Mother's downstairs."

Rebecca carried Matthew to the head of the stairs. She'd shifted him to her hip and that helped a little, but not nearly enough when she tripped over the loose carpet at the head of the stairs. The scream seemed to last forever, but it was only a moment. Jin felt the vision shatter around her like glass, and in another moment she was back on the cold stone, cradling the sobbing child in her arms.

"Matthew! Bring him back right now!"

Rebecca struggled against her, flailing with her small fists. Jin caught her hands and held them, forcing Rebecca to look at her. "That was not your brother! Rebecca, I don't know what you've been carrying all this time, but it was not Matthew. He's gone. He's been gone for a long time."

The child just blinked against the tears for several long moments as if she hadn't even heard, but Jin knew that she had. Just as Jin had been forced to watch before, now Rebecca had to listen. Those were the rules. Jin understood this, even if she still didn't really understand what the game was.

"Gone?" asked Rebecca, finally.

"Gone," said Jin, as kindly as she could manage. "He's gone, honey. You can't fix him. No one can."

The child looked away from her. "I'm sorry Matthew," Rebecca said. "I tried to find Nanny and she wasn't there and I didn't know what to do -- "

Jin took the child's face her hands and gently but firmly turned her back to meet Jin's gaze. "You never meant to hurt him, but gone means gone, Rebecca," Jin said. "It's all right -- you don't have to carry him any more."

"Gone," Rebecca said.

Rebecca was gone, too. Somehow, Jin knew it was going to happen before it actually did happen. First there was an odd sense of *absence*, then Jin felt the very solid child in her arms turn to something like mist, then nothing at all. That wasn't the strangest part. That was when Jin had the feeling that this same exact thing had happened before, but she could not remember who or when. In another moment Jin was alone in the passageway.

Well, almost.

The broken doll was gone, but the shadow that had infused it was not gone. It had taken the general shape of a man, but when Jin tried to focus her gaze on his face and form she found that she could not. The image of the shadow was constantly shifting, like true shadow under candlelight or a reflection cast on rippling water.

"Show yourself!"

"A fine thing to demand, Kannon, when you're the one who's been hiding," it said. "I've been searching for you for such a long time."

Jin blinked. "Why? What are you?"

"What am I? I'm a man, Kannon. Or I once was, and whatever I am now is what you made of me, so don't deny your part."

Jin took a step forward. Only later would it occur to her that perhaps this wasn't a wise move, but at that moment she was too full of anger and adrenalin to care. "I don't what you're talking about. I do know you were feeding that child's delusion. What kind of monster are you?"

The shadow took one step back, keeping its distance. "And now I'm a monster as well? So sure of that, are you? Quick to judge. I suppose one could expect that, considering your nature. Do you honestly not know who I am or why I am here?"

"I have no idea, and you've confused me for someone else. My name is Jin Lee Hannigan. I don't know who this 'Kannon' is..." Jin stopped when she realized this wasn't quite true. She had heard the name before, when Teacher was listing some of the names of Guan Yin.

"Since Kannon cannot lie then Kannon really does not know herself. This is very strange, and I must think about it."

"You know my name. What is yours?"

"If you're telling the truth, as you must be, then my name would mean nothing to you."

He sounded, no better term for it, hurt.

Jin walked toward the shadow. "Look, you can be stubborn if you wish, and you can *think* about my unfortunate situation all you want, but I've been rather short on answers lately. I'd like a few. Now."

"So would I," said the shadow. "But I guess we'll both be disappointed for the moment."

He was gone. Jin wasn't sure at first whether he just vanished or flowed back into the spaces between the stones and out of reach. She did know that there was nothing to be gained standing around in the empty corridor. She headed in what she hoped was the direction of Pepper Street, and when she found the door again she passed through into the alley beside Lovechild Florists. She could see the exit to the alley just a few feet ahead. Never mind that it or the doorway hadn't been there before; they were both present now. For the moment that seemed like enough.

Teacher was there, too. Standing on the curb in his too-big duster with the fresh carnation in the lapel. He stood under the harsh glare of a streetlight as the moths and nightbugs swirled and danced overhead. Jin staggered out of the alley.

"I see you haven't completely lost your touch," Teacher said, though I hope you don't think the next one will be that easy."

Jin took a deep slow breath, then decided maybe she would lean against the lamp post for a moment. It was either that or fall on her face on the concrete. "That was...easy?"

Teacher shrugged. "I suppose it's all relative."

"Are you going to tell me what just happened?"

"Are you going to pretend you don't know?" Teacher replied mildly.

Jin shook her head. "Dammit, I'm not an idiot! I was there! I know some of it. When I touched Rebecca it was if I knew her story even as I relived it with her. I knew what happened to her." She didn't mention Jeff, but she was thinking about him. It had been something like that when he kissed her, but this was much more intense.

Teacher nodded affably. "Remember that attribute I mentioned? After you punched me? This is the same thing, only in my case the vision just showed you what I was thinking, not what you needed to know to free me...for obvious reasons. It's up to you to know the difference and interpret what you see, and act on it, if the time has come to act. Part of you remembers, even if you still don't. You will."

Jin let her legs collapse under her and she sank to a sitting position on the sidewalk, her back supported by the lamppost. "That poor child...was in Hell?"

"*A* hell, and I wish you'd grasp the distinction. A little pocket universe all her own so small it was contained within the passageway from this plane to mine."

"She wasn't alone," Jin said, and described her meeting with the shadow after Rebecca had disappeared. "I touched it, too, before then, but I didn't get the same vision from it that I got from Rebecca. Just a swirl of images...I couldn't quite sort them out."

"The attribute of your touch is that it tells you the true situation of a person who is ready to move on. For someone else, someone whose time in a particular hell was not finished, that vision will be either empty or misleading or simply irrelevant."

"Misleading? You mean someone could lie that way?"

"Not exactly. It's more that you'd see what the person *believes* to be true, which is not always the truth. Be careful -- fetching a spirit out of hell is more art than science. I'm guessing Rebecca had some sort of attachment to that thing she was carrying? Is that how you freed her?"

"Yes," Jin said, because she knew it was true.

"Well, there you go. You broke the link, removed the obstacle, the obsessive attachment that had her trapped."

"So I basically take away what people want most? And they call me the Goddess of Mercy?"

Teacher laughed. "Never confuse 'mercy' with 'kindness,' Jin. As for the shadow...."

In another mood she might have taken some grim satisfaction in the obvious puzzlement on Teacher Johnson's face, but not now. Despite her annoyance with him, Jin realized she'd taken some comfort in the fact that *someone* seemed to know what was going on. That comfort was rapidly eroding.

"It seems to know you. I might know what that means. I'll have to give the matter some thought," he said finally.

Jin groaned. "That's what *he* said too. It seems there's a lot of question about what's going on around me, besides mine, I mean. I also turned into a demon for a little while," Jin said. She heard the casual tone in her voice, and wondered if it was there because the only other option was to start screaming. Oh, yes. By the way, I turned into a demon just now. Thought you'd want to know. Jin almost smiled.

Teacher brightened. "Oh, that. He's called Da Shi in some cultures, Pulan Gong in others. Another attribute. You were frightened at the time, yes?"

Jin nodded. "Terrified." She still was a bit, now that she thought about it.

"Well, there you go. Some hells are worse than others and most are no place for a celestial lady, even if she is a bodhisattva. Thus, your demon form. You'll find that aspect quite useful at times, but I would learn to control it, if I were you. I'm guessing you scared the crap out of that little girl."

"The shadow too," Jin said. "It hid from me when I was in that form." She finally managed to get back to her feet, though she felt a bit unsteady.

"Hmmm," Teacher said again, but that was all.

"There's something you're not telling me," Jin said.

"Because I don't know. I suspect much, but I'd rather be silent than wrong in this case." He glanced at his watch. "I have to go now," he said. "I have an appointment."

It was the first time Jin had been close enough to get a good look at Teacher's strange old watch. The first thing she realized was that it had four hands. The second was that, in place of numerals, it had the *kanji* for Earth, Fire, Water and Air at the 12, 3, 6 and 9 o'clock positions, respectively. Jin wondered for a moment what sort of time Teacher was reading. Then he was already walking away from her. Jin started to follow but her legs were still too wobbly to trust.

"Wait! You know I have a million questions, don't you?"

"I know I would, in your place, but I'm sorry to say that I don't have a million answers," Teacher called back over his shoulder.

"How about just one -- what do I do now?"

"Your job, of course. And about damn time, too. Have you any idea how crowded a hell can get?"

In another moment Teacher vanished.

CHAPTER 3

In the next three days Jin began to fully comprehend that there was a big difference between "data" and "information." Data she had, in multitudes: books, web articles, magazines all devoted to Buddhism in its various aspects and traditions. There was quite a bit on the subject of Guan Yin or GuanShiYin or Kwan Yin or Kannon, as the names varied depending on the location or sect/tradition. A lot of it was orthodoxy of various stripes, much else was in the realm of folk traditions: stories, legends, rumors, parables. In all that vast disorderly pile, there was not one jot that told Jin how to *be* Guan Yin.

So what did you expect, Jin? HOW TO BE A GODDESS IN FIVE EASY LESSONS?

Worse, a lot of what she learned was contradictory: Hell existed, hell didn't exist. There were thousands of hells. There were exactly two. There was only one, and every different punishment was just a different section of it. You were kept in hell until your sins were atoned. You were kept in hell until you had learned the lesson you needed to move on. You were kept in hell forever. Guan Yin was male. Guan Yin was female. Guan Yin embodied the feminine aspect of divinity but was neither male nor female. Guan Yin didn't exist. The Avici Hell was permanent. Nothing was permanent.

Jin sighed, and rubbed her eyes. She paused to adjust a teetering pile of books that was threatening to fall and crush her coffee cup, then turned once more to the open book in front of her. She tried to concentrate but the words were running together like a horde of centipedes. She glanced out the window of her apartment, saw a high full moon despite all the glare from the signs below the level of her tenth floor apartment. Jin put the books aside and went to bed.

Jin dreamed and, for a change, knew that she dreamed. She recognized that nothing she saw was real, just as she knew that what had happened to her in the alley *was* real. In the dream Jin got out of bed and dressed warmly against the chill, then glanced once out the window. The moon was still there, though no higher in the sky than it had been when Jin went to bed. Because, of course, it wasn't the real moon, just part of the dream. The moon winked at her as she passed the window, as if she needed a reminder. Jin just smiled and went outside.

The streets were empty. Jin looked around, not entirely sure what to expect. She knew that, even very late at night there was always some activity somewhere. Someone driving to a drug connection, a patrol car prowling, something. Not now. There was no one and nothing to be seen. The streetlights seemed to conceal more than they revealed, just little patches of light here and there along the streets, like the torches in the passageway to Hell that showed a section of the walls and hid the rest in darkness.

NOT TO HELL.

Oh, right. Her mistake. The passageway did not lead to hell; it led to the gateway which in turn lead to all the hells. It took a moment before Jin realized that someone else had supplied that answer, but she looked around and saw no one.

"Who are you?" she asked aloud. "It's very rude to talk to a person when she can't see you."

YOU MEAN IF I USED A PHONE IT WOULD BE DIFFERENT?

"Well...sort of."

ANSWER THE PHONE.

Jin's cell phone rang. She didn't remember bringing it with her, but there it was, in the pocket of her jacket. Well, it was and it was not her phone. It looked something like her phone. It also looked quite a bit like the strange watch that she'd seen Teacher Johnson wear. Around the faceplate were the kanji for earth, air, fire, and water. The display said CALLER UNKNOWN. Jin pushed the button to talk. "Hello?"

HOW'S THINGS?

The voice was familiar, but she didn't recognize it. "Tell me who you are, and I'll tell you how it is."

I'M YOU, SILLY.

Oh, right. Jin thought that, perhaps, she should have seen that one coming. It was, after all, a dream. "I'm confused and angry and scared shitless, that's how things are!"

DON'T BLAME YOU. BUT YOU HAVE TO GET OVER ALL THAT AND DO WHAT YOU HAVE TO DO. AND DON'T ASK ME "HOW." YOU'RE ON YOUR OWN. THAT WAS RATHER THE POINT.

Jin sighed. She didn't know why she had halfway expected the dream Jin to understand any better than she herself did awake.

"You're no help." Jin reached for the button to end the call.

NOT SO FAST, LUV. I HAVE SOMETHING TO SAY.

Jin hesitated. "Well?"

YOU NEED TO COME TALK TO ME. THAT'S WHY YOU'RE DREAMING.

"I *am* talking to you!"

IN PERSON...OR AS CLOSE AS WE CAN MANAGE, CONSIDERING THE METAPHYSICAL IMPLICATIONS. SOME THINGS AREN'T SAFE TO SAY OUT IN THE OPEN, SO COME MEET ME. AND DON'T ASK "WHERE" EITHER. YOU KNOW VERY WELL. DO YOU REALLY WANT TO SORT ALL THIS OUT?

"You know I do! Are you really going to tell me what's going on?"

IF YOU WANT TO KNOW THE ANSWER TO THAT YOU'LL HAVE TO COME SEE ME, WON'T YOU?

Jin got the "disconnected" message, then the display went back to idle. The kanji for fire and air, however, were glowing red. Jin didn't know what that meant, but she knew where the meeting was to be. Jin found the Pepper Street of her dream and headed down it as if she were going to work in the middle of the night, in the middle of the dream. She crossed over and entered the alley.

This time the alley didn't even bother pretending it was an alley. The bricks disappeared immediately, and Jin made her way down the passage she remembered from three days ago. She paused to look at the niche carvings, trying to decide if they looked exactly the way she remembered them because they were actually there, or just because, well, that *was* the way she remembered them. Then she firmly reminded herself that it was a dream and got back to walking, because she had things to do and the night wasn't going to last forever.

She came to the door at the end of the passage, and it was shut this time. Jin didn't bother with the lock, she just walked right through it as if it wasn't there, just as she'd fallen through it before. It felt strange, even in a dream, to simply walk through a door, to feel the wood part and flow around her.

The two guardians were waiting for her. Still massive, still stone, but now they watched her as Jin passed by. Fierce as they were, they didn't seem at all threatening. Jin stopped, and thought for a moment. It occurred to her that there was a question she wanted to ask, and now seemed like the time.

"Excuse me, but do you always stand at the doorway leading to Pepper Street?"

"Of course not," said the gigantic scowling warrior on her right. "We stand where we must to guard the way." His voice was coarse and grating, like stone on stone.

"What way is that?" Jin asked.

"Whichever way is the direction required," replied the demon figure on the left. "Guan Yin opens the way to a Hell and the barriers are weakened for a time. We must be certain that no one gets out save the one who gets out."

"Ummm...isn't the one who gets out by definition the one who gets out?" Jin asked, confused.

"What my addled companion *meant* to say," interrupted the warrior, "is that only those brought out of hell by Your Immanence."

"That's it," replied the demon. "Exactly."

"But you're made of stone. To do any of that don't you have to, well, move?"

They laughed together with a sound like rockslides. "Mistress is surely joking! We are not the statues," the warrior said.

"The statue is a symbol of our presence on the corporeal plane. Our existence and our power both are pure spirit," the demon added.

"We had heard your Immanence was...confused. We are sad to see that this is so," said the warrior. "We hope that you will feel better soon."

"Oh. Thank you." Jin left them then, unsure as to whether she had learned anything or not. It was a dream. Nothing was real. Or maybe all of it. She hadn't made up her mind yet.

"We haven't got all night, Jin. Morning's on its way."

Jin recognized the voice. She approached the dais with the statue of Guan Yin and her attendants. The braziers, the golden statue itself, everything was as she remembered. "It's you, isn't it? So it's true? I'm the mortal incarnation of a bodhisattva?"

"You've been studying," the statue said. It wasn't a question. "A bit of advice, though -- don't try to reconcile what you've been reading with you have experienced and are about to experience. Nothing fits in neat categories. Take us, for example: We're either the female form of an early male Buddhist deity from India, or the daughter of a Chinese nobleman who achieved Enlightenment through strength of character, or a native Chinese goddess who was hijacked into the Buddhist cosmos like the goddess Brigid in Ireland was turned into St. Bridget by the missionaries. Which story is the true one?"

"I don't know. Which?"

The image of Guan Yin smiled. "All of them, of course. Don't confuse the path with the destination. Clear?"

"As crystal mud," Jin said. "Bodhisattvas, gods, demons, avatars... It's hopeless! I'll never get all the rules straight in one lifetime!"

"This isn't about rules."

Jin put her hands on her hips. "Then what the hell *is* it all about? What's the secret?"

The Guan Yin That Was sighed. "You really want to know? Then I'll tell you: all living things come from the same place. We're all part of the same thing. And every single one of us, whether we realize it or not, whether it takes one lifetime or thousands, is just trying to get home."

Jin's jaw dropped. After a moment she closed her mouth, feeling foolish. "That's it?"

The statue nodded affably. "All the sects, cults, religions... all the theological squabbling, all the syncretic mish-moshes of gods and goddesses and demons, of buddhas and bodhisattvas. That's all it is, Jin. There ain't no more."

"Time for a reality check then--the nature of a bodhisattva is that he or she is an Enlightened Being, one who makes a conscious decision to forego Transcendence in order to remain of the world and help others along the path, yes?"

"More or less. What's your point?"

"My point is that, if I really were an Enlightened Being, I'd understand all of this already! Teacher Johnson is another Bodhisattva incarnation but apparently understands his nature. I don't. I free someone, I'm still just Jin Hannigan. I become a demon when startled, but I'm still just Jin Hannigan!"

"That's true -- We are Jin Hannigan. I incarnated to *be* Jin Hannigan. We're also Guan Yin. See, I did this to us on purpose, if you hadn't figured that out already. I incarnated without my memory. That's why I brought you here to talk about."

Jin sighed. "Finally. Answers."

"Actually, no. A warning -- stay away from the shadow. Now that he knows we've incarnated as a mortal he'll know where to find you. That was unfortunate but it can't be helped now. Karma has its own rules, as we should know."

"Why should I be afraid of him? When it came time to get serious I sent him packing! I bet I can do it again."

"And again and again and again for eternity? You don't understand," the image of Guan Yin said. "The problem with Shiro is you can't beat him—he has to beat himself."

"You're right, I don't understand," Jin agreed. "Explain, please."

"No," said the image of Guan Yin.

Jin's mouth dropped open for a second or two and it was a moment before she could trust herself to speak.

"What do you mean, 'no'?! You know the answer, don't you?"

"Of course I do, but you don't, and I'm sad to say, that's very important right now. If I told you how to defeat him, then you won't be able to do so."

"This doesn't make any sense! What if I just walk away? Did you even consider that?"

The image of Guan Yin shrugged her golden shoulders. In the distance Jin heard a stalactite fall. "You *did* walk away, Jin. For twenty years. You were Jin Lee Hannigan and that's all for those twenty years, but now you hear the voices, see the visions, and Shiro knows who you are. Try dealing with all that on your own or running away from it and I promise you either path will tear you apart."

Jin sat down on the dais and put her head in her hands. "You're as bad as Teacher."

"I don't suppose he gave you the 'Mercy isn't the same as Kindness' speech?"

Jin sighed. "As a matter of fact -- he did."

"He wasn't wrong. He seldom is. Though when it does happen, it's a beaut."

A shimmer passed through the cavern. Jin thought it was a flash of light for a moment, but then realized that the entire structure of the cavern had wavered for a moment, becoming less substantial. The image of Guan Yin sighed.

"You're almost out of time, Jin. If you've got any questions that I *can* answer, you'd better ask them now. Breaking the veil between Guan Yin as you were and will be and Guan Yin as you are now is tricky and dangerous, and I don't plan to do it very often."

"Why do you sound like me? I don't mean the voice, I mean the mannerism and slang. Seems out of place for a goddess."

"I'm speaking in my normal voice, Jin. I have no idea how you're hearing it, though I'd guess in a form and manner that you understand. Ask me something that matters."

"This is the Gateway to all the Hells, yes?"

"Yes."

"Then why does one of them lead directly to Medias?"

"Unless you're dumber than I think you are, you already know the answer."

"I was born...I live..." Jin couldn't quite finish.

"Scary, huh? It should be, but don't feel alone. On this side of Enlightenment, everyone lives in one Hell or another. There are places you'd consider Heaven, compared to Medias, that are no less a Hell than the deepest pit of all, and the people who dwell there are born and die and are reborn there just as the people in any of the other hells. Rewards can trap as surely as punishments. The trick is to learn the lesson you need to learn and move on."

"That's where I come in?"

"That's where you come in."

"But I don't know what to do! Dammit, I need help!"

The image reached out her golden hands and patted the heads of her two attendants, the young girl and the youth. "I thought of that. Do you know who these are?"

"Ummm, Guan Yin's attendants. Dragon Maiden and... Virtuous Youth? Yeah, that was it. I read about them."

"They followed you into this world. Now that you're awakening, they'll find you."

"How will I know them?"

"They'll know you. That's the important thing."

There was another shiver in the dream. The two guardian statues looked worried. "It's time to go," they said together, and Jin heard the image of Guan Yin sigh again.

"I wish we had more time."

"You and me both. One last question: if everything is illusory, where do dreams fit in?"

"Some illusions are more real than others. Later, luv."

Jin woke up. First she was standing in the cavern at the Gateway to All the Hells, then she was sitting up in bed, trying to focus as the clock radio buzzed in her ears. It was a moment before she could shut the thing off. She yawned hugely, and checked the time. It was 7 AM, right on schedule.

If I'd known I'd be taking a dream trip I'd have shut the silly thing off.

There wasn't anything she could do about that now, and a new day was starting with or without her. Little by little the waking day claimed Jin until she was showered, dressed, and nibbling toast at her kitchen table, in a small space cleared from all the books. That doesn't mean she'd let the dream slip away from her; she held onto every detail she could remember, and that was most of them. She still wondered how much of it was real, but the arrival of her promised assistants would be proof enough. If they arrived. Jin wasn't holding her breath.

Jin glanced at the clock again. She had a little time left before she had to leave, and she was almost certain that her mother had taken her laptop along on her latest assault on the forces of oppression and greed. Jin booted her own laptop and sent an email.

SUBJECT: GUESS WHAT?

Dear Mom:

I'm fine, and hope you are too. Give my best to the Forces of Darkness as you kick their hinies and what's this about a boyfriend? I want details. BTW, I've just learned that I'm the mortal incarnation of the Buddhist Goddess of Mercy, Guan Yin. Ain't that a stitch?

Love,

Jin

CHAPTER 4

The following morning Jin found this email waiting for her at breakfast:

SUBJECT: SAY WHAT?

Dear Lotus Blossom:

> Remember when you thought you were Death? You got over it, and I'm sure this will pass too. Preferably before the real Guan Yin finds out. Wouldn't want a goddess pissed at me! :)
>
> The Forces of Darkness send their regards. They're fine. They're also kicking me out of the country in a day or two so I'll see you before long. I've told Jonathan all about my lovely daughter with the identity issues and he's looking forward to meeting you. Be nice to him or I'll pull out your naked baby pictures.
>
> Love,
>
> Mom.

Jin blinked. Who the heck was Jonathan? Then she remembered--the new boyfriend. Jin shrugged. No doubt her mother's latest conquest, one more in a string of serial relationships that made Jin's own love life look cloistered by comparison. Which Jin admitted, was more or less the truth; Jin might as well have been a nun for all the difference it had made so far. Her lack of interest had quashed several promising friendships; Jeff was merely the latest. She shrugged. It wasn't something to worry about right then.

She could worry about other things, however. Jin decided that, when the time came, she would be nice as nice could be to her mother's new flame -- Jin knew her mother wasn't bluffing about the baby pictures.

While her mother's mention of Jonathan might be a mystery, the reference to Jin thinking she was Death wasn't. Jin had almost forgotten about it. Kissing Jeff had shook the memory a little but her mother's email finally jarred it loose. She flashed back on the little girl in the corridor, and finally understood why she had thought this incredible thing, this *vanishing* had happened before. It *had* happened before.

Jin was twelve. Her old ginger tabby, Missus Tickles, had crawled into Jin's lap while Jin was trying to do homework. Nothing unusual there; it is the role of a cat to demand affection at inconvenient times. Only this time Missus Tickles didn't head butt Jin's face or hands or any of her normal "drop whatever silly thing you're doing and pet me *now*" signals. Instead she just climbed into Jin's lap and sat there looking, so far as Jin could tell, confused.

Despite Missus Tickles making no demands, Jin had reached down to stroke her, absently, while pondering an algebra problem. In that precise instant something strange had happened. Jin had a very clear vision. It seemed that Jin *was* Missus Tickles, or at least a much younger and slimmer version, stalking prey through tall grass. And she wasn't alone -- an older female cat was close to her left shoulder.

She realized that it was Missus Tickles's mother, or rather *her* mother. It was all very strange, but it wasn't vague or hazy or even the least bit dream-like. It was real, or at least felt and looked that way. She saw the prey, a field mouse, grooming its whiskers just outside the entrance to its nest. Jin knew the time had come to pounce and she did so, without thinking twice about it, or whether it was proper for her to be a cat then and do what a cat was supposed to do. She simply pounced, and she missed. The mouse skittered away, and that was that. It got away. Which made Jin/Missus Tickles very sad.

As quickly as it came, the vision was over. Jin wasn't Missus Tickles anymore, but she remembered everything and, for some reason that she pondered for a long time, she still didn't think anything particularly odd had just happened. Jin just blinked, and looked down at the cat, who was still staring off into space. She scratched behind its ears.

SILLY OLD THING. IT'S NOTHING TO BE UPSET ABOUT. I BET YOUR MOTHER MISSED LOTS OF MICE IN HER TIME.

Missus Tickles looked at her. That was all. Then she curled up in Jin's lap and died. At least, that's what Jin assumed happened at the time, but there was more to it even then. Despite having the weight of Missus Tickles on her lap, Jin had a distinct feeling of, well, there was no better say this: *absence*. Missus Tickles was gone, just as, in the corridor, Rebecca was gone, even before her body went away. The cat's body likewise vanished; it simply faded away while she was looking right at it.

Jin told her mother what had happened later, and of course her mother told her that she was imagining things, including the cat. There was no cat and had never been a cat. Jin had insisted that there *had so* been a cat and thought her mother was playing a cruel trick on her, but that wasn't it. Turned out there was no sign of a cat at all. No cat bed, no cat food in its usual place in the kitchen cupboard; even the photograph of Missus Tickles that Jin kept on her dresser was gone. It was as if Jin had, truly, never had a cat, and she herself was the only one who knew better.

Just to be safe, Jin never got another cat, or any other pet. It was also five years or more before she could bring herself to touch another animal. Even a hug from her mom would terrify her, afraid that her mother, too, was going to disappear and her remaining relatives would come to her and say, Oh, no, you never had a mother, silly girl.

Jin realized now that this was exactly what she had done to Missus Tickles and that, when the cat disappeared, it was no different from the time she'd sent the little girl in the corridor out of Hell.

This is Hell.

Rather, she reminded herself quickly, Medias was "a" hell, one of many. Which, Jin was forced to admit, explained one awful heck of a lot.

Jin finished her toast and grabbed her purse. One thing she was certain of was that being a *bodhisattva* wasn't going to pay the bills. Jin wondered ruefully if that was one reason the job was usually done by someone of other than the mortal persuasion.

Elysium Fields Avenue was quiet as usual for that time of the morning. One or two stores were preparing for business but she didn't meet anyone on the street until after she'd stopped at Juney's Café for usual morning coffee. By then there were a few more people on the sidewalk, most coming from the commuter lot between Juney's and Resolution Park as the office workers came in from the suburbs of Medias. There was a young man in a black leather jacket standing at the corner. Jin thought he looked familiar and then remembered the man standing near Teacher Johnson the day before. Was it the same one? She tried to get a better look but he was gone now; Jin didn't see where he went. She shrugged and continued walking along the old brick wall lining the park to her left. When she passed the wrought iron gates that marked the entrance to the part someone spoke to her.

"Where do you think you're going?"

It was Teacher, on the other side of the gate, his hands gripping the bars as if he were in jail. Jin sighed, and stopped.

"To work, Teacher. Where else?"

"You're suffering under the delusion that your work resides in a single place on Pepper Street."

"Funny about that, considering they're the ones who pay me."

Teacher just looked a little forlorn. "You know that's not your real job and you go anyway."

"Well, I thought of following your example and exploring the homeless option, but frankly I like hot baths too much."

Teacher crossed his arms. "You're not looking at the big picture, Jin. This body of yours is a temporary inconvenience; frankly, the sooner you shed it, the better."

"I thought you'd say something like that. Teacher, did it ever occur to you that maybe *you* aren't looking at the big picture?"

Jin told him about the dream. "Whether The Guan Yin Who Was really came to me or not is debatable; maybe it was no more than a dream. Yet, as I recall, all you've done since you found me is complain about how irresponsible and inconsiderate it was for Guan Yin to incarnate without warning. Are those qualities you normally associate with Guan Yin?"

Teacher actually looked startled. "Well...no."

"So *maybe* you should consider the possibility that her warning to me was real and that she had a very good reason for incarnating as a mortal with no memory of her divine nature. I don't know what that reason is, but I do know she did not do it on a whim. Now, then -- until we know what that reason is, does it really make sense to talk so casually about this 'temporary inconvenience' that is my life?"

Teacher looked impressed. "That's actually a good point. I need to think about this."

"You do that. Right now answer a question: if I free someone from Medias, what happens to them?"

"Same as any other hell -- they go back on the wheel of life and death. They're reborn. Just not here. 'Where' depends on what lesson they've yet to learn."

"Suppose there are no more lessons?"

"Then they become Enlightened and escape the Wheel of Life and Death and move on to Transcendence. If they choose to remain behind, they become *Bodhisattvas*, like yourself."

"They just disappear from Medias? Poof? Gone?"

Teacher shrugged. "Pretty much."

"If Medias is a Hell, is there any place where people live that isn't a Hell?"

He sighed. "You do realize how ridiculous it is for the King of the First Hell to lecture Guan Yin on the nature of the cosmos?"

"Not as ridiculous as keeping Guan Yin ignorant," Jin replied affably.

"Fine, then -- there are six known states of being outside transcendence: humans, animals, ghosts, gods, jealous gods, and hell-beings. All six are trapped in *Samsara*, the cycle of Death and Rebirth. Even the demons, even the gods. The place where a god dwells is called a heaven, but it's really just another kind of hell. Humans are special only because they have the potential for self awareness *and* go through the cycle very frequently and thus, at least potentially, advance faster. It's tough for a ghost or a god to achieve enlightenment and even harder for a demon. Yet enlightenment does happen."

Jin didn't say anything for a while. She finally sighed. "Teacher, I'm late for work."

"Fulfill your materialist obligations if you must -- or can -- but don't forget what I told you about your Third Eye. Those whispers you've been hearing before now were just the beginning. You're going to start seeing things too as your Third Eye begins to open and you learn to control it. So try not to panic and assume your demon form every time you see something scary. Tends to frighten the natives."

"I'll do my best," Jin said. She turned to leave, then hesitated. "What did you mean, 'can'? Teacher?"

He was gone, of course. *For someone claiming to both mortal and an old guy, he moves damn quick.*

Joyce was already in the office by the time Jin got there. "Look, I'm sorry I'm late -- "

"What are you talking about? You're not late."

Jin glanced at the wall clock then and realized that Joyce was right. She had arrived on time almost to the minute. "Ummm, ok. *You're* early." Jin thought her assumption of lateness quite reasonable. Joyce was a punctual sort whom one expected to arrive at 8:00AM on the dot, so it followed that if Jin arrived after Joyce, then Jin was late. Only she wasn't.

Joyce just shrugged. "Got a tough case needs a referral. Thought I'd get going."

"Ok," Jin said again, since she wasn't quite sure what else to say. Joyce's early arrival had thrown Jin for a loop, and she wasn't sure why. It wasn't just the violation of routine. Joyce seemed...distracted. Joyce was never distracted. Jin had rarely met a more focused individual in her life, with the possible exception of her mother. Though in Kathleen Margaret Hannigan's case she tended to focus on different things at different times, and when the current obsession lost its magic, there was always another. Not like Joyce, whose attention and devotion to the Legal Aid Office was a measured, predictable devotion, which usually kept regular hours. Jin saw the empty coffee cup and crumpled bits on paper filling Joyce's waste basket and realized she'd come into the office quite early indeed.

"Have you seen Teacher lately?" Joyce asked.

Jin was startled out of her musing. "Oh...yes, a couple of times. Why?"

"No problems?"

"I told you, he's harmless." Jin knew she had been wrong about that much but, in this case, it wasn't the kind of 'harmless' Joyce was asking about.

"Well...maybe. But I meant what I said about being careful, mind you."

While Joyce said all this she wasn't even looking at Jin. She was staring intently at something on her desk. Jin managed to go for the coffee machine by such a route that she managed a glimpse of what Joyce was studying so intently. Which turned out to be a blank sheet of paper.

"Are you all right?" Jin asked.

"Fine. Just tired. Would you check on those filings from yesterday?" Joyce turned over the sheet of paper, which was also blank on the other side. After a moment she turned it back to the other blank side. Jin took her coffee back to her desk, since she wasn't sure what else she could do. Maybe Joyce would be willing to talk later, since she clearly wasn't in the mood right then. She concentrated on her own paperwork for a while, but found herself stealing glances at Joyce. One hour stretched into two. Joyce had put aside the blank sheet of paper some time before and now appeared to be doing actual work herself, but her mind was clearly elsewhere.

This isn't like Joyce. What's going on?

That's when Jin finally saw it. A little dark blob on Joyce's right shoulder. Startled, Jin found herself starting to change.

Da shi...?

She started to rise, find some excuse to get out of the room before Joyce saw her turn into a demon, but in that moment her vision blurred suddenly as if both eyes had been filled with tears without any warning. In another moment her vision cleared.

Her vision was, in fact, clearer than before. She noticed more than one strange thing in the next few seconds, but one most of all: perched on Joyce's right should was neither a shadow or a dark blob, but a very small creature. It was perhaps six inches high, jet black except for its horns and teeth, which were the white of bleached bones. The thing appeared to be whispering into Joyce's ear, for all that she seemed to take no notice of it at all.

What the hell...

Before Jin could rush forward or shout a warning, or any of the things she thought she meant to do, without actually *thinking* about either, of course, the thing straightened up from where it had been hunkered down by Joyce's ear and it looked straight at her.

YOU NEEDN'T SHOUT. I CAN HEAR YOU FINE.

The voice was entirely in her head, for all that she knew beyond any question that it belonged to the little imp perched on Joyce's shoulder. Jin's mouth worked silently. She raised her hand to point, or to ward the creature off, she wasn't really sure, and noticed dully that her *Da Shi* transformation had reversed itself.

OH, PLEASE. SIT DOWN BEFORE SHE SEES YOU!

Jin sat down, feeling rather foolish, but now she deliberately directed her thoughts at the imp. *You're hearing what I'm thinking*!

OF COURSE, BECAUSE YOUR INTENTION IS TO COMMUNICATE WITH ME. HOW ELSE CAN WE TALK WITHOUT THE CLIENT HEARING US?

Jin blinked. *Client*?

The creature nodded at Joyce. YOU HAVE ANOTHER WORD FOR IT?

She's my friend! What do you think you're doing?!

MY JOB, OF COURSE. MY LORD DID WARN US ABOUT YOUR CURRENT CONFUSED STATE, BUT FRANKLY I DIDN'T QUITE BELIEVE IT UNTIL NOW.

Your 'Lord'?

EMMA-O, YAMA...I THINK YOU KNOW HIM AS DAI SHI JOHNSON.

Teacher...

THAT, TOO. HE'S GOT ALMOST AS MANY NAMES AS YOU DO. LISTEN, I REALLY SHOULD BE GETTING BACK TO WORK NOW. IF YOU STILL HAVE QUESTIONS, YOU MIGHT WANT TO TAKE IT UP WITH HIM.

You think I'm going to just watch while you do...whatever?

THEN DON'T WATCH. CLOSE YOUR EYE.

Jin closed her eyes, but she still saw the demon. "Why..."

BECAUSE YOU'RE NOT SEEING ME WITH YOUR PHYSICAL EYES, OF COURSE. YOU'RE WATCHING ME WITH YOUR SPIRIT EYE, THE THIRD EYE. CLOSE THAT.

I don't know how!

The imp shrugged. WHAT'S TO KNOW? DO IT.

Jin opened her eyes. There was Joyce staring at her paper, there was the small demon looking disgusted. Jin took a deep breath and then just imagined an eye closing. She imagined the lid coming down, the view fading to black. In another moment the demon had disappeared. Joyce looked up and noticed Jin staring at her.

"Is something wrong, Jin?"

"Ah, no. Just worried about you, I guess."

Joyce grunted. "Nice for someone to worry about me for a change. Though I still think that Teacher guy needs watching."

Jin didn't disagree. Though she thought that, up till now, she could be forgiven for thinking more about here own role in this mess rather than the scope of Teacher's duties. Which, apparently, included "Boss of Working Stiff Demons."

There was something clearly blue-collar and no-nonsense about the imp on Joyce's shoulder. She could no longer see it, but she knew it could hear her.

What are you saying to Joyce?

I'M TELLING HER THAT SHE'S UNWORTHY OF THE JERK SHE'S LIVING WITH AND DESERVES TO BE TREATED LIKE SHIT.

That's a lie! She's the strongest, most together person I know!

SO WHY DOES SHE BELIEVE ME?

That stopped Jin cold for several seconds. *But...*

FOR PETE'S SAKE -- DO I TELL YOU HOW TO DO YOUR JOB, IMMANENT ONE? IF YOU'VE GOT A PROBLEM, TAKE IT UP WITH MANAGEMENT.

After a moment or two Jin remembered who "Management" was. *I believe I'll do that.*

Joyce closed the office early that afternoon, pleading a migraine. Jin just took a right into the alley by the flower shop. For a full minute as she walked there was nothing in the alley but trash, broken asphalt, and dirt. Jin was beginning to think that Teacher was trying keep her out again when the air seemed to shimmer around her and she was walking down the long corridor between double rows of grinning effigies on her way to the entrance to All the Hells. She found Teacher there by the dais as if he'd been waiting for her.

"Teacher -- " she began, but he didn't even let her finish. He glanced at his strange watch and sighed.

"Jin, didn't I tell you: 'no more questions'?"

"Teacher, did you think for one sodding moment I'd agree to that?"

In the distance the two guardians were in their usual poses, trying to pretend they weren't listening. Teacher leaned back against the dais and glanced up into the smiling, beatific golden face of Guan Yin as if seeking help. "Fuss all you want, I can't tell you how to be Guan Yin. Isn't that what you really want to know?"

"What I want to know is why you sent that imp to torment poor Joyce!"

"She's in Hell, Jin. Is there some part of the concept that you still don't understand?"

"Maybe all of it. She doesn't deserve to be treated like that!"

Teacher shrugged. "So why is she letting it happen? And when is she going to stop?"

"You're blaming the victim, Teacher."

He shook his head. "You're casting Joyce in that role, not me. For that matter, so is she. If you're so distressed by her suffering, why don't you free her?"

Jin seriously considered punching him again. "I don't know how," she said finally.

He nodded as if the matter were self-evident. "If you don't know how, then she isn't ready for Guan Yin. Do I sense a connection? Contrast that, perhaps, with the man in the fish and chips shop yesterday."

Jin blinked. "You know about that?"

"Yes, and so do you. Let's remember it together, shall we?" Teacher reached out an touched Jin on the shoulder before she could react. In that instant, Jin was back in Juney's Café on Jemmerson street. She heard the murmur of conversation at the surrounding tables, heard the sizzle as Karl slapped a burger onto the grill, smelled the meat cooking. There was a well-dressed, balding man at the condiment island. He was very calmly and methodically picking up lemon slice after lemon slice from the crisper and dropping them into a large glace of iced tea.

Weird old guy...

He was trying to get one more slice into a glass that couldn't possibly hold another when Jin reached for the ketchup and accidentally brushed against him.

"They're just lemons," she had said aloud after the shock of her touch had made him spill half his drink on the counter. "You don't need to possess them all."

In that instant he was gone as if he'd never been. In another instant Jin was back in the Gateway with Teacher.

"Your memory, Jin. Was his problem a fascination with lemons?"

She shook her head. "Of course not. It was greed and a lifetime in pursuit of things he didn't really want or need, just as a way of keeping score."

"Right. And in his case all it took was one simple statement from you to that effect, at the right time and the right place and he vanished from Medias and left no traces. If he had family, they no longer remembered him, or they did remember they believed he had been gone for some time. Business organization charts altered, payrolls and insurance rolls followed suit. You could practically see the hole closing around the place where the man had been."

"Just as it was as if I'd never owned a cat named Missus Tickles. My mother thought I'd made the whole thing up."

Teacher nodded. "Just so. They were ready. Joyce is not."

Jin knew that was the truth, even if she didn't want to. She tried another angle.

"Even so, if there's an imp on one shoulder, shouldn't there be an angel on the other? Isn't that fair?"

Teacher looked exasperated. "Fair? We're not dividing a pack of cookies here, Jin. Your friend has to be ready to understand, and to help herself or nothing is going to change for her. And just to be clear -- I didn't set the demon on Joyce, if that's what you think."

"Ummm, then who did?"

"*She* did. Not consciously, but she's trying to learn something, and strange as this may sound, the demon is helping her do it. There's nothing about her situation that requires a Guan Yin. Yet."

Jin scowled. "So what good is being Guan Yin if I can't even help a friend?"

Teacher shrugged. "I'm told that perfectly ordinary people help each other all the time. Or is there some other definition of 'friendship' that I don't know about?"

Jin just stared at him for several long moments before she shook her head wearily.

"Tell me, am I a complete and utter fool or do I just feel like one?"

Teacher's expression was pure joy. "Tempted as I am, only you can answer that one. I suggest you work on it."

CHAPTER 5

On her way out Jin paused at the two guardian statues. They merely looked large, fierce, and stony, as was their habit.

"You two were in my dream," she said.

They didn't say anything. There was still enough of the old Jin present to consider that, perhaps, she should feel a bit foolish about talking to statues, but that echo was fading rapidly. Now she only sighed, and decided to get a little more specific.

"You were there, weren't you?"

YES, they replied in unison, which is the way they seemed to do most things so far as Jin could see.

"So why aren't you two standing at the entrance to Medias? This isn't the way I came."

THIS IS THE WAY YOU NEED TO GO.

Actually, Jin had the same feeling. A kind of tug at the edge of her perception. That didn't change the fact that being told what she had to do or needed to do was getting a bit old. Jin put her hands on her hips. "And who, pray tell, said so?"

YOU DID. YOU MAY NOT HAVE BEEN AWARE OF IT, BUT YOU DID COMMAND US. WE ARE WHAT WE ARE, AND IN THE REALM OF DOORS AND PASSAGES, WE DO NOT MAKE MISTAKES. THE ORDER CAME FROM YOU.

Jin thought about it. "Suppose I commanded you to show me the way back to Medias?"

Jin heard a creaking sounds as if the stone of the guardians themselves was trying to turn and face each other. She got a definite feeling that the two statues were discussing the matter.

WE WOULD COMPLY, they said finally.

Jin crossed her arms. "Good to know, but I sense a 'however' coming. What is it?"

SOMEONE REALLY NEEDS YOUR HELP NOW. AND THEY ARE NOT IN MEDIAS. WHY WOULD YOU NOT WISH TO GO WHERE YOU'RE NEEDED?

Offhand, Jin could think of a lot of reasons, but none that didn't make her feel a little ashamed of herself. She was coming to terms with the idea that she was, in fact, the mortal incarnation of Guan Yin, since her only other option was to come to terms with the idea that she was barking mad. That meant that she could no more ignore the responsibility that came with that knowledge than a tiger could peel off its stripes. Mortal, limited, and all, she *was* Guan Yin, and she would do what Guan Yin needed to do.

She did not, however, have to like it.

"Just keep your guard up for anything coming back that isn't me," she said, irritably.

THAT IS OUR SOLE PURPOSE. WE EXPLAINED THIS -
-

"Yeah, yeah. I remember."

Jin stomped off toward the doorway the guardians were flanking and pushed on the door itself as if daring the thing to get in her way. It did no such thing, but rippled like water to allow her to pass through without even bothering to open.

Jin found herself in a corridor very much like the one that led from Medias to the Gateway to All Hells itself. The same flaring torches, the same carved monsters in the stone. The same dust and debris of ages settling on the stone floor.

I don't suppose anyone ever sweeps up.

It was a silly thought, but no more silly than a corridor with torches that apparently never burned out and never needed to be replaced. Her curiosity aroused, Jin made a conscious effort to open her Third Eye and then an immediate and panicky effort to close it again. For what seemed like one infinite moment she had stood on nothing at all over a space so vast and black that Jin knew without question it could have swallowed the universe with appetite left over. Then her Third Eye obediently closed and she was standing back on the solid stone of the passageway, squinting to see again in the weak torchlight, the dank scent of a long-closed space back in her nose. She'd never been so grateful for mold and eyestrain in her life.

It occurred to Jin that, perhaps, illusions were not always bad things. She'd suddenly become very fond of the one that made the passageways to Hell seem like simple stone corridors that allowed her to travel infinite space in the time it took to cross Pepper Street. Jin hurried down the corridor toward the far door.

Which wasn't there. Jin simply stepped through an open arch and into a cavern not unlike that containing the Doorway to All the Hells. The main differences that Jin could see at first glance was that this one seemed more elongated than round; she couldn't even see where it ended and she was fairly certain this wasn't simply because of the dim light. The other thing she noticed was that the floor of the cavern was strewn with small rocks and looked like the bed of a dried-out river.

She frowned. "This is a hell, too?"

"I suppose it depends on your definition."

Later Jin would think that, perhaps, she should be used to people just appearing and disappearing; Teacher certainly did it enough. As it was, she jumped back two feet and landed in a fighter's crouch in full demon form. A few feet away from her there stood a strange-looking little man.

He carried a staff with several rings set into the top of it. He was bald, and his earlobes were elongated exactly as those on many of the Buddhist images Jin had seen in her studies. He was maybe five feet tall in his sandals, and wore the robes of a monk. He looked about as dangerous as a fireplug with the water turned off.

"Damn it all, don't *do* that!"

The little man raised his eyebrows. "Immanence, your language has certainly gotten more... colorful, since our last meeting."

Jin stood up straight and abandoned her Pulan Gong form, feeling a little foolish. She racked her brains while she waited for her heart to stop pounding. "You're... O-Jizou, yes?"

He nodded. "You remember me, after all this time. I am honored, Kannon-sama."

Something in the way he said it led Jin to think that he wasn't honored at all. In fact, if it had been anyone other than the Enlightened Being O-Jizou was supposed to be, she'd have thought he sounded downright annoyed. He was a *Bodhisattva* like herself, and had something to do with children, but that was all she could remember.

"I'm in a mortal incarnation and my memory is faulty. Have I done something to offend you?"

"The Lord of the First Hell informed me of your condition. As for offense... those in my care have suffered because of you. Suffering may be the lot of all creatures, but usually it serves a purpose, however obscure. Does what you have done serve a purpose? Emma-O believes so, but I don't know for certain and neither, apparently, do you."

Jin said nothing. There didn't seem to be anything *to* say. Then the moment passed and the little monk turned on his heel and set out at a walk so brisk that Jin had to run to catch up. "Follow me, please," he said over his shoulder.

"I'm *trying*," Jin said, amazed that the man's short legs could move so quickly.

They hadn't quite reached the riverbed when a fierce-looking old woman appeared out of nowhere, blocking their path. Her hair was white and her eyes jet black, and those eyes glittered like cold wet stones. "Give me your clothes," she said to Jin.

Jin put her hands on her hips. "Excuse me??"

"Begone, Datsueba," O-Jizou said. "Do you not recognize Kannon the Merciful?"

The hag looked at her even closer. "I know guilt when I see it. Her clothes belong to me. That is the Law."

"I don't think so," said Jin. In another moment she was in full demon form again. The hag didn't appear worried at all, or even surprised. She did look a little puzzled.

O-Jizou sighed. "Stop that," he said to Jin, as if she were a misbehaving child, then turned back to the hag. "Whatever else this woman may be, she is mortal and alive. You're wasting our time, Datsueba."

"Mortal stink," said the hag finally, and made a sniffing noise. "I should have noticed. Didn't want to touch her anyway."

In another instant the hag was gone and Jin had returned to her normal appearance. O-Jizou started walking again and Jin hurried to catch up. "What was *that* all about?"

The little monk shrugged. "After their initial judgment, the dead, guilty and guiltless alike, come to this place to cross the river to the next realm. Those judged guiltless cross on a bridge. Those who are guilty must either wade or swim the river. It is the Datsueba's task to strip the clothing from the guilty."

"Just what am I supposed to be guilty of? Are all the guilty here supposed to stay naked?!"

"As to the first, I cannot say. For the second, no, they clothe themselves again in time," he said, as if the matter was of no importance.

Jin just hurried along for a little while, so intent on keeping pace with O-Jizou that the inherent absurdity of what he had said took a little while to catch up to her. When it did, she almost stopped.

"Ummm, O-Jizou, correct me if I'm wrong, but where we're walking is dry. There's no water here."

"Not a drop," O-Jizou agreed.

"So why does anyone need to wade?"

"Because they don't understand that the water is an illusion. If they did, they wouldn't belong here." Apparently seeing that Jin was about to ask something else he went on, "Even in your mortal form you should know this. Or has your Third Eye never opened?"

"Oh, right." Jin said. She did not, however, feel an overwhelming urge to open that eye just then and verify absolute reality.

As they walked along the riverbed Jin saw something very strange. All along the bank on one side were children, piling heavy stones one on top of the other. Some of them were in fact naked. Others wore tattered clothes of an overwhelming variety: kimonos, robes, jeans, dresses, jumpers. Their ages seemed to vary from those barely able to walk to pre-adolescents. All seemed to be working at the stones. Some were piling in groups, others worked alone.

"What are they doing?"

"They're too small to wade the river, or the older ones can't swim. They're piling up the stones to try and make a footpath to the other side."

"I don't understand. What can children so young be guilty of?"

O-Jizou just shrugged again. "Ask the one who judges them."

Even as they spoke Jin saw a ragged boy turn away to pick up another heavy stone and in that moment a small demon almost identical to the one on Joyce's shoulder dashed out of nowhere and shoved the pile of stones, scattering them and reducing the pile to nothing. The demon vanished before the child could return with the stone to find all his work gone to nothing.

"The poor thing -- "

Jin had started to turn back but without even looking at her O-Jizou had reached back and taken hold of her wrist. "Neither you nor your pity can help him, Kannon. Please concentrate on those who need you."

As scoldings went this one was very gentle, but it was a scolding none the less. Jin wanted to be angry, but couldn't. "This is what you deal with all the time, isn't it?" she asked.

"Yes."

"Can...can you do anything for them?"

"When the time comes -- and not before -- I help them cross the river."

"How do you know when the time comes?"

"How do you free someone from hell?" he returned, mildly. "It is, as Emma-O has taken to saying lately, 'my job,' just as freeing the punished is yours."

"So I've been reminded. A lot," Jin said dryly.

"If it were not so, Emma-O would not be doing *his* job. Granted, he has more than enough to concern him as it is."

That sounded like a scolding too. Jin sighed. "If it turns out that this incarnation is a mere whim of mine -- and your guess on this is as good as my own -- I'll be sure to apologize for wasting everyone's time. In the meantime can we just drop the subject of my incarnation?"

He just shrugged. "Your incarnation does not matter."

"Then why do you keep bringing it up?"

Somewhat to Jin's surprise, O-Jizou actually seemed to be thinking about her question as they walked. "I don't know," he said finally. "Maybe I'm just angry."

"Human emotion is an illusion," Jin said, even though she wasn't really convinced of that herself.

"'Show me someone who's never been bewitched by a pair of beautiful eyes and I'll show you a stone buddha,'" replied O-Jizou, smiling.

"Is that a real saying, or did you just make it up?"

"Yes," he said.

O-Jizou smiled again and Jin started to wonder if she was beginning to like the guy. She really could do without the scolding, though.

Jin thought of something. "You call me 'Kannon.' That's the Japanese form of Guan Yin, yes?"

"Yes."

"Shiro called me that, too. Maybe he's Japanese."

Jin took a few moments to describe her meeting with the shadow. Jizou listened impassively. He finally shrugged.

"Over the years I've known many shadows, but none of them spoke to me."

Jin sighed. She's known asking Jizou was a long shot, but she'd hoped for better. Neither said anything for a time. Jin followed the little monk up a narrow path on the opposite side of the dry river bed from the children. The land on the other side of the river didn't look very different from the river bed itself: it was flat, stony, and dry.

"What happens when a child finally crosses the river? Or is that something I should already know?"

"Of course it is but, since you don't... Then the child goes where it's supposed to go, just like anyone else who crossed over. Or rather, the child goes where it needs to go. I can't explain it any better than that. I can, however, show you. We're approaching Mariko's -- "

He didn't even get to finish. The air in front of them shimmered like one of the doors to the hell corridors and everything changed from one step to the next. One moment they walked in a dry, desolate place and in the next they were strolling down a narrow forest path in autumn. To either side of the path were maples in the full russet display marking the end of summer. There was a cool but not unpleasant edge to the breeze that made the pines whisper and the maple leaves rustle. They came to a place where a mossy stone bridge crossed a quiet dark stream, and there they stopped.

Jin knew that the way the place looked was not real, any more than the river keeping the children from crossing into their next destination was real. And yet, like that river, the appearance of the path was important. This seemingly tranquil place looked the way it looked for a reason, and that reason belonged to neither herself nor O-Jizou who, without preamble, had just sat down cross-legged under the larger of the two maples flanking the path about fifty feet from the bridge. He placed his staff across his knees and just sat there, not looking at her. He was looking over the bridge. After a moment Jin did the same and saw the figure approaching from the opposite side.

"Mariko?" Jin asked, and he grunted assent.

She wore a kimono of pure white, and it contrasted with hair blacker even than Jin's, and far longer. It trailed in two long braids down the front of her kimono almost to her waist; the rest spread from her head to fall down around her shoulders and black almost like a cape. Her face was in shadow but, by what Jin could see, it was almost as white as the kimono. She knew that Japanese women at certain times in history had painted their faces white, so thought little of it at first.

If Mariko noticed either of them she didn't show it. She started across the bridge with the tiny, shuffling steps that a formal kimono demanded. Jin had worn one once in a school play and couldn't understand how anybody could walk more than a few steps in the silly things, but Mariko managed just fine. She stopped at the highest point of the wooden bridge and looked down, gazing at the dark water, her long, graceful fingers resting on top of the railing.

Jin had been waiting, in a sense, for the other shoe to drop, but when it did she still felt a little sick. Mariko's fingers on the railing. Fingers too long, too thin. Jin remembered what little she had seen of Mariko's face and finally put it all together.

The skeleton is wearing a kimono. Jin almost giggled, though she didn't really think it was funny. She wasn't frightened -- she had seen far worse in her crash course in being Guan Yin -- but the sight was at once shocking and pitiful and for several long moments Jin could do nothing at all put stare at the poor girl, who still seemed oblivious to all except the water. When she finally did look up from the stream Jin thought for a moment that she'd finally noticed them, but soon realized that Mariko was looking down the path the way they had come. Jin glanced back that way but she saw nothing and it was clear that Mariko saw the same. The poor creature's shoulders raised briefly and lowered; Jin would have sworn the girl had sighed, even though she had neither lungs nor breath to do so.

O-Jizou made a slight noise, little more than a clearing of his throat, but Jin knew what it really meant -- her cue. Jin headed for the bridge, even though as yet she didn't have the slightest idea what she was going to do, and understanding that it was her nature to sort just such things out didn't make her feel the least bit more confident.

The understanding that Mariko was little more than a skeleton in a white kimono bothered Jin just a little, and not for the obvious reason. If all hells were personal -- and Jin knew that to be true -- then the particular torment, experience, and appearance of the punished one were all personal as well. Yet here was little more than an assemblage of bones and scraps of cloth pretending to be, as Jin perceived her, a young girl of about seventeen. Why? Jin could understand if Mariko was at a place where she would be subjected to horror and revulsion at her appearance; that was a torment that made sense, and Jin could look for understanding there. Yet Mariko was alone. Here there was no one to see her bones, her sorry pretense at being a living girl, so what was the point of it? It's not as if the girl carried a mirror to look at herself; so far as Jin could see she only carried a fan tucked into her sash, and considering the height of the bridge it was unlikely the water below could cast a reflection plain enough for Mariko to see.

Perhaps she merely wants it to be clear that she has died...but clear to whom?

Jin approached the bridge and Mariko didn't react. It was only when she stepped onto the wooden walkway that Mariko turned to look at her.

"Saburo -- " Mariko stopped. She sounded confused. "You're not Saburo-sama," she said, staring at her with the black holes where her eyes should be.

Jin took another step. "No. My name is Jin."

Mariko took a step back. "What are you doing here? Did Saburo-sama send you?"

"You're waiting on Saburo, aren't you?" Jin asked, dodging the question like a hurled stone. She took another step. So did Mariko, in the opposite direction.

"Stay back!"

Jin paused, her hand still on the railing. "I'm not going to hurt you."

Mariko shook her head slowly. "I know who you are. I won't go."

"Go where?"

The question seemed to confuse Mariko. "Where Saburo-sama isn't," she said finally.

"It would seem to me," Jin said dryly, "that *this* is a place where Saburo-sama isn't. How long have you been waiting?"

Silence, then Jin saw tears forming at the corners of Mariko's fleshless eyes. The idea that this was an impossible thing to happen came and was dismissed in a moment; it happened, so obviously it was not impossible. Not at that place, at least.

For a moment Mariko's fear and suspicion deserted her."I'm so tired," she said. Tears glistened on the bones of her face. "Please go away."

"Who do you think I am, Mariko san?"

"You are Blessed Kannon. You do not look as I expected, but it is you, I am certain."

Jin nodded. "You're an interesting girl, Mariko-san. I don't think you're confused at all about where you are and who you are. Yet you tarry here wearing a face like death itself waiting for someone who is never going to come. What was this 'Saburo-sama' to you?"

"Everything," Mariko said. "And he *will* come. We could not marry, but he said we would be re-united and we will. When that happens, he will see that I kept faith with him!"

Jin had a pretty good idea of what Mariko meant by that, but this was not the time for guesswork. She had to be sure. "Mariko, take my hand."

The ghost-girl took another step back. "I won't!"

"I'm trying to help you, Mariko, but I can't unless you help me, too. I promise I will not drag you away from here if you really don't want to go."

Expression was hard to read on the face of a skull, but Jin was sure Mariko was doubtful. "Well..."

"Kannon does not lie," Jin said.

Reluctantly, Mariko extended her bony hand and Jin grasped it gently. She felt none of the revulsion she had half-way expected to feel.

She saw what Mariko saw, felt what Mariko felt. In that instant she *was* Mariko as she had been a thousand years before. She stood on a small bridge in the garden of her father's house. Her father emerged from a small tea hut father down the path, and he had a guest. Jin felt her heart beating faster at the sight of the handsome young man accompanying him. Her normally gruff father was in a surprisingly good mood and he smiled at her.

"Daughter, come greet our guest."

As Mariko/Jin and Saburo bowed to each other, for a moment their eyes met. In that moment Jin finally knew what it was like to fall in love because, in the mind and spirit of a girl dead for a thousand years, for the first time and yet again she did fall in love. The sadness was almost more than she could bear. The details came flooding into her, filling in the small gaps that, to Jin, already seemed like a completed picture: Mariko was a girl of good family who fell in love with a scholar visiting her father's house. They spent one blissful night together but he was promised to another and told her so. In a moment Jin knew all this and more beside, no more or less than what she needed to know. When the vision ended Jin knew it was still up to her to put the pieces into place because her previous view of the matter was askew in one very crucial area.

Jin glanced at the ornate fan in her sash. "That was Saburo-sama's token to you, wasn't it?"

Mariko tugged her hand free and placed it protectively over the fan. "He will see that I have kept faith. I've waited for him here, he will see -- "

"The face you have chosen to show him. He will see your death. You didn't always wear this face, even after you came here, did you?"

"I-I don't remember."

"Oh, yes you do. Death doesn't come again to one already dead, but time still exists for all who cannot remove themselves from it, and you've waited a long time indeed. You became very angry with Saburo-sama over the years, didn't you? It was then that you started to let the memory of flesh fall away and now you're not waiting for him at all. You're waiting to show Saburo-sama what he did to you!"

Mariko didn't say anything, but she didn't have to. Jin smiled at her. "Break the fan, Mariko-chan. Let it go."

Mariko closed both skeletal hands around the precious fan and hugged it to her chest as if to protect it from Jin. "I won't! I will wait..."

Jin shook her head, slowly. "Did it never occur to you that maybe you misunderstood? You're not waiting on Saburo -- he's waiting on you."

Mariko just stared at her for a moment. "What are you talking about?"

"Saburo never understood what he meant to you. He didn't get word of your suicide until he returned to his father's house where his new bride was waiting for him. Because of his obedience to his father he tried to forget you but never managed, and that regret has followed him across the River of Souls numerous times since then."

"So why has he not come to me here?"

"Because he *can't*! This is not a meeting place. It is only where you wait for what will never happen while Saburo lives out his lives without the potential of settling matters between you, because you hide in this place."

"That's not true..." Mariko began, but Jin didn't let her finish.

"Kannon does not lie," Jin repeated. "Either break the fan or I will. Your choice."

"No you won't," Mariko said in triumph. "You promised!"

"I promised not to drag you from this place if you didn't really want to go. You do want to go, Mariko."

"No I don't! I will wait forever!"

"You don't have forever, Mariko. Sooner or later you will settle matters with Saburo, because you must. You've delayed that long enough. You've punished Saburo enough."

"No," she said, and that was all.

"You've got every right to be angry," Jin said gently, "But do you really never want to see Saburo again? If you can honestly say so, Mariko, I will leave you here. Only, for your own sake, tell the truth."

"I..."

Mariko's voice trailed off. She seemed puzzled again, and it was only then that Jin saw what she had missed the first time -- Shiro. He was in the fan. In that moment Mariko's manner changed and, for a moment, Jin saw the face in Mariko's memory, her true face and then it was gone again, replaced with something much colder and harder than bone

"He can rot in whatever Hell comes to him," Mariko-Shadow said then. "I will not go -- "

Jin took the fan. She never took her gaze from the ruined face, but Jin's right hand snaked out and snatched the fan from between Mariko's bony fingers.

"Get out of her you bastard!" Jin snarled as she snapped the delicate fate across her knee. Again, the visions. Brief, fragmented. There was no time.

Mariko howled like an enraged animal and lunged. Jin grabbed Mariko's wrists and held on as the girl snarled and tried to bite Jin with her skull full of teeth. Jin held her there as the shadow pooled itself and fell away. In a moment Mariko's bones clothed themselves with the memory of flesh just long enough to smile a little wistfully at Jin. In a few more moments she was gone, along with the bridge and the river and everything that had to do with Mariko's time in that place.

The shadow named Shiro, on the other hand, remained, but only fleetingly. It flowed away like dark water over the dry and desolate wasteland and Jin set out in swift pursuit of Shiro in her full demon form.

"I'll stick you in an ink bottle and write bad poetry with you, see if I don't!" snarled Jin as she ran. "I'll--I'll do worse than that! How *dare* you!"

Shiro eluded her by the time she reached the River of Souls. He seemed to have flowed away into the ground and under the rocks themselves, out of reach. Jin even dared opening her Third Eye to try and find him but, though she saw a great deal, there was no sign of the shadow creature at all.

She was hunkered down on the bank of the river of souls, her head resting on her knees, staring at nothing, when O-Jizou found her again. "Please don't do that, Jin. You're scaring the children."

"What? Oh." It was only then that Jin realized she was still in her demon form and the children on the opposite bank were cowering in little groups, hugging themselves and crying. She returned to being Jin again. "I'm sorry about that."

"Why is the Goddess of Mercy so angry?" he asked.

"That was Shiro. He was here!" He shook his head, and Jin went on, "When I first met him he was helping to keep a little girl trapped in one of the corridors and came very close to trapping Mariko as well. The blasted creature seems to reinforce whatever's keeping them from moving on. I don't know much else, but he used to be a man named Shiro. I know that much."

"Perhaps he's some sort of demon now. People do that, sometimes. I've known a few. But how did he get here?" O-Jizou asked.

"I don't know. It does seem to get around..."

The implication of what O-Jizou said finally got through to her. "...which should not be happening, should it? Only those who belong in a particular hell should be able to reach it. Perhaps he's following me somehow. I'll have to be more careful." Jin stood up. "I have to go now."

O-Jizou nodded slightly. "You'll be back soon. For now and on Mariko's behalf, I thank you."

"For doing my job?" Jin asked, a little shortly.

"For helping her," he said quietly.

Jin just nodded. "Sure... Listen, I don't mean to be rude, but I've got to go talk to someone. I can find my own way back, thanks."

Jin sat off at a pace that O-Jizou himself could only respect. In a short time she was back in the corridor leading to the gateways. She glanced neither left nor right but kept going until she passed through the door on the opposite end of the corridor.

The statue of Guan Yin and her attendants stood softly glowing in the torchlight, as they always did, but Jin didn't pay them any mind. She found the two guardians marking the way back to Medias and stopped there.

"Did you see a creature made of Shadow leave O-Jizou's realm?"

CERTAINLY, they said.

"And you let him go?" she asked, hands on her hips, glaring up at them.

OF COURSE. WE ALWAYS LET HIM GO WHERE HE WILLS.

Jin could barely believe what she was hearing. "Since you two are supposed to be guarding the doors, would it be too rude of me to ask why??"

BECAUSE THE LORD OF THE FIRST HELL HAS DECREED THAT HE MAY DO SO. IT IS NOT OUR PLACE TO QUESTION HIS WILL.

"Teacher...? Dammit, he *knew*!"

Jin sat down again. Not for the first time she wondered if she was going to be able to discuss a matter rationally with Teacher before she ripped his lungs out. On the far side of the cavern, the statue of Guan Yin smiled at them all.

CHAPTER 6

"Whatever the reason you've taken on this mortal incarnation, I really hope you don't do it again, Lady. You're not very good at being human."

Teacher was waiting for her at the dais after she left the two guardians by the passageway entrance as if he was merely keeping an appointment. He accepted her ranting with the same blend of weary patience and exasperation he seemed to be dealing with everything she'd said to him lately.

She shook her head. "The problem, if anything, is that I'm too damn good at it. Including mastering the finer points of losing my temper!"

Teacher sighed. He leaned back against the platform supporting the three golden statues. "Jin, Jin, Jin...haven't we been through this already? Anything I say to you about the Shadow Creature may interfere with your own divine plan which, for the record, you did not share with me."

She shook her head. "We can drop the 'Shadow Creature' spookiness. He has a name, as you well know. If you weren't in on the plan, then giving him access to all the hells wasn't *part* of the plan, now was it? You did that on your own, and now that thing is interfering with my duties; he almost prevented me from freeing that girl -- "

"Hmmm," said Teacher.

Jin crossed her arms. "Don't start, Teacher. I want the story. All of it."

"All right, but first you can answer a question of mine: why did you chase after this 'Shiro' when your Divine Self told you to avoid it?"

"She doesn't have to deal with him -- I do. This is the second time he's taken over what appears to me to be the functions of a demon, only he seems determined to find people who are ready to leave whatever hell they're currently in and *keep* them there. I have no idea why, but he's actively interfering with my work, so 'avoiding the shadow' isn't really an option now, is it?"

Teacher shrugged. "I don't know. I just know that the Guan Yin that Was must have had a reason."

"Fine. Now answer my question."

"All right, though there's not a lot to it. I did it as a favor to someone close to me...at least, I thought it was a favor. It was an appalling lack of judgment on my part; I admit that. But in case you were wondering, no, Guan Yin did not ask me to do it."

"All right, but I want some details."

Teacher hesitated for a good long while, but at last he lowered his gaze slightly. "There was once a man named Shiro. I don't think there's much left of that man now. Passing from hell to hell for centuries, untouched, untaught. I didn't do him or anyone a favor when I gave my word. But said is said, done is done. I can not and do not go back on my word, and more than Guan Yin would."

"In my dream Guan Yin said that when you make a mistake, it's a beaut. Was she referring to this?"

"More than likely," Teacher said, then glanced at his watch. "Judgment awaits, Jin. Make it quick."

"So how do I deal with this 'Shiro' if none of the hells can hold him?"

"I never said that."

"You did so! You said this Shiro person can travel between hells at will!"

"Yes, but not *all* of them. There's the Avici Hell, sometimes called the 'Hell of No Interval.' If he went there, he'd be trapped for so close to eternity that the difference isn't worth mentioning."

"I think I read a little about that. So how do I get him there?"

"Haven't you been paying attention? You *don't*. He gets himself there by his own actions, the way anyone else gets to any other hell. You want to know how someone ends up there? Look it up, but I don't think you really want to know. So. All done with me?"

"Not half. You're the one who judges the children in O-Jizou's realm, aren't you? How can children be guilty of anything? They're innocent!"

"I'm Lord of the First Hell which means I judge all the dead, Jin. And anyone on the Wheel of Death and Rebirth cannot be innocent by definition. If you're born, you're guilty. Case closed."

Before Jin could ask any more, Teacher shook his head, "I've got to go," he said and then he disappeared. Jin just sighed.

"Typical."

Jin rubbed her eyes. She was getting a killer headache and, worse, her time in O-Jizou's realms had left her more confused than usual. The place was what Jin thought of as a more traditional underworld, a gathering place for the dead, whereas Medias appeared to be the ordinary living world, but those who left Medias for good didn't *die*, strictly speaking, they just vanished. To go, perhaps, to places like the River of Souls? Jin didn't know, and wasn't sure it mattered, but she did know that there was a great deal about this cosmos and her role in it that she did not understand at all. Especially the shadow.

His name is Shiro.

She preferred using "Shiro" to "Shadow Creature." An actual name sounded more personal, more...well, human. Teacher, after all, said he was a man, or had been, but she didn't have a clue how one could go from human to the sort of shape-shifting thing that Jin had fought in the corridor and at the River of Souls. Neither, for that matter did she have a clue about a place called "The Hell of No Interval." Her function as Guan Yin was to get people out of hell, not put them in, and she'd seen enough to know that Teacher was right about what -- or rather *who* -- put a person into a hell in the first place. Yet if the *Avici* hell was the only thing that would hold this 'Shiro' person, what choice did she have?

Jin started back toward the corridor to Medias but hadn't taken more than a few steps when she found herself wobbling like a newborn calf. She staggered back to the dais and leaned there for a moment then decided it would be better to sit down. The adrenaline rush from her confrontation with Mariko and the explosion of emotion that had caused, and her clash with the shadow -- she was still having trouble thinking of the thing as a person, Shiro -- had worn off; Jin was left exhausted and shaky. She carefully lowered herself to the cold stone floor and sat there, her back against the dais.

I fell in love along with Mariko, and lost that love as well. It hurt like blazes. What else am I going to have to go through?

The answer was obvious: everything the Damned had gone through.

After a few minutes' rest she started to feel a little better. After a few more minutes she stood up just in time to see a familiar shadow emerge from one of the numerous doors and flow across the stone floor and up between the guardians who, Jin was sure, pretended not to notice. She hurried up to them.

"Where did he go?"

WHO?

"You know very well. Shiro."

After an uncomfortable silence, the guardian who looked more like a warrior than a monster said, THROUGH THIS DOOR.

Jin nodded. "Thought so. This is the door to Medias, unless I'm very mistaken."

IT IS, said the monster.

Jin glanced toward Heaven, or where she'd once imagined Heaven to be. Old habits died hard. "What's he up to?"

WE DON'T KNOW HIS BUSINESS.

"It was rhetorical, you...oh, never mind." Jin hurried through the door, her weariness all but forgotten.

There was no one in the corridor, but Jin didn't expect otherwise. She had no doubt in her mind that this 'Shiro' person was on his way to Medias. She did not think this was mere coincidence, especially since it was in that same corridor where she had met him in the first place. Neither did she think this a coincidence, any more than his appearance at the River of Souls was. In a sense he was stalking her, and doing it very, very well, finding her in places worlds apart, tracking her movements through multiple hells.

That was another thing that didn't make sense, now that she thought of it. She'd gotten the impression from the Guan Yin That Was that she'd come to Medias in the first place to hide from the shadow creature she now knew as Shiro. If that was the case, then it clearly hadn't worked. Shiro had found her and was now continuing to find her, no matter where she went, apparently at will. Was the Guan Yin That Was really so wrong about being able to hide in Medias? Perhaps...if that had indeed been her intention. But was it?

Jin as Jin didn't have a clue one way or another. Yet, if she really was the mortal incarnation of Guan Yin, then some part of Jin, some hidden niche, had to know exactly what the plan was, and her reason for being here in the first place.

Too bad the dream hotline is only one way --

Jin stopped. Was it, in fact, one way? She'd assumed as much, simply because as a mortal she did not have the full powers of a *Bodhisattva* or, in her own case, the knowledge. Still, she did know that dreams could work, had worked. Perhaps she could try.

Later, thought Jin grimly as she reached the end of the corridor. She stepped out of the alley by the florist's shop. It was dark out, and of course the shadow was nowhere to be seen. Jin glanced at her watch, and then felt a little foolish, remembering that she wasn't wearing one. She glanced at the sign on the bank branch at the far end of Pepper Street: 1:23AM.

Jin didn't see any point in chasing a shadow in the dark and headed for home. She passed one or two homeless sleeping in doorways and, despite keeping her Third Eye as tightly shut as she could, saw more than a few demons out and about their business. Yet despite the late hour or because of it, predators of the human sort were scarce. Which, Jin thought, was fortunate for them. She was just in the mood to go into full demon mode on some mugger's backside.

She reached Elysian Fields before she realized she was being followed. She glanced behind her, saw nothing, knew that what she saw and the reality of the situation were not the same. She kept walking.

Jin's first instinct was to head home by the shortest and most direct route possible, then she'd lead her stalker home as well. Plus the knowledge that she could turn into an eight-foot tall green demon at will lessened the urge. Instead she turned left onto Jemmerson, the first relatively well-lit side street she came to. Jin knew she should have been worried about a confrontation -- demon form on call or no -- since she didn't know what she was dealing with.

Juney's Homestyle Diner was on Jemmerson Street, just beyond the glare of the last street lamp. They kept a couple of ironwork tables with chairs outside for the lunch crowd overflow, said tables and chairs chained to a bolt in the side of the storefront now, after hours. Jin turned one of those chairs upright and sat down facing the way she had come.

"Don't keep me waiting all night," she said aloud to the empty street. "It's chilly out here."

She didn't have to ask again. A man came strolling out of the darkness and into the first of the three streetlights between the corner of Elysian and Juney's Café. His hands were stuffed into the pockets of his black leather jacket and Jin wondered if he was hiding a gun; he seemed awfully sure of himself. He also seemed familiar.

When he reached the second street light Jin finally saw his face clearly and knew she's been right about her first impression of his age. He was young, maybe Jin's age or a little older. Anglo, maybe six feet tall with long black hair pulled back in a ponytail. His skin was pale, almost ghostly, though Jin wasn't sure if this wasn't just a trick of the light. When he reached the third light Jin leaned slightly forward in her chair.

"That's close enough," she said, ready to assume her demon form if he took one more step. He didn't. He stood within the pool of light, waiting. Jin's other first impression likewise proved correct, in that he appeared neither nervous nor furtive. He must have known that she was scoping him out top to bottom and he just stood there, patiently. Jin knew the streetlight should have blinded him, but he kept his gaze fixed on her as if he could see her perfectly well. "All right then, who are you and what do you want?" She asked.

"Who I am depends on who you are," he said. His voice was a deep baritone, almost incongruous with his slim frame and pale features.

"Who I am doesn't matter to who you are. Tell me your name," Jin said.

"Not until you tell me *yours*," he said, softly, "and it does matter. A lot."

"I'm asking the questions," Jin said, irritated. "You followed me, remember?"

"Yes, but how can I be sure I followed the right person if I don't know your name?" he asked, all reason.

"For the love of... My name is Jin," she said. "Satisfied?"

He shook his head. "No. I mean your real name."

She sighed. "What do you want? My driver's license?"

"No, I want what I said I wanted. Your real name. Jin or Jin Hannigan or whatever variation you're using isn't it. Do you not even know your real name?"

Jin finally understood. "My name is Guan Yin."

To her considerable surprise, at the mention of that name the young man dropped to his knees in front of her and put his forehead to the pavement.

"Enlightened One, I am your humble servant."

Jin blinked. "Ummm...you are? And please get up. That doesn't look comfortable."

"As you wish." He got back to his feet in one smooth motion and just stood there, smiling at her. Close up, Jin realized he wasn't bad looking, though his deference was making her distinctly uncomfortable.

"Listen, did you say you were my servant? And how did you know my other name?"

"I didn't know it at first, though I had been told to meet you in this place. I thought I recognized you when I first saw you, but your fundamental nature was obscured, as I was told it would be. I've been following you for weeks waiting for you to notice me, since only an awakening of your true self would make this possible. I learned your current name while waiting."

Jin frowned. "Hey, I know you! You were standing near the alley by the florist shop a few days ago."

"Just so."

If the guy was telling the truth, Jin realized, then it was only the recent partial opening of her third eye that had made it possible to finally spot him. She held up her hand.

"Wait a minute. Who told you to meet me here? And who told you that my 'fundamental nature' would be obscured?"

"In answer to both questions -- You did."

"I did...?" Jin stopped. Oddly enough, it was finally starting to make sense. The Guan Yin That Was did say that her servants would find her. "Would you please tell me your name?"

"Your pardon, Immanent One. I am properly known as Shan Cai Tong Zi or, since I know you don't speak your father's language presently, 'the Celestial Youth of the Treasure of Merit,'" he said, giving a slight bow.

Jin blinked. "Could you repeat that?"

"Certainly," he said, "but maybe you should just call me Frank."

CHAPTER 7

Frank sipped his tea, looking around Jin's kitchen with intense interest, just as he had studied the rest of her apartment. The dishes in the sink and the unemptied garbage can that smelled faintly of used coffee grounds seemed equally fascinating to him.

"It's all so wonderfully ordinary," he said finally.

Jin wasn't sure if this was a compliment or an insult, but neither prospect concerned her overmuch at that moment. "You act like you've never seen an apartment. How old are you, twenty?"

"I've known everything from hovels to palaces, but nothing like this so recent. And I'm much older than that, Immanent One."

"Could you call me Jin? And I meant in this incarnation."

He frowned then. "As you wish, but Your -- Jin, I mean -- you're mistaken. I am not incarnate. I have simply taken an appropriate form."

Jin reached out and pinched his arm, hard.

"Ow!" said Frank, and Jin nodded.

"Feels physical to me," she said.

Frank rubbed his arm. "Your present circumstances must be confusing you, so I'll presume to explain: All *bodhisattvas* can assume corporeal form as appropriate or necessary. That's not the same thing as rejoining the Wheel of Life and Death."

Jin brightened. "Oh, you mean like my demon form?"

"Only one of many," he said, "but that's it exactly. I gather you've used this a time or two since your rebirth? You aren't actually reborn as a demon, are you? No. You simply change from one physical manifestation to another. In that form you are a demon just as I am a mortal youth now."

"Nice jacket, by the way," Jin said.

He looked at it as if he were seeing it for the first time. "Thank you. Judging appropriateness isn't one of my better skills, but I thought it was suitable."

Jin finished her own tea and put the mug down on her kitchen table. "All right, Frank, would you mind telling me why you're here?"

"To serve you, as I said. As I have been doing for some time."

"Yes, you did say. But is that all? Apparently I have some hidden reason to be here as I am now. I don't think it's beyond the pale to think that, perhaps, Guan Yin's trusted servant might know that reason and, indeed, might be present to help see that her -- my -- plan is carried out?"

As curious as he'd seemed before, Frank suddenly became even more interested in the kitchen and everything that was in it. He reached out and picked up an egg whisk. "What does this device do?"

"It disappears up your backside if you don't answer my question," Jin said sweetly.

Frank sighed in submission. "My being here is part of my service to you, yes, but your service has never been as simple as you seem to think."

"Frank, look at me," she said, and Frank obeyed. "All right now: do you know why I am here?"

"Yes, I do."

"Now we're getting somewhere. Tell me why I'm here."

"No," he said.

No...?

"I'm not exactly current on this whole mistress/servant thing," Jin said. "And the idea of having a servant in the first place makes me a little queasy. Still, are you saying I can't give you an order? Because that's what I'm doing."

"I understand that, but I fear my answer must be 'no.' I have strict prior orders from you -- the immortal you -- that I am to reveal nothing of your intention to anyone, and especially not to your mortal incarnation."

"Frank -- "

Frank didn't look away. "Mistress, my duty to you is clear and, if disobeying you in this one matter and suffering your anger is the price of that, I will pay in whatever coin you require."

Jin rubbed the space between her eyes, wearily. "I've got to go to work in four hours and this mortal body is very tired. I'm going to bed."

"Very well. I shall stand guard outside your door."

She blinked. "Shouldn't you go home?"

"I have no home. My place is with you."

"Now wait a minute. I hardly know you..." Jin stopped, aware of how silly that sounded under the circumstances, but she couldn't just banish common sense and appearances so easily. "Look, you can't stay here."

He shrugged. "Not necessary. I can stand guard outside your apartment."

Jin realized he was serious. Letting him stay was against her better judgment, but she just shrugged. "Ok, fine. You can sleep on the couch if you want. I'm going to bed."

Jin put the bedroom door between them and felt a sigh of relief. Not because she was concerned about Frank in her apartment -- she had no doubt that he was exactly who he said he was, and there was no harm in him anywhere. Mostly she just didn't want him staring at her with those puppy dog eyes; when he did that he reminded her too much of Jeff.

There had been no harm in *him*, either. Not really. But harm had happened regardless.

She needed to get to sleep, but there was still something she wanted to try first, even though she didn't have the vaguest clue of how to go about it. Then Jin had an idea. She called through the door.

"Frank? You awake?"

"Yes, Immanent-- Jin. Do you need assistance?"

"No, I need an answer."

"We did discuss this," he said.

Jin shook her head, forgetting for the moment that he couldn't see her. "No, I mean another answer. You can't tell me about Guan Yin's plans or purpose; I understand that. Can you tell me how to contact her?"

Silence for a moment, then. "But you *are* her."

Jin sighed and very quickly summarized her dream of Guan Yin. "You know how I did that?"

More silence. Then, "I think so. It's very difficult, though. Out of all the Guan Yins That Were, you'd have to find the right one."

"So how do I even start looking? Or are you allowed to say?"

"There were no instructions in this regard so I suppose so. You go to sleep," he said.

"That's it?"

"No. First you go to sleep. Then you open your Third Eye and search the past from the beginning of time."

Jin sighed. "Sorry I asked. Good night, Frank."

"Good night, Jin."

Jin got undressed and flopped into bed. She turned out the lamp on her night stand and stared at the darkness. If Frank was right she was beginning to see what Guan Yin meant about the difficulty in crossing the gap between them. Could she do it? She could try. But first she had to fall asleep and that, considering how tired she was, should have been the easy part. Only it wasn't.

Head's too busy.

The strangeness of the day itself and her encounter with the skeletal girl and Shiro the Shadow had left her much more keyed up than she'd thought. Jin stared up at the ceiling for a long time, wide awake.

Best do some reading.

She thought about the novel she'd abandoned on her night stand weeks ago, then changed her mind. It was a dog. Besides, the stelae in front of her was much more interesting. Something about Pharaoh Ramses the Great smiting some Nubians, or the like.

Stelae...?

Jin blinked. She was standing in front of a stelae of limestone, and she was reading it. And it made perfect sense. She saw other stones beyond the first one, thousands in fact, almost a virtual forest of stone. Some in Chinese, some Greek, some Latin and, further away still, something that looked like what she thought was Sanskrit. She could read them all.

This is interesting.

She thought, perhaps, it was even a little strange, but couldn't quite put her finger on why it should be. The stelae were all here, and of course she could read them -- the writing was plain enough. This one talked about a Han emperor's building projects. That one was a thank-you offering to Hermes for curing a case of gout. Another was just the Roman equivalent of "Eat at Joe's," though it certainly was a classier advertisement than any Jin had seen in a long time. Yet the thing they all had in common was how ordinary they all were, stripped of the mystery of time and language.

"People are all the same," she said aloud, as if it were a revelation. She knew it wasn't. Just one more of those ordinary facts, though this one wasn't written on any particular stone. Rather, in a way it was written on all of them, an echo of the human voices that survived from their time to Jin's.

"All time is the same," she said then, though she felt this was on shakier ground. According to her reading, all time was an illusion, but that didn't mean Joyce wouldn't fuss if she showed up late. Which reminded her that she'd have to get up soon. She wanted to check the time, illusion or no, but couldn't find the clock, or her bed.

I'll just have to look harder, she thought, even though she finally understood why her bed and her clock were missing, and why she could read all those normally impenetrable scripts. She held the thought at bay, afraid the sharp edge of her understanding would pop this particular bubble of illusion before she was done with it. Jin opened her third eye.

She later wondered if perhaps, in hindsight, it was better not to think about what she had done before she did it. If she had, truly, thought about what she might see before she did, there's a good chance she'd have refused. It was like the old story about movie monsters. Sooner or later the camera would always pull back and reveal what had been scratching at the door or lurking in the cellar, and such things were always as terrifying as the art of makeup and special effects would allow. Yet the monster revealed was never as frightening as the monster one imagined.

When she opened her Third Eye in her dream, she did not see monsters. She did, however, see herself. Guan Yin was there, standing alone among all the now ghostly and insubstantial inscribed stones. She did not look very much like all her statues, and yet Jin recognized her without any doubt. It was easy enough. Except for what looked like a plain white robe and an unearthly glow, she looked exactly like Jin. "You're real," Jin said, then glanced at the stones, "they're not."

"Ohhhh, bother," said Guan Yin. "I didn't think you'd catch me so easily."

"If I'm you," Jin countered, "how can you ever be really far away?"

Guan Yin laughed. She had a nice laugh, Jin thought. Not mocking. Delighted, rather. Joyous. Even though Jin wanted to strangle her.

"Good one, Jin. Well, don't worry. I won't be so close or easy next time."

"Next time?"

"Of course. Do either of us believe I'm going to spill the proverbial beans now? Do we believe that you'll be content to just let it go and not try to contact me again? No on both counts, Luv. We know us too well."

Jin shrugged. "You more than me, and I hardly think that's fair."

Guan Yin was still smiling, but there was a somber note in her voice when she said, "Jin, I would not put either of us through this if there was any other way to save him. Believe me, I've been trying for most of a thousand years."

"Save him? You mean *Shiro*?"

Guan Yin put a finger to her lips. "Oopsie."

Jin wasn't stupid enough to think her divine self had made an actual mistake. More likely Guan Yin was going to give her just a little more this time, like throwing a dog a bone to distract her from the side of beef. Fine. Jin would take the bone, but that didn't mean she'd forgotten about the beef.

"I suppose Emma-O told you about him. Typical," Guan Yin said.

"Shiro can pass between the hells at will."

"Not quite as easily as that, but close enough. He has mobility, yes. Almost as much as we do. That's been a problem for a long time."

"He's somewhere in Medias, or was. That's another," Jin said.

"It will make avoiding him more difficult."

"Difficult? It's impossible! He shows up wherever I need to be! How the blazes am I supposed to avoid him, especially if I'm supposed to 'save' him somehow?"

"Hmmmm," was all Guan Yin said. Jin knew that sound. It was the exact same tone that Teacher took when he wasn't going to say any more on a particular subject.

"Look, can you at least tell me why I need to try and avoid him?"

Guan Yin laughed. "Jin, that's the one thing I really can't do. And by the way, we're almost out of time again. Pick better questions."

"Try this one, then: You've sent me a servant who withholds vital information. Why should I trust him any further than I can toss your sodding statue?!"

Guan Yin put her hands on her hips in gesture that reminded Jin a great deal of her friend and boss, Joyce. "For pity's sake, Luv, buy a clue! If the Celestial Youth tells you that it's raining gumbo, you better grab a bowl! He can withhold information at my command, but he can't lie. Not ever."

Jin groaned. "You're making my head hurt. Ok, fine. You can't tell me what to do about Shiro. You can't even tell me *why* you can't tell me. I'm up against something extremely nasty and you say I can't beat it!"

Guan Yin wasn't smiling now. She said, very slowly and clearly, "I never said you couldn't beat him. You already have the only weapon you need, but if I tell you what it is and how to use it then you won't have it anymore."

Jin looked at her. "Isn't there anything you can tell me? Anything at all?"

"Try trusting yourself a little more."

"Meaning you?"

"Meaning *you*," she said. "It's almost but not exactly the same thing. I'm counting on that 'not exactly,' by the way."

Jin sighed. "That's it?"

Guan Yin grinned. "One more thing, Luv. Close your Eye and open your eyes. It's time to wake up."

CHAPTER 8

Jin dragged herself out of bed when the alarm rang, though she didn't remember much of what happened right after that. She had some vague memory of cooking breakfast, then a slightly less vague memory of an argument with Frank the Celestial Youth when she sent him out to locate Shiro.

"I'm not sure that's wise," he had said.

"I'm not sure I care at the moment," she said. "I'm not supposed to look for him. Did the previous me command *you* not to look for him?"

"Well...no."

"Then do it," Jin said. "Don't confront him, don't attack him, don't even get *near* him if you don't have to. I just want to know where he is."

Frank put on his nice leather jacket and left. Jin poured herself a third cup of black coffee and got ready for work. It occurred to her that the idea of having someone entirely at her at her disposal was a very strange one, and that it should be making her a lot more uncomfortable than it was. Yet any help she could get, she wanted.

Jin sipped her coffee, now wondering when her other promised assistant was going to show up... what was her name again? Dragon Princess? Something like that.

Jin had halfway expected to run into Teacher again on her way to work, but there was no sign of him. She arrived barely on time to find Joyce already there. She waved hello and then went to her own desk.

The demon was still there, but Jin hadn't really expected otherwise. She ignored him and he went on with his work. Joyce, for her part, looking rather pensive but not particularly angry or upset. They worked in silence for a while, but Jin could only stand so much of this. She knew the demon was there. There had to be a reason.

"Feeling better today?" Jin asked finally.

Joyce frowned. "Hmmm? What are you talking about?"

"You were a little spaced out the last time I saw you. Thought perhaps there was something wrong."

"Oh. Not really. I mean, the usual."

Jin hesitated. "I know what 'the usual' means in my case. What's the usual for you?"

Joyce didn't say anything for several long moments. "You just askin', or do you really want to know?"

"I really want to know."

"I threw Lucius out. Third time this year. It's getting old, to tell it plain."

Jin sighed. "Joyce, you don't have to tell me the *reason* you threw Lucius out if you don't want to, but I'm guessing it's not too far from all the other times?"

"Got that right, girl."

"Then I understand why you threw him out. What I don't get is why you let him back in."

HEY, WHAT YOU DOING? Jin heard the demon's voice in her head.

I'm being a friend.

DON'T HAND ME THAT. YOU'RE INTERFERING!

Damn right, and as completely and deeply as possible. Listen to me, imp, cause I'm not going to repeat this -- we both have a job to do. You do yours the way you think best, but don't presume to tell me how to do mine.

BUT --

Jin cut him off. She'd rather suspected that she could do that. She was pleased to be right. The demon on Joyce's shoulder looked annoyed, but he finally shrugged and went back to whispering.

Joyce, oblivious to all this, shook her head. "Listen Jin, you're a nice kid and all, but you're young and cute and you have no idea what it's like for someone like me."

"You're right," Jin said. "I also don't pretend to be the smartest person in the world, or even in this office, but I can listen."

Joyce smiled a tentative smile. "Tell you what -- finish logging those eviction notices before half of downtown Medias is out on the street, and we'll talk. 'Kay?"

"'Kay."

They did talk for a good bit of the afternoon. It wasn't much that Jin hadn't heard before, at least in bits and pieces, but Jin had the distinct feeling that Joyce talking about it mattered more than Jin listening. Joyce clearly needed *someone* to listen, and had needed that someone for quite some time. Jin was more than a little chagrined that she had been too distracted by her own problems to notice, even granted that those problems were a little unusual. At the end of the day she was rewarded by the sight of the little demon sitting, not on Joyce's shoulder, but on the paperweight on her desk, looking thoroughly frustrated.

Sorry 'bout that, Jin said.

WE'RE ON THE SAME SIDE, BELIEVE IT OR NOT. I'LL JUST BE BACK TOMORROW, the demon said grimly.

So will I, Jin said, and cut him off again. The door to their office opened and Frank strolled in. Jin hurried up to meet him before Joyce could get up.

"My apologies, Immanent -- "

"Jin," she corrected in a harsh whisper.

"Again, my apologies. I forgot. About the shadow -- " he began, but now Joyce was there.

"Jin, you've been holding out on me. Who's this?"

Jin thought quickly. "This is Frank...Celeste. He's a friend of mine."

Joyce smiled and nodded. "About damn time, too. Hi, I'm Joyce Masters," she said. "Jin has told me absolutely nothing about you."

"Pleased to meet you," said Frank, looking a little nervous. He glanced at Jin who shook her head slightly. She mouthed the word "careful."

"So. How long have you two been seeing each other?" Joyce asked.

"Just a few days," Jin said before Frank could answer. "I met him in the library. I've been doing some personal research."

Joyce glanced from one to the other. "Riiight. Well, time to go. You two have fun." Joyce pulled Jin aside as they left, whispering. "Tomorrow I will have details or else."

Jin just nodded, wondering what sort of details she'd have to make up. Maybe Frank couldn't lie but there was nothing to stop Jin from doing so, even if she didn't feel right about it. It's not as if she could give Joyce the true story.

"Let's walk," Jin said to Frank when Joyce had left. They set out down Pepper Street toward Elysium. Frank looked confused.

"What was this Joyce person talking about?"

Jin stifled a grin. "She thinks we're a couple."

Frank blinked. "A couple of what?"

"Lovers," Jin said, and Frank actually blushed. Jin thought this was the cutest thing she had seen in weeks.

"We must correct this misapprehension," Frank said and started to turn around, but Jin pulled him back.

"No, that is one thing we must *not* do. I've been thinking about this a bit. I can't operate openly as Guan Yin. The people of this Hell would try to lock me up for a loon, and then how would I function? No. As long as you're with me, we need a cover story, and this is it: you're my boyfriend."

"But I'm not -- "

Jin raised a hand. "I know. I also know that it's not your nature to lie, according to that other Guan Yin. However, I already know you can withhold information and refuse to answer."

"Well... yes."

She nodded. "That's all I'm asking now. Try not to reveal your true nature or the nature of our relationship unless there's no alternative. Ok?"

"I will do my best," he said. "The appearance of carnality has precedent."

Jin stopped so suddenly that Frank had taken a couple of steps past her before he realized.

"Now what are *you* talking about?" she asked.

"Just that there were traditional aspects of your divine self that used your beauty as an enticement, though to tempt men to the True Path rather than toward their baser natures."

"Frank, are you saying that in some times and places I'm essentially a Divine Cock Tease?"

Frank looked horrified. "If I understand the term correctly, certainly not. You are blameless, Jin. Your nature does not change and is always pure, but human perceptions are faulty at best, and it's possible for anyone's actions to be misinterpreted. You always act for the good."

"Maybe, but right now there's a great deal of me that's not divine at all. I'd remember that if I were you. There's also a saying here, that 'the road to hell is paved with good intentions.' I'm betting that things don't always turn out right, no matter how good my actions are; that's common sense."

"It's hard to say how anything has turned out, when so much has yet to be decided," Frank said, "even -- " He stopped.

Jin saw a thread of understanding and she grabbed for it. "You were going to say 'Even Shiro' just now, weren't you?"

"I mis-spoke, Jin. Please don't ask me to explain, because I cannot."

"You don't have to. The implication is that I had something to do with why Shiro is the way he is now. He said as much himself."

Frank looked so distressed that Jin felt a little sorry for him, but she grinned anyway. "You can't lie, even with your expressions. I'm right, aren't I? You don't have to answer that, but considering Guan Yin's attitude and the way Shiro keeps turning up I had my suspicions already."

Frank didn't say anything. He just started whistling a tune Jin didn't recognize. She sighed.

"All right, be that way. What about Shiro? I mean, did you find him?"

"No," Frank said. "I did not."

A direct statement. Unless what Guan Yin had told her and Jin's own instincts were way off, he was telling the truth. "You're saying he's not here?"

Frank shook his head. "No, just that Shiro's time skulking between Hells has made him very good at concealment. If he's here I *will* find him, but it may take time."

"That's fine," Jin said though, for the moment, her mind was elsewhere. She started walking again and Frank fell into step beside her. "Frank, tell me something -- are there any unforgivable sins?"

He frowned. "It's not a question of forgiveness. It's a question of correcting error."

"Fine, then -- an error that cannot be corrected. Does such a thing exist?"

"No."

"Then what about the Avici Hell?"

Frank brightened a bit. "Ah. I think I understand. Emma-O -- Teacher, that is, told you of this?"

"Yes. He seemed to be saying that to be trapped there was so close to forever that the difference wasn't worth squat."

"There is a vast gulf between forever and 'almost.' Granted, this is the absolute worst Hell there is. It does take an extreme level of error to gain entry."

"For example?" Jin asked.

"Well, deliberately harming one's own parents would do it. Pretending to be a *bodhisattva* and using the position to cheat honest believers..."

"Anything else?"

"Well...killing a *bodhisattva*."

Jin felt a chill in her gut. "Aren't they immortal?"

"Anyone or anything in corporeal form can be killed, and that includes you or me," Frank said. "Though with beings such as ourselves, it's barely an inconvenience."

"Then why would the punishment be so great?"

Frank sighed. "Again, it's not a crime being punished, it's an error being *corrected*. Harming an Enlightened Being directly is to work against the eventual unity of the Divine Consciousness of which we are all part, and in a very tangible, deliberate, and serious way. There is no greater mis-step on the Path that a person can make, and the correction must likewise be great. Thus, the Hell of No Interval."

"I think I see. Let's talk about something else, then. Where are you taking me for dinner?"

He blinked. "Dinner?"

"For all anyone else knows at the moment, you're my boyfriend, remember? The least you could do is take a girl out for a meal. It's late and I'm starving."

"But... I have no money. I have had little use for it."

Jin sighed. "Figures. Ah, well. It's on me, then. Won't be the first time."

Supper was delayed, though it wasn't because Jin got shanghaied into another Hell tunnel. This time the feeling that had helped lead her to the previous sufferers was much more explicit, and easier to define. It was no longer the simple tug at the edge of perception that she had felt just before her trip to the River of Souls; now Jin had a very strong and undeniable sense that there was somewhere she needed to be, and that somewhere was right there in Medias. This understanding nagged at her with a forceful persistence that Jin's own mother would have admired; she felt as if she were being pulled. Jin turned right across Pepper Street instead of left toward Juney's Diner as she'd originally planned, with Frank close on her heels.

"You've been called," he said, hurrying to keep up. "I've seen this look before."

Jin sighed. "I think before now I've really been more pointed and led than called," she said, "but if I understand your meaning, then yes -- I think I have definitely been called."

The only questions remaining so far as Jin could tell were "where" and "who." She already knew why. If she didn't yet know "where," she did know which direction to go, and for the moment that was enough, though she did wonder why she also felt an extreme sense of *urgency*.

"What's the hurry?" she asked aloud.

"You're setting the pace," Frank said. "Or was that question rhetorical?"

"Not exactly. I feel we need to hurry."

"Then I suggest we do so," Frank said, maddeningly calm as usual.

Jin gave up her brisk walk and started running. She didn't like the direction her running was taking her. Pepper Street wasn't exactly upscale, but compared to some parts of Medias it was downright posh. Just a few blocks from the legal aid offices Medias became a war zone. They ran through garbage littered streets, past boarded up windows and derelict cars. She sensed many pairs of eyes following them, and the intelligences behind those eyes were not friendly. She ignored them; the sense of urgency that had driven her to this place was getting stronger by the moment and didn't allow room for caution. If she didn't hurry they would be too late.

A young man dressed in what looked like some sort of gang costume ran past them, going in the opposite direction. He was screaming, a look of absolute terror on his face. Jin barely had time to take this in when, a bare second later, two more young men streaked past them in a much similar state as the first, but only the third one was making any noise; the second one's mouth was frozen open like a stuffed bass. The third kept up a rapid and repetitive monologue as he flashed past them.

"OhGodohGodohGodohGod...."

Jin turned the corner and skidded to a stop. There, lying half in and half out of a gutted storefront, was a shabby old black man. Jin thought he was dead at first, but no, he was struggling feebly against what pinned him to the ground -- a green dragon.

Jin couldn't tell how large it was; it was coiled twice around the old man's body but most of the rest of it disappeared into the empty building behind it. It was about three times as thick as the largest python Jin had ever seen, and covered with iridescent green scales. Two green whiskers flowed back past the head as if blown by a high wind, and the head itself was crowned with a pair of stag-like antlers. The shock and surprise of it sent Jin immediately into her demon form but Frank called out.

"I was wondering when I'd see you," he said.

The dragon vanished. Where the dragon had been there was now a young girl of about fifteen who kneeled protectively beside the old man. Her hair was as black as Jin's and much longer. She was dressed in retro fashion hip-hugger jeans and a red blouse with long, trailing sleeves.

"About time you two got here," she severely. "We almost lost him."

"We almost lost...?" Jin resumed her normal form. "Who's we... I mean, you?"

Frank sighed. "My apologies, I should have realized you didn't recognize her. Jin Lee Hannigan, Mortal Incarnation of Her Immanence Guan Yin, may I present your other servant: Lung Nu, sometimes called the Dragon Maiden."

"I prefer 'Dragon Princess,' you oaf. My father is a king after all," the girl said.

Jin just stared. She did remember what Guan Yin had said about the person known as "Dragon Maiden," but she hadn't expected such a literal rendering of the name. She thought of many things she wanted to say, most of them questions, but what came out first was, "Wow, you can turn into a dragon! That is so cool!"

The girl frowned and shook her head. "Your pardon, Immanent One, but you are mistaken -- I don't 'turn into' a dragon. I *am* a dragon."

The old man groaned and Frank looked down at him. "I think he's regaining consciousness."

"He's likely to be a bit confused," Lung Nu said. "Things were a little chaotic, there at the end."

"Several disreputable young men ran past us," Jin said, "I assume that was your doing?"

"They were harming this gentleman. I intervened."

"Intervened and a half," Jin said, remembering the terror on their faces.

"Very timely," Frank said. "This man is the one who called our mistress. I assume you heard this call as well?"

She nodded. "The time of my arrival in this plane was nigh in any case. The surest way to find you both seemed to be that I simply go to where you two must surely appear." She glanced down at the old man. "Unfortunately, I may have been too late. He appears to be dying."

Jin reached for her cell phone. "I'll call..." She stopped. Both Frank and Lung Nu were staring at her, looking puzzled. "That's not why I'm here, is it?"

"If those brigands had killed him before you came to help him, then he would have been reborn here again and possibly gone through yet another lifetime to little purpose. He's ready to move on. You can sense that."

"Don' tell me what my life's about, boy."

The old man's eye's were open. He struggled to sit up. Lung Nu was closest, she went to help him but he pulled away from her. "What do you kids want?"

"Are you all right?" Jin asked, though that was just to be polite. Clearly he wasn't.

"Hell no. Those sorry-ass bastards kicked the crap out of me... Where'd they go?"

"I chased them away," Lung Nu said simply. "They won't be back."

"You? How in the hell... Wait. I remember...there was this big snake? No. That wasn't real. No big snakes, no ants crawling all over me. I got the horrors, that's all. My drinking is catching up with me."

Jin was close enough to smell his breath. "I'd say so."

He groaned. "Nobody asked you, missy."

"My name's Jin. I'm here to help you."

"Then buy me some proper sippin' whiskey. Hadn't had a taste of the good stuff since ninety-seven."

"You don't need it," Jin said.

"Don't tell me what I goddam need! Stupid bitch..."

Frank and Lung Nu glanced at each other. "Could there be a mistake?" Frank asked.

Jin just shook her head. There was no mistake. "What's your name?" she asked.

"Buster," he said. "And don't ask me if my last name is 'Brown' or I'll smack you one."

"Were you this polite to that gang? No wonder they beat the shit out of you."

"Thas' none of your damn business," Buster said. His tongue didn't seem to work right. Most of the words were getting slurred. Jin didn't think it was just the booze.

"Wrong," Jin said. "At this moment, it's as much my business as yours. Show me why you're so angry."

"Dammit, I said -- "

"Now, Buster."

Maybe it was the tone of command, which surprised even Jin, but Buster's mask of anger seemed to have shattered. He sat in the doorway looking old and frail and tired, his shabby clothes hanging off of him like rags on a bush. "Nothing you can do for me," he said. "If you kept them boys from hurting me...thanks. But please go away and leave me alone now."

"Can't do that, Buster," Jin said kindly. "I need to know what you're holding onto that keeps you mad at the world."

He laughed then. It turned into a harsh, rasping cough. "Old. No job. No family. Feet swollen, lungs rotten, liver poisoned, dick don't work no more...you keeping a list, missy? I got a ton of 'em."

"I'm not greedy, Buster, I'll settle for just one. The one that actually matters." She reached out and put her right hand on his shoulder. Buster tried to pull away but Jin held on, and his strength was no match for hers. After a time that seemed to Jin very long indeed but could not have been more than a few seconds, she let go. Touching Buster's life wasn't pleasant for her but her *Bodhisattva* mojo or whatever it was still worked fine. She knew what she had to do.

"This isn't about your liver, or feet, or even your dick. You've been waiting at least two lifetimes for me and almost went for a third. I owe you an apology for that. I hope you'll believe that I am very sorry for what I put you through."

Buster frowned. "What you talking about? I don't even know you!"

Jin touched him again, this time atop his filthy head as if bestowing a blessing. "Oh yes you do. Not my name, maybe, or even who I am. But you know why I'm here. Give me the bottle."

"I need it," he said simply.

"No, you don't," she said. "You keep repeating the same mistake. It's not the liquor, Buster -- it's the bottle."

"Bottle just holds booze," he said. "That's all it's good for."

"Bottle holds *you*," Jin said, "and that's not good for anyone." She held out her hand.

"Save the preachments, missy! I've gotten holy rolled by the best of 'em and I ain't impressed. You can't have my whiskey! It's all I got left."

"You mean it's all that's holding you here. Let it go."

He tried to pull away, but Jin was faster. She shoved him backwards, saw the bottle in an inner coat pocket and snatched it away.

"Why, you hateful bitch -- " He started for her and Frank and Lung Nu both took a step forward, but Jin waved them back.

"That's right, Buster. I don't 'do' kindness. I do this."

Jin flung the bottle against the brick storefront where it shattered into a thousand or more pieces. The whiskey ran down the bricks and puddled into the dirt. Buster's anger was gone. He was in tears now.

"That was all...I got nothing now!"

"Buster, that's what you had all along."

The old man looked puzzled for a moment, then another, then it was if a light bulb had gone off in back of his eyes. "Well, I'll be damned..."

He was gone.

"Not likely," Jin said, to no one in particular.

Better late than never to hear the truth, I suppose, but we've got a lot to answer for, Guan Yin, Jin thought, for herself and all the Guan Yins who ever were or would be.

CHAPTER 9

Jin was almost too tired to eat by the time they made it to Juney's, but that didn't stop her from tucking into a soyburger and fries when they finally showed up. Lung Nu and Frank sat at the table with her, but they weren't eating.

"I 'pose," Jin said to Lung Nu around a mouthful of burger, "tha' there's limits on what the Guan Yin who sent you here will let you tell me?"

"Correct, Mistress," Lung Nu said.

"Call me Jin," Jin said, glancing at the other tables. They were mostly empty this late in the day, but Jin didn't want to take chances. "You call me 'Mistress' around here and someone's going to get the wrong idea."

Lung Nu frowned, then shrugged. "As you wish...Jin."

Frank hadn't bothered to brief Lung Nu on the situation with the shadow as they walked to Juney's, except for one telling phrase, "She calls him 'Shiro' now," he had said. It didn't take a master detective to know that Lung Nu knew as much as Frank did about Shiro, and wasn't going to say any more.

"I would ask if you already know about the shadow, but of course you do. So. Frank doesn't eat. You don't, either?"

"We can," Lung Nu said. "Though, strictly speaking, it isn't necessary." She neither confirmed nor denied Jin's assumption about the shadow, but then Jin didn't need confirmation now.

"Did either of you notice anything strange about our encounter with Buster?"

Frank and Lung Nu exchanged glances. They actually looked perplexed. Jin almost smiled.

"No shadow," Jin said. "Shiro wasn't there. I can only think of one previous instance when that wasn't the case." She told them about the Lemon Man in Juney's earlier. Frank looked thoughtful.

"The only thing both instances have in common was that they both took place in Medias," he said.

Jin nodded. "Any idea why this might be? What's different about this particular hell?"

Lung Nu shrugged. "It's a fairly mild one as hells go," she said. "And it is the one in which you chose to incarnate. Other than that, I don't know. Perhaps he is constrained in some way?"

"I thought of that, but I can't imagine why. His scope of operation extends to almost all the hells, thanks to Teacher. He's come this way before."

Now Lung Nu looked puzzled. "Teacher?"

"Emma-O," Frank explained. "Teacher is his mortal form."

"Oh," said Lung Nu.

"While we're on the subject, I'm surprised you two didn't incarnate as well. Teacher said it had some advantages."

"From his standpoint, certainly," Frank said. "He was looking for you -- "

Too late he saw the warning in Lung Nu's face. Jin pounced on the slip. "Whereas you two were not. You knew where to find me."

Frank glared at Lung Nu, but finally shrugged. "Yes, we did."

"Guan Yin That Was implied as much," Jin said. "No point in sending either of you if it took a hundred years to track me down. Still, it's just nice to have confirmation, reluctant or no."

"You're clever," Lung Nu said admiringly, "but then I would expect no less. Just don't think you're going to trick me as easily as Celestial Youth tricks himself."

"Now wait a minute -- " Frank began, but Jin cut him off.

"Bickering? Is this any way for *Bodhisattvas* to behave?" Everything she had read about Enlightened Beings said they were above desire and human emotion, but in the short time that she'd known them, Lung Nu and Frank gave her the impression of squabbling siblings.

"It's impossible to remain in the cycle of Birth and Death and be unaffected by it," Frank said. "Taking corporeal form makes things bad enough even without actually incarnating. If I try hard enough, I can even convince myself that I'm hungry."

For a moment Jin could have sworn that Lung Nu wanted nothing so much as to stick her tongue out at Frank. Jin almost wished she had done so; it would have made Frank and Lung Nu both seem more like comfortable dinner companions than what they really were, and that was two beings of tremendous power and understanding temporarily slumming it in approximations of mortal form. Jin finished eating while Frank and Lung Nu waited patiently. "Unless you two have some insight you'd care to share, I need to decide our next step, yes?"

Frank and Lung Nu looked attentive, but that was all. "We await your will," Frank said.

Jin turned back to Lung Nu. "First of all, what should I call you? I'm sorry but, in this time and place, 'Lung Nu' sounds like a respiratory disease. I need something simpler."

"It's not actually my name," Lung Nu admitted. "More a description."

"You mean like 'Celestial Youth of the Treasure of Merit'?"

Lung Nu smiled as Frank scowled. "Something like that. My real name wasn't made for a human voice to speak. You may call me Ling, if you wish."

"That's a pretty name. Ling it is, so long as that's ok with you. Now then. I want you both to search for Shiro... and Ling, I know you know who I mean, so I won't bother explaining further. If you do have any questions, probably best to ask Frank. Find Shiro, preferably without letting him *know* he's been found."

"No questions, Mist-- I mean, Jin. We go."

Ling started to glow, but Frank put a hand on her arm before anyone noticed. "I believe Jin meant us to use the door," he said, trying not to smirk.

Ling cocked her head. "Really? How odd. Well...as you wish."

Jin watched them go. Whatever early questions she had harbored about Frank's motivations and loyalties, they were pretty much answered, and she saw no reason not to extend the same courtesy to Ling. Jin knew very well that the previous Guan Yin still pulled their strings. Jin only hoped that, in time, she could catch wise to precisely what strings were being pulled.

Jin checked the time, saw that it was almost midnight. Juney's would be closing in a few minutes. Jin laid a tip on the table and paid her tab on the way out.

I've got a dragon working for me.

Say what she would about the entire situation, Jin still thought that this particular notion was pretty damn awesome. Jin wondered if Ling could breathe fire and was still thinking of a tactful way to broach the subject when she arrived back at her apartment. The message light on her machine was blinking, but she was too tired to deal with it.

She did take a moment to check her email. Somewhere mixed in among all the penis and breast enlargement ads was a note from her mother:

SUBJECT: STATE OF ARRIVAL

Dear Lotus Blossom:

Arrived this morning. Sorry for the delay; I thought they were going to deport me directly but the Forces of Evil were nice enough to simply ask me to leave. Ok, so it wasn't a request, but that gave us some flex. Jonathan and I took a side trip to the Great Wall and then stopped in Japan on the way back. You should go, you know? The Great Buddha at Kamakura is really something. Anyway, come to dinner tomorrow night. Bring a date if you have one, and you darn well better.

-- Mom

P.S. You still think you're Guan Yin? Jonathan's a psychologist. He can help. Gives great back rubs too.

Jin sighed. At least she didn't say he was "great in the sack"; her mother's sex life was extremely high on the list of things that Jin most emphatically did *not* want to know about. She brushed her teeth and went straight to bed and, as before, lay there for some time while the noise of the day gradually subsided in her mind. She didn't go looking for the Guan Yin That Was this time, but she wasn't terribly surprised when the Guan Yin That Was came looking for her.

They were on the field of statues once more. Multiple images of Guan Yin through all the times and ages. Jin had to admit some were pretty impressive, especially the one known as "Kannon of the Thousand Arms." She didn't wonder how she knew what the particular image was called. It was more a case of not being able to *not* know. Just as she knew the Guan Yin perched on the shoulder of a statue labeled "White Robed Guan Shi Yin" was her own past self.

"I thought you said this communication was dangerous," Jin said.

"Not nearly as dangerous as you are, luv. Mind telling me what the blazes you're thinking?" The Guan Yin That Was still looked and sounded exactly like Jin, even though she obviously wasn't pleased with her mortal incarnation just then.

"If you're talking about Shiro, avoiding him doesn't work, and I've got to find something that does. This is *your* mess I'm trying to clean up, you know."

"Oh, I know, luv. Doesn't change anything, though. You're taking a big risk hunting him. A simple word to the wise, which we are alleged to be. In your case, I wonder."

"Like I care. Look, Miss High and Mighty -- I take a big risk either way. I'd rather stalk than *be* stalked. That's just the way I am."

Guan Yin smiled. "Even with Teacher and...Frank, is it?"

Jin crossed her arms over her chest. "That was different. Teacher and Frank are harmless. Shiro isn't."

The Guan Yin That Was laughed out loud. "The King of the First Hell, Lord of the Underworld, Judge of the Dead? Harmless? Oh, Jin, you crack me up, you really do. What next? Skinny dipping in the River of Souls?"

Jin reddened slightly, but kept her temper in check. "Save it. Look, either drop me another of your patented 'hints' or just go away. I need some rest, being mortal and all."

Guan Yin shrugged. "Say hello to your mother for me."

Jin was stunned. "You...you know my mother?"

"As well as I know my own," Guan Yin said. "She won't remember, of course."

"This is what you came to tell me, isn't it? One more tiny, maddening bit of information that does me absolutely no good? Thanks for nothing, I guess."

Guan Yin smiled a little sadly. "Oh, no, Jin. Thank *you*. You have absolutely no idea just how grateful I am."

The Guan Yin That Was disappeared and, in Jin's dream, it began to rain. The statues slowly dissolved as if they were made of salt. The rain remained after the last trace of the statues were gone and Jin managed to forget about both the statues and Guan Yin for a little while. She strolled happily along a stark, black and white city scape carrying a bright red umbrella on her way to meet the coming dawn.

CHAPTER 10

There was no sign of either Frank or Ling the next morning. Jin dragged herself out of bed, but only because her alarm insisted. She washed her face and got dressed, slowly. It was Friday but it didn't feel very much like Friday was supposed to feel. Partly because Jin knew that there would be no real rest for her on this weekend or any other for the immediate future, but mostly because tonight meant dinner with her mother and, as much as Jin looked forward to seeing her mother again, she was not so sure about Jonathan.

History's against you, Mom.

Her mother, to say the very least, did not have a very good track record with men, and that emphatically included Jin's own long gone father. It took a lot of years and much unpleasant water under the bridge before Jin had finally realized that her mother really did love her and was doing the best she could as a parent. Yet her mother's admitted incompetence in that area left Jin feeling just a little cheated at not having a dad around. All Margaret Hannigan had needed to do, in Jin's opinion, was find a man slightly less screwed up than she herself was. How hard could that have been?

Apparently, pretty darn hard. The last Jin heard, her biological father had moved to the Pacific northwest and married an ersatz-Indian "holistic medicine woman" named Bambi Spotted Fawn, or some such nonsense. Which, Jin knew, just went to prove that she probably got the better deal in the roll of the parental dice. Not that she had ever admitted this to her mother.

Jin thought she had a clean blouse, but in the end had to settle for one that wasn't too grungy. She made a mental note to try and fit some overdue laundry into her divine schedule. Then she checked the time and settled for toast and coffee as something approaching breakfast before heading out to work.

Joyce was relatively cheerful that morning, and Jin was suspicious at first. "You and Lucius make up?" she asked, dreading the answer just a little.

Joyce grinned. "Hell no. Why do you think I'm in such a good mood? And don't change the subject, even if the subject was a holdover from yesterday: what happened between you and this Frank guy? He's damn cute."

"He is, and nothing," Jin said, and added quickly when she saw the frown forming on Joyce's brow, "Honest! Look, we're...we're still working out what our relationship is going to be, ok? I don't want to rush into anything and end up with a repeat of Jeff."

It was true enough so far as it went, but taking lovers didn't seem the sort of thing an Enlightened Being did anyway.

"Smart girl," Joyce said. "That doesn't mean I don't want details if anything *does* happen, you understand, but yeah, probably best to take it slow. He coming to see you today?"

Jin blinked. "To tell you the truth, I'm not sure. He's doing an errand for me and I'm not sure how long it will take. Hope he does get back, though. I'm due at my mom's tonight."

"I thought she was off in India?"

"They kicked her out."

Joyce just sighed. "Your mom's a smoking pistol, you know that?"

"Frankly, I'm surprised she didn't tell them to bite her fanny. Maybe she's mellowing."

"Maybe she realized how sharp their teeth were."

Jin laughed. It felt good. "That would imply both common sense and the concept of self-preservation. This is my mother we're talking about, after all."

Both Frank and Ling appeared at the office that afternoon. Jin introduced Ling to Joyce as a visiting cousin then herded the pair of them off to her desk to confer.

"Any luck?" Jin asked, keeping her voice low.

"No," they both said, and Frank added, "There's no sign of him. Perhaps he's since left this place. That would explain why he wasn't present at that last old man's release."

Jin absently bit a fingernail. "Maybe."

It was reasonable, but Jin didn't believe it was true for a moment. Shiro hadn't gone to Medias on a whim, and then just slipped right back out again.

"If he left the same way, the Guardians would know. Ask them."

"Shall we keep searching if he hasn't?" Ling asked.

"Yes, but only until six this evening," Jin said. "Celestial Youth, you've got to be my boyfriend Frank Celeste when we have dinner with my mother this evening."

Ling raised an eyebrow but didn't say anything. Frank didn't look happy. "I am your servant in all things, but it will be difficult for me to succeed in this deception. The very idea is ludicrous."

Jin nodded. "Yeah, but better that than showing up at my mom's tonight without a date."

"I don't understand," Frank said.

"You will when you meet my mother. I'll do as much of the talking as I can, but just change the subject if she backs you into a corner...which she probably will. Most likely on the subject of grandchildren."

Frank's expression was sheer terror, but Ling's face contorted as if she was in pain. It took Jin only a moment to realize it was because the dragon girl was fighting like mad to keep from laughing. Ling finally got herself under control.

"Shall I keep searching while Shan Cai plays his part?"

"I hope you don't mind," Jin said. "The evening's going to be complicated enough with just Frank present."

"As you wish, though I will regret missing the Celestial Youth's performance."

Jin noticed the beginnings of a glow about Ling's face and simply said, "Door."

The glow died before it was more than a spark. "Oh, yes. Sorry," Ling said. Jin glanced at Joyce's desk but she was hard at work, though Jin was pretty sure she'd been trying to hear them. They'd kept their voices low enough that Jin didn't think Joyce had managed to make out more than a word or two. When Ling and Frank were gone Joyce was looking thoughtful.

"What's the conspiracy about?" Joyce asked. "Anything I should know?"

"Just a strategy meeting for dinner with my Mom tonight. I could tell you the plan, but then I'd have to kill you. Or make you come along, which would be worse."

Joyce laughed, though Jin had the distinct impression that her boss wouldn't have minded being a fly on the wall during dinner. The walk home from work that evening was uneventful. It occurred to Jin that she hadn't seen Teacher in a day or two. She wondered if, perhaps, she should have been concerned, but offhand couldn't think of a good reason. He tended to make her angry, and Jin was very tired of being angry.

Frank presented himself at her apartment promptly at six. As long as he was pretending to be her boyfriend, it seemed appropriate to let him wait in the foyer while she dressed for dinner.

Not too formal, not too casual...

She finally settled on a plain black dress with matching shoes and bag, then collected Frank from the foyer and headed out. They headed north on Elysian Fields, away from downtown. Her mother's house was in the neighborhood, barely a twenty-minute walk. Jin made use of the time.

"Now then, Frank, my mother is going to ask you questions. I cannot possibly prepare a contingency for all of them, so I'll just have to count on your discretion for some things. Otherwise, here's what I expect." Jin ran down the list of likely questions and acceptable answers. Framing each so that Frank wouldn't have to actually lie was the tricky bit, but she managed. "Now, do you have all that?" she asked.

"I believe so," Frank said.

"Fine, but let's review: My mother asks what you do. What do you say?"

"I'm an eternal student, but well provided for. I'm not attending school at the moment."

"What do you say if she asks how long we've been dating?"

"I say I've known you for a long time, but I've been away and we've only gotten back together in the last few days. That's an implied lie, I think."

"It's a side-step. We arranged to meet at a particular time, for a particular activity -- this dinner. By most definitions, that's a 'date.'"

Frank blinked. "Oh. Then can I say, 'I've known your daughter for a long time, but today is our first actual date' instead? That's all true."

Jin shrugged. "Close enough. We've just been 'hanging out' together before now...that just means being together. Which we have, technically speaking, so that's also true."

Frank looked a little doubtful, but didn't dispute this. Jin went on. "All right, what if my mother asks who your parents are?"

"I will give their proper names, but point out that both are long deceased. Now, may I ask *you* a question?"

"Sure."

"What if she asks for specifics, such as precisely how long I've known you? That's somewhat over a thousand years."

"Say you have trouble believing in time as a linear construct. She'll like that."

Frank brightened. "Actually, I don't believe in time as a linear construct. It's an illusion."

A few blocks further north on Elysian the neighborhood turned from "downtown" to "old and settled." They turned onto Kindle Avenue.

"You seem apprehensive," Frank said. "Is something wrong?"

"Not yet," Jin said, "but wait a while."

"You love your mother," Frank said, and it didn't sound like a question.

Jin thought about it for a moment. "Yeah, I do, but the one doesn't change the other." Jin walked up and knocked on her mother's door, which was thrown open in welcome almost immediately.

"Hi, Mom," Jin said.

Kathleen Hannigan smiled as she stood aside to let them in. "Hi back, Lotus Blossom. Introduce your friend."

"This is Frank Celeste. And no, we haven't been dating long. We've just sort of hung out together before now."

Jin's mother smiled and held out her hand. "My daughter thinks she can head off the third degree by answering all my questions up front. Silly girl. I'm Margaret."

"Call me Frank," Frank said. "Pleased to meet you." He took her offered hand briefly.

Margaret turned to Jin. "He's much cuter than Jeff. Nice move."

Jin sighed. "Mom!"

Her mother patted her cheek. "Well, of course I'm going to embarrass you -- it's my duty as a mother. Come on in, both of you. Jonathan may be delayed, but dinner will be ready in a few minutes."

Margaret left them in the living room by the couch and disappeared back into the kitchen. "Can I help?" Jin called after her.

"Not unless you've been practicing, dear."

Jin sighed and sat down heavily on the couch. Frank stood, looking around curiously. "Your mother has a nice home."

That was true enough, though Jin had hardly taken the time to notice. The house wasn't exactly a mansion, but was furnished impeccably. There was an overall Asian theme, with a wide-screen television hidden behind sliding *shoji* screens, bamboo print on the couch, and authentic Japanese wood block prints on the walls. Some of them quite valuable, as Jin recalled.

"My mother has money," Jin said simply. "She was a corporate lawyer for fifteen years, working on 'the system' from the inside. She quit."

"Why?"

"Because I realized I was making more money than difference," Margaret said. She had appeared in the doorway bearing a tray of cookies.

"I didn't mean to pry," Frank said, but Margaret dismissed that.

"I'm not ashamed of having money; it's useful," she said, setting the tray down on the glass-top coffee table. "Nor of what I was. A mistake is only a mistake if you don't correct it."

"Was that why you went to India?" Frank asked.

"She told you about that? Well, it's true. I'm a hippie activist forty years too late." She smiled then. "Better late than never. Can I get you something? I think the cookies are a bit dry."

"I'll take a Chablis, if you have any," Jin said. "Frank doesn't drink..." She turned to Frank. "Water? Would that be ok?"

Taking his cue from Jin, Frank nodded. "Water. Yes. That would be fine."

"A teetotaler? Well, well... Be right back then. Talk about me some more if you'd like."

Jin put her head in her hands. "It's starting," she said.

Frank frowned. "What is?"

"Mother is a bit...passionate. We usually end up arguing."

"I like your mother," Frank said. "She's interesting."

"That's a good word for it."

Margaret appeared with the drinks, then hurried away. Jin sucked down her wine in one long gulp and followed her mother to the kitchen.

"Frank's a sweet guy, but a little naive," Jin said when they were out of earshot. "I'd consider it a personal favor if you went easy on him."

Jin's mother seemed to consider this as she adjusted the burner under a covered pot. "Is he gay? I mean, I don't mind and all, but it's not doing much for my plan to be a grandmother in this lifetime."

Jin blinked. "What makes you think he's gay?"

Margaret Hannigan turned away from the stove and faced her daughter. "I could be wrong. I'll admit he has a sort of puppy-dog devoted look on his face whenever he looks at you, but there's not much else so far as I can tell in the personal chemistry department. Surely you noticed?"

Jin hadn't noticed, but then she wasn't looking. "Frank is...special."

"What do you mean, special? Is it serious with you two? Have you slept with him?"

"Mother!"

Margaret shrugged. "I'll take that as a 'no.' Figures."

Jin put her hands on her hips. "Mom, with all due respect, you're a fine one to lecture me on men."

Her mother just sighed. "Touche, Lotus Blossom. I just worry about you, that's all."

"I know, but you don't need to. I'm fine."

Jin's mother looked her up and down again. "You're not getting much sleep; that's obvious. Is work going ok?"

"It's just a bout of insomnia. It'll pass. Work is fine."

"You don't have to, you know. Work, I mean. You could stay here. I'm not underfoot most of the time anyway."

"That's not the point. If I weren't working, what would I do?"

"Anything you want. Travel. Meditate. Go to law school, if that's what you want."

Jin almost smiled. "I like working at the Legal Aid Office, Mom. Perhaps that's not very ambitious, but what I'm doing it important."

In Margaret Hannigan's world view that was the one irrefutable argument, and Jin used it with that full knowledge.

"And the judges award the stubborn daughter another full point," Margaret said, and then she sighed. "What you could have done in a courtroom... Look, Jin, I can't be too upset that you've rejected a path that I abandoned myself, but for a while now I've had the feeling you've just been waiting for something to happen. Life doesn't work that way."

"I know, Mom. Lately I've been thinking about what I want to do long term and, you'll just have to trust me on this, it's not going to be a problem. Grandchildren, on the other hand -- "

"Just floating a trial balloon," Jin's mother said, smiling. "You're still young, so no rush. You better get back to your guest. The table's already set."

The doorbell rang before Jin had turned around.

"Get that, will you? It should be Jonathan."

Jin dutifully went to open the door.

"You must be Jin," said the newcomer. "I'm Jonathan Mitsumo."

Jin just stared for a moment. It wasn't just that the man was handsome, though he was. His features were Asian but it was obvious he was of mixed ancestry, as she herself was. He was tall and slim and looked maybe forty, just slightly younger than Jin's mother, and had wavy black hair only slightly peppered with gray. That wasn't what got Jin's immediate attention. It was his eyes. They were very dark, and glittered like small stones. They were also very, very familiar. Jonathan Mitsumo smiled at her, and Jin knew.

Jin knew that it didn't matter what he looked like now, or what he called himself, or how it had come to be. She only knew that the man calling himself Jonathan Mitsumo and currently her mother's lover was one and the same with the shadow man she had first met in a little girl's version of hell.

Shiro.

Jin didn't change into a demon, or run screaming, or lash out, or any of the things she thought she might do. What she actually did was quite different.

Jin smiled. "Won't you come in?"

CHAPTER 11

Jonathan smiled at her, but he didn't offer his hand and was careful to keep some distance between them. Jin noted his caution for what it was.

"Nice to meet you," Jin said as she escorted him inside. This is my friend, Frank Celeste."

Shiro did offer his hand as Frank stood to meet the newcomer. "Pleasure," Frank said.

"Likewise."

Jin glanced from one to another but there seemed to be no more to the greeting than polite interest on both their parts.

"Mom says dinner is almost ready. Have a seat," Jin said, but Jonathan smiled.

"Thanks, but I better go apologize to your mother for being late. You know how she is."

She watched him go through the door, and in the instant the door closed Frank was at her side. "Jin -- " he started to whisper, but Jin stopped him.

"I know," she said, keeping her own voice low.

Frank shook his head, looking crestfallen. "I sensed him, but not until he was very close. He's taken corporeal form. I didn't know he could do that, and for one like me, a spirit is easier to find than a man. I have failed you. If he had attacked..."

"If he'd attacked I'd have gone medieval demon on his sorry ass. My demon form scares him. I've seen it."

"Since demons are the normal persecutors of beings in hell it stands to reason he'd have a healthy fear of them, from the time before his bargain with Emma-O."

"Maybe," Jin said, "but I don't think that's the whole story. Do you know what he's up to now?"

Frank frowned. "Jin, I honestly do not. He's been making a habit of appearing wherever you have work to do as Guan Yin, but I don't know how that applies to this. I mean, developing a relationship with your mother? It doesn't make sense."

"It makes perfect sense if the goal is to get to me," Jin said, "but I'd bet you anything you'd care to wager that it's not a whim. Apparently he was seeing my mom even before Teacher told me who I was. If it was really the plan of Guan Yin That Was to keep me away from him, then it never had a chance. This 'Jonathan' person -- Shiro -- knew who I was before I did!"

It was simply beyond belief that Shiro would assume corporeal form in Medias and then in turn find Jin's mother entirely by accident. It wasn't, Jin reminded herself grimly, that small a hell. No, if Jin was his real target -- and both the Guan Yin That Was and Teacher apparently believed so -- then it stood to reason that Jin's mother was simply a means to that end. But what was his purpose?

As always, too many questions and not nearly enough answers. Jin glanced at the door, but the kitchen was silent. Jin strongly suspected that Jonathan and her mother were making out like schoolkids, but the kitchen timers her mother had set would ring them out of it soon enough.

"Frank, now that we know were Shiro is, he's going to need watching. Go find Ling and tell her what we've found out. I want you both to come back and watch the house. More specifically, watch *him*."

Frank shook his head. "I will not leave you alone with that creature, Jin."

"Look, if he intended me physical harm by any direct means he's had more than one chance already."

"He wasn't corporeal before now. He could have a gun," Frank pointed out.

"Which wouldn't be much good against my demon form, and that's what I'll be wearing if he even hints he's going to get cowboy on me. Look, just do as I say, for now. I'll make up some excuse for you."

"Deception comes easily to you in your current state," Frank said. "If you don't mind me saying so."

"Go!" Jin ushered him out the door. He shrugged, then walked into a circle of light that suddenly appeared and then he vanished, as did the light. Jin glanced up and down the street, but there was no one around. She had no sooner sat back down on the couch when her mother appeared at the door.

"Dinner's ready...say, where's Frank?"

"He got a call on his cell phone. Urgent family business, I'm afraid. He sends his regrets."

"I didn't hear a phone ring," said Jonathan from behind Jin's mother.

"His cell's set to vibrate," Jin said without missing a beat. "Don't you hate it when someone else's cell phone is always going off?"

"I know I do," Margaret said, and then she sighed. "Are you sure this wasn't some lame attempt to get out of the parental grilling I've been so looking forward to?"

"No," Jin said, "That part was just a bonus."

Margaret laughed. "All right, but I will insist on a raincheck. Shall we?"

They went into the old-fashioned dining room where Margaret, apparently with Jonathan's help, had laid out the feast, and it was no less than that. Roasted turkey, ham, dressing, three kinds of vegetables. For a moment all Jin could do was stare.

"Wow, Mom, you'd think it was Thanksgiving or something."

Margaret just shrugged. "In a way it is. How often are my two favorite people in the world under the same roof?"

Jin smiled, as did Jonathan, who winked at her. Jin kept smiling, but it was more like grinding her teeth than an actual smile. "Mom tells me you're a psychologist?" Jin asked. "Where do you work?"

"I'm in private practice in Sumter," he said, naming a smallish town about twenty miles north of Medias. "I'm listed. Come by and see me if you'd like."

Jin accepted a dish from Jonathan, but their hands never touched. "Professionally?"

He smiled. "That would probably be a conflict of interest. And unnecessary. I'm sure you're no more nutty than your mom."

"No, though I had my hopes," Margaret said. "Jin, pass the carrots if you're through staring at them in disgust."

"Gladly," said Jin, who had never been able to develop a taste for carrots, despite her mother's best efforts. "I've been thinking about what you said earlier."

Margaret raised an eyebrow. "About carrots?"

"About moving back home. At least for a while." Jin was speaking to her mother, but it was the man calling himself Jonathan who had all her attention. She looked for any sort of reaction from him: fear, pleasure, worry, surprise, but he was unreadable.

Her mother was grinning like a possum. "Really? You're serious?"

Jin nodded. "It's silly to live apart when we live this close together. There are better things I could spend the rent money on, you know?"

"I know," Margaret said. "Now. What are you up to?"

Jin blinked. "Up to? Nothing."

"Honestly Jin, I'd love it past your ability to understand if you were to move home, but I never expected you to do it. Are you having trouble at work? Do you really need the money?"

Jin just sighed. "The answer is no and again, no. I'm fine. My moving out served its purpose. As you said, you're gone most of the time. We're both adults. So long as you're good with that, I don't see a problem."

Margaret raised an eyebrow, but she didn't argue the point further, for which Jin was very grateful. After all, she couldn't tell her mom the real reason, could she? What would she say anyway? That her mother's boyfriend was some sort of shape-changing shadow creature escaped from his own hell and here in hers to... what, exactly?

That part was puzzling Jin greatly. One thing she did know beyond doubt -- there was no way she was leaving her mother alone with Shiro, Jonathan, or whatever he was calling himself, if she could help it. Jin didn't want to move home, but at that moment she didn't see a good alternative. Nor did she quite know what to make of the warm smile that had finally blossomed on Jonathan's face. It looked entirely too much like the one her own mother was wearing now.

"It's for the best," Jonathan said brightly. "Perhaps it's not my place to say, but you know how your mother worries about you."

"And vice versa," Jin said grimly, idly wondering if Shiro was a poker player. He'd be a natural. "I won't let anything happen to my mother if there's anything I can do to prevent it."

Margaret actually looked touched. "How sweet. But I'm a grownup. Just as you are, Lotus Blossom."

Jonathan frowned. "'Lotus Blossom.'?"

"It's been my nickname since I was seven," Jin said. "Don't ask me why."

Her mother shrugged. "Because you are. My Lotus Blossom, that is."

"She's gone zen again," Jonathan said, which was something of a shock to Jin, who was thinking the exact same thing. Not that her mother really understood zen or was even a serious student of it, but that she tended to go through periods when she expressed herself in zen terms. It was just part of the glorious spiritual mish-mosh that was Kathleen Margaret Hannigan's world. Jin and Jonathan exchanged glances and it was as if, for a moment, they were old friends sharing a secret. Jin looked away, confused, almost blushing. Jonathan just kept smiling.

"Your room's just the way you left it, you know," Margaret said, apparently taking no notice. "Like a shrine to my Lotus Blossom. You can move right back in."

Jin shook her head. "That's exactly what I can't do; shrines aren't for the living. I'll need to rearrange things a bit."

"Suit yourself," her mother said. "Now eat. Your tandoori chicken is getting cold."

Jonathan looked thoughtful. "You say Jin's room is exactly the way she left it?"

Margaret looked stern. "You will not analyze me on this, Jonathan Mitsumo. Whatever else I may be or how good or poor a job I've done, I'm still a mother. I won't apologize for acting like one."

He raised his hands in mock surrender. "Perish the thought. It's just that Jin's room might give me some insight into Jin as a person... or at least the girl she used to be. I need to get to know you both if I'm going to be involved in your lives."

Margaret's expression brightened. "Oh, you want to analyze *Jin*," she said. "That's all right, then."

"Mother!"

Jonathan's smile was totally disarming. "Do you really mind, Jin? I promise not to form any crackpot theories."

Jin was not disarmed in the least. "I'd rather you didn't," she said, tearing off a piece of chicken like a lioness ripping into her kill.

"I suppose it rather was too personal of me," Jonathan said. "I apologize."

"Nothing to apologize for," Jin said. "In fact, I think I will show you my room after all." She swallowed what she was eating and dabbed her mouth with a napkin. "It's upstairs, second door on the right. I go first, though. Thanks for dinner, Mom."

"You didn't eat much," Margaret said.

"Not much for a teamster, you mean. I'm stuffed." Jin got up from the table. "I'll go on ahead," she said to Jonathan. "Or do you need help with the dishes?"

"Thanks for the offer, but I can manage. I wouldn't want to stand in the way of boyfriend/daughter bonding. Up to a point, that is," she said pointedly.

"I'll be up in a minute, and I promise to keep my hands to myself," Jonathan said, directing the last bit to Margaret.

"Good, if you want to continue to have hands," Margaret said. "A word to the wise -- my Lotus Blossom is fierce when cornered."

Mother, Jin thought grimly, *You don't know the half of it.*

Jin left the dining room, crossed the living room into the foyer and took the stairs two at a time up to her old room. Once inside the door Jin saw that, like her mother's usual view of the truth, her remarks about keeping Jin's room as a shrine were sort of true but only up to a point. Oh, the poster of some long-forgotten schoolgirl crush was still on the wall, and the ruffled bedspread and comforter hadn't changed, but Jin's algebra book had been placed in the bookcase instead of under the bed where she'd kicked it after graduation, and the various minor ribbons and trophies she'd won in debate and talent competitions had been hauled out of their box in the closet and proudly displayed. The room wasn't exactly untouched but it was, in essence, a shrine to Jin.

Guan Yin *has so many, but here's one to me alone.*

Something glittery on her old dresser caught her eye, and Jin took a closer look. It was a candlestick in the shape of a green Chinese dragon, about eight inches high. Jin frowned. She did not remember this item at all. Then the candlestick winked at her, and her mouth fell open in surprise. It was several long moments before Jin got over her shock enough to realize what was going on.

"Ling?" she whispered, and the candlestick nodded at her.

HERE, MIST... I MEAN JIN. CELESTIAL YOUTH SAID YOU WERE LOOKING FOR ME.

"For both of you, really. Where is he?"

CLOSE. HE ISN'T SHOWING HIMSELF.

"Good. Listen, Ling... Jonathan, I mean Shiro, is coming. Don't do anything unless I tell you."

Ling didn't have a chance to reply, because there was a knock on the door and, after a pause, Jonathan let himself in. "Did I hear voices?" he asked.

Jin reddened slightly, but didn't look away from him. "Talking to myself. Or the past. Make of that what you will."

He just shrugged. "What is there to make of it, other than what it is? I've been known to do it myself. So. I assume you changed your mind for the purpose of getting me alone. What do you want to say to me, Jin?"

Jin blinked. Jonathan or Shiro or whoever he was had called that one right. The problem is, presented with the reality of being alone with the creature who'd been dogging her steps since Teacher's revelation, Jin wasn't entirely sure what she wanted to say to him. She started with one simple truth, though it might not have been the first one on her mind.

"My mother and I haven't always gotten along, no surprise, but I won't let anyone hurt her. I don't know what your game is..."

Jonathan was busy looking around the room as if he hadn't listened to a word she'd said. "What did she tell you about me?"

"Mom? Not a lot. She said -- "

"Not her, Jin. You know who I mean."

Jin did know. "So. We're not even going to pretend, are we?"

He just shrugged. "Why should we? You know I am not simply Jonathan Mitsumo, and I know that you know this. No need to take it any further than that if we don't want to sound like an old Abbott and Costello routine." He smiled at her. "Or do you? I'm game."

"You're Shiro," Jin said grimly.

He nodded. "Also true and I do not deny it. But who is Shiro? What does that name mean to you?"

She frowned. "You're the shadow creature who helped trap that little girl in hell, the one who helped keep Michiko in hers. Doubtless there are others I haven't discovered yet. Let's not play games then -- I intend to stop you."

"Stop me from what?"

Jin couldn't tell if he was mocking her or not. So far as his expression was readable, he seemed puzzled. Jin put her hands on her hips. "From interfering, for a start. From making some unfortunate soul spend one moment longer in hell than they need to!"

He shook his head sadly. "Why are you so angry at me, Jin? I really would like to know."

Jin blinked owlishly. "Why...? I just told you!"

"You told me I was interfering. I admit I've been going to the places I know you must go. I can follow the golden threads as well as you can. But I was not interfering."

Jin had no idea what 'golden threads' he was referring to, and at that moment could not possibly have cared less. "What would you call it then?"

"Being near you. That's all I wanted. That's all I've ever wanted."

Jin felt her fact flush in anger and embarrassment, and there wasn't a thing she could do about either. She was barely able to keep her voice below shouting. "My work is not your concern. Neither, for that matter, am I."

"I disagree, but let that be for now. You incarnated to hide from me, but I know there's more to it than that. But I've had some time to think about it, and I'm thinking that, perhaps, I know the real reason. Or at least more of a clue than you have, I'll wager."

Jin kept her temper, but it was hard. "Speaking of that, I want to know how you found me, how you knew who I was."

Shiro grinned. "That was easy -- Emma-O told me. Oh, right. I believe you know him as 'Teacher.'"

Jin started to deny it, but she couldn't. For all she knew it was true. Shiro went on. "I'll be glad to answer any question you put to me, but I do think you should choose them better. And I would like an answer to mine: who am I?"

Jin's hands balled into fists. She didn't want to answer him, but not answering seemed worse. Driven to the wall, she fell back on the truth. "You call yourself Jonathan Mitsumo, but you're Shiro...but aside from that, I don't know."

Shiro just nodded. "You really don't know, do you? I thought as much. She sent you in blind, didn't she? Yes, that fits. Unfortunately for both of us."

Jin didn't have to ask who "she" was. He meant the Guan Yin That Was. And he was absolutely right. For a moment Jin considered assuming her demon form, just to escape the feeling of being at such a complete disadvantage, but it was as if Shiro sensed her thought. "Go ahead if you want. Hardly anyone can stand before you in your Prince of

Demons form. It won't make any difference. I will, as they say, be back. I will go where you go, and I will do whatever it takes to be near you."

"Dammit all, who *are* you? I mean really. Forget the names which, so far as I can tell, mean less than shit. Who are you really? What do you want?" she asked finally.

"I am Shiro, and I told you what I want. Whatever you call yourself now, whatever flesh you wear, it makes no difference to me. What I want," he said, "is you."

Jin just stared at him. "I'm the mortal incarnation of **Guan** Shi Yin! What am I to you?"

"The same thing you are as **Guan** Shi Yin in all her glory. My love," Shiro said. "My wife."

Jin just stared at him for several long moments. "Don't you dare move," she said finally, and reached out and touched Shiro on the shoulder. To her surprise he didn't attempt to escape. He didn't so much as flinch.

"It's about time," he said just as her fingers brushed his shoulder, but by then it was too late.

Jin had a vision. Or perhaps the vision had her. There didn't seem to be any difference. Jin was no longer in her old bedroom. She was now at a place totally new to her and yet somehow totally familiar. She was in a dream. She was not in a dream. She was the one who acted. She was the one who watched, all her selves present and immersed in what was happening, had happened, would happen. All caught, for now, in time's net.

The temple was dark despite the lamp glow and the man's face was in shadow. That didn't matter; Jin knew him. He kneeled before the gilded statue of Kannon that Jin knew to be herself; flesh of stone and jeweled eyes notwithstanding. All of what was happening made perfect sense, because it was all part of the dream that Jin was a part of, too. He was praying to himself or to the statue. Jin heard a phrase over and over. She understood it and that understanding made her feel very sad. Was that a memory too? Part of the dream?

She didn't know. She only knew that she could no longer endure his prayers.

"Stop praying," she heard herself say, but it was the statue speaking.

The kneeling man was clearly stunned. Perhaps that's why he shut up. He finally looked up at the statue and Jin got her first good look at him. It was Shiro, of course. Not the same as the Jonathan she knew, but recognizable enough as a slim young man in robes of silk. "Have -- have I displeased you?" he finally managed.

"You have mistook me," Kannon and Jin said together. One and the same. Jin did not think this was strange. She was Kannon. She was Jin. If she were more Kannon than Jin at the moment, did it matter? This was Shiro. He was a problem. Nothing had changed at all.

"How? I will atone," Shiro said.

"You do not pray to me," Kannon said. "You're praying for me. Your prayers are snares. Admit it."

"I love you," Shiro said.

"I love you," Kannon said. "I love all who suffer. You are suffering, Shiro. You are confused, that is all. I am the gate, not the goal."

"You are my goal," Shiro said. "You are all that I want, all that I can imagine. There is nothing that is not Kannon. I am nothing. Though I linger a thousand years or die and am reborn a thousand thousand lifetimes, I will love you."

"Yes," Kannon said, and her voice was sadness distilled. Jin wept. Kannon wept. The look on Shiro's face was beyond rapture.

"I love you," he repeated. "I always will. Cast me into any hell of your choosing and block the way forever, I will always love you."

"Yes you will," Kannon said. "And no you won't. This ends, Minamoto no Shiro, and here is the beginning of it."

"What will you do?"

The statue disappeared. In its place was a living, breathing woman that Jin knew was Kannon, Guan Yin, GuanShiYin, Jin Hannigan, hair long and glossy black, her face at once luminous and no more than mortal. She wore the white kimono of a bride. She stood before the man who loved her in the flesh, because flesh was required.

"I will marry you, Minamoto no Shiro. I will be yours. That is what I will do."

I WILL SHOW YOU THE REST.

The voice was Shiro's, and Jonathan's, but it was outside the dream. Jin was having trouble listening. The dream moved from one scene to another with no interval at all, which was the way of dreams. Jin as Kannon as Guan Yin and as a mortal girl who was not Jin at all but called herself Mei accompanied Shiro home as his bride. She found herself blushing. She felt a strangeness in the pit of her stomach, a rush of blood to her face and belly. She felt something that she had never felt before, for anyone.

Shiro... did I... love him?

YOU LOVED ME. YOU KNOW IT'S TRUE.

Jin frowned. That sounded like Shiro, but it could not be Shiro. Shiro was on her arm, leading her to where the sleeping mats had been prepared and where she went, willingly, joyfully. Almost eagerly. Part of her was screaming that this could not be true, but the loudest voice within her, that *was* her, stood firm: it was true. This is almost how it happened.

"Almost?" she wondered aloud, and Shiro the groom smiled at her.

"What are you whispering?" he asked.

"Nothing," Jin said, blushing again. The thoughts were unbidden and confusing. She was where she needed to be, where she wanted to be. A new life was starting for her, a life with the man she loved. She wanted to embrace it just as she embraced him. They kneeled together. Flesh called to flesh and would not be denied.

IMMANENCE, PLEASE WAKE UP.

A new voice. Jin frowned. There was a little green dragon wound around her wrist. She could have sworn it spoke to her. But there was no little green dragon in this dream. She banished it with a thought, but it returned as soon as her attention wandered to her groom.

I HUMBLY SUGGEST THAT YOU WAKE UP NOW, the dragon said. Jin made to slap at it like a pestering fly, but the thing merely turned to smoke and then reformed.

AS YOU REQUIRE...

It bit her on the thumb. Jin shouted and flung it away from her and in that instant she was standing back in her own bedroom, in the now that she understood to be now. The image and the feelings of that other Jin, and that other Kannon long ago retreated to memory, all save one. Jin stood looking into Jonathan's handsome face, and she blushed again.

It had all been Jonathan...Shiro's, vision. Perhaps not a true vision in the way of a mortals ready to graduate from their current hell, but was any of it true at all? Did she... love him? Jin looked hard at the man in front of her, and there it was: the feeling that, until now, she had not believed herself capable of feeling. It was so much like what she had felt when she had been Mariko meeting her Saburo for the first time. Was it the same? She didn't know. It was so close. She asked herself what, she feared, might be the real question:

Do I love him?

"You know who I am, what we shared," Shiro said, gently. "You can't deny it. For now, that's enough."

CHAPTER 12

Shiro smiled at her and left without saying anything else. When he was gone, Jin sat down on the edge of the bed. Or rather her knees buckled and the bed happened to be there, fortunately. Otherwise she would have sat down on the floor. Hard.

"What the hell just happened?" she asked, in a small and frightened voice.

Ling appeared first in her green dragon form, then as the mortal girl Jin had come to know. In a moment there was a shimmer of light and Frank appeared as well. "What happened?" was Frank's question as well.

"She was almost trapped into sharing Shiro's delusion," Ling said. "An artifact of the flesh, I think, so I attacked the flesh in response. I apologize for the bite, Immanence. Does it hurt?"

Jin looked at them as if she didn't quite understand the question. Hurt? Of course it hurt! But the pain in her thumb was the least of it. She felt as if she'd been punched hard in the stomach by someone with very good extension who knew how to rock the fist forward into the gut at just the right moment. She looked from one to the other for a few moments before she could trust herself to speak again. "He was telling the truth, wasn't he?"

Now Ling and Frank looked at each other, and that was all the answer Jin needed. "Son of a bitch...you were both in on it!"

Ling frowned. "'In on it?' What do you mean?"

"Guan Yin's plan. Teacher's plan. Hell, everybody's fucking plan!"

Even then, shaking in shock and confusion, Jin realized how silly she sounded. Of course they were in on Guan Yin's plan. After all, they were there on the other Guan Yin's command, not hers. "Why didn't you tell me?"

"Could you be more specific?" Ling asked. "What should we have told you?"

"That you knew who Shiro was, for a start! I mean, I knew there was more to the story but... married? I mean, Shiro and Guan Yin? Goddess of goddam *Mercy*?"

"There's a legend in Japanese folklore concerning this marriage," Frank said calmly. "We're not privy to most of the details, but there's a seed of truth in it."

"We serve and obey," Ling said primly. "We do not anticipate. In all fairness to us we never told you this part of the story because you never *asked*."

"Get out," Jin said.

Frank nodded. "You're upset. We understand. If you would like to take a moment -- "

"Get out!!!"

Frank looked shocked, Ling just shrugged, but they both immediately disappeared in separate flashes of light. Jin wanted nothing much more than to get out of that room, that house, that reality, but she still didn't trust her legs to hold her. There was a knock on the door.

"Jin? Honey, are you all right? Who are you shouting at?"

"No...no one. I'm... I'm all right. Just let the past catch up with me, I guess."

"Happens to me all the time," Margaret said, as she opened the door. "Are you sure you're all right? You look pale." She suddenly frowned, and sat down beside Jin on the narrow bed. "I was joking earlier, but did Jonathan...?" She didn't finish.

It took Jin a moment to understand what her mother was asking, then she almost laughed. "No, nothing like that. We just talked."

Her mother looked relieved. "Ok, so I didn't think he was like that, but then you know my judgment in men isn't always the best. Still, I knew I was right about Jonathan. He's a good man."

Tell her.

For a moment Jin thought she'd spoken aloud but no, the thought was still confined inside her skull, though it was clamoring to get out.

Tell her what? That I really am the incarnation of **Guan** *Shi Yin and that man she's dating was my husband a thousand years ago*? Jin shuddered. No, now was not the time. Not until Jin finally pulled herself out of the dark that everyone from Teacher and the Guan Yin That Was on down to Ling and Frank seemed determined to keep her in.

"Is Jonathan still here?" Jin asked.

"He had to eat and run. Always some excuse or other when it gets serious, but he's probably afraid of commitment."

Jin frowned. Something in the way her mother said this sounded like a hint. "Mom...pardon me for asking this and I'm not even sure why I want to know, but I do -- are you sleeping with Jonathan? I mean, before I just kind of assumed you were. Are you?"

Margaret looked decidedly uncomfortable. "I'm not sure that's appropriate -- "

Jin put her hand on her mother's shoulder. "I really do need to know. I can't explain why, but I think it might be important." Her mother just looked at her for a few moments, but finally shrugged. "No, we haven't been intimate. Jonathan says he's old-fashioned and doesn't want to rush. I'm beginning to think it's me."

"Couldn't be." Jin leaned closed and kissed her mother on the cheek. "I need to go now." Jin stood up carefully, feeling brittle and weak, but her knees held this time. She stretched and yawned, feeling as wrung out as a bar dishrag. "Listen, I'll try and bring some of my things over tomorrow, ok?"

"Looking forward to it." Jin's mother looked around. "I guess it's silly to keep all this if you're going to be here yourself. Just pack up what you don't want and we'll put it all in the attic. I'm not quite ready to purge your childhood just yet. Uneven as it was."

"I wasn't always the center of your universe at the time I wanted to be," Jin said. "But I know you were going through some rough times, too. I'm sorry I didn't make it as easy for you as I could have."

Her mother just smiled wistfully. "Ditto."

Jin let herself out and headed back toward downtown. She glanced at her apartment building but, weary as she was, she didn't stop to rest. She didn't think this was the sort of weariness that sleep might relieve and, even if it proved possible, she wasn't ready to speak to the Guan Yin That Was just yet. She stalked the streets of downtown Medias. She remembered it was Friday night. Here and there were couples walking, but Jin knew those were locals who had little more than their own company, else they wouldn't be downtown in the first place. Now and then she would hear a whisper on the wind, a voice of pain. It was not pleasant to hear, but she could manage. She had to hear them, even when there was nothing she could do to help them yet. She was Guan Yin.

The crowds thinned and Jin moved into areas she knew weren't safe. Jin didn't think she had a choice. She had to find Teacher, no matter where he was, and she wasn't about to summon Frank or Ling to do it for her. It was only when she had covered all his known haunts that she was satisfied that he was not in Medias.

Jin turned a corner and there was a young man there in a shiny new leather jacket. "Frank?"

"Maybe next time. You're out of your place, Jin."

Jin got a better look and knew she'd been mistaken. This young man was about four inches taller than Frank, and heavier-set. He had a scraggly beard and goatee, and what Jin supposed was meant to pass as a knowing smirk. She knew him through the legal aid office. His real name was Marshall Simmons. His street name was Baby. After his tenth arrest and fourth conviction, mostly minor stuff, Joyce was just about ready to give up on him. Jin hadn't made up her mind yet.

"Place? I was born here, Marshall."

"'Baby' to you, sweet cheeks. Or you can just call me 'lover,'" he said, moving to block her path.

"I don't have time for this," Jin said, but that wasn't exactly true. She had time. What she lacked at that moment was patience.

"Don't tell me what you got and don't got," Baby said. "You're in my world now. You gotta pay the toll."

Jin blinked. "Don't you think mugging part of your legal aid team is just a little stupid? I mean, even for you?"

He scowled. "I ain't playing, Jin. I'll take it out of your purse or that sweet pussy of yours. Makes no difference to me."

Jin looked around. They were alone of course, on a seedy street that saw little enough traffic during the day and almost none this time of the evening. "Why hang out here, Baby? The big boys won't let you play with them?"

Baby actually flushed red, though whether from mere anger or because she'd nailed him with the truth, she didn't know. She didn't care. "Look, Baby. I'm sorry I dissed you.

I've had a rough few days, ok? Now let me by and I'll forget this nonsense you've been talking."

Baby pulled a knife. It was a long, shiny and new. He reached out and grabbed Jin's wrist. "Don't tell me what you will or won't do, bitch! I own your ass -- "

Jin pulled him in. She didn't want to. It wasn't his time and she wasn't here for him, but there was a vision when the fool touched her. He was too unaware to make that vision into anything but the truth and Jin saw it plain -- Marshall Simmons was no street kid, nor was he an orphan as he had always claimed. His parents were solidly middle class, stable and boring. Marshall Simmons fell in love with an idea, an image that, to him, promised excitement, and danger, and all the things he thought he wanted. They called him "Baby" on the street because that's what he was. The real gangs laughed at him. He was a wannabee, a poseur, but he was heading for deep trouble and it had been coming for a long time.

Marshall staggered back. "What the hell did you do?"

Jin shrugged. "Think of this as your wake-up call."

"What are you talking about, bitch?"

"Your manners, for a start." Jin faced Marshall squarely and assumed her demon form. "Baby needs a spanking."

Then, before he had time to scream even once, Jin beat the living crap out of him. When she was done with him she left Marshall slumped against an alley wall, bruised and barely conscious but alive, with his fancy new knife shoved into the dirt inches from his crotch. Jin resumed her human form and kept walking.

I didn't kill him. How's that for mercy, Teacher?

She found the guardians in their usual place, flanking the entrance as she emerged into the central sanctuary. The huge golden statue of Guan Yin with her assistants/servants smiled at all as always, but Jin ignored it. "Where is he?" she asked the guardians.

HE? YOU MEAN SHIRO?

"I know where Shiro is, thanks. Tell me where the King of the First Hell is. That was not a request."

The guardians reluctantly moved to flank a new door. NOW MAY NOT BE THE BEST TIME, they said as one. HE IS IN JUDGMENT.

"I don't care if he's in the john," Jin said, and walked right past the two huge stone figures and into a passageway to another hell.

Jin walked down a corridor that seemed, if anything, longer than usual, and she wondered what hell it led to. She'd learned better than to open her Third Eye while in transit, but she couldn't help but wonder what the reality of this corridor looked like. For one thing, instead of the silent carved monsters and demons in their niches, this corridor had what looked at first like thousands of tiny circles carved into the stone. At one point Jin hesitated, then actually stopped, plucked one of the ubiquitous flickering torches from the wall, and moved closer to examine the niches.

Scrolls. The walls were full of regularly spaced niches stacked with carved stone scrolls. Jin reached out and touched one, gingerly, then immediately drew her hand back, startled. The scroll looked like stone, but it didn't feel like stone. It felt a lot like parchment. Jin reached out slowly once more into the niche and pulled out a long roll of parchment.

"Here now, put that back!"

Jin almost dropped the parchment. She whirled around just in time to see a brown hooded blur flash past her. She looked down and realized she wasn't holding the parchment any more.

"...took me ages to find the right place to file that. Honestly, some people..."

What looked like a short, squat little man in a plain brown robe stood in the front of the niche, muttering. He let out one "Hah!" of triumph as he apparently found the hole he was looking for and slid the parchment back into place. Then he very carefully removed two other parchments which were, so far as Jin could tell, identical to the one he'd just put back, and turned around.

Now that she could see him better Jin realized that he wasn't a man at all but a short demon, but at this point Jin would have been more than a little surprised if that had not turned out to be the case. He had large eyes, pointed ears, long sharp teeth, and a round hole in the middle of his face where a nose should have been.

"Listen, I'm -- "

"You're Guan Shi Yin and should know better than to muck with the records." He cradled the two parchments in his arms and started back down the corridor, Jin a step or two behind.

"I'm looking for Teacher...I think you know him as Emma-O."

"Teacher, Emma-O, Yen Lo, Yama... I know nearly all the names, including that first one. That's what I do," he said. "Since you don't remember me I don't suppose you remember that, either?"

Jin had misplaced her anger briefly are her meeting with the bureaucrat demon, but it was starting to come back. "Listen you little -- "

"Oh, fine," he said. "Take your problems out on me. It's not like everyone else doesn't, so why should the Bodhisattva of Mercy be any different? Still," he said, and sniffed, "some of us know what our jobs are. I'm doing mine. Why are you here?"

"I need to see Teacher. It's important."

"No you don't and no it isn't, but if you must then I can take you to him."

"Oh. Thank you... Umm, may I ask your name?"

He rolled his eyes. "Oh, fine. Throw that up at me, why don't you? That's gratitude."

Jin just frowned. "I beg your pardon?"

The demon stared at her for a moment or two, then shrugged. "So you forgot that as well? Madame Meng really gave you your money's worth, didn't she?"

"Madame Meng? Who's that?"

"The Mistress of the Ninth Hell, of course. She brews the potions that make people forget their past lives before they're reincarnated. Your memory has been erased, obviously, so you must have visited her. Or did you think that just happened on its own?"

Jin blinked. "I hadn't thought of that."

"Obviously. Listen, Immanent One, none of those who serve Emma-O remember who they were, so names are rather a sore point with us. You may call me the Keeper of the Names if you must. Follow me, please."

The demon was fast for someone with such short legs; Jin had to hurry to keep up.

"Wait," Jin said. She reached out and grabbed the Keeper of the Names by the shoulder. "I've changed my mind."

"You don't wish to see Teacher?"

"Later. Right now the person I really want to see is Madame Meng."

CHAPTER 13

Jin passed the niches of parchment with no more than a glance in either direction. Perhaps it was her focus on the destination that shortened the trip, but it seemed almost no time by comparison before she emerged back into the Gateway of All the Hells where the guardians were patiently waiting.

"Show me the way to the Ninth Hell," she said.

WE CANNOT, they said. YOU FORBID IT.

"I...?" Jin stopped. Yes, of course she had, or would have. It was so like her. She thought for a moment, then smiled. "The Guan Yin That Was forbade you to show me the way to the Ninth Hell, yes?" They nodded. "Did she forbid you to tell me how to find Madame Meng?"

Silence for several long moments. NO, SHE DID NOT.

"Very well, *that* is my command. Do not show me how to reach the Ninth Hell, for lo, Guan Shi Yin has forbidden it and we can't muck with her Word and in truth I give rather less than a rat's ass about the Ninth Hell as such anyway. What I really want is to talk to Madame Meng. How do I do that?"

DYING WOULD WORK.

Jin glared at them. "Assuming I don't want to shuffle off the mortal coil just yet, how else? Can't you just show me the correct door?"

THAT WOULD BE THE SAME AS SHOWING YOU THE WAY TO THE NINTH HELL, SINCE THAT IS WHERE YOU WILL FIND HER. IF YOU REALLY WISH TO SPEAK TO MADAME MENG, THE ONLY OTHER WAY I CAN THINK OF WOULD BE TO EITHER HAVE EMMA-O OR YOUR SERVANTS SHOW YOU THE WAY.

"They know? Oh, of course. I should have figured that they would."

Jin left the guardians by the door to the First Hell and walked toward the center of the chamber, toward the statues of Guan Shi Yin, Celestial Youth, and the Dragon Maiden, and she considered the situation as she did so. She was still looking forward to tearing Teacher a new one, but she had put that pleasure off for the sake of this new lead and so didn't think that this was the best time to be asking him for favors.

Jin looked up a the statue of Guan Yin again, at its great height, glory, and richness. It was just a statue. Metal, wood, artistry. Probably no more real than the torch-lit corridors between hells; Jin could open her Third Eye and see for herself, but she didn't trust what she would see any more than she trusted Frank and Ling.

"I know you can hear me, Frank. Ling. Front and center." There was a pause, and Jin sighed. "Stop being so literal. What I meant was, show yourselves!"

They manifested in their equivalent statues on the dais, Frank with his palms pressed together in an attitude of prayer, Ling dressed in flowing robes and carrying a pearl that glowed with its own light.

"Has the Goddess of Mercy forgiven us?" Ling asked. Jin didn't know if Ling was being sarcastic or not, but decided that she didn't really care.

"I dunno. Ask her the next time you see her. For my own part, no, I'm still fairly pissed."

Frank frowned. "But you *are* Guan Yin!"

Jin smiled a grim smile. "Yes and no. Guan Yin is not a mortal girl, and that's what I am. Yet as we both know, that is what Guan Yin intended me to be, and without her divine understanding. So. We are stuck with the notion that this mortal girl is in charge of Guan Yin's duties, Guan Yin's power -- such that a mortal can bear, anyway -- and Guan Yin's servants, correct?"

Frank and Ling glanced at each other. "Well...yes," Frank said. "Though I should point out that Guan Yin was once a mortal, as you are. She remembers."

"But I don't. Funny how that worked out."

Frank and Ling exchanged another glance, and Jin sighed, "Never mind, so long as we understand one another. Now get down from there, I want to talk to both of you."

Ling and Frank appeared in front of her in their street clothes and their statues reverted to their former inanimate selves. Jin nodded approval. "Much better. Now, then -- do you two know the way to the Ninth Hell? The dominion of the entity known as Madame Meng? And no consulting with each other; I just want a straight answer."

"Yes," said Frank. "We do."

"Fine. Will you take me there?"

Ling frowned. "Why would you wish to go to the Terrace of Oblivion?"

"That's my own business. I just want to know if it's forbidden."

"We have no prior instructions on this," Frank said. Ling said nothing.

"Yet I'm almost certain that the Guan Yin That Was knew I might ask. Interesting, but I'll think about that later," Jin said. "Very well. Show me the way."

"We can take you there instantly," Frank said.

"I know. I want you to show me."

For a moment Frank just looked as if he didn't understand, and Ling just sighed. "This way, Jin."

She led Jin to one of the doors that looked like all the other doors. Jin stopped long enough to pick up three small stones and placed them on the right side of the door. "I know these aren't real, strictly speaking, but they look like stones and I'd like them to remain here so I can find this place again at need. Understand?"

"Yes," Ling said. "You think we might move them. Which seems rather pointless on our part if all you have to do is command us to show you the way again."

Jin stepped through the door with Ling and Frank close behind. She started walking. "I want to be able to find this place on my own if I have to. That's all."

Ling just shrugged again. Jin seriously considered addressing her attitude, but she knew Ling would simply say something about not being responsible for Jin's interpretation of Ling's communication, or whatnot.

Jin knew that Lung Nu was a Bodhisattva too, and clearly being so didn't excuse one from all human emotion, at least when wearing a corporeal form. Ling was obviously feeling aggrieved; Jin knew the signs. Ling might be a many thousands of years old dragon, but she was acting like a sullen teenager, and Jin was more relieved than annoyed. "Sullen teenager" was a world-view that Jin understood.

"You think I'm being unfair," Jin said. "Well, put yourself in my place. When Shiro dropped his bombshell, what would you have done?"

"I would have torn him apart and devoured the better pieces," Ling said, though there was just a hint of a twitch at the corner of her mouth that suggested she wanted to smile when she said it.

Jin did smile. "Given that this wasn't an option for me, what then?"

Ling seemed to consider the question while Frank kept pointedly silent. "I don't know," Ling said at last. "Perhaps...perhaps I would have gotten angry."

Jin shrugged. "Well, obviously that was the way I went. I thought I was justified at the time. I still think so, so far as my limited understanding allows. You'll have plenty of chances to prove me wrong."

Unlike Jin's hike through the record vaults of the First Hell, they arrived at the opposite end of the corridor very quickly, and Jin opened the door to a far different hell. For a moment she was stunned, and could say nothing. She just stared out into the place called the Ninth Hell for several long moments.

"This..." she managed at last, "this is wonderful."

Even as she said it Jin knew that "wonderful" was a lame, inadequate word for what she was seeing. For sheer scale it was a match for the First Hell, but there the resemblance ended. Jin and her companions stood on a mountain ledge. Far below them was a vast green valley, though it was sometimes hard to see for the thick fluffy clouds floating by. On the far side of the valley was another mountain much like the one they stood on now, grass and trees growing wherever the niches and ledges allowed and all sorts of blossoming plants taking root in crags and the cracks in stone. Flocks of white cranes soared across the gap between the mountains and the peaks, and the air was filled with the scent of flowers. Jin knew that, realistically, trees should not grow on mountains this high, that she and any foolish flowers should be freezing from cold and there should have been nothing to see but snow, but Jin didn't care. She was perfectly willing to believe that such a marvelous place could exist, must exist, *should* exist.

"Is this a paradise?" Jin asked.

Ling frowned. "This is the Ninth Hell," she said. "Madame Meng's dominion."

Jin shook her head in wonder. "If this is a hell I can't imagine what a paradise must look like."

"There are several and we can show you those, too," Frank said. "Though, except for a few more celestial palaces, they look a lot like this."

"Maybe later," Jin said, forcing her breathing back to normal. "Where is Madame Meng?"

"Across the valley. The Terrace of Oblivion is on the far side of that mountain. Shall we go?"

"Umm," said Jin, looking down into the mists, "how do we get across?"

"On the bridge of course," said Ling.

Jin looked across, then down, then across again. "What bridge?"

There was a gleam in Ling's eye as she took hold of Jin's left hand and Frank took hold of her right. Before Jin realized what they were up to they had taken two quick steps off the edge of the mountain and out into nothing.

"Are you crazy?" Jin shrieked, before she realized that they were not falling. Her feet had come down on something solid and it took her a moment to realize what had happened; they stood among the clouds Jin had seen floating between the mountains, but this particular set of clouds were not moving. They stretched in a long tumbly, puffy line from across the long space between the peaks. Ling and Frank released her hands and she reached out and felt something much like a railing on either side of them. It felt cold to her touch, and looked like impossibly white marble.

"What was that, payback?" Jin asked. "You nearly gave me a heart attack!"

"We merely showed you where the bridge was," Ling said, but Frank was almost hugging himself to keep from laughing.

Jin was angry for maybe three seconds. She finally smiled despite herself. "Ok, fine. But do anything like that again and odds are your old mistress will have to get herself a new patsy."

Ling just looked innocent, though Frank had a little difficultly getting back in control. "I'm not sure what you mean, Immanent One, but we promise not to be so abrupt in future," he said finally. "Shall we?"

"Oh, no," Jin said. "You two go first so I can keep my eyes on you. All three of them, if I have to."

They're children, Jin thought. She wondered if it had some deep symbolic meaning that Lung Nu and Shan Cai were always shown as youths and perhaps that was what she was interpreting as horseplay but there seemed to be an almost sibling rivalry between the two *bodhisattvas*. If the Guan Yin That Was ever showed her face again in Jin's dreams, she resolved to ask her about that.

Now that she was aware of the railing, Jin kept her hands on it as she walked. Despite the solid feel underfoot, it still looked to Jin as if she was walking on clouds, and it was a very long way down. She glanced over the side once and decided that this was a bad idea, not to be repeated for the rest of the trip. She kept her eyes firmly fixed ahead on Ling and Frank as they led the way.

Ling glanced back. "Is the Bodhisattva of Mercy afraid of heights?"

"Nope. Just falling from them. Illusion or not, physical bodies tend to go splat when that happens. I have no wish to be the illusion of a big splat."

Ling smiled. "No need to concern yourself. These bridges have stood for many aeons, subjective time."

"All time is now," Jin said, not entirely sure where her words were coming from. "No new action in the future nor in the past. I will not fall in the past, or future, but I very well could fall now."

For an instant Ling actually looked impressed, but Frank shook his head. "That chaos of divinity and mortality, of transcendence and human desire and fear within you... I don't know how you stand it."

"As if I have a choice," muttered Jin.

They were approaching the other side. Jin glanced over the side once more despite her better judgment and was rewarded with the sight of a majestic flock of white cranes flying past the cliff face far below them. She had to shut her eyes and stop for a moment until both the dizziness and urge to throw up faded.

"I told myself not to look down again. I should have taken my own advice."

"Your wisdom is legendary," Frank said. "Personally, I would listen to you in future."

Jin couldn't tell if he was making another joke or just being sarcastic, but she didn't really care. She concentrated on reaching the far mountain and, after what seemed like hours on the bridge of clouds, they made it. Jin stepped gratefully onto solid rock. If it, like most existence, was simply illusion, Jin didn't care. It was a solid enough illusion, and that was all that mattered to her then. She leaned against the rough bark of a cedar, breathing its refreshing scent.

They stood on a broad ledge that looked and smelled a lot like the one they had left, only this one was wider and marked with a winding path leading up the face of the mountain. Frank and Ling started up the path immediately and Jin followed. They walked through what seemed more garden than road; if anything the vegetation was more lush here than it was on the first ledge. Many different types of colorful birds were singing; monkeys chattered at them from the treetops.

"This is a really pretty hell," Jin said.

"The people who come here are due a little respite, so I imagine it was tailored to them. It seems little enough considering what they're about to go through," said Ling.

People?

Jin was concentrating so much on the magnificent views around her that she'd completely overlooked them. There were other people on the path, though none where she and her companions were at the moment. She could see them further up the path, walking either alone or in small groups. Some were wearing strange clothes. Some wore nothing at all, but all marched up the path with what seemed to Jin a rather resigned air, barely taking notice of what was around them. Jin glanced back the way they had come; the other mountain was still visible on their left and, as Jin looked closer, she noticed that theirs was not the only bridge across the valley, and there were more people on the other bridges. They were arriving at different heights along the cliff face, but every bridge connected to a place where the same path snaked past the face of the mountain. As Jin walked with the others they eventually passed one or two of the slower people, while a few faster ones passed them on their way up. Upon closer inspection, Jin's first impression was affirmed: everyone, despite the beauty of their surroundings, was either looking very grim or simply resigned. After one particularly sour-faced young man hurried past, Jin turned to Frank and Ling.

"What's the matter with them?"

"I'm not sure I understand you," Frank said. "This is the Ninth Hell and all is going as it should."

Jin glanced skyward and sighed. "I *mean* why does everyone look so glum? As hells go this one is very pleasant."

"Not everyone," Ling said, and nodded her head toward an old woman hobbling up the path. She seemed positively cheerful by comparison. She even nodded pleasantly to the three of them as they stepped to the side to let her pass. "To most people who come here, the Ninth Hell is just about the worst there is. Some, like that old woman you just saw, think it as splendid as you do. The only difference between those two reactions is this: those who look sad do so because they know what's about to happen to them. Those who look happy, do not."

"Oh. Just what is about to happen to them?"

Ling looked astonished but Frank shook his head. "We beg your pardon, Immanent One, but we sometimes forget the extent of what you do not remember. You know about the Terrace of Oblivion?"

"Yes, but only since today. It's why I need to speak to Madame Meng. Isn't it where a person's memory is blanked out before they are reincarnated?"

"Exactly," Frank said. "Those who look unhappy do so because they still remember their old hell and, even though they will soon forget, they know they're going back again, that they are not ready to move on. Those who are happy have been released, like that old woman. They more than likely will be going to a hell also, but a *different* one, so they don't know what will happen, just that they are going on to something new. They're making progress. Their time on the Wheel of Life and Death is getting shorter."

"But I don't remember releasing that old woman. And if I'm the only one who can..."

"You don't remember releasing her," Ling said. "That doesn't mean that you didn't. The fact that she's here at this particular *now* and not in some age long gone "now" doesn't mean she was released recently. She took her own path here, as everyone must. If you went and touched her, you'd remember."

Jin thought of racing ahead and placing a hand on the old woman just to see if she would remember being the Guan Yin That Was as well, but she knew the visions didn't work that way. They would be about the old woman, not her redeemer.

"Fine. So where are the animals?" Jin asked. "I released my own cat, Missus Tickles, back before I even knew who I was. If that's so, then why isn't she here, or some other?"

"Humans are at an advantage in this," Ling said. "The greater the sentience, the more possibility of understanding error. Animals do move on, as you discovered, since all living things share this burden. That doesn't mean it's common. I believe the fact that Missus Tickles did appear here was Teacher's final proof that you were who he thought you were."

"She gave me away, huh? I wondered about that. Do... do you know what happened to her?"

"Missus Tickles? She was reborn in a different hell, of course. As a human this time. Progress," Frank said.

"I know some cat lovers who would dispute that point," Jin said dryly.

"I would dispute that point as well," Ling said. "Before my Enlightenment, there were those who argued that a woman could not, in fact, achieve Enlightenment. That I was a dragon besides and not human at all was doubly astonishing to them."

"Grrl power," Jin said, smiling.

Ling flexed her arms, grinning. "Indeed."

Frank just shook his head. "I look forward to the day when we can shed these corporeal forms again. Having a body makes one silly."

Jin smiled. "There are advantages. Though when I'm trudging up some infernal corridor or path trying to get somewhere I need to be, it's hard to remember what those advantages might be." Jin stopped a moment to rest on a large stone. "How much farther?"

Frank studied the path ahead. "Fifteen steps."

Jin looked up the mountain path as it meandered upward.

"More like fifteen miles."

"Appearances deceive. In hell, doubly so. Please count."

Jin rubbed her aching legs and then stood up again. "All right. One," she said as they took a step together.

"Two," said Ling.

"Three," said Frank, and by the time they all called "Fifteen!" they stood at a massive door of bronze, silver, and gold.

"On the nose," Jin said. "Nice job."

"Oh, he can count," Ling said. "I'm so impressed."

Jin sighed. "Don't start, you two. Where is Madame Meng?"

"Inside," Frank said. "But this is as far as Ling and I can go."

Jin blinked. "You're not coming? Why?"

"It's hard to explain," Ling said. "You could say it's outside our jurisdiction."

"Then... isn't it outside of mine as well?"

"You are Guan Yin." Frank said, as if that explained everything. Not that Jin was particularly worried about going in alone; in fact she much preferred a private audience with this Madame Meng, whoever she might be. Yet it was just one more reminder of how much she had yet to understand. She was hoping that Madame Meng could help with that.

"Wait for me, then. I'll be right back," Jin said, though at the moment she had no idea if that was true or not. Jin opened the door.

CHAPTER 14

It's just like Grand Central Station!

Jin had only been to New York's Grand Central Station once, but the similarities with Madame Meng's domain were remarkable. Jin stood in one vast central space ringed by numerous doors disgorging people. There were high windows of colored glass that let the sun in, and everywhere was the bustle of people trying to get from one place to another. Everyone seemed to know where they were going except for Jin.

She stood just inside the doorway for a moment, then moved to one side as more people came through while she continued to study all the activity for a time. Soon Jin was able to make out patterns: when people first arrived, they all moved toward what looked like a vast waiting room off to the left, only no one waited there for very long. After a fairly short while they milled back into the main section, looking somewhat confused but still moving with purpose toward a huge open doorway on the far side of the central chamber opposite Jin. In time Jin began to think that the comparison with Grand Central Station wasn't totally accurate. In many ways it was more like the Gateway to All the Hells, except people were coming in through different doors and all leaving by the same one.

Jin left the wall where she had been watching everything and found one of the new arrivals, a rather depressed-looking old man. "Excuse me, do you know where Madame Meng is?"

"Here, of course," the man said and kept walking.

That wasn't very helpful, but it seemed to be all the help Jin was going to get. All the depressed-looking people said more or less the same thing with slight variations, and all the confused looking people just said, "Who?"

The Terrace of Oblivion, Jin thought. *If I were double-jointed, I'd kick myself.*

Jin had thought of the Terrace of Oblivion as a metaphor, but she thought now that, perhaps, that was an error. She fell in with the people heading out toward what she'd first thought was the waiting area. They shuffled through great open doors, far larger than that those of an aircraft hanger, and out onto a vast balcony of marble and granite. In the distance Jin could see another mountain, much like the one where her path from the Gateway to All the Hells emerged, and there were so many bridges spanning the gulf from that side to this one that Jin was a little amazed that she hadn't noticed them at first. That aside, the view, as it was from the other side of the mountain, was simply breath-taking. Jin even noticed waterfalls on the opposite side, fed, she assumed, by high mountain lakes and rainfall. They emerged through fissures in the rock to fall in long white plumes toward the valley below, creating permanent rainbows in their wakes.

Jin thought of the central hub where the people had been going after visiting the balcony; she wondered if, perhaps, it was a stairway down to the Tenth Hell. Maybe the valley below was the Tenth Hell.

A large group of men and women shuffled past Jin, and something about them got her attention. Or rather, something missing: voices. The place was filled with people and no one was talking to each other. Even the people who moved in groups seemed to do so more from some sort of unconscious flocking instinct than any real interest in each other's company. They were simply bodies moving from one place to another as if by stage direction: go there. Stand here for a moment, then go over there.

There were multi-level fountains that looked like stacked marble mushrooms, and this was the "there" where most people were headed. They would walk up, take a ladle from the basin, and drink. Some seemed to drink eagerly, some drank looking resigned, and others still looked angry and sullen. Yet once they had drunk, all assumed the slightly bewildered look that Jin had noticed in the main hall. Then they would shuffled back into the main hall and proceed toward the central hub and its huge black doors.

All but one. She stood with her hands on the balcony railing. Her hair was long and pure white, her hands spotted and wrinkled with age. She did not drink. She did not speak. She simply looked out over the valley toward the far mountain. Jin approached, hesitantly.

"Excuse me... are you Madame Ming?"

The woman turned then. Jin's impression of age was not mistaken; the woman was ancient, her face lined and care-worn. Yet she stood straight and there was a dignity about her that made Jin feel more than a little awkward.

"**Guan** Shi Yin. It is you, isn't it? Let me look at you, girl."

The old woman frowned, then sniffed the air. Jin thought for a moment that maybe she needed a shower, but the old woman was smiling. "Real living flesh. Impressive. I'm surprised you made it here intact. Everyone else is dead, you know."

Jin did, in fact, know that, but the blunt way the old woman said it rather startled her. "Ahh, excuse me, you *are* Madame Meng, aren't you?"

"That I am. Sorry to go on so. Rude of me, but of course you didn't recognize me and I should have realized. It would make no sense at all if you did. Not even a bit. How have you been?"

Jin, confused, just stammered out the conventional reply. "Uh, fine. And you?"

"The same. Always the same." She was looking back at the far mountain again, and Jin joined her at the rail.

"Beautiful, isn't it?" Madame Meng asked after a short while.

"It's incredible," Jin said. "Though most of the people who come here don't seem to appreciate it. Frank... I mean, Shan Cai and Lung Nu said it was because they were dreading what was about to happen to them."

"I'm sure that's part of it," Madame Meng said, "but this is my realm, and I have my own theory."

"May I ask what that is?"

"They're dead, Immanent One. It's not that dying removes your sense of esthetics; I simply believe your priorities change. Now, take us by contrast -- we're alive. This sight means something to us. I've been here for longer than most glacial epochs and I never get tired of it. Which is fortunate, else I think I would go mad."

Jin wondered if she should say something, but Madame Meng didn't seem to expect it. Jin waited for her to say something else, but she didn't do that either. She simply leaned against the rail, looking out, just as she was when Jin found her.

"Listen, I hope you don't mind my asking -- "

"Not at all, and the answer is 'yes,'" Madame Meng said, not even waiting for Jin to finish the question. "Your divine self came to me to be reborn on the Wheel of Life and Death. That *is* what you came to ask, isn't it? Once your mortal incarnation found out that I and this place existed?"

Jin just stared at her for a moment, then blushed. "Well...yes."

Madame Meng just sighed. "I thought as much. You don't remember any of that, of course. Your choice. How I envy you that."

"You envy me? Why?"

The old woman smiled. "Well, not you as such, Guan Yin. Your responsibilities are grave and, despite my complaints, I would not wish to trade mine for yours. Just the 'forgetting' part. I wish I could do that."

"I don't understand."

Madame Meng looked back into the distance. "The nature of my responsibilities is that I must remain here, brewing the Elixir of Oblivion. It's my gift, you see. Or curse. It has to be done, and only I can do it. I have been doing it for a very long time, and I remember everything. One day, one time, one 'now' pretty much like another, and I think what a joy it must be to forget the journey, the path ahead and behind and all that has gone before."

"Like the people who come through here?" Jin asked.

Madame Meng nodded toward the confused-looking men and women shuffling out on their way to the Tenth Hell to be reborn. "Yes, and that's the true rebirth, not the taking on of crude flesh one more time -- the rebirth of the spirit. To start over fresh, your sins and errors all forgotten, to see the world with new eyes..." Madame Meng closed hers for a moment as if trying to imagine it. She finally shook her head, and opened her eyes once more. "I'm supposed to be beyond all that now, yet sometimes I think it would be worth all that I am to forget, just once." She smiled at Jin then. "Forgive my rambling. I get so few visitors. Or rather too many, but none of them are much for conversation. I gather conversation is what you had in mind? Answers?"

"Yes... I was hoping you would help me."

Madame Meng leaned over and patted Jin's hand in a grandmotherly fashion. "Let's have some tea and talk about it." She turned away from the railing. "It's not good for me to stare out like this for too long anyway. I start to believe I can fly, like those silly cranes who are always flittering around out there."

Jin followed the old woman to one side of the balcony, where a small door of iron-bound wood appeared. At least, Jin was pretty sure the door had suddenly appeared, since she was certain that it had not been there a few moments ago. They went up a spiral iron staircase into what looked like the den of a very comfortable apartment. While Madame Meng put the kettle on in the adjoining kitchen, Jin looked around.

There was an overall vaguely Eastern theme to the decor but, except for the lack of electronics the, place didn't seem much different than any other modern apartment. There was an overstuffed red sofa and chair, a small iron table and chairs by a big bay window. There were a few books, but they all seemed to be in Chinese.

"Nice apartment," Jin said as Madame Meng emerged from the kitchen.

"I must say I do prefer the current manifestation," Madame Meng said, smiling. "There was a time it was little more than one drafty room with a central hearth. Amazing how the perception of progress sometimes leads to the real thing. Please. Sit." The old woman lowered herself into the chair and Jin sat down on the couch.

"So," Madame Meng said, "what do you want to know?"

Jin thought about it for a moment. "First, I want to know if I... if the Guan Shi Yin who came to you, I mean, expected me to turn up?"

Madame Meng laughed. "Oh, child, it does get torturous, doesn't it? To be you and yet not 'you' at all." She looked thoughtful. "What do you call yourself now?"

"Jin. Jin Lee Hannigan."

"Well then, Jin Lee Hannigan, I have to tell you that the answer to that is also 'yes.' Guan Yin considered the possibility that you would find out about me and the Terrace of Oblivion."

Jin felt her hopes sink. "Damn...pardon my language, Madame Meng, but I hoped your answer would different. She forbade the Guardians to show me the way, so I thought 'maybe if I find another way..'"

"You're a clever one, incarnated or no," Madame Meng said. "And I must admit there's more than a little entertainment value watching you trying to outsmart yourself. I have so few diversions here." She apparently noticed the stricken look on Jin's face and patted her hand again. "Oh, don't look that way. Things aren't so bad as you fear. They may actually be worse."

"That's not exactly comforting," Jin said.

"Did you come to me for comfort? I thought you came here to find out the truth. While I don't claim to know it all, I believe I can give you a piece of it."

Jin frowned. "But you said -- "

"That Guan Yin had anticipated the arrival of her mortal incarnation here, and so you did. You're assuming that I promised not to reveal your own intentions to you."

"Well... didn't you?"

Madame Meng chuckled. "Oh, not at all, because you did not confide in me. Not that it would have made an ounce of difference -- you simply asked me as a friend for the gift of oblivion and I gave it to you. Do you think me such a poor sort of friend that I would turn about and take it away?"

Jin slumped back against the couch, defeated. "Then I'm wasting your time...or whatever it amounts to. I'll go now—"

The tea kettle started whistling, and Madame Meng shook her head as she got up to attend to it. "Nonsense. Stay and have a cup of tea. We'll talk."

Jin wanted to make her excuses and go, but the sofa was comfortable and she was suddenly very tired. Getting up and going back outside seemed altogether too much bother, even for another glimpse of the wonders of the Ninth Hell.

"Do you take lemon or milk?" asked Madame Meng from the kitchen.

"Neither. Just a little sugar if you have it," Jin said absently.

"I have everything I want or need," Madame Meng said, as she emerged from the kitchen bearing a tray with a tea service and what looked like small cakes with chocolate and white icing. "Save the freedom to leave, other than for very short periods. It goes with the position. Let's take our refreshment by the window, shall we?"

Jin got up, feeling brittle and old, and trudged behind Madame Meng to the ironwork table by the window. Madame Meng set down the tray and went to pull open the curtains while Jin chose a seat and fell into it.

"You must be tired," Madame Meng said. "One of those limits of the flesh we have to deal with."

What Madame Meng said now and before on the terrace finally registered. "Are you incarnate too? Like me?" Jin asked.

"Since the day I was last born... I think you'd call it Han Dynasty China."

"But...aren't you a Bodhisattva?"

Madame Meng seemed to be having a bit of difficulty getting the curtains open. "No, just a very old woman." She glanced back at Jin. "That surprises you, doesn't it?"

"Well...yes."

Madame Meng nodded. "I wasn't the first to say this, but it's true: Never be good at something you don't want to *have* to do. The sad fact is, in order for the Ninth Hell to function, my elixir is required. I was a mortal woman but the only person with the skill to make that elixir. So..." She shrugged. "One bite of the Peach of Immortality and here I am -- immortal and in demand, but no more 'enlightened' than a tree stump. It's rather like one who maintains the path but can't walk on it. You might think of it as job security."

"I know you said you wouldn't trade," Jin said, "but I think you have a very difficult job."

Madame Meng smiled, then shrugged. "Sweet of you to say, but I'm suited for it, and that's the truth. I couldn't do what you do. But then you can't do what I do, either. Best for both of us that things worked out the way they did, yes?"

She finally got the curtains unsnarled and pulled them aside. Jin was reaching for a cake when she got her first good look at what lay beyond the window.

"Holy crap."

Madame Meng sat down and began to pour the tea. "That's a rather colorful way of describing it."

Jin had expected the window to show the same mountain view she'd seen on the way up. By her reckoning it pointed in the same direction, but the view was very, very different. Jin looked out over a blighted landscape, marred by smoking pits and lava flows. Demons were hard at work grabbing screaming, writhing people and dumping them headfirst into what looked like, and probably were, cauldrons of molten lead. Jin wondered dully if any of them were the unfortunate person that the Keeper of the Names was gathering the records for back in the First Hell. Madame Meng seemed to sense her thought.

"Hard as we both have it," she said, "I don't think either of us has anything on Emma-O. Did you know that he'd been demoted for a time?"

Jin just shook her head, staring with a mixture of horror and fascination out of Madame Meng's window, and the old woman went on. "It's true. To the Fifth Hell. Too lenient, it was said. That is his instinct, bless him. He's really a gentle sort. Yet he was not performing his function. We all serve in our fashion."

"It's horrible," Jin said.

Madame Meng shook her head. "Necessary."

Jin tore her gaze from the window. "Could you do this? Condemn a person to something this horrible?"

"No," Madame Meng said. "I could not. That's one reason I'm here and not King of the First Hell."

Jin glared. "I'm not sure I'd call that a failing."

Madame Meng smiled. "Suppose someone you loved was sick, and you knew a way to cure them. Would you do it? Whatever it was? Whatever it took? I know for a fact that you would."

Jin looked out the window. "Why doesn't this window show you the Ninth Hell?" Jin asked. "And for heaven's sake, why don't you keep those curtains shut?"

"Because I have everything I need," Madame Meng said, "Remember? And one thing I do need, and often, is a reminder that my burden, no matter how onerous, may not be so great after all. It's the sort of thing we can all do with, now and again. So. Drink your tea before it gets cold."

Jin wasn't really interested in tea now, but she stirred in a spoonful of sugar and took a sip. It tasted faintly of jasmine, and the aroma was heady. For a moment she closed her eyes and tried to forget about the horror outside Madame Meng's big bay window. She couldn't do it for long, despite the splendid tea.

"Is that the Avici Hell?"

Madame Meng just shrugged. "Possibly. The view changes now and again. I'm never really sure....ah, there it goes."

The scene did change, almost like someone had flipped a channel on an infernal remote. Now Jin and Madame Meng looked out on rolling hills that were covered in wicked looking black spikes. Men and women were impaled on those spikes but did not die. They twitched feebly but were unable to move.

"The Hell of Needles," Madame Meng said. "That one's easy to spot... Well, this has been a lovely visit and I appreciate your patience, Jin. So. Let's get down to business."

Jin blinked. "I don't understand. You said there was nothing you could tell me."

"Not a bit. I said that I didn't know your original plan, and that's true -- I don't. But I do know what you were running from."

"So do I," Jin said, "though I don't think I was supposed to. His name is Shiro. He's taken physical form in Medias and he's found me."

"Naturally," Madame Meng said.

Jin just stared at her for a moment. "What do you mean, 'naturally'?"

"I mean it was inevitable. Once Emma-O found you, it stood to reason that Shiro would, too."

"You know about Shiro? And Teacher... I mean Emma-O betraying me?"

Madame Meng had to put down her teacup, she was laughing so hard. Jin just stared at her with her brow furrowing in annoyance until the old woman regained control of herself. "Oh, child...is that what you think? That Emma-O betrayed you?"

Jin stiffened. "Of course. Shiro said that Emma-O told him where I was!"

"So first you believed he meant that literally, and then you jumped to conclusions. Did it not occur to you that he may just have meant the obvious? That he knew Emma-O was looking for you and if he'd chosen to incarnate in a particular hell, it could only mean that he'd found you?"

Jin started to argue, but stopped before she'd gotten the first word out. "Oh," she finally said. I didn't think of that."

"You haven't thought of a lot of things, Jin. You don't really know what's at stake here, do you?"

Jin nodded, looking glum. "It seems odd saying it, but I seem to have covered my tracks very carefully...at least so far as keeping the incarnate me in the dark. Every other aspect of my vaunted 'plan' seems to be a massive screw-up. If the idea was to keep me away from Shiro, then it didn't work. If there's more to it I haven't a clue as to what it might be."

"Still," Madame Meng said, and Jin reddened.

"I'm doing my best! Ok, so I'm not the brightest -- "

Madame Meng was laughing again. "Oh, Jin, you are priceless. You actually believe what you're saying... Jin, whatever you have been or will be, 'dim' is not one of them. Read your own legend sometimes."

"I have been!" Jin protested, but Madame Meng wasn't impressed.

"Well do it again, and pay attention this time. Take a good long look at your reputation: you're wise, powerful, compassionate... and I can personally swear to the truth of all of them."

Jin frowned. "But... didn't Guan Yin make a mistake? She married a mortal! And why? Did... do I, love him?"

"Of course. What do you think this has all been about? You're trying to help him."

"I mean as a woman loves a man," Jin said, and she realized she was blushing.

Madame Meng looked thoughtful for a moment. "At first glance, no. You're an Enlightened Being, remember? You've seen through the delusions of the world, including desire. That's what an Enlightened Being is."

"But I -- "

Madame Meng held up a finger for silence. "I wasn't finished, Jin Hannigan. Remember what I said above? 'Whatever it was. Whatever it took'?"

"You were talking about Emma-O."

"I was talking about you, too. If Guan Yin decided that the only way she could help Minamoto no Shiro was to fall in love with him, she would do it. I'm not saying you did; I don't know. But don't say it's not possible."

"But... even if that was the plan, it didn't work! That was thousands of years ago and he's still obsessed with me!"

"No, he's still in love with you. You really don't know what's at stake now, do you?"

Jin didn't know what to say. As infuriating as it had been to be kept in the dark, she had taken some comfort in hoping that, perhaps, the Guan Yin That Was knew what she was doing and that everything would work out. Yet after her discovery by Shiro and the little bombshell he'd dropped on her, Jin was having a harder and harder time hold on to this notion. With Madame Meng's help, that slim lifeline was unraveling completely.

"Does... does that mean you do know what's at stake?"

"Not entirely," Madame Meng admitted, "but I may have a better grasp than you do at the moment. As you may have guessed, I have a great deal of time on my hands and at my leisure I've given the situation some thought. Would you like to hear what I think?"

Jin just looked at her, and when she spoke her voice was barely above a whisper. "Please," she said.

Madame Meng nodded. "Fine, then. We'll start with Shiro, but you first. Tell me everything you think you know." She took a sip of tea and settled down to listen.

CHAPTER 15

"It's worse than I thought," Madame Meng said, and that was all she said for a long time.

Jin didn't mind the silence; her throat was sore from talking and she was content to sip her tea and rest. She still felt tired and worn, but talking to Madame Meng came as a great relief; speaking to Teacher always felt like a confrontation regardless of whether it actually was. Jin, by contrast, felt no fight or flight stress from the Queen of the Ninth Hell. She felt almost like an old friend which, by what Madame Meng herself said, might even be true.

Still, Jin held onto her caution--it was one of the few things she still trusted. "You were right when you said that I didn't know what was at stake. I thought I did, when Shiro first appeared. He was like some great evil darkness, the way he was trapping that poor little girl in her own hell. Was I wrong about that?"

"About Shiro as a great evil darkness? I accept that his desires are so strong that they might affect others. That doesn't mean he was doing what you say on purpose."

Jin shrugged. "He must be. He seeks out those ready to pass over because he knows I must go to them too."

Madame Meng nodded. "Yes, but that doesn't explain why he would interfere. Not that the little girl wasn't trapped already, I suspect, but you're saying he was deliberately feeding her delusion."

Jin put down her tea and rubbed her eyes. "I only know what I saw."

"No argument, Jin. And if that's the case, then Shiro's actively interfered with the work of freeing souls for advancement. For that alone he could be condemned to the Avici Hell. Yet that hasn't happened. I don't suppose you've wondered why?"

Jin looked a little sheepish. "Madame Meng, in all honesty I don't understand enough of what's going on to reach that level of suspicion. I barely know that the Avici Hell exists. I barely know what my function in all this is."

Madame Meng looked thoughtful. "Which, I believe, was the whole point of reincarnating without your memories. Now, you're a quick learner and you're doing your best to fulfill your basic duties as Guan Yin, despite the handicap of your mortal form. That essentially satisfies Emma-O's interest in you for the moment and he seems content to leave matters as they are. Yet that leaves you without any greater understanding of the context in which you work or even the true point of it. Yes?"

Jin nodded. "It's true. Teacher gave me the big picture but he wasn't particularly keen on specifics."

"That's what I mean when I say you don't have a clue what the stakes are now."

"Then what is at stake?"

Madame Meng sipped her tea and Jin was left with another long silence. "Many things, Jin, but I think the most grave may be your ability to function as the Bodhisattva of Mercy."

"Well, it's true that I feel limited, but you said yourself that I was managing -- "

"You don't understand, Jin. I mean your ability to perform these duties, period. In whatever form you may inhabit. I think the cosmos is in danger of losing Guan Shi Yin entirely."

Jin almost dropped her cup. "Because of Shiro? How?"

Madame Meng shrugged. "I don't know. I don't pretend to understand the events that Guan Yin has set in motion. But I'm sure that I'm right. Marrying Shiro was a dangerous act."

Jin felt a chill. "Which I don't understand at all. How could Guan Shi Yin marry in the first place? She renounced the world!"

"That's where you're wrong. A Bodhisattva specifically does *not* renounce the world. That's what makes them Bodhisattvas."

"Well, ok, they remain active in the world, but all the rest goes away, doesn't it? Love? Physical desire?"

Madame Meng shrugged. "Not being Enlightened, I wouldn't know. Love certainly does not go away. You've always had that, Jin, in abundance. That's why you are who you are."

"It might help me understand if I knew more of Guan Yin's history with Shiro. Are there any details? I'll settle for a broad outline."

"I'd be surprised if the legend is unknown, even in your time."

"I don't want a legend. I want the facts."

Madame Meng smiled and freshened their cups of tea. "I wasn't there, Jin. You were. Since by your own choice you no longer know the facts, then I guess you'll have to settle for the legend."

Jin sighed. She kept hoping there was a way out of the maze of good intentions and hidden agendas that the Guan Yin That Was had laid out for her, but so far she wasn't finding it. Still, hope refused to die. "I'd be grateful," she said, "for anything you can tell me."

"For a start, according to most legends this didn't happen to you at all."

Jin blinked. "Huh?"

"This story is actually told about a Japanese goddess of luck named Kichijoten."

"Kichi...what? Does she really exist?"

Madame Meng sighed. "Kichijoten. And you're having tea with the ruler of the Tibetan Ninth Hell and you're asking me?"

Jin smiled then, despite herself. "Sorry. It was a silly question."

"Anyway, the story is that a worshiper became obsessed with a temple image of Kichijoten, to the point that he fell in love with the goddess herself. So she showed up in person and agreed to marry him, on the condition that he remain as devoted to her as he'd been to her image. Specifically, no fooling around."

"And he fooled around?" Jin asked.

Madame Meng laughed. "You know he did. Found this sweet young thing on a business trip and broke his word. When he got home his wife the goddess was waiting for him with two buckets full of semen. It was, apparently, every ejaculation he'd had with her while they were married. She gave it all back to him before she left forever."

"That is the most disgusting thing I have ever heard," Jin said.

"Not even close for me," Madame Meng said, "though I agree it's disgusting enough. Yet that is the story."

"But if this really did happen to this Kichijoten person, what's it got to do with me?"

"Well, for one thing it makes more sense if it did happen to a goddess of luck and not the Bodhisattva of Mercy. Especially since, in some traditions, you weren't female at all."

"You mean Guan Yin started out as male Indian deity named 'Avalokitesvara.' I already knew that...sort of. I've been trying not to think about it."

Madame Meng shrugged. "In some traditions a woman cannot be a Bodhisattva at all, yet mercy is widely believed to be a primarily female trait -- mostly by people who don't understand women that well -- so the perception of the Bodhisattva who became Guan Yin changed. If the world is an illusion it follows that perception and illusion orders the world, Jin. No need to dwell on it."

"I won't," Jin said. "It makes my head hurt."

"I did warn you. Anyway, what I think happened was this--the person you know as Shiro was captivated by an image of the divine, much as most men are captivated by their mortal loves, but it was you, not Kichijoten. His ardor was such that it was the image and physical form itself that enthralled him. In that sense you were an obstacle to his eventual enlightenment. You manifested physically in an attempt to cure him of that error. Needless to say it didn't work at the time, and so now here we are."

"So my incarnation as a mortal was Plan B? I have to slay the monster of love all on my own?"

"I don't know what you have to do. I'm sorry," Madame Meng said, and she looked like she meant it. Jin smiled a little wistfully.

"You may have been more help than you know. Thanks for the tea and conversation. I do appreciate both."

Madame Meng pulled back the sleeves of her robe and Jin noticed that she was wearing one of the strange timepieces that Jin had seen on Teacher.

"What is that?" Jin asked.

"Hmmm? Oh, this thing? It's the closest object I have to a manifestation of time," Madame Meng said. "It tells me when it's time to brew up another batch of the elixir... and it is time. Ah, well. Can you see yourself out?"

"Sure," Jin said. "Good bye, then. I hope I see you again."

"You will, and soon," Madame Meng said. She didn't sound happy.

Jin started to ask what she'd meant by that, but Madame Meng wasn't there. Jin decided not to dwell on that, either. She made her way back down the stairway and out onto the terrace, where thousands of people were forgetting everything they had ever known on the Terrace of Oblivion. Just for a moment, Jin thought of taking another sip herself and just wandering off to a new life via the Tenth Hell.

That didn't work the first time.

Jin just shrugged. Sooner or later Teacher would find her again, or Shiro. There was no escape that way. She wondered if there was any escape at all. Fight love? How the hell was she supposed to do that?

Frank and Ling were waiting right where she'd left them. For all she could tell, they hadn't even moved.

"Was Madame Meng of any assistance to you?" Frank asked.

"Yes," Jin said, not really sure if it was true or not. It had felt good just to talk to someone who understood, even if at the end she'd said no more than Teacher had. "Frank, remind me of something you said earlier. That a Bodhisattva could be killed? Is that true?"

"Of course," Frank said. "I never -- "

"Yes, yes, you always tell the truth as you understand it. I wasn't doubting you, just making sure I understood correctly."

"He's right," Ling said. "A physical form can be destroyed, no matter its power. Even your demon form, if you were injured gravely enough, though there are not many who could do that."

"'Not many' implies someone could. Who?"

Ling looked thoughtful. "Well, I think I could. My true dragon form is quite effective against demons. Also possibly Emma-O; he's very powerful."

"Well, assuming neither of you have any such notions, what about one of Guan Yin's more typical manifestations?"

"Then it would not be so difficult," Frank said. "If someone was really determined."

"Thought so. Never mind, then."

Jin sighed. For awhile she had thought the idea might be to trick or goad Shiro into killing her human incarnation and trap him in the Avici hell but, apparently, that wasn't it. Guan Yin could have managed that without incarnating as Jin Lee Hannigan.

Both Frank and Ling looked as if they wanted to ask the reason for her strange questions, but neither said anything.

"Do either of you know what time it is back in Medias? Feels like I've been visiting various hells for days."

"About 10:30PM of the same night you left," Frank said. "You really haven't been gone that long, in linear time."

"Seems like ages. Take me home, please. I don't feel like walking any more."

"Best to keep your Third Eye shut," Ling said. "You probably don't want to see this."

"I know I don't," Jin said. "I'm tired of looking at anything at all."

Frank and Ling reached up into empty air in front of the ledge and pulled to either side as if they were opening curtains. A rift appeared in the sky that grew into a circle of light. Jin stepped into the rift without thinking about it, since if she *had* thought about it she'd have probably changed her mind about walking. She walked through another corridor that was much brighter and not nearly so long as the ones between hells, and in seven steps she was back in her own apartment. Frank and Ling appeared behind her as the door of light closed.

"Your command?" Frank asked.

"You know where Shiro is now, so Keep an eye on him. If he tries to harm my mother you have my permission to rip him to shreds. But only if."

"Ripping him into shreds now might avoid any more unpleasantness later," Ling said.

Jin smiled. There was a touch of bloodlust in Ling's makeup -- or at least this manifestation of it -- and Jin could relate to that. She even wondered, for a moment, if Ling might be right. She didn't know. Once again, there was still too much she just didn't know.

"Watch him for now. I'm tired and I'm going to bed. Good night."

"And to you, Jin," they said, and vanished through separate flashes of light.

Jin ate a snack, showered, and crawled into bed. She didn't intend to seek out the Guan Yin That Was or to do anything other than sleep. The Guan Yin That Was had other plans.

"Jin," the other Guan Yin said, as soon as Jin was safely asleep, "We need to talk.

In her dream, Guan Yin was sitting on the edge of her bed. She was manifesting as a living statue of ivory and gold. Jin thought that rather showy, and in either case she just wanted to sleep. Jin dreamed of pulling a pillow over her head. "Go 'way."

"You've been talking to Madame Meng," Guan Yin said.

"Did you honestly think I wouldn't, once I found out about her? Well, don't worry. She didn't know your plan, so no harm done. You win again."

"You think this is a game, luv?"

"Isn't it? You made the rules, you set the pieces in motion. If your pawn is feeling a little grumpy and put upon...well, tough. Now let me sleep. Mortals need their rest."

"So do Bodhisattvas, luv. You cannot imagine how weary I am."

"Then that's another thing we share. Other than soul or a consciousness or whatever you want to call it. So how does sending Shiro to the Avici Hell earn our rest?"

"Who said it did anything of the sort? You're guessing. Bad idea, but then you've had so many."

"You give me one option and then fuss if I use it? Bite me," Jin said. "Better yet, go bite Teacher. I still think I owe him one."

"Yes, but not for the reason you seem to think. Didn't Madame Meng tell you about Emma-O being demoted for a while?"

Jin blinked, and pulled the metaphorical pillow off her head. "She did. What about it?"

"Why do you think it happened? Who do you think Emma-O showed excessive mercy to?"

"Shiro," Jin said instantly, and knew it was true.

"Shiro," Guan Yin confirmed. "If you're really determined to do things your way, you might ask him about that."

"But -- "

Too late. Guan Yin was gone. Jin sighed and went back to her pillow.

I'm beginning to really dislike that other me.

CHAPTER 16

Jin woke after a night of vague, troubling dreams. Not including the one where Guan Yin came to visit her, however. *That* particular dream was as clear as a glass bell, though troubling in its own right. The other dreams were more of the night phantom variety -- ghostly artifacts that slipped through her fingers when she tried to grab on and look at them. In the end she gave up and concentrated on the dream that remained.

Jin yawned and finally glanced at the clock. It was after 9AM. *Son of a...Joyce is going to kill me*!

Jin was late. Over an hour so, and there was a stack of working waiting for her that Joyce in turn would be waiting for, and Jin was holding up everything because, after all the *Sturm und Drang* of the previous day, she'd forgotten to set her alarm. Jin flung the covers aside and dressed as quickly as she could. She was munching the last of a piece of dry toast as she headed out the door.

The morning was humid and warm. Jin was sweating by the time she reached Pepper Street, and it felt like the last of her toast had stuck in her throat. She hurried to the front door of the Legal Aid Office and grabbed the handle. "Joyce, I'm so sorry!" Jin said before she was even well inside the door, but Joyce just waved Jin to her desk without even looking up.

"I remember what it was like to be young and have a brand new boyfriend. Just finish checking those depositions as soon as you can."

"But I -- " Jin began, then thought better of it. Let Joyce think whatever she wanted about Jin and Frank's relationship; it was certainly easier than explaining the real reason Jin was late. "Right away," she finished, lamely. She made a detour past the coffee pot for something to overwhelm the toast and then got right down to work.

For a little while there was nothing but the sounds of the mutual shuffling of papers, but then Joyce's clients began trickling in. Joyce greeted several clients in turn and then directed them to the private conference room, finishing just in time to meet the next appointment. They were the usual sort that Jin saw almost every day: pensioners contesting evictions or rent increases, one or two parents with sullen teenagers in tow destined for Family Court, poor, frightened people in trouble with the law and distrustful -- often rightly so -- of court-appointed counsel. The Pepper Street Legal Aid office had only a small network of *pro bono* volunteers; Joyce had to take a lot of the cases herself. It was at times like these that Jin half-way considered taking her mother up on her offer to send her back to law school. She thought that, maybe, she could be more help that way. Then she looked at the mountain of paper work that Joyce was depending on her to finish and concentrated on the task at hand.

At 11:30 the same morning Jin's phone rang.

"Hello?"

"Hi, Lotus Blossom. When are you moving in?"

For a moment Jin blanked, then she remembered. "Mom, I'll bring some of my things over tonight and we'll try it out, ok? I'm keeping my apartment for now, though."

"I never thought otherwise, dear."

Jin shook her head, grateful that her mother couldn't see her. "One thing, though -- I may be fairly late. I've got an errand to run first."

"You have your key," Margaret said serenely.

"Listen, Mom..."

"What is it?"

"Ummm, oh nothing. Later, Mom."

Jin hung up the phone and took a deep breath. Joyce happened to be passing Jin's desk at the time, and apparently noticed the look on Jin's face.

"Trouble?"

"Not yet," Jin said. "I'm moving back home for a little while. Mom needs me."

Joyce looked a little wistful. "At least you still have a mom. I'd love to be able to talk to mine sometimes."

Jin grinned. "I've got one you can borrow any time you want...oh. Joyce, can I ask you a personal question? I'm afraid it's going to sound a little weird. And this is just hypothetical, understand. I mean, it's not about Frank and me."

"Out with it, girl."

Jin took a breath. "If you wanted to... I mean, you thought it was for the best and all, how would you make a man fall out of love with you?"

Joyce didn't answer her for a while, and Jin was starting to think she'd offended her friend somehow when Joyce finally smiled. "Haven't a clue, but then I don't know why a man falls in love in the first place. If they do. Sometimes I think that's just a big misunderstanding all by its own self. As you may have guessed, the only question I've really pondered lately is 'how do I stop loving someone I shouldn't?' Don't know the answer to that one, either."

"Lucius... yeah, I see that. Love is complicated," Jin said wistfully. "I just had no idea how complicated before now."

Joyce smiled again, but it didn't last. She looked hesitant. "Listen, Jin..."

Jin looked up. "Yes?"

Joyce paused, then finally shook her head. "Oh, nothing. Forget it. I've cancelled my last appointment; I've got to meet someone. Can you hold down the fort until five?"

Jin frowned. "Sure, no problem. Ummm... are you sure there's nothing else I can do?"

Joyce shook her head. "No, girl. Some things you have to do for yourself, you know?"

"Try telling my mother that."

Joyce laughed, though Jin thought it sounded more polite than real. Joyce stopped by her desk just long enough to pick up her purse and she was out the door. Jin stared after her for a little while. She had the feeling that Joyce really had wanted to talk about something. Maybe she'd just been in too much of a hurry, but Jin made a mental note to see if she could draw Joyce out about it later. She suspected man troubles again, but she hoped she was wrong. Jin got back to work.

About 4PM Ling came by to report that there was nothing to report. Jonathan Mitsumo was seeing clients in his office and had been doing so all day.

"Sorry to give you such boring work," Jin said, but Ling smiled.

"You're talking to someone who once meditated upon a giant pearl for two hundred and ten years. Boredom is an illusion."

"I keep forgetting that," Jin said dryly.

Ling just shrugged. "Most humans do. Constantly."

Jin had no answer to that, nor did one seem required. She sent Ling back to her post. When five o'clock came around she summoned Ling again.

"Ling, do you know where Teacher is?"

"It's Monday, so I believe he's feeding pigeons in Resolution Park," Ling said. "I can take you there if you want."

"No, thanks. I just wanted to know before I wasted time hiking through the corridor to the First Hell."

Ling started to leave, then hesitated. "Jin, would you mind summoning Shan Cai... I mean Frank, next time? I think he's getting jealous."

Jin tried not to smile, and failed. "Sure, I'll do that, if it'll make him feel better."

Jin locked up the office and headed toward the park. She found Teacher where Ling said he would be, sitting by himself on a shadowed bench under an ancient water-oak, throwing bits of bread from a little brown sack to a flock of squabbling pigeons gathered at his feet.

"Teaching the birds about the sins of avarice?" Jin asked.

He didn't even look up. "Nope. Waiting for you," he said. "Seems I did that for a lot of years, though not so much lately."

Jin brushed off a few fallen acorns and sat down on the bench next to him. "So you knew I was looking for you."

He shrugged, and the carnation in the jacket of his lapel shed a petal. "Pretty much. Keeper of the Names told me he ran into you, and how you went off after he mentioned Madame Meng. I was rather hoping that wouldn't happen, but it seemed inevitable."

"I was very angry with you," Jin said. "I think it's better that I found her first."

He smiled a little wistfully. "Maybe. Hard to see all the ends. Maybe a knock down, drag out fight would have done us both some good. Cleared the air, perhaps."

"I've got a couple of very specific questions for you, Teacher. If you don't answer them, you may get your wish."

Teacher looked unhappy. "It's not that I don't *want* to answer them, Jin. Besides, I don't have all the answers; I told you that from the start."

"See if you have this one," Jin said dryly. "Did you or did you not tell Shiro that I was in Medias? He says you did."

"Speaking to him a lot these days?"

"Just answer the question. Please."

Teacher fumbled for another piece of bread. "He found out I'd incarnated and was hanging out here, so he came to Medias and waited, and was ready when your nature began to manifest." Teacher said. "So maybe from his point of view I did tell him. Your real question is: Did I deliberately betray you to him? The answer is 'no.'"

Jin took a piece of bread from Teacher's sack and threw it to one of the smaller birds. "Madame Meng says you were sent to the Fifth Hell for a while. I don't pretend to understand all the hierarchy, but I take it that was not a good thing?"

"I didn't enjoy it, if that's what you mean."

"It was because of Shiro, wasn't it?"

Teacher tore a larger piece of bread in half and expertly flipped the pieces toward opposite sides of the flock. "Sometimes you ask questions just like a lawyer, you know that? I see it when I get hauled in for vagrancy every so often. I see it when I sit in judgment in the First Hell: if you're asking the question, you already know the answer. The point is not to get an answer. The point is for the person questioned to damn himself. Is that what you want me to do, Jin?"

Jin thought about that, something that would not have been possible had she found Teacher before speaking to Madame Meng. "No, I want you to explain yourself. And before you start dodging, I thought I better mention that the Guan Yin That Was told me to ask you about it. That's the truth. I do know you got into trouble for helping Shiro. I really want to know why you did it."

"I didn't help Shiro," Teacher said.

"You showed him leniency, as I understand it. That looks like help to me."

Teacher smiled. "And you'd be right. I was trying to help someone, I still believe. But who?"

"You're being cryptic. Stop it."

"Am I? You throw a crumb at that sparrow and the pigeon next to him gets it. Who are you helping?"

"The pigeon, obviously."

"But was that your intention? No? Do you accept the obvious fact that sometimes we do things that don't work out the way we meant?"

"Sure. Now will you accept the obvious fact that I want to *know* what you meant? I'm rather at a loss about the matter otherwise."

Teacher looked thoughtful. "Jin, at any time during your childhood, did you ever come across stories of star-crossed lovers? Those who were meant to be together but the fates, nay, the very *universe* itself was against them?"

"Sure. Romeo and Juliet, Pyramus and Thisbe, Heloise and Abelard, to mention a few. They usually end badly."

"Leaving aside the fact that very few things end in the first go-round, I'm betting that not even once did it occur to you that, just maybe, the universe was right?"

Jin stared at the squabbling birds. "Teacher, what on earth does the notion of star-crossed lovers have to do with Guan Yin and Shiro? Whatever Shiro thought, whatever Guan Yin's reasons for indulging him, I think we can safely assume that her agreement to marry him wasn't about love, at least not the kind Shiro was hoping for."

"Irrelevant. Do you know what Karma is?"

"Fate?"

"More like consequences. Every volition, every act, good or bad, is what we call Karma. It accumulates over several lifetimes, and what Hell or Paradise one is reborn into is determined ultimately by it. Now, as an Enlightened Being,

Guan Yin no longer accumulates Karma, but Shiro certainly does. With me so far?"

"I think so," Jin said.

"Good, since here's where it gets hazy. In some traditions you hear of people who died for love in one life who are reborn in another, where they get a second chance."

"Sounds too good to be true."

Teacher smiled. "That's because it is. See, their second chance is not to find love again. Their second -- or third or thousandth -- chance is to free themselves of it."

Jin sighed. "Ok, now you've lost me. What's wrong with love?"

"Nothing, except when it becomes an end in itself, when two people cling to each other above all else, that is not a virtue. They become centered in each other. They cut themselves off farther from spiritual progress."

"Even if I buy that," Jin said, "Guan Yin was certainly not building her world around Shiro."

"As you say. But I think it's a safe bet he was building *his* around *her*. Once she agreed to marry him, even though her intention was to cure his obsession, at that point his Karma was linked to her. He's been tying himself tighter and tighter to Guan Yin through thousands of cycles of death and rebirth. I think he was very close to trapping her again on the Wheel of Death and Rebirth with him. I hate to say 'I told you so' but I said as much to her at the beginning."

Jin sighed. "Madame Meng said marrying Shiro was a dangerous act."

"And she was right. That's why I didn't send Shiro to the Fire-Jar Hell or tip him into a vat of molten lead or any of the things that he certainly deserved."

"So instead you gave him the keys to all the hells. Why?"

Teacher sat quietly on the bench, ignoring the birds at his feet. Jin reached over and took the last piece of bread from the sack and threw it toward the sparrow. Then,

"Teacher, I'm fully prepared to concede that you meant well. What I really need to know is why you thought giving Shiro free range of the entire cosmos was going to help, because I just don't see it."

Teacher shrugged. "I'd have thought that was obvious. It's beyond my power to give Shiro or anyone Enlightenment, but I could do the next best thing -- get him out of the cycle of death and rebirth. He's not really beyond it... more 'in between.' Despite what he's done or failed to do, he no longer accumulates Karma. He neither progresses nor devolves. He just is."

"So there's no chance of his trapping Guan Yin within his own little universe of delusion? I'm here to tell you, Teacher -- that didn't work. It almost happened yesterday."

Teacher nodded, looking glum. "I applied a band-aid when clearly a tourniquet was required. I goofed."

"No shit, Sherlock."

Teacher looked at her. "You're still angry."

"One of the advantages of the being mortal. Maybe Guan Yin reincarnated as me just so she could be properly pissed at you. She may be beyond passion, but I'm sure not."

Teacher smiled a weak smile. "Don't think that didn't occur to me."

The pigeon flock and the few sparrows milled about for a while, hopefully, but when it became obvious no more bread was coming, in twos and threes they started to fly away. Soon they were all gone.

"I have one more question," Jin said. "If you're right about the danger of love then Madame Meng is right again I'm risking the very existence of Guan Yin, and not just this mortal incarnation. All well and good, but in the meantime Shiro has the full run of Medias, and he's capable of anything."

"Not anything," Teacher said. "But quite a lot. You're having your servants keep an eye on him, I suppose?"

"You bet."

"Remember what Shiro was like when you first saw him that day in the corridor? Just keep in mind that, whatever he looks like at the moment, he can become that same shadow again at a moment's notice. If you think love's hard, try getting a grip on a shadow."

CHAPTER 17

The next morning the door to the Legal Aid office was locked when Jin arrived. She just stared at it curiously for a moment or two, then realized that the blinds were still pulled and the lights, except for the few they habitually left on, were off. Jin fumbled through her bag until she found her key and let herself in.

No Joyce. The message light on her phone was blinking, but no Joyce. Jin checked her own phone, but there were no messages, especially nothing from Joyce explaining her absence, or "hold the fort until I get there," or anything of the sort. Jin dialed Joyce's number and got her answering machine, but that was all. She hung up without leaving a message.

Jin pushed the code into Joyce's machine that forwarded her calls to Jin's phone and tried to get on with her work, but it was hard to concentrate. After about an hour Jin couldn't stand it any more. She called Joyce's apartment one more time and, when that only got Joyce's answering machine, she took a photo she had of Joyce and scribbled Joyce's address on a sheet of note paper. In that instant Ling appeared in a blink of light, just in front of Jin's desk.

"Jin, I'm afraid the person calling himself Jonathan Mitsumo has eluded us."

Jin, her mind still on Joyce, shifted gears slowly. "Shiro? How?"

"We're not entirely sure," Ling said, a little defensively. "He went to his office this morning as usual, and then he just wasn't there."

"Can he open one of those gateways like you and Frank do?"

"Certainly not," Ling said. "These means are not for the likes of him. We're searching for him now. We will find him."

"No," Jin said. "I have another errand for you. I was going to call Frank, but since you're here..."

Jin handed her the paper and a photo Jin had taken of Joyce having lunch in the park the year before. "Remember Joyce, my boss? I've written down her address. First I want you to find Frank and tell him to go watch my mother instead. If Shiro's up to something I want her guarded, understand? Then go to Joyce's apartment and see if she is there. Don't let her see you or anything, just come back and tell me. I'm worried about her."

"As you wish."

Ling vanished through the familiar doorway of light. She wasn't gone five minutes before she reappeared in almost the exact same spot. "Frank is watching your Mother now; there's no sign of Shiro. And no one is at Joyce's home."

How very strange...

Jin nodded absently. "Thanks... uh, do you think Frank will be all right on his own for a little while? It isn't like Joyce to go missing without letting someone know. I want you to find her."

"If that is what you want, I am ready. As for Shan Cai, he can take care of himself," Ling said which, Jin thought, might be the closest thing to a compliment the girl had ever paid to him within Jin's hearing.

"I'm glad someone can. Get going, then."

"Going now, Jin," Ling said, and in another moment she was, in fact, gone. Jin thought it might have been her imagination, but Ling seemed to give her a lot less attitude when she was given a clear task to perform. Jin resolved to keep that in mind.

Jin thought she was worrying for nothing. Doubtless Joyce had car trouble or needed to run an unexpected errand. Jin repeated the thought often, but it didn't help. She tried to concentrate on her work as best she could, but the minutes seemed to crawl by until Ling returned about an hour later.

"I've found her," Ling said.

Jin realized she'd been holding her breath, and let it out. "Great! Where is she?"

"On her way to the Terrace of Oblivion."

"Terrace...? You mean she..." Jin suddenly couldn't see very well; Ling's face was blurring like a badly focused presentation.

"The Ninth Hell, yes. She is dead."

Ling said it so calmly, with neither malice nor sorrow. It was simply a fact, and she was reporting it as Jin had requested. That was all.

"What...what happened?"

"I do not know. You did not instruct me to question her about her absence."

Jin rose a little unsteadily from her desk and went to lock the door to the office entrance. "Please take me to her."

"Do you really think that's wise? The process is working as it should -- "

"Now," Jin said.

Ling made no further protests, but opened a doorway as Jin rushed through. They were at the entrance to Madame Meng's palace. "Joyce has already entered," Ling said, "I can't go to her directly now."

"Wait here," Jin said unnecessarily, and passed through the doorway as she had done the day before. Nothing had changed so far as Jin could tell. People still arrived, shuffled toward the Terrace and its fountains, while others shuffled back toward the entrance to the Tenth Hell and their next chance -- or rather their next obligation -- in life. Jin looked about frantically, but of course it was like looking for a needle in a haystack the size of a mountain.

Jin gave up and ran out onto the terrace. Madame Meng was there, in almost the exact same spot she'd stood the day before. "Madame Meng, you've got to help me! I'm looking for a friend..."

"Yes, I know," the old woman said sadly.

Jin staggered to a stop as Madame Meng's words sank in. Now she remembered what the old woman had said before Jin had left the Ninth Hell after her first visit, something about "visiting again soon." Jin hadn't thought too much of it at the time. Now and for a little while it was all she *could* think about.

"Son of a..."

"I don't see how insulting someone's mother is going to help," Madame Meng said. "Nor really what you hope to accomplish now, Jin. Lovely as it is to see you again, I think you should go home."

"I have to talk to Joyce!"

Madame Meng regarded her with an expression of polite curiosity. "Why is that?"

Jin stopped. She had no idea what the answer might be. She thought furiously. "I need to know that she's all right!"

"All right? She's dead, child. Dead, that is, until she passes through the Tenth Hell and returns to Medias. She's not ready to move on, but of course you already know that."

Jin realized she did know that since, if Joyce had been ready to leave Medias, Jin would have known, just as she knew about the man hoarding lemon slices in the diner. "She died too soon, then! It shouldn't have happened!"

Madame Meng sighed. "Several lifetimes are often required before a person is ready to leave a particular hell, and this was merely one. Even in your currently confused state, you know this, too."

"She was my friend," Jin said softly.

"I'm sorry, Jin, but the one doesn't change the other."

Jin took a long slow breath, and let it out again. "Madame Meng, I need to know what happened to her. Why... why she's here. Please, it's important."

"To whom? Joyce?"

Jin met the old woman's gaze. "It's important to me."

Madame Meng nodded. "So long as you understand that, I'll help you. Go to the third fountain to your right. She is there."

Jin took off at a run. She passed the first fountain, then the second. She skidded to a stop by the crowd clustered around the third fountain, waiting for their turn to drink. Jin took a closer look at the fountain and realized what she'd thought was water was really a very fine mist, almost like smoke. It pooled and swirled as the people there cupped their hands and drank.

Where...?

There. Just at the edge of the crowd, calmly waiting her turn, was Joyce.

"Joyce! It's me, Jin!"

Joyce didn't look at her at first. She seemed fascinated by the fountain. She moved closer as the people closer in took their turn and left the terrace. She finally turned around when Jin rushed up, breathless.

"Oh. Hi, Jin."

For a moment Jin thought she was going to burst into tears of relief. "You still know me!"

"Of course I know you. Listen, can we talk later? It was a long walk here and I'm just so thirsty..."

"Please don't drink yet," Jin said, "I need to find out what happened to you. Was it an accident? Did... did someone hurt you?"

Joyce just stared at her for a moment. "I don't know what you're talking about."

"Don't you know where you are?"

"I'm where I'm supposed to be. Ain't that weird? I've never been here before and I don't really know why I'm here now, but I'm supposed to be here. Are you supposed to be here, too?" Joyce glanced at the water. "I'm supposed to drink. I need to drink, Jin."

Jin knew it was impossible now, but she wanted to grab Joyce's shoulders, hold her, make her understand. More even than that, she wanted to hug her tight and say how sorry she was, for everything. For not being there. For not stopping it, whatever it was. For not being able to help. For not being a better friend. For not... Jin stopped, and she felt ashamed. This couldn't be about Jin. Now now.

"Joyce, listen to me just for a moment. Can you do that for me? Do you remember what happened to you? Try hard, please. Just before you found yourself on this mountain, where were you?"

Joyce frowned. "I was with someone. Then I wasn't..." Her expression cleared. "Oh, that. Yes, I remember, Jin. It doesn't matter."

"It does matter!"

"Not to me, not to nobody. It happened."

"What happened?"

"Jin, let it go. I think I'm about to."

The way in front of the fountain was clear, and Joyce reached down and took the smoky liquid in her hands and drank deep. Her expression didn't change for several long moments, then noticed Jin staring at her. "Oh. Hello. Do I know you?"

Jin shook her head, slowly. "I was looking for a friend. You reminded me of her."

Joyce nodded politely. "I think I have to go now. I... I hope you find who you're looking for."

"Thank you. So do I," Jin said, as Joyce joined the crowd shuffling off to the gate to the Tenth Hell. Jin remained by the fountain. She wasn't sure how long she stood there, but that's where Madame Meng found her.

"Did you get what you wanted?"

"No," Jin said.

"I'm sorry she wasn't more cooperative, but dying does change one's perspective, I'm told. It's been so long since I've done it that I quite forget," she added a little wistfully.

"You knew Joyce was going to die, didn't you?" Jin asked.

"Of course, since everyone mortal dies at some point. Perhaps even I will, if my job here is ever done. Did I know your friend was going to die and didn't warn you? No. I'm not omniscient, Jin, and there's just too much going on to keep track of it all; even Bodhisattvas have to specialize and, as I already told you, I'm not one. But I can see ahead, just a little, now and then. I knew you would be back, and it would not be for a happy reason. I shouldn't have said anything."

Jin went to the terrace railing and Madame Meng followed her.

"Why not?" Jin asked after a while. "You should have told me more! Maybe I could have figured it out -- "

"There was nothing to 'figure out' Jin. All my comment did was make you think there was something you could have done to change what happened to your friend. That's why I shouldn't have said anything."

"There must have been something I could have done!"

"Why? Because you would have it so?"

Jin smiled a grim smile. "You said it yourself -- you're not omniscient."

Madame Meng sighed. "True enough. But I still don't think I'm wrong. And I am sorry about your friend."

"Me too."

Jin didn't say anything else about it. There didn't seem to be any point. Joyce was dead and, somehow, Jin had let it happen. Nothing could change that now, but there was still something she could do. There had to be. Jin said goodbye to Madame Meng and went back to where Ling was waiting for her.

"You don't look pleased. Were you too late?" Ling asked.

"Apparently. Please take me back to the office...wait." Jin looked around.

"What's wrong?"

"I felt as if someone pulled on my hand."

"There's no one else here," Ling said.

Jin knew this was true. She had even risked cracking open her Third Eye for a quick peek, but there was no one. What there was instead was a shimmering golden thread tied around her left wrist, invisible when she looked with her two human eyes. "So that's what that tugging was... That's how I know where I have to go. I just didn't see it before... I think I've been summoned."

"Yes. Shall I take you there?"

"I don't know where 'there' is yet, but I have no doubt I'll find it. Please go on back and help Frank."

Ling frowned. "Are you all right?"

"I'm fine. I'll call if I need you, thanks."

Ling looked doubtful, but Jin smiled at her and after a moment Ling dutifully opened a circle of light and vanished. It was only after Ling departed that Jin started shaking. She stumbled to a rock next to a weeping willow a few feet off the pathway and sat down hard.

Ok, so I lied.

Jin wasn't sure how long she sat there, staring out into the depths of sky between Madame Meng's mountain palace and the cliffs leading to the hell corridors. She didn't cry. Jin had expected to, indeed taken it for granted that, once she found a quiet place to sit alone, she would cry: for Joyce, for herself, for everything in her life that seemed to call for mourning, but none of it happened.

Not yet. I don't have the right.

Was that it? Or was it simply not the right time? Jin wasn't sure, but as she sat there the constant faint tugging at her wrist finally brought her back from the beautiful abyss in front of her and back to more practical concerns. She stared at her wrist, ruefully.

"I don't suppose you'd mind waiting until I feel more like myself? No? I thought not."

Jin tested her legs and, when they didn't wobble overmuch, she got back on her feet and started down the mountain path, always led by the tug of an invisible golden chain.

CHAPTER 18

Jin was rather hoping for another Japanese garden, like the one that had surrounded Michiko, but no such luck. This was a more hellish sort of hell. Jin stood on a high ridge overlooking a plain of black sand and what looked like the charred skeletons of burnt-out trees. Here and there across the landscape firepits erupted like the craters of volcanoes, throwing ash and molten rock into the air to fall like searing rain onto the sand. Jin felt another tug on her wrist. As she had done so many times before, she peeked with the Third Eye just enough to tell which way the golden thread was leading. She was in the right place, though she wasn't particularly happy about it.

Dante would have loved this place.

Jin had taken two steps down the slope before she realized that she was in full demon form. She stared at her taloned feet for a moment, curious. She didn't feel frightened, especially, despite her surroundings. Just now Jin didn't feel much of anything. Why had she changed, other than this obviously was not a nice place to be? Jin was wondering whether she should change back. Despite its strength and ferocity, or perhaps because of them, Jin didn't especially enjoy her demon form most of the time, and the few times she had, such as when she used it to pound that mugger back in Medias, she'd felt a little sick afterwards. Then one of the nearby firepits threw a small lava bomb that struck her squarely on the side of the head and exploded into steam and tektite shards.

"Shit, that hurt..." Jin reached up and rubbed the spot where she had been struck. It was another full moment before the meaning of what had just happened got through to her, and it was simply this -- if that lava bomb had hit her mortal human form, it would have killed her stone dead. At that point Jin surrendered all notions of walking through this particular hell in her human body.

When it comes to being Guan Yin, *my instincts are smarter than I am.*

Jin realized that, buried somewhere deep inside her, the same irritating Guan Yin who appeared now and then to bedevil her dreams was alive and working and, when it came to the duties of the goddess, she was in charge, not Jin. She still could not remember being Guan Yin and perhaps never would, thanks to Madame Meng's skillful brewing, but she had to be grateful that there was a part of her who knew how to be Guan Yin at need. It had never failed her before. Jin hoped it wouldn't fail her now.

Hear that, Guan Yin*? Don't screw this up... whatever it is.*

Jin followed the trail of the golden thread. She wasn't in a particular hurry, despite her awful surroundings. Now and then she caught herself dallying, such as the time she paused to watch a pack of demons flogging several people into climbing one of the seared trees. Embedded in the trunks and branches of those trees were the same volcanic shards that resulted from lava bombs like the one that had struck Jin; the people climbing the trees were being cut to ribbons. Jin wanted to feel sorry for all the people being tortured, except they weren't making it easy for her. They screamed, they cried, but through it all Jin saw no fear, only anger. They cursed at the demons driving them, cursed the trees, cursed at Jin as she walked by, and through it all lashed out at each other even as the demons lashed them.

All that torment and pain, and all they can feel is rage?

As much as she wondered about this, she wondered even more why she had stopped to watch it. Jin wondered if, perhaps, there was a principle here that she was overlooking, but for the life of her she couldn't quite see it. She shrugged and kept walking.

The tug at her wrist was persistent but not frantic. Jin knew that there was no particular urgency, so why did it feel wrong to her that she did not want to proceed with any urgency? After all, her whole purpose here was to free someone suffering in hell and help them move on to whatever came next for them. Shouldn't she want to hurry? Hadn't whoever it was suffered enough, or at least enough of this particular hell?

One quick trip to Madame Meng's fountain terrace and they'll just be back in hell...well, a different one, anyway. What difference does it make?

Jin thought of the little girl she'd freed from the corridors of hell on her first day on the job. It had made a difference to her. It had made a difference to Michiko, and Buddy, and even that silly man counting lemons. It mattered, even if she didn't pretend to understand precisely why.

Jin's taloned feet sank a bit into the sand under her weight with every step. Jin paused for a moment to look behind her at the trail of dark footprints she'd left behind her. Jin almost giggled. It looked like pictures she'd seen of a volcanic sand beach in Hawaii. Certainly nothing at all like Ship Island...

Jin stopped. Ship Island. Footsteps in the white, white sand. She'd gone with Joyce on a quick weekend trip...what? A year ago? Didn't seem so long. It was Joyce's idea. She'd said Jin was much too gloomy for someone her age. She needed to get out, have a little fun...

Jin finally understood why she was dragging her feet in this unnamed hell. It was because, when she finished here, it was back to Medias and what was waiting for her there. And who wasn't. Suddenly the current hell didn't seem quite so bad.

Maybe I'll just stay here. It's sort of like being on the beach. Except for the firepits and no ocean, but that's ok. Just as well Joyce isn't here, though, she loved the ocean... oh, damn.

Jin had a thought. She didn't want it; she'd have given anything that was hers to offer to be rid of the horrid thing, but it was too late for that. The thought Jin had was that, perhaps, Joyce was there after all. Oh, Jin knew it was almost certainly not true. As she understood things, Joyce would be reborn in Medias, to try again to learn whatever lesson her premature death may have prevented her from learning the first time. Madame Meng had said as much. Still, Jin couldn't not be entirely sure. It wasn't as if Jin had known for certain where Joyce was going to go after her visit to the Tenth Hell. She could be anywhere. She could be one of those screaming people bleeding on one those jagged-edge trees. Jin walked a little faster from that point on, and she took far less interest in what she might see to the left or right as she followed the golden thread.

The place it led her to was not quite so full and noisy as the plain she'd just crossed. There were still the blackened trees, but they were empty of either people or the bloody remnants of them. Jin wondered, when she thought of the bloody wounds on the people she'd seen so far, if they would die there, and then be reborn right back where they'd started, just in time for their next turn on the tree. Perhaps, that seemed to be the way most of the hells worked, though the idea of someone giving birth in that place struck Jin has highly unlikely.

Maybe they just reappear, just as those who finish with a hell simply vanish. Different hells, different methods?

Possibly. Perhaps that was why all hells had devils, but not all devils were visible. Even though Jin had the unshakeable feeling, somewhere deep in that Guan Yin inside her, that at heart all the hells were the same. She knew it wasn't true, at least not on the surface, yet she had a hard time shaking the notion and didn't see any particular reason to try.

In the distance Jin saw a dark mountain spire of what looked like granite rising from the plain. She thought perhaps the person she was looking for was there, since that was the way the thread was pulling. It was only when she got closer that she realized that her path led down, not up. Around the base of the mountain the sand had either sunk in or blown away to reveal a deep valley; it reminded Jin just a little of the vast valley system that almost surrounded Madame Meng's mountain palace in the Ninth Hell, but this one was not nearly so grand; she estimated it was no more than about a hundred feet deep, with slides that sloped fairly steeply down but were more rock than sand. Jin stepped to the side as a nearby firepit shot ash and lava bombs in all directions, then picked her way through the resulting smoking piles of slowly cooling rock as she made her way down toward the valley floor.

Now that Jin was a little more acclimated to her surroundings, she noticed something definitely odd about the section of valley floor in front of her. Rather than the haphazard arrangement of firepits, black sand, and old lava fragments that made up the rest of the landscape, the valley floor in front of her, a section about forty yards wide that abutted the base of the mountain, had a certain...ordered, quality about it, something that she had seen nowhere else in that hell. Yes, there were some large stones and the ubiquitous black sand, but there was also an almost total lack of small bits and rubble. More, the sand itself was ordered. Rather than flat and windswept, it was arranged into long narrow ridges that seemed to almost flow past the few large stones there, as if she were looking at miniature islands in a black water sea. For a moment Jin just stopped and stared at it in wonder, idly rubbing the spot on her head that was still sore from being smacked with that lava bomb. She was certain that she'd seen something very much like this before, if only she could remember!

Oh.

Jin did remember, though she was having a great deal of trouble believing that what she saw once on a trip to Memphis years ago was the same thing she was looking at now -- a zen garden.

In hell.

Jin ignored the faint tugging at her wrist for a few moments as she carefully traced out the limits of the garden. She was very careful to stay just outside the boundary as she paced off the length. It was around forty feet long and about the same across, and bordered on three sides by a line of flat stones, almost like paving stones. They were rough and unpolished, but apparently carefully selected for the purpose. The base of the mountain itself formed the fourth side, and within those boundaries the chaos of hell was kept at bay. Here and here alone all was ordered and serene. Jin just stared at it for a very long time as if the meaning of it would unravel before her and the place would explain itself to her, but nothing happened. Jin finally shrugged and let the golden thread tug her further down the valley to where a demon was torturing a little girl.

"Mommy used to whip me too," said the child, who appeared no more than eight or nine years old. She lay draped over two dead limbs of one of the cutting trees. Her voice was weak, and blood dripped from her arms and legs to pool in the dark sand beneath the tree. Yet, faint as the voice was, Jin heard every word.

"I'm sure she meant well," said the demon. "Try not to think too badly of her. Is that the highest you can go?"

Jin was too stunned to move. The demon, a big green thing looking somewhat like an ape crossed with a bulldog, held the whip that it had just used to drive the child up to a higher branch; Jin could see the dark bloodstains on the limb just below where the child lay now. Yet, for all that was clearly happening, the two seemed like old friends. The child was not upset, not crying, and the demon, for all his ugliness and the whip in his hand, sounded like someone's indulgent grandfather. The strangeness of the scene held Jin in horrid fascination even though her every impulse was to rush forward, dash the demon against a convenient rock, and rescue the poor child. Wasn't that what she was there for?

"I'll try," the little girl said. "You might need to whip me again."

"I don't think I can," the demon said.

"I must climb this tree," the little girl said. "Please help me."

Jin could barely believe what she was hearing, and she could not reconcile it at all with what she saw. The demon raised the whip again and snapped it expertly at the girl's battered legs, raising an angry red welt across her foot. The child winced and reached for the next branch. That was as far as she got. Her bloodied hand lost its grip as she overextended, trying to go higher. She fell.

The demon rushed forward as if he meant to catch her, but he was too far away, as was Jin, who finally shook off her immobility and ran to the base of the tree. She found the demon kneeling beside the still form. It glanced at Jin, but that was all. Its attention was on the girl.

"I'm sorry," the girl said, her voice barely above a whisper. "I tried."

"It's all right," the demon said. "You can try again when you're feeling better."

"I think..." she began, and that was all.

Jin fervently hoped with every ounce of her being that the child had merely fainted. "Get out of the way if you're not going to do something!" she said, but the demon didn't even look at her.

"Very little one can do at this point," the demon said. "She's dead."

I'm...too late? Jin drew back to strike the demon, but her arm froze in mid-blow: the demon was very carefully picking up the tiny body to cradle it tenderly in its arms. Then he slowly stood up and very carefully bore his burden along a well-worn path. After a moment Jin lowered her fist and followed him.

"If you've come to help me with my duties," the demon said over his shoulder, "it's really not necessary. As you can see, I can manage my tortures very well."

It was only when they had gone just a little further Jin began to realize just how long the demon had been managing. The valley floor beyond the one torture tree was littered with cairns of stone, several hundred of them, and Jin knew it didn't take the sharpest knife in the drawer to realize that they were graves. The demon lay the child's body on an empty patch of sand and started gathering stones. Jin watched him as he worked.

"Who is in all the other graves?" Jin asked, furious. "Where they all children, just like her? Is that your specialty?"

"Of course they were just like her," the demon said calmly. "They *were* her."

Jin didn't know what to say. The thought that the poor child had been tortured to death in the same hell by the same demon for incarnations almost past counting was almost more than she could bear. If only she had gotten there sooner! If only she hadn't stopped to look at that stupid garden. She still didn't know why it was there or who made it, but it seemed so pointless now, compared to her horrible failure, and the reality of what had just happened there and, apparently, was going to happen again.

"I'll stop it next time," Jin said. "Count on that."

"I don't think that's within your power, but please do try."

The demon finished his work and now there was one more grave among all the others. It dusted off its hands like any other workman after a job well done and then started back down the path. This time the demon paused when it passed Jin, and stared at her with some curiosity. "You are an odd one. I'd think a Demon Lord of your obvious stature would have more pressing matters than watching one poor demon at his infinite work. Didn't I torture her well enough?"

"She's dead," Jin said. "No one's faulting your...enthusiasm. Though one might ask why you bothered to bury her."

"I don't like bones lying about," the demon said. "It's untidy."

Jin just stared. "In the depths of hell, and you talk about 'untidy'? Are you insane?"

"I've often wondered that myself," the demon said. "Excuse me, I have work to do."

The demon trudged past the tree while Jin just watched him. No point in hanging around there, really. If it was true she'd missed her chance this time around, then the time would come again.

"I'm sorry," Jin said aloud, and to no one in particular since she didn't even know the little girl's name. Jin left the path and started up the slope to go back the way she had come.

She felt a tug.

Jin just stared at her wrist for several long seconds. The tug had been fierce this time, and there was no mistaking it. But... that couldn't be! The girl was dead! It was too late.

The tug wasn't coming from the grave. Jin opened her third eye just a bit, and ignored the infinite nothingness it showed her long enough to see what was in front of her there, what was real. The golden thread was real, it was there, and it led to someone. Not the girl.

I'm here...for the demon?

Jin couldn't believe her eyes -- any of them -- but there was no mistake. The thread connected to Jin's wrist played out through the smoke and ash of hell to connect to the demon's wrist. The one who had killed the child even as she watched like a useless lump was the one she had come to this hell to free.

"I don't believe this," she said aloud. "This makes no sense!"

"Were you talking to me?" the demon asked over his shoulder.

"I-I don't know."

Now the demon stopped, and turned back to look at her again. "You seem confused," it said, "Come with me and let's talk about it."

CHAPTER 19

While Jin had been watching the demon and his victim several lava bomb fragments had landed within the boundaries of the garden. First the demon scooped up the erring rocks and flung them out of the valley entirely with its powerful arms. Then the demon fetched a crude rake from a cleft in the mountain and began to make the sand right again. Jin sat on a stone further up the slope and watched him work.

"This is your garden," Jin said. "I didn't know."

"Even a demon can get bored," it said. "And there will be a delay until Azuki-chan can return from the Tenth Hell."

"And then you torture her to death again. I guess it's a good thing that she won't remember you," Jin said.

The demon shrugged. "That doesn't matter. I have my role to play. She has hers."

"Such a good way to avoid responsibility for what you do."

The demon grunted as it raked up and discarded another stone. "No one avoids responsibility for what they do, though it pleases many to think otherwise. The only uncertainty is when payment will be demanded and in what form."

"Azuki-chan? That was her name?" The demon just went on raking, but Jin didn't really need his answer. She was beginning to wonder what answers she did need. "Why her?"

The demon paused in its raking. "What do you mean?"

"I mean most demons here work in packs, torturing people who also suffer in packs. Yet here we have one demon, one tortured denizen of hell. You've devoted all your time to one person, this 'Azuki-chan.' Why?"

The demon shrugged. "Have there been complaints?"

"Please answer my question."

The demon shrugged again. "Why should I? The fact that I am a demon and I am here means I am serving my function. There isn't much leeway for our kind."

"Did you enjoy torturing Azuki-chan?"

"The question is meaningless. I did what I had to do, as did she."

"Yes. Quietly, with dignity on both sides. No screaming. No fear. No anger. What would you have done had she screamed at you? Begged? Cried? Think of this, then tell me it's a meaningless question."

The demon raked harder. "I would have done my duty. That is all there is, and all I am. As a servant of hell, what I want doesn't matter."

"What if you were wrong?"

The demon stopped raking. It looked at her for a moment, then shrugged and went back to raking. "I see. You've come to torment me. That's a little unfair," he said. "Those graves attest to how attentive I am to my duties."

"It was a simple question."

"Simple?" the demon bared its tusks. "If I tortured Azuki-chan and there was any other option then it was for nothing. How shall I dance around the thought that what I did was wrong, that I picked up her broken body from under that same tree so many times for no reason? That I did what I did --" He stopped. "Please go away," he said.

"Why her?"

"It doesn't matter. I told you that."

"If it doesn't matter, then you can answer my question as well as not. Tell me what I want to know, and I'll go away."

"Demons lie. I know."

"That doesn't mean I'm lying now and that doesn't mean you'll lie to me."

The demon stood on the edge of its garden and leaned on its rake, examining its handiwork. "Because she asked me to," he said. Jin didn't say anything and after a little while it went on. "Frankly I expected you to challenge me on that, but it's true. I don't understand it, myself. When she came here she wasn't like the others. They are all angry, almost as fierce as demons themselves. Not Azuki-chan. You saw. It was no different *then* than from her first time. I remember. I had just struck her particularly hard and she looked at me. She just said. 'I want you to be my teacher.'"

"Teacher? Did you know what that meant?"

"No, and I still do not. I don't even know why I agreed, but from then on I was the one who drove her up this killing tree in our own corner of hell. I had to. And to answer your previous question truthfully: Yes. I-I enjoyed it."

Jin shrugged. "You didn't look like you were enjoying it today. Oh, I admit you were unflinching, but that's not the same thing."

"At the time," the demon said, "all I could think was that I had my very own poor fool to torment. I didn't have to share her with any of the other demons. I practiced with my whip until I could strike her body any place I wanted. Sometimes I killed her quickly, using the whip as much as the tree. Sometimes I killed her slowly, let the tree do its work. Sometimes both equally. I was a master at torturing Azuki-chan."

"What did she do through all this?"

"The same as now. Bore it all and came back to me for more. Never afraid, never angry. In pain, yes. Sometimes she would cry out. Then she would apologize." The demon shook its head. "Can you imagine? Apologizing to a demon?"

Jin took a long slow breath. "When did it change for you?"

"I don't understand."

"Yes you do. When did you get tired of being angry and cruel?"

"I never -- "

"When did you become tired of being a demon?"

"One cannot tire of one's fundamental nature! It's ridiculous!"

"Unlike, say, a demon tending a garden in hell?"

Jin wasn't entirely sure where her words were coming from, but she'd learned to follow her instincts in these matters. She knew what she said was true, but she also knew that, so far, it was not enough. What was she missing? After a moment that understanding came to her, too.

The demon shrugged. "This is a diversion, nothing more, as I await Azuki-chan's return. I'll destroy it if you like."

"You'll just rebuild it again. You are a demon in hell and yet you insist that this one little patch of sand be something more than hell. How many times have you tried to destroy it before today, only to make it anew?"

The demon was so startled it nearly dropped its rake. "How...how did you know that? Who are you?"

"Let me borrow your rake for a moment, and I'll tell you."

The demon frowned, but held the rake out to Jin, who rose from her stone seat and walked down the slope to grasp it. She wasn't looking forward to what she was about to do, but so far she had not learned what she needed to learn, and there was only one way she knew to do it. Jin reached out for the rake, and deliberately brushed the demon's hand.

The knowledge was there, and it was even worse than Jin expected. For that moment she was the demon, a true demon, and carried a thousand years of memories of *being* a demon. The things it had done, and what it had felt as it did them. Watching the sufferers die and now and then dying and being reborn itself once more as a demon in this one hell.

"I'm called Palun Gong," Jin said. She made a show of studying the crude rake, but she did not give it back.

The demon frowned. "I have heard this name, I know, but I can't think where. Why did you want to see my rake?"

"I didn't. I wanted to see *you* a little more closely," Jin said, and she shuddered to think just how very close she had, in fact, been to the demon. But she had learned what she needed to know, including the demon's name.

"Are you done with your questions then, Palun Gong? If so, please return my rake. Azuki-chan will be returning soon and I have work to do."

"I only have one more: when did Azuki-chan start torturing *you*?"

"Nonsense! You saw what I did to her! That's -- "

"The truth, Gnasher. You hate what you do to her. You hate what you are. No matter what you do to that poor child she does a thousand times worse to you every time you lift that whip."

"Please go away, Palun Gong. Leave me..."

"To suffer in peace? Was that what you were going to say? See how well Azuki-chan taught you."

"I am a demon! What else is there for me?"

"The same as for anyone else, Gnasher -- Everything."

Jin lifted the rake in her demon's hands and she shattered it. Gnasher screamed in anguish. "My garden...!"

"Doesn't belong here," Jin said firmly. "And neither do you."

There is a certain stubbornness in the mind of a demon that resists reordering, so it took a moment or two for understanding to dawn, but when it did it arrived like a clap of thunder. Gnasher stopped being a demon. He wasn't exactly human, either, but he had changed. Jin dropped the remnants of the rake down the slope onto Gnasher's garden.

"I think I know you now, no matter what you call yourself. Yet what about Azuki-chan?" Gnasher asked. "Who will perform the duties of hell for her now?"

"She'll be fine, I promise. You have a long journey ahead of you, but say hello to Madame Meng for me, will you?"

Another few moments and Gnasher was gone. Jin went back to her rock to wait. She noted with mild interest when a shadow detached itself from the rake from and flowed across the sand, barely visible as a darker patch of blackness as it slipped into the crevices of the mountain.

Shiro.

Jin was not particularly surprised at his appearance there; there had been something familiar about the touch of the rake. Not intense, not vivid nor full of images as her contact with Gnasher had been, or even as much as her first contact with Shiro, but very familiar for all that. Faint, by comparison, and easy to overlook in the rush of *knowledge* she had gained from Gnasher, but Jin did not overlook it. She knew Shiro had given both Frank and Ling the slip, nor in turn was she surprised that he didn't hang around; Jin had already established that her demon form gave him the screaming willies, and after her conversations with Frank and Ling, Jin even had a pretty good idea as to why that was.

Still, it occurred to Jin that perhaps she had been wrong about what she had seen back on that very first day. Was Shiro helping to trap Rebecca in that corridor, or was he just there because he knew that, sooner or later, Jin would be too? After all, Gnasher hadn't needed any help from Shiro or anyone else to trap himself in hell -- he was a demon and by definition that's where he belonged. The difficult bit was for Gnasher to learn that he didn't have to be trapped, or belong. Shiro hadn't changed any of that, nor really interfered so far as Jin could tell; he was just there....

Oh.

It occurred to Jin that maybe, just maybe, she knew what that meant. The differences in this rescue pointed to something about Shiro that perhaps she had misunderstood before now. She wasn't sure this knowledge changed anything, but it was something she needed to think about later. For now, she had other fish to gut.

Jin didn't have to wait very long. The reborn Azuki-chan soon came wandering out of the plains of hell. When she saw Jin sitting there in her demon form she stopped, looking confused. "Who are you? Where is Gnasher?"

"Gone. Promoted, moved on, not-quite-but-more-so-enlightened, whatever you want to call it. You can drop the act now."

Azuki-chan started to glow. She never changed into anything else, but her clothes changed from rags to flowing white robes. "Well. Took you long enough," the girl said.

With her face no longer smeared with blood and ashes, Jin finally got her first good look at Azuki-chan. Jin nearly fell off her stone.

"You're me!" she said. "Well, at least you look like I did, when I was about ten years old. Why do you look like that?"

Azuki-chan hid a smile. "You knew what I was and you don't know that? Maybe you're not as wise as people say."

Jin just stared for another few moments, trying to reconcile what she saw with what she understood, and after all the possibilities where considered and discarded, she was left with only one.

"You don't look like me. You *are* me."

"In a sense. I'm another incarnation of Guan Yin. Brought here ages ago for the purpose of Gnasher's salvation."

"What do you mean, 'another incarnation'? How many times has Guan Yin reincarnated? How bloody many of us are out here?"

Azuki-chan frowned. "I didn't say 'reincarnation.' I said 'incarnation.' Guan Yin wasn't physically reborn as me. I'm simply an aspect of her, given physical form for a purpose, as you are."

"'Aspect'?" Jin dropped her demon form, just for an instant, then resumed it. "Guess again," she said.

To Jin's considerable surprise, Azuki-chan immediately dropped to her knees. "I crave your pardon, Immanent One. I didn't know you had resumed mortal form."

Jin sighed. "No, of course you didn't. So. Gnasher is gone, you've won. What will you do now?"

"My purpose has been fulfilled. I must cease."

"You mean die?"

"I mean surrender this temporary form and rejoin that from which I was sundered."

"That would be me," Jin said, feeling suddenly uncomfortable.

Auzki-chan smiled. "What you are now is not all that Guan Yin is, or what she will be, or what she was. We are all the same, sooner or later, but not necessarily at the moment. Good fortune in whatever task you have before you."

"Thanks. Listen, one question before you...whatever. How did you bear this, and why? You went through all this for a demon! I saw what he was, I felt it, and, for what seemed like forever, I lived it!"

"And yet you, too, went through that for a demon."

Jin thought about that. "But... does it matter? I really would like to know."

"We are all the same, so how can there be someone, even a demon, who does not matter? Goodbye, Immanent One. Until we are reunited."

The girl did not so much open a doorway of light as *become* a doorway of light. Then she, too, was gone. Jin just stared at the empty spot where Azuki-chan had been for a very long time, trying to get her mind around what she had seen over the past few hours and not succeeding very well.

Jin tried to imagine herself, or anything that was even remotely an aspect or reflection of her, being brave and selfless enough to suffer torture and death repeatedly through hundreds of centuries, and all for the benefit of something as vile and degraded as a demon. Jin tried to see any part of herself in someone like Azuki-chan and, except for appearance, Jin just couldn't find it there. What little she had suffered when, for that moment, she had become Gnasher, seemed like a hangnail by comparison to what the centuries in that place must have been like for Azuki-chan. Besides, it was not like Jin had a choice if she didn't want that invisible thread tangling behind her for eternity.

We are all the same.

Jin stared at Gnasher's lovely zen garden. Which, to her mind, was another point. How many demons could or would do that? She made a fairly confident guess that, other than Gnasher, that was pretty much an empty set. All the same? What a complete load of crap!

"It is, isn't it?" Jin said aloud.

YOU KNOW IT...OH, ROT.

Jin smiled a grim smile. "Gotcha."

Jin figured the odds were fifty-fifty, so she opened her Third Eye just a bit and glanced at her left shoulder, and there he was: a little imp identical to the one she'd seen riding Joyce's shoulder. Jin grabbed it by the scruff of its neck and held it in front of her at arm's length.

"Just what did you think you were doing?!"

The imp shrugged. WELL, YOU WERE THE CLOSEST MORTAL. I HAD TO TAKE A SHOT. IT'S NOT JUST ANY DEMON WHO'S HAD A CHANCE TO BEDEVIL THE BODHISATTVA OF MERCY.

"I have enough self-doubts and wrong-headedness of my own, thanks," Jin said. "I don't need you making it worse!"

The little imp struggled in her grip. HOW DO YOU KNOW THAT? MAYBE YOU SHOULD JUST STOP TRYING TO

BE A GODDESS AND GO WITH THE MORTAL FLOW. IT'S NOT LIKE YOU'RE VERY GOOD AT THE GODDESS THING, the creature added slyly, and Jin shook it until she fancied she could hear its teeth rattle.

"Try that *once more*," Jin said, "and I'll see to it that you spend the next few eons reincarnated as a dung beetle. And believe me, that *is* mercy compared to what I'd like to do to you." Jin didn't actually know if she could arrange such a thing, but it felt good to think that she might. The imp, for what it was worth, looked like it had no doubts at all.

I WON'T, I PROMISE! it said.

"That's better. How long have you been here?"

SINCE YOU LEFT THE OFFICE.

"Since I... oh."

Jin understood, then. The imp didn't just resemble the demon who had tempted and led Joyce away from believing in herself -- he was that demon. Which at once infuriated Jin even more, but also gave her an idea.

"Were you with Joyce when she died?"

I WAS ALWAYS WITH HER. YOU KNOW THAT.

"Then why didn't you help her?"

There was open astonishment on the demon's ugly little face. YOU KNOW WHAT HAPPENS TO A DEMON WHO INTERFERES WITH KARMA? IT MAKES YOUR 'DUNG BEETLE' THREAT SOUND LIKE A VACATION.

Jin hadn't really expected anything different, even though she didn't pretend to know all the rules of Karma. That did leave something else, though. "If you were there, then tell me what happened," Jin said.

WHY SHOULD I?

"We've discussed dung beetles. You want to try for toilet paper?"

FINE, IF YOU MUST KNOW. IT WAS HER BOYFRIEND.

"Boyfriend... you mean Lucius?"

YEAH, THAT'S THE ONE. HE STRANGLED HER.

CHAPTER 20

In Jin's work with legal aid she'd made more than one contact in the Medias police department. She called one of them as soon as she got back from hell. She'd have called sooner, except for the "out of service" message. Thinking back on it, Jin knew she shouldn't be surprised.

"Detective Mabus? This is Jin Hannigan. From Legal Aid, right. Listen, I know who killed Joyce Masters. I can't prove it, but -- "

There was a bit of static, but the voice was clear enough. Jin pictured John Mabus at his desk: balding, overweight, overworked. "We all know who killed Joyce Masters," he said. "And proving it is not an issue. He confessed."

"He... confessed? Lucius Taylor?"

"At the scene, Jin. Hadn't you heard?"

"I've been...away, for a little bit. I'm-I'm sorry I wasted your time."

He sighed wearily. "Forget it. Listen, I know you're under stress. She was your friend and all. I'm sorry. But we got the guy already. It's over."

Jin thanked him and rang off. On her way back to Medias Jin's mind had been whirling with plots and stratagems to prove what she knew to be true: that Lucius Taylor had murdered Joyce, but it was all for nothing. There was no mystery, no dramatic revelations. Everyone already knew what Jin knew -- that Joyce had gone to Lucius' apartment, and they had argued. Lucius became violent. Neighbors had reported a "domestic disturbance" but it was far too late when the police arrived.

Why did you go there, Joyce?

Jin had no answer to that. As for the demon, he had told Jin only what everyone else in Medias who bothered to listen to the radio already knew. If Jin had hers turned on that morning she would have heard about Joyce's murder before she'd even sent Ling to find her.

Jin received a call from Karl Simon, the Chairman of the Board of the Legal Aid Office, right after she returned -- first supposedly breaking the sad news, then adding that the office was to be closed pending the appointment of a new director which, the Chairman said, could take months. It wouldn't be easy to find a lawyer -- or anyone, really -- willing to do what Joyce had done, day after day.

"Mr. Simon? Have you considered Margaret Kathleen Hannigan?" Jin asked.

"Your mother? You're kidding, right?"

Jin smiled despite herself. "Only a little."

"Well... her heart's in the right place and she's certainly got the skills. But she was involved in setting up the charity in the first place, remember?"

"I do. Why is that a problem?"

"It's just that your mother and the Board go way back. And not in a good way, you know?"

Jin knew, unfortunately. Margaret Kathleen Hannigan was many things, but a politician wasn't one of them. She didn't suffer fools gladly, or much at all, whereas Joyce did it all the time out of necessity. When your life's work depended on dealing with people who had money and the urge to do good but not much else going for them, there really wasn't any choice.

"Will you at least float the idea?"

"I will, Jin. And it will be shot full of holes and sink like a stone. But you and I know she'd be great."

"Yeah. She would. Pity."

Jin thanked the man and hung up. She found an empty box and started to clean out her desk. She heard the bell over the office door before Jin was even through cleaning out her desk. "I'm sorry, but we're closed..."

"I know, Lotus Blossom. Jonathan called me. I came as soon as I heard," said Margaret Hannigan.

Later Jin would wonder how she had let what happened next, happen. Later Jin would remember who had told her mother about Joyce and why, perhaps, that was important. Later. Right at that moment she understood one thing and one thing only.

Mom?

Jin dropped a plastic Bay St. Louis souvenir mug and it clattered on the linoleum, but she paid it no heed. Her mother just stood there for a moment, a sort of sad half-smile on her face. Then Margaret Kathleen Hannigan held out her arms and Jin didn't even hesitate. She took three quick steps and then burst into tears as her mother hugged her tight.

"...sucks, Mom. Just sucks!"

"I know, hon. It'll be all right."

Jin didn't think it would be all right at all. Even though she had *seen* Joyce at the Ninth Hell and she knew beyond any doubt that the person who was Joyce Masters had survived and would go on, would *have* to go on, none of that seemed to make any difference.

"Why now, dammit..."

Jin's mother just held on, swaying gently. "I don't know why Joyce had to die now, Jin. I don't think there is an answer."

But that wasn't what Jin meant. The question that burst out in Jin's anguish wasn't about Joyce at all -- it was about herself. She was crying. She knew it was right to cry for Joyce, for what she might have achieved *as* Joyce with more time, with more help. Many more years of the good she had done as Director, as Jin's friend. Maybe, just maybe, Joyce could have done whatever she had come to Medias to do and moved on, but that wasn't going to happen now, not for a very long time. All that deserved Jin's grief, but why now? Was it because she had been so busy, so angry since Joyce's death? Or was it because her mother was there, and it was all right to cry now? Jin didn't think that was the answer either. It was always all right to cry, when there was enough reason.

Not all right, Jin realized. *Safe. That's why I'm crying now.*

She would not cry in front of Shan Cai, or Lung Nu, and certainly not Teacher, nor even before Madame Meng. Yet, in her mother's arms, it was safe to cry and she did just that, until her face was hot and flushed and no more tears would come. She finally regained her breath and composure and took a step back.

"Better?" asked her mother, handing her a handkerchief. Jin blew her nose and managed a weak smile.

"Much."

"All right. Are you ready to talk about what comes next?"

Jin frowned. "You mean the funeral?"

"I mean you cleaning out your desk. What's the status of the Office?"

Jin told her mother about her conversation with the Chairman. Margaret just laughed. "Typical. I helped set up this office. I guess I wasn't as polite about it as I should have been. That doesn't explain why you're packing up. The office will reopen, sooner or later."

"I know. I'm just not sure I want to come back, Mom. Even now I keep expecting Joyce to come around that corner and ask me about a mis-filed deposition, or my love life. I don't think I could take that."

"You're a strong girl. You can take anything you have to," Margaret said. "And pay it back with interest."

Jin shook her head. "You make it sound so easy. I'm not you, Mom."

"No, you're not," Margaret said very seriously. "For which I thank whatever god, goddesses or universal forces allowed that to happen."

"Ummm, what are you talking about?"

Margaret Hannigan looked at her daughter with open admiration. "You, my beautiful Lotus Blossom. I've made a lot of messes in my life; I'll admit that under oath in any court you'd care to name. But you're the one thing I got right."

Jin thought maybe she was blushing, but her face already felt red and puffy from crying and she just couldn't tell. "Flatterer."

Her mother sighed. "Not even a little. Jin, I know this may not be the best time to tell you this, but frankly I don't know when *would* be a good time. Probably never, so I'm going to be selfish and say what I have to say, all right?"

"Tell me what, Mom?"

"Why do you think I'm the way I am? It's you, Jin. It's all and only because of you."

Jin took a deep breath, let it out. "Mom, you're not going to pin that on me. Not now."

Margaret smiled grimly. "Yes, now, because I don't know if I'll have the courage to do it later. Just be quiet and listen to your mother for a minute, then you can talk. Deal?"

Jin sat down on the edge of her desk. "All right, Mom -- I'm listening." Jin felt a tug at her wrist. She ignored it. Whoever it was could just wait, that's all. She listened. Jin figured she owed her mother at least that much.

Margaret hesitated, then plunged right in. "When you were born, I was a corporate lawyer. And I was damned good at it, too -- made partner before I was thirty. Six years after you were born I quit, and I've never looked back."

Jin glanced toward heaven. "Mom, I *know* all that. You quit because you wanted to make the world a better place for me, so much so that you were almost never there..." Jin saw the stricken look on her mother's face and went on, a little defensive, "Well, it's true. You know it and I know it. Maybe I was angry about that when I was growing up. Maybe I still am a little, but it's water under the bridge. Several bridges, even."

Margaret frowned. "Who told you that rubbish? About quitting to make the world a better place, I mean."

Jin just stared at her mother for a moment, wondering if she was joking. "You did, Mom."

"Did I?" Margaret smiled a sad little smile. "Yes, I suppose I did. Sounds like me, anyway. It was a lie."

Another tug a the wrist, which Jin ignored. She barely felt it as she blinked at her mother in confusion. "Excuse me?"

"A lie. False. At odds with the facts. See also: fib. Do it under oath and it's perjury."

"What on earth are you talking about?"

Her mother sighed. "Well, maybe I didn't lie to you on purpose. For a long time I believed that bit about the world and all myself, but I haven't done much but think about this when you said you were moving back for a while. I was trying to figure out why you'd agreed."

"It's complicated, Mom."

Margaret shrugged. "No doubt. Yet at first I thought perhaps the bad old world was getting to be a bit much for you, but I knew that wasn't it, and it was silly to even think that. So I started to think about why I *knew* that it was a silly idea. That's when I finally figured this thing out."

"Figured what out?"

"Jin, I didn't stop being everything I was to make the world a better place for you. I stopped because I wanted to *be* you."

Jin just stared. "You're not making any sense!"

Her mother shook her head. "My mind has never been clearer in my life. Jin, you have no idea what it was like for me, watching you grow up, loving you, seeing in you everything that I was not."

Jin could barely believe her own ears. "Like what?"

Margaret grinned. "Lots of things, but first and most of all: fearless." When Jin just stared at her she went on, calmly. "It's true. I once came to pick you up from first grade and found you facing down two second-grader bullies by yourself. And why?"

Jin did remember. She remembered how hot her face had been, how angry she was. She remembered the confusion on the two louts' faces as she hurled herself between them and her playmate David, who was lying bruised and crying in the dirt. She remembered taking blows and giving them back harder for every blow struck and crying with rage, not fear, and then the hand on her shoulder that she tried to tear away from before she realized the hand belonged to her mother. The two bullies ran away then, leaving Jin with a bruised cheek and a black eye, but Jin remembered the next day with some satisfaction as the two bullies showed up for school, one with two black eyes and the other with one shiner and a split lip. From a girl. Neither of them was quite as effective as a bully from then on.

"Why? Because I didn't have enough sense to run?"

Margaret shook her head. "Because they were hurting your friend. You were always like that, Jin. From the time you could walk until now: fearless, and with an innate sense of justice that had me ashamed of the things I had to do every day. I kept asking myself, 'what would Jin think' and knowing I wouldn't like the answer."

"All kids know about justice, Mom. The problem is they think it applies to everyone else."

"*You* didn't think that way, and give me a little credit here, please. You weren't a little pipsqueak goody-goody saint, hon, and maybe you didn't get half the paddlings you deserved. You were simply *better* than me, and deep down I knew it every time I looked at you."

Jin felt her knees wobbling, and she was glad she was sitting down. "I don't know what to say."

"Neither did I, for a long time. You know, it's funny the lies we make up about ourselves. What we're willing to believe in order to keep up the illusions we cling to. I'm not ashamed of the things I've accomplished, Jin, but I am a little ashamed of why I did them and throwing it all in your lap now. I know something's going on with you above and beyond the loss of your friend. I wish I could help."

Jin stood up, a little unsteadily, and now it was she who opened her arms and enveloped her mother in a tight hug. "You already have.... oh.

Margaret buried her head for a moment in Jin's chest. "What is it, Lotus Blossom?"

It was the last thing on earth Jin expected or wanted to feel or know just then. She did not feel it the first time she had embraced her mother, but now it was all there, laid out for her like the petals on a rose. Jin felt the tug at her wrist again, and now she knew it for what it was. The touch and the tug together brought a complete and unwelcome understanding.

I won't. I can't...

"Honey, what is it? What's wrong?"

Jin said the words, though she wanted with every iota of her being not to have to say them. It was too much to ask of her, and yet she did it anyway because, well, it was what she did and who she was, like it or not.

"It wasn't a lie, Mom, you just didn't understand -- you weren't trying to be me, you were trying to be *you*, and you didn't know how. You started wrong, and it just took you a while to figure that out. I was a clue, an example, perhaps even a hint, but that's all. The rest you did on your own."

"All...?"

There wasn't anything to break. There were no external symbols of the confusion that had ordered Margaret Kathleen Hannigan's life. She's just been waiting for an explanation, the one it was Jin's fate to give. She kissed her mother on the forehead. "If I was fearless, ever, I learned it from you. Goodbye."

"Goodbye?" Margaret Kathleen Hannigan looked confused for just a moment, but that moment passed quickly. "Oh. It is goodbye, isn't it? I think I understand, now."

With that understanding the last links to Medias were severed. Margaret Kathleen Hannigan was already fading out of Medias forever, but she did smile fondly at her daughter one last time.

"I said you were better than me, Lotus Blossom, but I didn't know the half of it. I thought you were kidding. About being Guan Yin, I mean."

"I wish I had been," Jin said.

"You don't mean that, Jin."

"I don't know if I do or not, but I had to say it... Mom, I'm sorry."

"Don't you dare be sorry. I'm not. Goodbye for now, Lotus Blossom." Then she was gone.

Jin found she had a few tears left after all, but even these could not last for long. There was too much left undone and she tried to concentrate on that, since she had no tears left to cry with.

I assumed Shiro made contact with my mom in order to get to me, but it was no different from all the other people who were waiting for me: Rebecca, Michiko, Buddy... Dammit, Shiro knew! Why didn't I?

Jin sat in her chair in the empty office. Elsewhere, she knew, the world was being reordered to account for the absence of both Margaret Kathleen Hannigan and Joyce Masters. The difference was that Joyce would be eulogized, mourned, and buried, while those whose lives she affected, including Jin, would rearrange the pieces as best they could on their own. For Jin's mother the process would be very different -- the world would reorder *itself.* Jin wondered if, for instance, she called up the Chairman of the Legal Aid Board, he'd even remember Jin's mother at all or simply remind Jin that she'd died years ago. Which way was the world going to turn? Jin found herself oddly unconcerned, really. How the world reformed itself didn't bother her so long as it didn't try to make her forget her mother.

That wasn't going to happen. She remembered Buddy, and Rebecca, and Missus Tickles, and even the Lemon Man, who had a real name that Jin knew and could say aloud if need be. Everyone from Medias who had caused a shift in the world to accommodate their loss. She realized that it didn't work the same way in every hell; she rather doubted that the hell she'd just come from would or needed to bother much to replace one working demon out of millions. But in Medias it was different and, though she really didn't understand why, she knew it was so. She also knew she wasn't going to forget her own mother, even though -- or because -- she was the one who sent her out of the world forever.

I'm sorry I couldn't do as much for Joyce.

It felt strange to think that way. For all that she knew in her mind that what had happened to her mother was supposed to be a good thing, it was hard to see it in those terms. Jin felt the way she had felt at age twelve with Missus Tickles -- she felt like Death. After all, death wasn't a person; it was a portal from one world to another and that was how Jin felt, and that was what she had done, and kept doing, and was going to continue to do even after the mortal part that was Jin Lee Hannigan was long gone.

"How did she do it?" Jin asked aloud, but there was no one there to answer. At least, she didn't *see* anyone, but Jin wasn't fooled. "I asked a question," Jin said. "I know you're there. At least, you damn well better be. Those were your instructions. Come out."

Frank and Ling appeared. "Forgive us. We didn't realize you were speaking to us."

"Of course I forgive you. I have to, don't I?"

"You would forgive anyone almost anything," Ling said. "That's not the same thing."

"I'm glad you said 'almost.' I want to reserve my options on that. Anyway, it was a serious question. Guan Yin, I mean. How did she do it all those centuries? When I free someone from Hell I feel like I've killed them, even though I know it's a good thing, and to keep my sanity I must believe so too. You saw what happened to my mother."

They nodded, though neither spoke.

"So why do I feel like complete and total shit?"

Ling shrugged. "Because you're mortal. The part of you that is Guan Yin knows, but the part of you that is mortal must interpret what is happening in terms that make sense with its limited understanding."

"You know that for a fact?" Jin asked. It made perfect sense, but that didn't mean she was prepared to accept anything on faith just yet.

"No, it is just what I believe," Ling said. "When my mistress -- the full, divine form of her -- did what you do, there was nothing but joy on all sides. You, if you'll pardon my saying so, seem more confused and sad than anything else. This is a time to celebrate! This is not a time to grieve."

"And yet I'm going to, and for a long time. One more problem with being mortal. I'm beginning to wonder if there *are* any advantages." Jin rubbed her eyes, wearily. "All right. Thank you both for protecting my mother; it made me feel somewhat easier. But now I need some time alone."

They both winked out without another word. Jin finished loading her cardboard box and prepared to lock up the office. She hesitated, then opened her Third Eye the slightest bit.

The imp was there, sitting alone on Joyce's desk, looking morose. Jin wanted to be angry but she just didn't have the strength.

"Oh, shoo! The office is closing, and Joyce is dead, and you already know what's going to happen if try anything else with me!"

The imp just sighed. SHE WAS CLOSE, YOU KNOW.

Jin almost dropped her box. "To what? A total breakdown?"

TO GETTING OUT.

"If this is some kind of sick joke -- "

YOU KNOW IT'S TRUE. NOW I HAVE TO START ALL OVER WITH SOMEONE ELSE.

"Why don't you wait for Joyce? She's coming back."

IT'S STILL STARTING OVER. THAT'S THE PARADOX, BUT THAT'S HOW IT WORKS. KARMA BUILDS, BUT EVERY LIFE IS THE FIRST ONE, THANKS TO MADAME MENG.

Jin almost smiled. "You're starting to sound like Gnasher."

The little imp shook his head, and sighed. TOO MUCH PRIDE IN MY WORK YET. TOO MUCH JOY.

Jin frowned. "Can there ever be too much joy?"

IN SUFFERING?

Now Jin did manage a smile. A weak, pale one, but a smile nonetheless. "Good point."

STILL, WE ALL DO OUR PART. LISTEN, IMMANENT ONE -- IF I DO MEET YOUR FRIEND AGAIN, I PROMISE NOT TO BE ONE BIT HARDER THAN I HAVE TO BE. THAT'S NOT AN EASY THING FOR A DEMON.

Nor for Guan Yin, *when she's me.*

"Thank you," Jin said, and meant it.

CHAPTER 21

Jin got her first hint of how the world had reordered itself when she got back to her apartment and found that it wasn't her apartment anymore. She didn't even have a key. The harried-looking young mother who answered the doorbell thought she was lost. After a moment Jin decided that was probably true. She asked directions to Kindle Avenue and was a little relieved to discover that it still existed. She let the poor woman get back to dealing with a squalling toddler and walked back down the stairs.

I wonder if I have a home at all?

Not that Jin had really expected that. The changed world might not have been able to change Jin, but despite that Jin had a pretty good idea of what the new reality had wanted to do. Acclimating would not be hard. Still, one thing to know and another to feel, as Jin already knew. By the time Jin had walked box all the way to Kindle Avenue she was getting a little anxious, but the key fit the door to her mother's house just as Jin knew it was supposed to. Jin walked through the door and recognized things that belonged to her mother: a small brass statue of the Hindu goddess Tara, a Japanese print in sumi-e style of a running horse, a rickety plant stand. There were one or two things she recognized as her mother's.

So. She hasn't disappeared totally.

Jin carefully went over the house from top to bottom, noting each change: her old bedroom was a guestroom now. Jin found her own clothes in what had been her mother's bedroom. She also found pictures that were indisputably of Margaret Kathleen Hannigan.

Jin found the actual obituary in newspaper clippings in a scrapbook in her night stand. Apparently her mother had been hit by a car about five years before, in Jin's junior year in high school. Jin grunted. Honestly, was this the best the universe could do? A car? For Margaret Kathleen Hannigan that seemed much too ordinary an end. Jin wasn't sure what she'd expected, perhaps something more along the lines of 'buried by a bulldozer in Israel' or murdered by government thugs in India, but no. The obituary stood firm: hit by a car on Pepper Street. There was one other difference, too -- in this version of the world, her mother had served as director of the Pepper Street Legal Aid Office until her duly recorded death; it was only then that Joyce Masters had taken over, apparently. Although, in this new version of the world, Joyce was still dead.

As for her mother, Jin felt very strange to be reading about the death five years previous of a woman Jin had hugged barely an hour ago. Jin thought that, perhaps, she should be immune from strangeness after what all had happened to her in the past few weeks, but that didn't seem to be the case.

Jin quickly tracked down bank statements and other basic items of life and gave herself a crash course in what it meant to be Jin Hannigan now. She didn't have a job so far as she could tell. If the bank statements were accurate she didn't need one, at least for a good long while. Both realities seemed to have agreed that she'd be without a job, since in the one she'd just left there was no working Legal Aid Office, at least temporarily. It wasn't very different from before, really. Hardly worth mentioning except for the part about feeling absolutely and utterly alone.

The odd part was that Jin didn't think that being alone was an altogether bad thing. For example, she didn't how she would have coped if the reordering of creation had gifted her with a live-in lover, or caused her mother's sister Aunt Bernadette to move in, a relative so smugly self-righteous and humorless that Jin had trouble believing that she and Jin's mother were from the same gene pool. Jin took some grim satisfaction when she came across a letter in her files from Aunt Bernadette berating Jin for not moving in with her or another relative after Margaret's "death."

Good for me, thought Jin. Then she felt a tug at her wrist and she groaned. *Dammit, not now! I've got my own shit to deal with.*

The tug ignored all that. Yes. Now. It was gentle but persistent. Firm. Implacable. Jin sighed. How was she supposed to solve someone else's problems when she was such a wreck herself?

You're not a wreck.

For an instant Jin thought that the Guan Yin That Was had intruded into the reality of Medias, but no. The thought was solidly her own, and Jin knew it for truth. She couldn't use weakness as an excuse, much as she wanted to. She was grieving, yes, but that wouldn't stop her from doing what she had to do. Jin spied the golden thread at her wrist and she followed where it led her, or rather followed willingly as it pulled her along.

It seems such a fragile thing.

Jin risked opening her Third Eye enough to take a good a look at the thing as she dared. At first this didn't tell her any more than what she already knew -- that the thing was normally invisible, that it appeared to have a luminous golden quality when viewed with the Third Eye and took on the appearance of a delicate thread, almost like silk. It was only on closer inspection that Jin saw the individual strands that made up the thread, almost like a tiny rope, and that there were small points of light moving along those strands, and that in turn those pinpoints of golden light were made of things that were neither thread nor gold: Jin saw what looked like tiny people moving in repeating patterns. She wondered if she was looking at memories, or things that were currently happening in the person's life, but past this point her perception failed her. Jin knew there was understanding to be had within the golden thread but, at the same time, it was just beyond her reach.

I bet the real Guan Yin *would understand.*

Jin squelched the thought. Just now, *she* was the real Guan Yin, and as the real Guan Yin there was a part of her that did understand, and that she could trust to do the right thing when the time came. Annoying as she was, she hadn't failed Jin yet.

The thread led her down to Pepper Street and toward the familiar alleyway leading to the Gateway to All the Hells, but then it did something strange -- it went right past the alley. Jin frowned, but kept following. After a few yards the thread actually doubled back. Just when she reached the alleyway once again, the thread did the exact same thing except it went beyond the alley in the other direction before again doubling back.

"What the blazes is going on here?" she asked aloud, to no one in particular. "It's almost as if..."

Jin dismissed the thought at first, but when the thread again proved capricious and its true direction elusive, Jin had to consider her conclusions once more and she finished the thought. "It's almost as if whoever is on the other end of this thread knows I'm coming and doesn't want me to find them... but that doesn't make any sense!"

It also wasn't going to work. Jin opened her Third Eye and followed the thread again, only this time she ignored the tangles, ignored the circuitous route, and looked beyond all that. If she were correct, then she knew where the thread was really going and the Third Eye verified it. Jin saw much more of the *nothing* underlying Medias than she really wanted to, but the thread itself, after numerous switchbacks, did indeed disappear down the corridor to the Gateway.

Jin ignored the tangles and went straight down the corridor. In a few moments the thread resolved its contradictions and led her unerringly forward, while the tangles vanished behind them. Jin glanced behind her and saw them melt away. Before that, the pull she had felt made Jin think of the thread as an "infinitely elastic" cord, and that it simply compressed as it pulled her on. Now she saw the thread dissolving once she passed the place it had been but, in either case, it had to lead eventually to the right person.

Assuming someone wants to escape, could they?

Jin had her answer when she reached the Gateway to All the Hells. The cord led to one of the numerous doors, but did not pass through. Jin found it lying in a tangle on the ground and, like all the other tangles, it vanished when she stepped past it.

"Guardians!"

In a moment they were there. YES, IMMANENT ONE?

"Who passed through this door a moment ago?"

WE CANNOT SAY.

Jin nodded. "Which only means one thing -- it was Shiro."

WE DID NOT SAY SO.

Jin smiled grimly. "No, you did not say so. I did. Where is Teacher? Back in the First Hell?"

HE'S HERE.

Jin blinked, then looked at where the three statues stood. Teacher leaned against the dais. He was barely recognizable at that distance and Jin couldn't tell if he was looking her way, but she was pretty sure that he was. She left the guardians and set out on a brisk walk toward the dais. Jin realized she hadn't been there in a while but, as she got closer, she also realized why. It wasn't that she had no real need or reason to go there; she was actively avoiding it. The sight of her own serenely smiling self was annoying in the extreme, and every time the Guan Yin That Was had managed to visit her Jin's reaction had just gotten worse. She tried to take that into account as she considered what to say to the King of the First Hell. What she had not and could not have taken into account was Teacher's first words to her.

"I heard about Joyce. I'm sorry."

Jin blinked. "I don't understand."

Teacher looked a little wistful. "Which part? That I knew, or that I'm sorry?"

"Why would you be sorry? Don't you deal with people like Joyce every day? It's just one more turn of the wheel, isn't it? She's reborn into Medias and gets another shot at whatever she didn't get the first time."

Teacher shrugged. "Well, not automatically. It's possible for a person to make things worse and be sent to a lower hell. That's my call. Umm, that didn't happen, in case you were wondering."

"I'm glad for that much. But I still don't understand why you say you're sorry."

"I say it because it's true, Jin. I know what you're feeling, simply because that's the way humans feel when someone near to them dies. I'm expressing concern and sympathy like any other human would, because there's really nothing else I can do."

"It's different for me. I saw Joyce after she died," Jin said. "Down in the Ninth Hell. I know she survived. I know death isn't the end."

"I saw her too. The one doesn't change the other."

Jin smiled a faint smile. "You're right, it doesn't." Jin leaned back, put her hands on top of the dais and hoisted herself up to sit there, her legs dangling over the sand. "I was following Shiro," she said.

"I suppose you expect me to deny that it *was* Shiro?"

Jin shrugged. "I wondered."

"You're a smart girl, Jin, when you're thinking clearly. Who else in the known universe wants to be near you and yet lives in fear of you? Shiro. Who would flee Guan Yin in her aspect as Deliverer? Shiro. There was no other possibility, really."

Jin took a deep breath. "Are you finally ready to help me, then?"

"I've been trying to help you from day one, but if you mean 'am I going to risk interfering in what I don't understand,' then the answer is still 'no.'"

"Then why were you here waiting for me? You were, weren't you?"

"I told you that part already. Because of Joyce. Because it was the human thing to do. For what little it's worth."

Jin thought about that for a moment and then nodded. "For what little it's worth: thank you."

"You're welcome."

"I do have a favor to ask, though. I want to talk for a minute. You don't have to say anything you feel you shouldn't, but I want you to listen to me. Will you do that?"

Teacher glanced at his strange wristwatch again, checking each hand's position against the symbols of Earth, Air, Fire, and Water. "I'll be glad to, at least for a little while. Hell doesn't wait on anyone, and that includes me."

"All right, then: Shiro, apparently against his will, has reached a point where he's vulnerable -- a strange use of the word -- to Guan Yin as Deliverer, and made a conscious decision to avoid me as surely as he avoids my demon form. Besides the ability to physically destroy him in my demon form, as Guan Yin I also have the power to send him on to you for his next judgment. Killing him I could do anytime provided I was willing to risk the consequences, but the fact that he broke the connection between us tells me that the state of 'being ready for deliverance' is not either on or off, as

I had thought. Opportunities can be lost or, apparently, discarded. Why did Shiro discard his?"

Teacher finally went off script. "I'm not going to tell you that, Jin. Not because I can't or won't, but because I don't have to. By now you know the answer, or you're an idiot. And you are not an idiot."

Jin nodded. "He doesn't want transcendence. He wants me."

Teacher grinned. "Duh."

Jin smiled a grim smile. "Careful, Teacher. You're coming close to interfering."

"Not a bit. It's not interfering to tell you what you already know," Teacher said, looking a little affronted. "Though, like most mortals, you don't always *realize* what you know. And I say that on good authority."

Jin smiled. "Let's go with that for a moment. Guan Yin married a mortal. Why would she do that? It makes no sense until you realize that the answer is obvious. She did it for the same reason she does anything -- to release someone suffering from torment. And Shiro was and is suffering. It's a hell of his own make and design, but he's in it. He carries it with him wherever he goes."

"Yes, but what she tried to do didn't work."

Jin shook her head, slowly, and she grinned. "Nice try, Teacher. Sure, as a mortal it's very hard for me to take the long view, but it's safe to say the Guan Yin That Was did not have that problem. I no longer think this is 'Plan B' or anything of the sort. I think Guan Yin's original plan has not failed -- *it's still going on*, and we're in it."

Teacher sighed. "Even if you're right, and let's, for the purpose of this delightful discussion, assume you are. So what? All this doesn't solve your problem."

Jin smiled. "I didn't want to solve it, Teacher. I wanted to understand what it *was*, and I think I do now."

Teacher smiled. "Really? Would you put a wager on that?"

Jin didn't even blink. "Name the stakes."

Teacher just stared at her for several long moments, then shook his head. "No, I don't think I will take that bet. But I really would like to know."

"My problem is this. Or rather, the question I have to answer: what can I can do for Shiro as Jin Lee Hannigan that I can not do as Guan Yin?"

Teacher was silent for several seconds. "You'd have won, you know. I do not know the answer and wouldn't tell you if I did. I will tell you just one thing, though, for what little it might be worth: Shiro already believes he knows the answer, and I pray with everything I have that he's wrong. He believes that Guan Yin, as the mortal woman that you are now, can finally and truly love him the way he loves you. That he can 'fix' whatever went wrong the first time."

"I felt something for Shiro that I'd never felt for any mortal man I've ever met. I thought it might be love. I was afraid it was. It wasn't, was it? It was the karma we share, he and my mortal self. You said that Guan Yin doesn't accumulate karma, but she was mortal then just as she's mortal now. But she's never going to love him the way he wants."

"I hope that's true," Teacher said, looking thoughtful. "I'll even go so far as to say that I think it's extremely unlikely. Yet we're both mortal at the moment Jin, with all the hormones and confusion and delusions that naturally go with that state, so don't tell me it's impossible -- I know better and so do you. So, I think, does Shiro. He believes this is his chance, and he's not going to let go of it."

"He damn well is; I'm going to make him let go."

Just then Frank and Ling appeared in separate doorways of light.

"Immanent One," Frank said, "we followed Shiro, but he proved elusive. We believe he came through here -- "

He stopped, blinking in surprise, when both Teacher and Jin burst into laughter. Ling just shook her head, looking disgusted.

"Mortals..."

CHAPTER 22

After Teacher returned to the First Hell, Ling and Frank remained behind. Jin, for her part, remained perched on the dais, looking thoughtful, for some time. She finally rose, stretched, and started to walk around on top of the dais among the statues of Guan Yin, Lung Nu, and Shan Cai.

"Down to business, then," Jin said. "Do either of you have any idea where Shiro might be now?"

"No," Ling said. "Even if we knew which hell corridor he went down originally, he wouldn't have had to come back the same way. These doors lead to all the hells, but they are not the only ones. He could be almost literally anywhere."

"Could be, but isn't," Jin said. "He's never going to be very far from where I am."

Ling nodded. "We know, and Frank and I have discussed this. We don't think we should leave you again. We move very quickly, but not infinitely so, and we can protect you better if we are with you. Now that..." Her voice trailed off.

"Now that my mother and Joyce are gone, yes?" Jin said evenly. "You can say their names; I won't break. But what if your function here is not to protect me?"

Ling and Frank glanced at each other. "We don't understand," Ling said

Jin shrugged. "It's simple enough. You're assuming your function is to prevent me from being harmed. What if it isn't?"

"But...what else? We serve Guan Yin, whatever her form. We would never allow you to come to harm willingly."

"I believe you," Jin said, because it was the truth. "I also believe you'll intervene if you think I'm threatened. But what if it becomes necessary for me to put myself in harm's way?"

"You mean deliberately?" Frank asked. "Why would that be necessary?"

"I'm just saying 'what if?' What if I ordered you not to interfere with a course of action I've chosen?"

"We would obey," Ling said. "Even..."

"Even if you thought I was being a damn fool?"

"Yes," Ling said evenly. "Even then."

"Good, since before this is over I may have to do some very foolish things. Just so we understand one another."

"Fine, but may we suggest that at least one of us stay with you while you send the other to search for Shiro?"

Jin didn't say anything for a moment. She finally nodded at no one in particular. "That won't be necessary, since I know where he is." Jin held up her left wrist. "He's at the end of this golden cord. You see it, don't you?"

"Yes, though it was a broken fragment a moment ago," Ling said.

"I know. I just noticed the pull myself. Shall we?"

Jin followed the newly reformed cord and Frank and Ling followed her, Frank a step to her left and Ling just behind her. Jin had the feeling that one would have walked in front of her if they could have figured out how to do so without getting in the way. She didn't know for certain that the new cord was leading her to Shiro; in fact after they had walked for some time Jin was pretty sure that it was not. The cord led her straight and true but, when they came to another door and passed through to a barren, rocky wasteland with a sun the color of burnished copper, the path remained straight and led them on in a direct line to whoever was on the other end of it.

Not Shiro, but I'll wager he's not far away.

The heat was terrible. There was no sign of water, or shade. There were no trees, no weeds, not even so much as a single blade of grass. No birds flew in the shimmering sky and, so far as Jin could see, she and her two companions were totally alone. After a few steps Jin put on her demon form to gain some relief from the sun, though neither Frank nor Ling seemed overly affected. Still, Ling nodded when she saw what Jin had done.

"That was well done. I think we are in the realm of Hungry Ghosts; it is no place for a mortal of any sort."

"A 'hungry ghost'? What's that?"

Frank looked surprised, but then blushed. "Your pardon, I still forget sometimes."

"That I don't know what I'm doing?" Jin asked sweetly.

"That you do not *know* all that you know," Frank said. "A hungry ghost is usually a person who was overly covetous of food, drink, or possessions. They are reborn here with none of these things. They can find nothing to eat nor to drink, yet they cannot die since they are not really alive. They tend to become somewhat...desiccated and abnormal-looking. I think you'll find a prime example over there," Frank said, pointing near an outcrop of stone jutting out of the barren ground.

For a moment Jin could not comprehend what she was seeing. What she'd taken for a tangle of debris near the base of the rock was moving. She got a little closer and saw that the debris vaguely resembled a human, but only vaguely. Its neck was thin and long, and tied into a large knot at the base of the skull. Its eyes were large and staring, it's limbs almost literally pencil thin and its body at once wrinkled yet bloated so that it was very difficult for its very weak limbs to move it about. Yet it was gamely trying, making slow progress around the rock in a sort of crawl, roll, and flop technique. The sound it made filled Jin with horror and pity.

"Is it looking for shelter from the sun?" Jin asked.

"And food and water," said Ling. "Well, anything, really. It won't find any, of course. There is none in this place."

"Isn't there something we can do?"

"Not that I'm aware of," Frank said. "Nor should we."

"Should...? Can't you see it's in torment?"

"It's in the Hell of Hungry Ghosts," said Ling, and she shrugged. "And it's here for a reason. Your tendency to mercy and your empathy for those who suffer does you credit, Jin, and as the mortal incarnation of Guan Yin it's entirely natural. Yet I must say those feelings are misplaced here."

Jin held up her wrist. "Not entirely."

Ling shrugged again. "I admit it is very strange to see that; only a demon is less likely than a hungry ghost to progress beyond its own hell."

Jin shook her head. "It used to be human. Doesn't it know what happened to it? If such had happened to *me* I'd be going to any length to escape this place, including finding and correcting my spiritual error. Why is it so difficult here?"

Ling's smile wasn't pleasant. "A fair question that deserves an answer. You there!"

The pitiful collection of rags and twisted limbs shuddered as if it had been struck. It moved its head and they could hear its joints popping and cracking like dried-out leather with the effort. The voice, though faint and whispery, was audible. "Who calls?"

"I am Lung Nu, servant of Guan Shi Yin. My mistress wishes to speak to you."

"What does she offer?" asked the hungry ghost.

Offer? Jin frowned, and stepped forward. When the hungry ghost saw the demon approaching it shrank back against the stone. "I won't hurt you," she said. "I only want to ask why you are here."

"Give me gold," the ghost said.

"I don't have any," Jin said. "And what would you spend it on if I did have some and gave it to you? Do you see merchants? Wine shops? Inns? Restaurants? What is gold to you, so long as you remain in this place?"

"Everything," the ghost said simply. "It would be everything to me. I would eat it. I would drink it. I want nothing else. There *is* nothing else. Give me gold!" The thing tried to crawl its way toward Jin, but there was too much distance to cover quickly in its crippled form. Even so, in that instant Ling was between Jin and the ghost in her full dragon form. She hissed and spat steam at the ghost, who cried out but did not retreat.

"Dragon? Dragons have gold. Give it to me!"

The creature frothed and snapped like a rabid animal, now trying to crawl roll flop its way over to Ling. Ling paid it no more heed than an ant. She reverted to human form and looked at Jin. "Now do you understand why this creature is here?"

Jin nodded, feeling a little ill. "This is not the one. Let's keep going."

"They're all like that," Frank said, when they were well past the first hungry ghost. "If it's not gold it's something else. The overwhelming desire is common to them all, and it consumes them as much as their eternal hunger and thirst. Still, even they are not beyond redemption. Or else why are we here?"

Jin glanced at her wrist as they moved at a steady pace "I'm curious about that myself," she said, trying not to listen to the creature's pitiful cries until they finally and truly faded in the distance.

They passed others like it. It was hard to tell if they had been men or women; they all seemed alike, though some were even more grotesque than the first one. One had no less than three knots tied in its neck. Another's head was so large that it hung to its waist, though the creature seemed to be better off to the extent that it could stand on two stumpy legs and move upright with a very slow, shuffling gait. All had wrinkled skin and misshapen limbs, all were searching for things they would not find, whatever they might be, because there was simply nothing there. They shrank away as Jin and her companions approached.

"Why are these afraid of us?"

Ling smiled. "You're a demon now and these people are in hell, of course they're afraid of you. As was the first one, until it because fixated on what it thought we had, rather than what it thought you were. We have nothing they want."

Almost nothing, Jin thought, after they had trudged to the top of a small ridge. On the other side there was an unmistakable flash of green. Jin looked closer. It was a tree. A fruit tree of some sort, though Jin did not have a clue what sort of fruit it might be. The golden fruit hung ripe and round and heavy; when Jin sniffed the air she could smell its heady scent. The aroma made her a little hungry herself; she could only imagine what it would to any of the starved spirits who came near it.

From the rise she could see that there were hungry ghosts gathered around the tree, which made perfect sense. What didn't make any sense at first was that they were neither mobbing the tree nor trying to pull the fruit from its branches. Instead they mostly milled about in a rough circle around the tree as if an invisible fence kept them from approaching the tree. It wasn't until they were a little closer that Jin saw why.

Demons guarded the tree.

Jin counted ten of them, each as black as coal and about seven feet high and armed with a vicious-looking trident. As Jin watched, one of the hungry ghosts, apparently overwhelmed by the scent and sight of the fruit, made a frantic crawl toward the tree, but two of the demons simply jabbed it with their cruel forks, forcing it back. They did not pursue the ghost once it retreated, nor strike at anyone else unless they got too close to the tree. The rest of the time they simply waited, calmly leaning on their tridents planted firmly on the bare, hard-packed ground. Jin stopped, and stood watching the scene for a moment.

"Rather cruel of them, don't you think?" Ling said, glancing at Jin.

Now Jin smiled an unpleasant smile. "You know I do. And by the way, don't be coy. You're not very good at it."

The dragon-girl actually blushed, but she didn't back down. "It is not my place to instruct Guan Yin, even in her current limited form. Yet misplaced mercy in this place can do more harm than good. The demons are simply serving their appointed role."

"You think I don't know that?"

"Your pardon," Ling said, "but you can understand why one would wonder."

Jin shrugged. "That's fair enough. Yet right now I'm more curious about the tree than the demons. If such a thing would exist in this place, then of *course* demons would guard it. What I don't understand is why it's here."

Jin started down the slope toward the tree and Frank and Ling followed her, but now Frank was looking puzzled.

"Isn't it obvious? The hungry ghosts spend their entire existence looking for drink and nourishment in various forms, and here they find it, only to be denied. It's an intensifying of the basic punishment by teasing them with what they cannot possess."

Jin had to admit that, yes, that was exactly the way things appeared, and it certainly was in perfect accord with the purpose and operation of a hell as she had come to understand the concept. Yet her instincts told her that there was more to the matter of the forbidden fruit than what appeared on the surface.

"Maybe so. And also maybe it's just a coincidence that the thread has led us here, but I just don't think so."

Ling looked around. "You know where the thread leads? I cannot see it clearly in all this confusion."

"I can," Jin said. "He's right there." She led them on.

That was the first difference that Jin recognized -- he. Jin thought of this hungry ghost as a 'he' and not an 'it.' At first glance he didn't look any different from all the other hungry ghosts gathered around the tree: a distorted head. Huge, staring eyes, misshapen limbs, wrinkled, desiccated skin.

The crowd of hungry ghosts parted around them as they got closer to the tree, though not without considerable wailing and hissing, and the crack of dry joints and skin as they moved aside. The demons guarding the tree glanced at them with some curiosity but nothing more than that, and they didn't fail their duty when another tormented ghost made an attempt at the fruit.

Unlike the other ghosts crawling about, this ghost sat on a rock as he stared hungrily at the tree. Yet he did not reach for it, nor try to attack the tree with the others. He simply sat there, his grotesque form arrayed in a position that, if not identifiable as comfort, at least gave the poor wretch some support as it regarded the tree.

"Wait here," Jin said. "If any of the ghosts try anything with you, kick them or something."

"Do not concern yourself about us," Ling said. "Just be careful."

Jin didn't need the advice. She was being very careful indeed or, rather, cautious. She sensed something greatly important and yet very delicate was happening, and she did not want to make a misstep. She needed to speak to the ghost and, more than likely, touch it -- though she was certainly not looking forward to that part. Yet she strongly suspected his reaction to her demon form might make both of those goals very difficult. Yet she could not assume her normal form, not in that place.

I need...

Jin knew what she needed, and in another moment she had it: her body changed from demon to Hungry Ghost.

Jin felt her head droop on a long, scrawny neck, felt the hot sand burn her and felt, for a moment, a thousand years worth of hunger and thirst and longing, but she knew it was an illusion. In another moment she could function, albeit poorly.

This is interesting.

Jin wasn't especially surprised -- once your body has transformed from human to demon one time, nothing else it might do seemed especially strange -- but it was the first time this had happened. Jin wondered if this was merely because she needed it to happen, then decided none of that mattered. Whatever had transformed her, it was all part of the same thing. As with her transformation to demon, she could only hope and believe it served her purpose, and not another's.

Jin sat down on the rock next to the ghost.

"My rock!" said the ghost.

Jin shook her head, and immediately regretted it, as her head swayed too and fro across her flat, dried out breasts like a pendulum. "Do you really care about the rock?"

The ghost frowned at her. After a moment he turned that stare back toward the tree. "Can't drink it. Can't eat it. It burns my butt. Still mine, but I don't care. Sit. Go. Don't care."

"What do you care about?"

"The tree. Mine. Fruit. Oh, how sweet the scent. Mine..." He turned to stare at her again. "What are you?"

Jin blinked eyes as large as his. "Just one more poor wretch banished to this place, like you."

"No," he said. "Not like me at all."

"Oh? Don't I look like you? Like everyone looks at this place?"

"Look is not be. I have been here...*without* for long, long, long -- " The word seemed to get stuck in his throat and struck himself hard on the side of the face, cracking the skin. The wound leaked some dry powder, but no blood. "Long time. No one. Ever. Asked another what they care about.

Everyone cares for themselves alone. You are different. Like him."

"Like who?"

The hungry ghost looked back at the tree. "I don't know. He comes and talks to me. I don't know why he comes. I don't know why you're here. I just want the fruit. It's mine."

"What would you do with the fruit?"

"I would be happy."

"How? Would you eat it?"

"Silly thing, whatever you are. Of course not. Then it would be gone. Not mine."

"So you're hungry and you cannot eat the fruit."

"Mine," he repeated after a while, as if he hadn't heard. "It's mine. I want it."

"Why?"

The hungry ghost's face distorted. Jin was both horrified and puzzled when she realized he was trying to smile. "You sound. Him. Like him."

Jin had a hunch and followed up on it. "What does he look like?" Jin asked.

"Darker than a demon. Sneaky. Talks to me. Makes me listen. I get angry, I get more hungry than I have ever been and his words mean nothing. Then he goes away, and I think about what he said. I like it when he's gone, but I like the fact that he was here. It is strange... Are you trying to make me listen too?"

"No. I'm the one listening," Jin said. She was also trying very hard to understand what she was hearing.

You don't suppose...

"I want the fruit," the hungry ghost said, and Jin forced her attention back to where it needed to be.

"What's your name?" Jin asked.

The ghost looked puzzled. "Name? I can't give that to you."

Jin almost laughed. "Never mind. So. If you had the fruit you wouldn't eat it. What would you do with it?"

It looked at her if she were insane. "I would keep it!"

"You can't. In this heat the fruit would rot in your hand within a day. You can't hold it and you won't eat it. What good is the fruit to you?"

"I would keep it! Keep it sweet, keep it forever -- "

"No," Jin said firmly, "you wouldn't."

The hungry ghost didn't say anything for a little while, and Jin thought at first it had turned its attention back to the tree and forgotten she was even there. Then he spoke again. "I know," he said. His voice was clear and distinct. "I can't keep anything. I try and I try and I just can't."

Even later Jin wasn't sure if she'd touched the ghost's hand because she needed to or simply because it sounded so sad. It flinched away from her, but in that instant Jin had everything she needed. Strangely enough, it was what she suspected even without the touch.

"The fruit is to be eaten," she said. "Or not. In neither case is the fruit the problem. You know that, don't you?"

"Yes," he said softly. "I want everything and I have nothing. I can't get the thought out of my head. That's the one thing I do want to give up, but I don't know how. Strange, isn't it? For someone who has nothing at all?"

"Not strange at all. You look thirsty. I know where you can get a drink that will actually help you. Would you like to go there?"

"More than anything," he said.

"Good, because you're already on your way," Jin said, and in another moment she was alone on the rock. She sat there for a while, gazing at the fruit on the tree. Frank and Ling finally approached her.

"The person is gone," Frank said. "Do you expect Shiro to appear nearby?"

"Shiro's already been here. He's the reason that there was any need to come," Jin said.

"What do you mean?" Ling asked.

Jin took a deep breath. "I mean Shiro came here many times, and while he was here he taught a hungry ghost that, no matter how hungry or thirsty he was, no amount of food or drink would satisfy him."

"That can't be -- " Frank started, but Jin didn't let him finish.

"I touched the ghost and I saw who came here to teach him. It was Shiro. There is no doubt. His influence was not altogether positive, but that's something I need to think about later. For now, I know he helped that man."

"Why would Shiro do that?" Ling asked.

"Good question." Jin looked thoughtful, and Frank and Ling looked nervous.

"What are you going to do?"

"The only thing that makes any sense to me whatsoever," Jin said. "I'm going to talk to Shiro."

CHAPTER 23

Jin wasn't surprised that Frank and Ling tried to talk her out of talking to Shiro. She was surprised that they positively would not shut up on the subject. They kept hammering at her through the long walk back. Jin thought of having them open a doorway to get them all back sooner, but wondered if, perhaps, it was better to let them talk themselves hoarse.

She had apparently misjudged their capacity for nagging. When they passed beyond the doorway and into the corridor, leaving the Hell of Hungry Ghosts behind, they were still talking when Jin took the opportunity to revert to human form. Her demon form's horns tended to make her head itch.

"Did not Guan Yin Herself forbid you to seek Shiro out?" Frank asked.

"I am Guan Yin Herself," Jin pointed out. "A fact you two seem determined to forget. Besides, the answer is 'no,' she did not. She simply said it was a bad idea."

"And in your human form you think it a good idea to go against your own Divine Self's advice?"

"I've already spoken to him twice and the world didn't end," Jin said.

"Close enough," muttered Ling, but Jin ignored that.

"There are a lot of reasons Shiro might have done what he did, but I have to know the real one. Can you think of any other way?"

"We could beat it out of him," said Ling.

"Probably fun, but not necessary. He knew I'd find out what he did in the Hell of Hungry Ghosts. In fact, I think he wanted me to know."

"I still say that seeking him out is madness," Frank said. "Your mortal form is clouding your judgment. I'm sorry, but I must say what I think is true."

"Noted," Jin said. "Now drop it."

To her surprise, they actually did drop the subject, though not without one last try. "Will you at least allow us to accompany you?" Ling asked.

"He certainly won't talk to me with you two hovering around. I'll call you if I need you, but I can take care of myself if that proves necessary."

"So you say," Frank said, but there were no further argument from either of them. "What are your instructions?"

"For now? Find Shiro again and let me know where he is."

"As you wish," Ling said, and they disappeared, leaving Jin to emerge into the Gateway to All the Hells alone. She passed the Guardians but didn't say anything. She was about twenty feet away when something occurred to her, and she turned back.

"I know that Shiro made many trips to the Hell of Hungry Ghosts. Has he been doing that anywhere else? And surely you can tell me that without giving away his current location."

PLEASE DEFINE 'MANY,' IMMANENT ONE.

Jin sighed. "Are you two going literal on me?"

WE'RE SIMPLY SAYING THAT 'MANY' IS A CONCEPT WITH MORE THAN ONE INTERPRETATION. WE WANT TO KNOW YOURS.

Jin thought about it. "All right. How about 'more than three separate trips within the space of a month.'"

There was a long silence that Jin took to mean the two were conferring. Finally they spoke to her again. HE HAS DONE SO FOR BOTH THE FIRE JAR HELL AND THE MOUNTAIN OF NEEDLES.

Jin thought that, between the hell that was nothing but fire and black sand and the Hell of Hungry Ghosts, she had visited enough hot places for a while and the thought of a "Fire Jar Hell" did not entice. "Show me the entrance to the Mountain of Needles. I won't ask if Shiro is there, though if you can comply I'll assume he isn't. Is this acceptable?"

YES.

Jin thought that she should be getting used to the way inanimate statues moved without seeming to do so. After a moment -- and it was barely more than that -- the two Guardians were standing flanking another doorway that looked just like all the others, except for the one Jin had marked. There were no markings here, and Jin was fairly certain she had never been this way before.

ONE THING, IMMANENT ONE -- WE WOULD ADVISE TAKING DEMON FORM BEFORE YOU OPEN THE DOOR AT CORRIDOR'S END.

Another dangerous hell. Why do I ever assume anything different? "Thanks," Jin said aloud, "I'll do that."

Though as Jin entered the doorway she thought about the nature of hells. They weren't always physically dangerous, or at least not all the time -- Medias certainly wasn't. Some even seemed outwardly pleasant, such as Michiko's Japanese garden. Yet however they looked or felt, they were always of an appropriate nature given their task. That made her wonder at hells like Medias, which seemed to serve different purposes at different times if the Lemon Man and Buddy and even Joyce were any indication, while a place like the Hell of Hungry Ghosts was more specialized. Maybe this meant that more extreme cases called for more extreme measures.

Or maybe it just means that Hell isn't fair.

Jin didn't know the answer. She had a very hard time conceiving that there was a part of her that did know. Jin, musing, almost forgot to switch forms before she emerged from the other end of the corridor, but one glance beyond the door had her in full demon mode before she stepped across the threshold. This was a very good thing, considering what she stepped in.

Needles?

Needles, yes, but for some reason she hadn't taken the description of the Guardians literally. Now Jin realized her mistake as she stood at the base of a mountain every bit as huge as the one in the Ninth Hell, and it was covered in spikes, from small ones no bigger than rose thorns on the bare earth, to massive spikes thicker than her waist and a dozen feet tall. There was almost nothing else around -- no other mountains, no other landscapes, nothing. Just the mountain. Everything beyond it passed into haze and smoke. Jin started to summon Ling, then belatedly remembered their little talk...how long ago? She'd forgotten that part.

"Frank!"

In a moment Frank was there. "You summoned me, Jin?"

"What is the purpose of the Hell of the Mountain of Needles?"

"Well, strictly speaking it's not a hell at all. Or rather, it exists in many hells simultaneously. People are forced to climb it before being cast into the deeper parts of the hell."

"So someone here could be on his way to practically anywhere?"

"As long as by 'anywhere' you mean the blackest, deepest hells? Yes."

"That is interesting. Thank, you Frank."

Frank understood he'd been dismissed and immediately vanished. Jin watched demons driving wretched sufferers up the mountainside to impale themselves on the countless spikes; the sight made her feel more than a little ill. She also realized she didn't have any way to identify who she was looking for. Jin rather doubted there would be any external sign at all. Jin risked a step onto the mountain and, even with her hard-scaled demon's feet, it was like walking on a stubble field so she didn't go far. She spied a little red demon with a wicked-looking spiked whip who was idle for the moment and spoke to him.

"You there. I need to ask you a question."

"There's no one here," it said defensively. "I can't drive anyone up the mountain if they aren't here!"

"That wasn't what I wanted to know. I'm looking for a man called Shiro. I believe he appears as a shadow most of the time. Have you seen him?"

"I've seen many shadows, Lord, but none that had a name."

At that moment a blinking, confused, and terrified old man appeared out of a tunnel at the base of the mountain and the little demon ran off to drive him up the mountain with its whip. Jin watched them for a moment, but quickly decided she'd had enough of the place and withdrew to the corridor.

"Not very nice, is it?" someone asked out of the darkness.

Jin did not jump, though it took an effort. She didn't bother to ask who was there, however. She knew.

"Shiro. I want to talk to you."

"Took you long enough," he said. "I gather you're ignoring good advice to do it."

Jin took a deep breath. "I said I wanted to talk to you. Are you willing to do so or are you going to behave like a sixteen-year-old boy on hormones?"

"Probably both," Shiro said. "But I'm listening."

"Then show yourself," Jin said. "I'm not talking to a shadow with an attitude."

"While we're on that subject, I'm not talking to any demons," Shiro said.

Jin realized she was still in demon mode. "Fine then. Meet me halfway."

Jin reverted to human and so did Shiro, after a fashion. He took the form of Jonathan Mitsumo though he looked younger, perhaps closer to thirty than forty. Was that his age when Guan Yin knew him that first time? She wondered if she was right about that or merely a trick of the poor light.

"You're looking very beautiful, Jin. You always did."

Jin sighed. "Spare me the silly lines, Shiro. Why have you been in the Hell of Hungry Ghosts?"

Shiro looked unhappy. "I was beginning to hope that you finally understood, Jin. Apparently not."

"I know that you think you're in love with me."

"Then you don't know anything," Shiro said sadly.

"Ok, I don't know anything. Now please answer my question."

"I was trying to help you, of course. I've always been trying to help you."

Jin had a sudden suspicion, and only cursed herself because it *was* a sudden suspicion. Considering what she had learned in the Hell of Hungry Ghosts, it should have been obvious.

"Were you helping my mother the way you helped that man in the Hell of Hungry Ghosts?" Jin asked.

"Of course. My interest in your mother was purely spiritual."

He said it so easily. It took every ounce of self-control that Jin possessed not to revert to demon form and rip Shiro to ragged shreds then and there. Shiro watched her closely, and finally nodded.

"You're furious. Good."

Jin blinked. *Good*? It wasn't for the first time, and Jin was sure it wouldn't be the last, but once more she had the strong suspicion that she didn't have clue one as to what was really going on. "I'd really like you to explain that, Shiro. Are you saying you helped my mother shorten her time in Medias to make me angry?"

He laughed then, but it wasn't the mocking, taunting laughter she'd envisioned from him. It was at once good-humored and rueful. "Oh, Jin... of course I didn't do it to make you angry! I did it because I wanted to help you, and that's the truth. And I can help you; you've seen that I can."

Jin sighed. No point denying the obvious. "Yes. Your point is?"

"Simply put: I want to be with you, and to be whatever it is you need. I love you."

Jin shook her head. "Even assuming I believe that, what you've said still doesn't explain why you think my being angry was 'good.'"

He smiled at her. "Because it was so human, Jin. What have I really done? I've helped your mother shorten her time in hell, albeit a relatively pleasant one. The Bodhisattva Guan Yin would be pleased, but the mortal Guan Yin is so angry she could spit. Why? Because Jin Hannigan has just lost her mother, and that's all she can see, and all she can understand. That's love, and loss. That's human."

Jin nodded. "You've told me something you think you know, Shiro, and you've spoken the truth to the degree you understand it. Fair is fair. I'm going to tell you something that you don't know."

He frowned. "And what would that be?"

"You think I'm here in mortal form so I can fall in love with you. Even though that didn't happen the first time."

"That was the first time, and it's in the past. This is now," he said.

"Why do you think I was so angry with you, that first time in the corridor? Even though at the time I had no idea who or what you were?"

"That? I didn't understand at first, but in time it became clear that it was because you misunderstood! You thought I was harming that child, or some such nonsense."

"Shiro," she said very calmly and clearly, "that is exactly what you were doing."

"No," he said. The smile faded.

Jin went on, relentless. "I may be mortal, but I am also Guan Yin, and I am not wrong about this. Your presence made it harder for Rebecca to pass over, and Mariko, and, yes, even Gnasher."

"That's not true!"

"I say it is."

"A mortal can be mistaken," Shiro said softly. "A mortal can lie. I'm sorry, Jin, but I don't believe you."

"Of course you don't. I never thought you would."

Shiro frowned. "I admit it -- I'm intrigued. Tell me why I don't believe you."

"Because in order to believe me, you'd have to believe the *reason* your presence harms those people. They catch your desire, your obsession, like a child catches a cold," she said.

He shook his head. "Jin, I know you came into this incarnation with your memories erased. You're confused, clearly, because surely you realize that what you just said made absolutely no sense?"

"Oh, no, Shiro. It makes perfect sense. "What you feel for me -- call it love if you want -- is very powerful. Frankly, Shiro, I've never seen a greater desire, a greater fixation on exactly the wrong thing in any hell I've visited. Your desire is so great that it affects everything around you, and especially all other ties to the Wheel of Death and Rebirth. Rebecca's doll, Mariko's fan, even Gnasher's rake! You're like a jumpstart to a dying battery -- you keep it alive past its time."

"Then how do you explain the hungry ghost?"

Jin was ready. "I'll answer that if you'll explain why your words only reached him when you were no longer present. Or did that not occur to you?"

Jin didn't need the stiffening in Shiro's posture to know she'd nailed that one. "All right then... what about your mother?"

"That was different," Jin said.

His look was all triumph. "Rubbish. I helped her. I did not strengthen her 'chains.'"

"I *was* her chain, Shiro. Just as I am for you. You were able to help her because of what you shared. She moved on when she realized what held her. Perhaps she helped you a little too, but then you already knew what held you. Stop embracing your chain, Shiro. It's time."

"Another lie."

Jin held up her wrist. "The broken thread tells me otherwise."

"Then why was I able to break it?"

"I don't know the answer to that. Do you?"

He did know. She saw it in his eyes.

"I was once a man, Jin. At the heart of it that's really all I am now. I make mistakes. Sometimes I'm weak, even after all this time, all my patience, all my fighting. It never more than a moment, and never enough to turn me from my goal. I love you, Guan Shi Yin. You love me, too. I can prove it! Do you know why, in your demon form, you never tried to destroy me? Even though you thought I was this terrible threat?"

Jin sighed. "Let me guess...because I love you?"

"I don't deserve your sarcasm, Jin. It's because, in your mortal form, you cannot kill me with the pure heart that such an act requires. You yourself could be trapped in the Cycle of Death and Rebirth again. It would be a rare thing for a Bodhisattva, but it could happen. By becoming mortal again you've taken a terrible risk. I know you've asked yourself why. I've been asking myself the same thing, Jin, ever since I found you again."

Jin didn't know if Shiro was telling her the truth or not, but she did know that Teacher had said essentially the same thing.

"That's why up until now I've kept mostly to the shadows, even though I longed to be near you. See, it took me some time to work out why the Guan Yin that I knew would take such a horrible risk, and I've finally worked it out. You'd have done the same, in time."

"Tell me," Jin said softly.

"Before I do, there is one confession I have to make: I've eavesdropped once or twice when you were talking to Teacher. I know it was wrong of me, but I had to find out what you knew."

Jin just sighed. "I can't be any angrier at you than I already am, Shiro. That sort of thing is no more than I expected."

He smiled a bit ruefully. "I don't blame you. What you must have thought of me! What you still must think. That won't make this any easier. We still have a long way to go."

"'We' aren't going anywhere, Shiro. I may be the mortal Jin Hannigan, but I'm also the Bodhisattva of Mercy, Guan Yin, GuanShiYin, Kannon, take your choice. There is no 'us'! You know that has to be so."

Shiro just cocked his head slightly, regarding her as a student might regard a particularly vexing problem. "Do I? Don't forget -- I know something you don't know. I know why you're a mortal."

"Stop stalling, blast you! Either tell me or shut up!"

Shiro's smile did not falter. If anything it got wider. "You became a mortal, Jin, because only a mortal can fall in love."

Jin shook her head wearily. "That's it? That's the best you can do?"

"It's a start. That's enough."

Jin started to argue but she made the mistake, though she would often wonder if it really was a mistake, of looking into his eyes. The look told Jin the truth; she had seen it the vision Shiro had shown her the second time she'd touched him, and she saw it now. She did finally understand one of the few things the Guan Yin That Was had told her, though.

Things *were* much worse than she had thought.

Shiro stood by patiently, apparently waiting for her to say something, or to do something, or both, and Jin didn't have any idea of how to go about any of that. She thought furiously but, for several long moments, nothing came.

"What? No questions? Are you saying you finally accept what I'm telling you?"

"I accept that you think you're telling me the truth."

He smiled. "And I accept that, at the moment, you are not doing the same."

Jin was almost grateful. He'd given her a bit of her anger back, and it was certainly better than nothing. "I don't want to throw cold water on this fantasy of yours -- all right, that is a lie -- but it doesn't add up."

Shiro shrugged. "Really? How so?"

"Well...there's the thing about my memory. Even assuming you're right about my reasons for reincarnating, why visit Madame Meng and seek oblivion? Wouldn't I want to keep my plan uppermost in my love-besotted mind?"

"Sarcasm again... I take you for all you are, Jin, but I'm not loving that aspect of your mortal form. As for your memory, that's obvious -- without your memory you couldn't put up all the reasons why it wouldn't work or was a bad idea. You'd be fully mortal, and love as a mortal would. It's only because Emma-O found you first that this didn't work as you planned. I was too slow, and I failed. No matter; you may have good and sensible reasons for objecting, but you are a mortal woman and they will not stop you. In time, you will come to love me."

Sure of ourselves, aren't we?

What Jin didn't dare put into words was the horrid realization that she was none too sure of *herself* just now. Was it possible that Shiro was right? And if so, what did that mean? Jin remembered what Teacher had said to her about the idea of falling in love with Shiro -- it might be unlikely, but it wasn't impossible.

"I need time to think," Jin said, and Shiro just shrugged.

"Take all the time you want. I am a very patient man. If you don't realize that yet, you will."

"That almost sounds like a threat."

"It's the truth. No more and no less," Shiro said evenly. "I accept that you believe I'm harming your work. I'll be more careful. Until later, my love."

Shiro returned to shadow form and flowed away into darkness, leaving Jin shaken but still standing. She felt as if she'd gone three rounds with one of the Guardians. She summoned Frank and Ling. "Please take me to Teacher. Emma-O."

"He is -- " Frank started, but Jin wasn't listening.

"I don't care where he is! Take me there."

Ling shrugged, and Frank sighed. "As you wish."

CHAPTER 24

In a moment they were standing inside the men's public bathroom in Resolution Park. The smell was indescribable, which Jin decided was a very good thing. Fortunately there was only one stall in use, and the door, though it barely hung together on rusty hinges, was in use. Frank looked unhappy but Ling was clearly trying her best not to laugh, and didn't look like she would succeed for very long.

Jin glared at the both of them. "Don't. Say. A. Word."

A surprised grunt from the stall. "Jin? Is that you?"

"I need to talk to you," Jin said, "but I'll wait outside."

Jin left the men's room, though not without a quick glance out to make sure no one was looking. "Fine, I should have listened," she said as she sat down on a nearby bench. "Add that to my tab of mistakes for the day."

Frank and Ling, as per her wishes, didn't say anything. Teacher finally emerged from the men's room, looking puzzled. "The demands of this mortal body can't always be ignored, but I must say I wasn't expecting visitors."

Ling made a noise, barely stifled. Jin ignored her. "Sorry, I was a little impatient. I've just talked to Shiro."

"I see," Teacher said. He sat down beside her. He obviously hadn't bathed in days or changed his clothes in longer than that. The smell wasn't pleasant but, compared to the men's room, it could have been rosewater.

"I see? Is that all you have to say?"

Teacher sighed. "No, that was merely a conversational pause while I wait for you to get to the point."

Stung, Jin did get to the point. "I'm sure about this, Teacher -- Shiro's in love with me. Not obsessed, though sometimes it's hard to tell the difference. He is really and truly in love with me."

Teacher slumped in his seat. "I thought so too, and I'd hoped it wasn't true. A simple obsession would have been easier to deal with."

"No shit! But Shiro is not crazed obsessive, or insane, or any of the things you'd expect from someone who has literally crawled out of hell to find the object of his affection. I see it in his eyes when he looks at me, and I can't mistake it for something it isn't, try as I might. He loves me. Angry as I am, worried as I am, I can't help but think that it's...well, a little sweet."

"Sweet," Teacher said, and slumped down on the bench. "And you still don't see why the Guan Yin that Was told you to avoid him?"

"I see all to well, but that was never really an option. I know that, and I think the Guan Yin That Was knew it, too. Also, if I realize that Shiro is in love with me it's a safe bet that *she* knew it, too."

Teacher nodded, looking glum. "Almost certainly. That would explain the danger."

"Would it? I'd really like to know why."

Teacher looked thoughtful. "Think about it and, while you do, know this: I love you, Jin."

She just stared at him for several long seconds. "You...?"

He snorted in laughter. "You should see the panic in your eyes. Relax. But it's true -- I do love you. I also love

Shan Cai and Lung Nu. I even love the guy I condemned to be boiled in his own urine this morning."

"Boiled in..." Jin kept staring. "Sometimes I wonder if I'm on the right side."

Teacher smiled "There's only one side and we're all on it, Jin. Even Shiro, though he's confusing the goal with the symbol at the moment. Now, the love I feel for you and everyone else I've mentioned is what allows me to help them, and makes me *want* to help them, painful as that help sometimes is. It's the same for you, Jin."

"But not Shiro?"

"No, Jin. Shiro is a man who escaped hell with his own determination and my bad judgment to be with the one he loves. In human terms that's an incredible love story, a romance for the ages. In karmic terms, however, it's a bloody disaster."

Jin sighed. "All right, already. I get that.

"Good, because otherwise I'm still explaining karma to Guan Yin. If this wasn't so dangerous, it'd be funny. Blast it, Immanent One, why did you do this?"

Jin didn't have to ask what he meant by that last bit. "I wish I knew," Jin said softly.

Teacher took a deep breath. "Sorry, Jin. Sometimes the ridiculousness of this situation just hits me. I've said before that you were in great danger, but I don't think I knew the half of it."

"Is that all love is? An obstacle? Something to be avoided?"

"No, only when it becomes an end in itself, and not a step along the journey, that it becomes an obstacle. It's an obstacle for Shiro, make no mistake. What is it for you?"

Jin blinked owlishly. "Me?"

Teacher watched her face closely. "Are you in love with Shiro, Jin? Please tell me the truth."

Jin thought very long and carefully before she answered. "For awhile I thought I was. Yet I remember love,

Teacher, through the feelings of a girl dead a thousand years. I felt it. Touched it, tasted it, just as Michiko did. I also felt what it was like to be in love, as the first mortal incarnation of Guan Yin. It was like that... and it wasn't like that. No, Teacher. I am not in love with Shiro."

Teacher let out a great sigh of relief. "Praise All for that much... all right, Jin. You've had a close call. Now what? Do you have a plan?"

"No." As much as it pained her to admit it, Jin did not. She sat there for a moment, looking glum. Teacher glanced at his strange watch, but made no move to leave. Frank and Ling remained at the same discreet distance they had maintained since Jin first sat on the bench.

"Are you thinking about Shiro?" Teacher asked finally.

"Actually," Jin said, "I was thinking about being in love. I mean, I don't want another lecture, but before... you know, before I found out who I was, it was always something I thought would happen. I even went looking for it a time or two. And with all the hassles and disappointments, there's a part of me that feels very sad to give up the idea of ever being in love."

"Karma doesn't care about romantic love one way or another, except for the cause and effect aspect," Teacher said. "And yet I'm mortal now too, and there's a part of me -- not the Emma-O King of the First Hell me, but the sixty-six years old homeless and ugly Teacher Johnson me -- that still wants to believe in love. For what little that's worth to either of us."

Jin leaned over and kissed him on the cheek. He rubbed the spot, thoughtfully. "What was that for?"

"No reason," Jin said. "Though I do think I owe you a thank you.'"

"You're welcome."

"One thing I forgot to mention." Jin told Teacher about the fact that, for a while, she had a connection with Shiro just as if he'd been ready to move on. "He gave me the slip, finally, and when I saw him next the connection wasn't there."

"I don't know anyone else who could do that. If you want my opinion, it means that somewhere there's a deeper, wiser side of him that can still be reached. Maybe that's my optimism talking."

Teacher was looking at his watch again. "No rest for either the wicked or the judgmental; I've got to go. Oh, by the way." Teacher reached into his duster and pulled out a rather wrinkled piece of torn newsprint. "I know you've been busy. I've got the details here for Joyce's funeral. It's tomorrow. I thought you'd want to know."

Teacher left her holding the scrap of paper and walked off into the trees. Jin stared at the announcement for a little while.

"You're going, aren't you?" Ling asked. It sounded like an accusation.

"Of course I am."

"Why?" Ling asked. "I have it on good authority that the person you knew as Joyce Masters was reborn into Medias just this morning."

"That doesn't matter. My friend is gone, and I'm going to mourn that properly. It's a human thing, I guess. Teacher understood that."

"Teacher is trapped in his own body at the moment. His advice may not be the best," Frank said. "With all due respect to his Hellish Majesty."

Jin just stood up. "I'm going to take a walk. You two aren't coming."

"What do you wish of us?" Ling asked.

At the moment she just wanted the both of them out of her sight, but she didn't say that. "For now just do whatever you want."

Ling and Frank exchanged one more of those glances that made Jin think they were talking behind her back in front of her face and then both vanished, this time through the same portal of light. When she was certain they were gone, Jin sat back down on the bench. She looked at the funeral announcement again. There wasn't a lot to it. Four column inches about Joyce and her work for the Legal Aid Office, and no cause of death listed. Then the date, place, and time: April 23rd, Willowbrook Memorial Chapel, 2:00 PM.

You'd think there'd be more.

Jin wasn't really sure what she'd expected, she just knew that this wasn't it. There was so much more to Joyce's life. How could anyone sum it up in four inches of newsprint? Or forty, for that matter? Yet here it was, short and to the point. A life gone. They may as well have said, "She's dead and you're not. Say goodbye and get on with it." Maybe that was the point. Maybe they were even right, given all that she had learned in the past few weeks. That didn't change the need to mourn.

Jin felt a tug at her wrist. She ignored it as long as she could, but that wasn't long. It was rather insistent. Jin peeked with her Third Eye and there was the golden thread, right where she knew it would be. She sighed.

No rest for the merciful. Just don't look for mercy from two to four o'clock tomorrow.

She got up slowly and let the cord guide her. When she emerged from the entrance to the park the tug was to the left, down Elysian toward Pepper Street. Jin didn't need the cord to guide her for a while after that. She only paused when Elysian crossed Pepper Street to be sure that the cord was, in fact, pulling her toward the Gateway to All the Hells and not onward to a destination in Medias itself.

The tug got even more insistent. Jin frowned. She didn't remember any of the previous instances feeling like this, even the ones that had been fairly time critical. She thought of summoning either Frank or Ling in an attempt to speed things up, but that was no good. Jin knew from before that only Guan Yin -- or rather, her current incarnation -- could get direction from the cord. Frank and Ling could see it but they couldn't go directly to where it led because they didn't know where that was any more than Jin did, at least until she had followed the cord to its end. Jin found herself almost at a trot, trying to match the pull of the cord as she ducked into the alley. When she emerged in the Gateway she was running.

"Where?"

Jin realized she'd asked the question aloud even though she hadn't expected an answer. She still got one, of a sort. The Guardians sounded unhappy. IMMANENT ONE, WE CANNOT...

"You can't... mark the way?" Jin said, already short of breath.

NO.

Jin understood what that meant. "Bloody hell..."

She took off at a dead run and the cord kept pace. She passed through the door without bothering to opening it. Jin felt the familiar instant of *shimmer* and disorientation that followed and then she was off down the corridor with barely a pause.

Don't let me be late, not this time. This is my chance!

Jin knew the corridor itself wasn't real; she didn't need another disorienting peek of the Third Eye to remind herself of it. She also knew that the distance she was covering was at once illusory and yet far vaster than it appeared. She didn't know how to travel instantly the way Frank and Ling did, but she also knew that being in a hurry actually did help. She focused on reaching the door at the opposite end of the corridor and, though her impatience made it seem a very long time indeed, in seconds she was there and through the door and out into --

The Mountain of Needle--oww!

Jin staggered and nearly fell. She leaned against a bare spot of stone long enough to tug a wicked-looking thorn about an inch long from the bottom of her foot. Her blood trickled into the rubble and debris at the bottom of the mountain even as the cord pulled her to go higher. Jin changed to demon form but that only helped a little. The spikes were cruel even to her hard scaly demon feet and when they touched the fresh wound on her foot it was even worse, but she kept moving. She moved through a forest of spikes as she climbed; changing to demon form had at least given her a second wind. Up ahead she heard what sounded like a fight.

Jin did not understand this. The victims of demons might wail and writhe and protest, but she had yet to hear of any of them fighting back. Jin hobbled along as fast as she could. She emerged from a thicket of spikes on a high plateau and found the battle.

Shiro?

Shiro was the only one Jin recognized at first. He was changing rapidly from human form to shadow as he tried to avoid his attackers, but he was losing. Two luminous beings floated in the air above him. One bore a trident of light that pierced and tore at the shadow that was Shiro and he cried out in pain, the other struck as well with extended claws and also found its mark.

The other, Jin realized dully, was a dragon.

Shiro became aware of her first. He smiled bitterly. "Come to see your handiwork, Jin?"

The dragon glanced in Jin's direction and she could almost swear that it uttered a curse.

"STOP!"

The force of Jin's demon voice actually shattered several spikes like glass, and in that instant everyone did stop, frozen in place like a photograph, but it didn't last. Shiro reverted to purely human form and fell to his knees, bruised and bleeding. Lung Nu and Shan Cai, for their part, looked at once defiant and as guilty as children caught with their hands in the cookie jar.

"We were so close!" Lung Nu said, ruefully.

"You damn well were. What were you two thinking?"

"We were thinking," Lung Nu said, "that we would obey your command."

"I never told you to attack Shiro!"

"You told us to do what we wanted," Frank said. "We've wanted to do this for a very long time."

"And if the Guan Yin That Was had wanted it settled this way she'd have done it! Don't try to tell me you two didn't understand her wishes!"

"There are mysteries," Frank said righteously, "even to the Enlightened."

"I can see," Jin said very slowly and distinctly, "that I'm going to be much more careful of what I say around you two. Shiro, listen, I -- " she began, but there was no one to talk to. Shiro had vanished.

"Blast it, he got away," Lung Nu said.

That was plainly true. Jin checked the cord on her wrist, but she didn't really need the glance of the Third Eye to know what she already knew -- the cord was broken once more. What she still didn't understand was why it was there in the first place. And why, specifically, was it there when Shiro was in trouble? The time it had happened before, Ling and Frank were with her; it couldn't have been them. Was he threatened then, or --

Jin remembered the way Shiro had looked at her before she'd stopped her servants. That wasn't love in his eyes then, that was anger. Betrayal. Hurt.

Cause and effect. That's karma, Jin thought grimly. She looked at Guan Yin's servants. She no longer really thought of them as hers.

"Did you two tell Shiro you were here on my command? And get down here; I'm getting a stiff neck looking up at you!"

Frank had actually looked embarrassed, but Ling didn't bat an eyelid, even after she had reverted to human form and floated down to hover just over the spines of the mountain.

"Of course we did, Immanent One. It was the truth," she said.

Jin sighed. "Maybe, but you stretched it almost beyond recognition. If that's not lying its close enough."

"Immanent One -- " Frank began but Jin held up a hand.

"Right now my foot hurts, my head hurts, I'm tired and I'm thoroughly pissed at the both of you. I'm sure you can justify your actions nine ways from Sunday but I just don't want to hear it, ok?"

Ling and Frank kept a sullen silence while Jin tried to think about what had just happened. From a human perspective it made perfect sense; such a betrayal would give any human being second thoughts about their beloved, if not convert that love directly into hate.

Jin smiled.

Cause and effect. No more and no less.

Frank frowned. "Immanent One, may one ask why you are smiling?"

"Why do you want to know?"

"Because it frightens me," Frank said grimly and Ling, for all that Jin could tell, seemed to agree.

"Take me home," Jin said. "And I promise I'll stop."

CHAPTER 25

Stopping smiling was the easy part. Jin spent a big part of that afternoon in her kitchen with her violated foot in a tub of hot water and rock salt, and even longer after that sitting on the couch with her foot bandaged and elevated on a throw pillow as she went back to her neglected books. After a while she remembered why she'd stopped her studies in the first place; her head was in almost as much pain as her foot.

Jin hadn't forgotten how simple it all was at heart: Whether it was called the Divine Consciousness or Nirvana or Heaven, it was all the same. Everyone started as part of it and everyone now separated from it for whatever reason and trapped in the Cycle of Death and Rebirth was just trying, no matter how clumsily, to get home. Yet she knew one case where it emphatically was *not* true.

Shiro.

TOOK YOU LONG ENOUGH.

Jin blinked. There was no one else there. A quick glance with the Third Eye proved that, but Jin could not escape an extreme sense of *presence*. A familiar one in fact.

"Guan Shi Yin. Look, we've both been on this page a dozen times or more. Either tell me what I need to do or get out of my head."

NOT POSSIBLE ON EITHER COUNT, JIN, BUT AFTER ALL YOU'VE BEEN THROUGH, I THINK I CAN AT LEAST TELL YOU WHY ON THE FIRST ONE. SO. WOULD YOU LIKE THAT?

"What about the second one?" Jin asked.

Jin could almost picture the Guan Yin That Was smiling. IT'S LIKE TEACHER SAID: EITHER YOU ALREADY KNOW THAT OR YOU'RE AN IDIOT. AND YOU ARE NOT AN IDIOT.

"Hard to prove by the mess I've made of things so far," Jin said, rubbing her eyes, "but I'd be glad for a bone, a scrap, any hint at all."

DON'T BE SO DRAMATIC. WHATEVER HAPPENS NEXT, I'M PROUD OF YOU, JIN. I JUST WANTED YOU TO KNOW. BEING BORN AGAIN AS YOU WAS WORTH THE RISK.

Jin actually blushed, but quickly recovered her composure. "That's nice, but what's your point?"

JUST THAT LOVE, IN KARMIC TERMS, IS TOUGHER THAN FEAR, ANGER, AND OBSESSION ALL ROLLED TOGETHER, AS YOU'RE JUST STARTING TO DISCOVER. THE FACT IS THAT I COULDN'T DEFEAT LOVE, JIN. NOT AS Guan SHI YIN OR THE MORTAL GIRL THAT MARRIED SHIRO IN THE FIRST PLACE. BUT YOU CAN.

Jin tried to let that last bit sink in. "But... why me? And why won't you tell me what to do, blast it?"

BECAUSE, BLAST IT, IF I TELL YOU WHAT TO DO, YOU WON'T BE ABLE TO DO IT. LOOK, I KNOW THAT'S A PARADOX, BUT FORGET IT FOR THE MOMENT. THINK OF SHIRO. YOU KNOW HE REFUSES TO MOVE ON. WHY?

Jin frowned. "Why? He's in love with me!"

GRANTED. BUT WHY NOT MOVE ON? HE'LL ACHIEVE ENLIGHTENMENT, AND THE TIME WILL COME WHEN ALL THE WANDERING ONES HAVE RETURNED AND THERE IS NO MORE NEED FOR Guan Yin, OR HELLS, OR ANYTHING. HE'LL BE WITH US FOREVER.

"Together in spiritual harmony or whatever is not the same thing at all as being alone with the one you love, and you know it."

SURE I DO. SO WHY DON'T YOU?

Jin felt as if a door had closed, and the sense of presence was gone. Not that Guan Yin was really gone. Jin knew better. But for now Jin was as alone in her own head as it was possible to be at the moment.

She didn't think she'd learned anything particularly useful, but the conversation did get her thinking about Shiro, and progress toward transcendence. Jin thought again about the Golden Cord, and the precise moment it had appeared, linking her to Shiro. Jin frowned as she considered an entirely new possibility. Maybe she wouldn't have to convince him to move on. Maybe all she had to do was be in the right place and time when the link formed again, when, despite himself, Shiro was vulnerable.

When his spiritual ass belongs to Guan Yin.

Jin wasn't certain that what she had in mind was possible, but she was certain enough that it was worth a try. All she had to do was be present and in place when the link formed, as it eventually would. She had two choices there: she could either follow Shiro the way he had been following her, which seemed nearly impossible on the face of it. Or...

Or I can make the link happen.

Jin sighed. The devil was always in the details. Jin yawned and swung her legs over the edge of the couch. She put weight on the injured foot before she remembered and grimaced in anticipation, but it wasn't so bad as she'd feared. Jin laced on her sneakers and tried the foot again. It was tender still and Jin knew she wouldn't be running any marathons any time soon, but the foot was serviceable enough, so long as she put most of her weight on her uninjured left foot and didn't mind limping a bit.

It did occur to Jin that this might be Shiro again, but even if it was and especially in her current condition, there was no way she could catch him before he'd managed to shake off whatever transient state of mind or emotion was making him vulnerable. Jin followed the thread out of the front door. It was late afternoon, but there was still an hour or two of daylight. She paused to lock up and then continued to follow the thread in as brisk a walk as her condition allowed. This time when she reached Pepper Street the thread pulled her to the right, toward the courthouse.

This one's in Medias, whoever it is.

There were patrol cars in evidence, something you didn't see so much on the far side of Pepper Street. The courthouse itself was Greek Revival, modeled on some of the more posh antebellum mansions in Natchez. Jin walked past the portico and went through the metal detectors at the main entrance. An armed guard checked her bag and then sent her through. She paused for a moment by a directory. She'd been there once or twice for jury duty so everything was at least vaguely familiar, but it wasn't a place she thought about much. She was near a bank of two creaking elevators and the central stairwell. Upstairs were the actual courtrooms and the DMV was down the hall. The golden cord pulled down. Jin blinked. What was downstairs in the basement? She checked the directory.

Prisoner holding cells.

Jin glanced at the creaking elevators and took the stairs. Her foot was still a bit tender and she moved slowly. There was a guard station at the bottom. A bored-looking young man with thinning hair glanced up at her. "May I help you, Miss?"

Jin hesitated, glanced around, then checked the cord. She was definitely not there for the guard; the cord looped past him and through a door of iron bars to the holding cells beyond. "Oh, sorry," she said finally, "I must have taken a wrong turn. Is the DMV on the ground floor?"

"At the end of the hall."

Jin thanked the guard and went back up the stairs, slowly. She had never come across a situation where she couldn't reach the person that was ready to move on from their current hell. There was one case where said person had given her the slip -- Shiro -- but that wasn't the same thing.

Jin knew she'd have had to call on Lung Nu and Shan Cai sooner or later for her strategy against Shiro, but she'd hoped to put off calling on them in any capacity for a while longer. Jin glanced around; there was a fairly steady stream of people going about their business, including the occasional uniformed bailiff or police officer, but followed the hallway until she found an alcove to one side of a portrait of the governor. She looked around quickly to make certain there was no one in sight at that moment, then summoned Frank and Ling. Just after she did so she realized in horror that she hadn't specified their appearance, but they appeared in their standard human attire.

"Have you forgiven us?" Frank said.

"Have you learned your lesson?" Jin asked.

Ling frowned. "I don't think so. Your pardon, Immanent One, but your spiritual perspective may be... uncertain, in your present form, but ours is not. Ending Shiro's shadow existence and putting him back into the Cycle of Birth and Death is the right thing to do."

"No argument from me," Jin said, "but we disagree on how to accomplish this. Maybe if I'd been a few seconds later the point would be moot, but once I did know, I had to stop it."

Now Frank looked puzzled. "Why?"

"Because then I would have been a party to his murder, because that's what it looked like to me." Jin noted several people approaching along the corridor and lowered her voice. "My 'spiritual perspective' may be wonky, but that doesn't mean I can ignore it. Besides, if Guan Yin thought that was the answer don't you think she'd have told you to kill him long ago?" She didn't, did she?"

"Our Mistress has a kind heart -- " Frank began.

"Bullshit. If Guan Shi Yin thought destroying Shiro was the right thing to do to help him, she'd have turned him into fishbait herself and whistled while she did it. Do you doubt this?"

Frank and Ling exchanged glances again and this time Jin was a little amused to see that they actually looked a bit guilty. "Well, no," Ling was forced to admit.

"So trust her judgment, then, if you don't trust mine. The easy, simple way isn't always the right one."

"Then what is the right one?" Ling asked, and Jin shrugged.

"I have the beginnings of a notion, but I'll tell you about it later. Right now I need to get into the prisoner holding area down in the basement, preferably without being seen. I went down earlier but couldn't get past the stairwell. Is there another way?"

"More than likely," Frank said. "Let me scout a bit."

Frank vanished, and then a doorway of light opened and closed.

Jin sighed. "He's invisible now, isn't he?"

"Of course," said Ling.

"I always suspected you two could do that. I haven't been alone as much as I thought, have I?"

"This is true for all beings," Ling said piously, though she looked like she was trying not to smile.

"I'll take that as a 'yes,'" Jin said. She glanced at her watch. "Frank needs to hurry. The courthouse closes in thirty minutes."

Frank was back in five. They saw the flash of light and then Frank reappeared. Fortunately the number of people walking by was diminishing and no one saw him. "There's only one guard, which I assume you saw. There are security cameras at each end of the holding area. Could you tell if the cord was pulling you left or right from the stairwell?"

Jin shook her head. "There wasn't time, and I couldn't see far enough to get a fix on anyone."

"There are only three prisoners currently in the holding area -- two on the right side, one at the far left. I overheard the guard on the phone calling for the Sheriff's department to transfer them back to the county jail. The court is apparently finished with them for today. We have perhaps fifteen minutes before that happens."

"Can you get me in there?"

"We can persuade the light to ignore you for a time," Ling said.

"If by that you mean 'make me invisible too,' fine. Take me to just beyond the inside door. I'll take over from there."

"As you wish."

Jin thought she would feel a change when she turned invisible: a tremor, a tickle, something, but when she held up her hand the process was already complete. She waved what she thought was her hand across her face, saw nothing. Her reaction was pretty much the same child-like excitement she'd known when she saw Ling switch from true dragon to her human form for the first time, but she managed to keep it to herself this time.

This is so farkin' cool!

Jin felt herself blush and was glad Frank and Ling couldn't see her. Still, what was wrong with a little delight? It's not as if the role of Guan Yin in a human suit gave her much else besides a ton of aggravation; Jin was a bit relieved that she could still feel joy over what, compared to some of the other things she'd experienced lately, had to be the metaphysical equivalent of a card trick.

A doorway of light opened. Jin hesitated, then she felt a hand on each arm as Frank and Ling guided her through. Again Jin felt that moment of total dislocation and once more she risked a glance with her Third Eye into the void. It only lasted a moment, but that was quite long enough. In another moment they reappeared in a dim hallway.

You'd think, as much as that sight unnerves me, I'd stop looking. Maybe she wanted the reminder of the reality beyond all the appearance. Or maybe she wanted to wonder if the void was what was actually real after all.

Jin banished the distracting thought and concentrated on her surroundings. Her first impression of the dimness beyond the cold iron door didn't change. She glanced up and saw that the overhead florescent light was barely flickering. Behind her by the much brighter guard's station she could see the stairway leading up to the ground floor, and the guard at his desk idly flipping through a newspaper. Jin turned away from the door and looked down the hallway.

The cells were laid out as Frank described. Jin saw two men sitting in the rightmost cell, speaking in low voices. She didn't feel anything at first. Jin glanced toward her wrist and saw the golden cord right where it was supposed to be. Her passage through the doorway seemed to have confused it for the moment, but Jin waited patiently and, after a short time, it began to pull on her wrist again.

Good boy, Jin thought, as the cord led her past the first cell. So it wasn't either of those two. Jin kept walking. If Frank was correct, there were only three prisoners in the holding area, and no one else besides the guard up front. Her goal had to be the final prisoner. She went to the last cell.

A large black man with flecks of gray in his hair sat on the bunk. Jin stopped. She had not seen the man in some time, but she knew him beyond any doubt.

Lucius Taylor.

Jin shook her head. No. This wasn't right. It was a mistake. This particular hell wasn't through with him yet, and when it *was* he was going to one that made this one look like Paradise. All the things that Jin believed, but hadn't realized she believed, came rushing over her as she stared into the stony face of Lucius Taylor.

The cord tugged at her.

Jin shook her head. *No. You can't make me.*

The cord tugged, stronger this time. More insistent.

It's too much. Can't you see it's too much? Stop it.

The cord paid her no heed. It tugged again.

"I said stop!"

Before she even realized what she was about to do, Jin grabbed onto the cord with her free hand and tugged. She had to keep staring into the void opened by her Third Eye to keep a grip on it, but she did not let go, even when she felt that the darkness beyond the hell was staring back into her. There was an instant of unbearable pain.

The cord broke.

Jin just stared dully at the severed end of the cord that was slowly fading into nothing. Lucius looked around, startled.

"What the hell was that?" the guard was at the barred door, "Who's there? Dammit, Lucius, I know that wasn't you!"

Lucius didn't answer the guard, who fumbling with a security code pad by the door. Jin just kept staring as the remnants of the golden cord faded to nothing. She almost didn't see the shadow that moved in the corner and then faded into the greater darkness.

I can't let my anger go. Shiro, you taught me this.

There was a harsh whisper at her left ear. Jin recognized Frank's voice. "Jin, what just happened?"

"Nothing," Jin said softly as the iron door opened. "Take me home."

"But -- "

"Take. Me. Home."

They stepped through the doorway of light and vanished into the void.

CHAPTER 26

Jin woke from a troubled sleep and lay staring at the ceiling. She finally yawned and checked the clock. It was after 10:00AM, but she didn't get up immediately. There was no need to hurry.

The funeral wasn't until two.

She had halfway expected the Guan Yin That Was to show up in her dreams to rip her a new one, or Teacher to come pounding on the door demanding an explanation, but neither happened. Jin wondered if, perhaps, she had triggered the end of the world and no one noticed.

Would it matter if I had? There are many more hells than this one.

Jin pulled back the drapes. The glare made her look away, but when her eyes adjusted she could see that the world was pretty much as she'd left it. The sun was shining -- intently, in fact -- and outside her window there were trees with birds singing in them, just like yesterday. Jin stumbled to her desk to check her email but there was nothing. Not even spam. On a whim she scrolled down looking for the emails she'd gotten from her mother over the last several weeks, but of course they weren't there.

Your mother's life was rearranged to explain her absence. Why did you think you were immune?

Maybe, Jin thought, because she still remembered all those things that didn't happen, at least in this version of the world. Jin knew that, if Joyce had been freed as her mother was, the world would have rearranged itself for her as well. As things were, funeral arrangements had been made and Joyce's killer was now in jail and, thanks to Jin, he would remain there pending trial. The Board would be looking to replace Joyce, just like before. The only real difference was that now Jin's mother wasn't a candidate for the job, even if the board did happen to run out of other options. But at least no one was pretending the last several years of Joyce's life hadn't happened. Jin took some small comfort from that, so she didn't really know why.

Jin remained at her computer long enough to type out and print a letter to Frank and Ling, though she used their more formal -- and correct -- names Lung Nu and Shan Cai. She slipped this into an envelope before she called them.

"Yes, Jin?" Frank asked when they appeared. Jin handed them the envelope.

"What's this?" asked Ling.

"That is a set of very precise written instructions for how you are to proceed the next time I confront Shiro. Just so there will not be any confusion as to my intentions when and if I summon you. Read them carefully."

"Jin..." Frank began hesitantly, but Jin raised a hand.

"Frank, if whatever you're going to say is about yesterday, I've already said that I do not wish to discuss it, now or ever."

"Actually, I was going to ask if you wanted either of us to accompany you to your friend's funeral," Frank said.

Jin frowned. "You're assuming that my apparent betrayal of Shiro has turned love to hate. I only wish that were so, but I know better. And assuming Shiro is angry with me, do you really think he will attack me there?"

"If Shiro intends you physical harm now he'd attack you wherever he could. I simply think there are times when one does not wish to be alone," Frank said softly.

Jin nodded. "That was almost sweet. Thanks, but I'm pretty sure I won't be alone. I think Shiro will be there. That's why it was important to give you your instructions now."

"We will consider them very carefully," Ling said.

"You will do more than that. You will follow them to the letter...please. This is important. All right, you can go. Just be ready when I call you."

"Always," Ling said, and they disappeared.

Jin sighed. No matter how many times they did that, it still made her feel a bit like a white rabbit was going to rush by at any second, pull out his watch, and fuss about being late. Jin grinned. She had a sudden image of Teacher in his duster, sporting long white ears and a fluffy tail, checking his karmic timepiece. My, my. Everyone's late for judgment. This won't do at all.

Jin couldn't keep the smile going for very long, but she tried. She forced herself to eat a little soup when it was lunchtime, and soon after it was time to get dressed for Joyce's memorial service. Jin felt a moment of panic when she realized she had no idea if she currently owned a black outfit of any kind, but a quick sort through her closet came up with at least two outfits appropriately somber. Jin selected a demure knee length black dress and found a matching bag and shoes without having to dig too deeply.

Dammit, I should know these things.

It wasn't the uncertainty about her wardrobe as such that was so annoying. It was more the fact that this was the second time her life had been rearranged without her permission, she was more than a little sick of it already, and the only way that she could see to stop it from happening again was to never, ever have any meaningful contact with another human being as long as she lived.

"Well," she said aloud, though there was no one there, "At least that way I wouldn't have to attend any more funerals."

Her Miata was in the garage but she didn't trust herself to drive it. She thought of having Ling or Frank transport her to the service, but in the end she'd just called a taxi.

Willowbrook Funeral Home was about five miles north of the subdivision where Jin lived now, past the point where Elysian turned into State Highway 501. There were several cars in the parking lot of the chapel when Jin arrived for the viewing, though the service itself wasn't scheduled to begin for another twenty minutes. Jin recognized some of the people there. There were one or two members of the board of the Legal Aid Office, plus several former clients of Joyce's who had come to pay their respects as well. Jin knew that Joyce had few living relatives in the area and was, apparently, on the outs with most of those, but Jin was surprised that no more of her family seemed to be present.

Jin took a deep breath and went in to where the casket rested on its platform. There were flowers. Jin realized she hadn't ordered any herself. She knew she had an excuse, but that didn't seem to matter just then; she should have remembered. She glanced at one nice wreath of yellow roses and was shocked to see her own name on it.

But I didn't...oh. Shiro.

Or rather, Jonathan Mitsumo. He was standing at the back of the room; she hadn't even noticed him when she came in. He was looking at her, expressionless. Jin turned her back on him and went to see Joyce's body.

What did they do to you, Joyce...?

It wasn't just the heavy makeup the undertakers had used to cover up what must have been massive bruising on her neck. It took Jin a moment or two to realize that they had also put Joyce in a wig. Joyce had always favored very short styles because they were no trouble to take care of. The wig made her look matronly, and Jin had to resist the urge to reach in and pull the silly thing off.

"There you are, missy."

A small black woman had walked up beside Jin and was peering down at Joyce's body, and Jin realized the woman had been speaking to Joyce, not her. Jin started to leave, but she wasn't even well into her turn before the woman's next words froze Jin in place.

"I was right, missy. Don't you lie there dead and try to tell me I wasn't right."

Jin saw the resemblance. The woman looked about seventy and she might have been as heavy as Joyce was at one time, but age seemed to have burned it away and left little but skin and bone and wrinkled behind. She looked down at Joyce Masters with hard, dry eyes.

"Excuse me," Jin asked. "Are you a relative?"

The woman nodded, but she didn't look away from the body. "You could say so. I'm her mother."

"Oh, I'm sorry," Jin began, "I'm Jin Hannigan. Joyce didn't talk about her family a great deal."

"Luella Masters. How did you know my daughter, Miss Hannigan?"

"I worked with her. She was very dedicated."

The old woman sniffed. "Oh, yeah, and see where it got her at the end of her days. My Franklin worked himself to nothing to get her into that law school. She could have made it all back in no time. She had good offers. So what did she do? Threw her life away on one charity or another, not to mention that waste of a free law clinic."

Jin stiffened. "I wouldn't call that a waste."

"Call it what you want, Miss Hannigan. You don't know."

"No," Jin said, "I suppose not. I would like to ask you something, though it's none of my business."

"People always say that when they're gonna ask anyway. I'm listening."

"If you had a chance to speak to your daughter one more time, is this what you'd have told her?"

Just for an instant Jin thought she saw a softening in the old woman's features but it was no more than a hint, and soon gone. Luella Masters just shrugged. "And more besides, you just believe. She never listened no way. At least now she can't walk off when I talk to her. That's what I get to do now, rickety old bones and all. Good day, Miss Hannigan."

And I thought Joyce only had one devil on her shoulder.

Jin opened her Third Eye just a little as Luella Masters walked back out of the room and out the front door. She saw what perched on the old woman's shoulder. She was a little ashamed of herself for doing it, but not much.

If Joyce didn't listen enough I think you listen a little too much, Luella Masters. It's a pity you don't know who's doing the talking.

Jin saw a movement at her right elbow. She turned and found Shiro standing beside her in his Jonathan form.

"I see you've just met Joyce's mother. Lovely woman."

Jin just shrugged. "Lots of people get distracted by things that don't matter. You should understand that."

He smiled. "Jin, you have no idea what I understand. I sent the flowers for you, by the way. Do you like them?"

"Yes," Jin said, and added because she felt she needed to, "Thank you."

"You're welcome. See? Not impossible to have a pleasant conversation with the devil himself."

"You're not the devil, Shiro. You're not even *a* devil, though there was a time I thought so."

"That's almost a compliment," Shiro said.

"Not in my book. A devil at least is doing his job. That's more than I can say for you."

Shiro frowned. "My job? You mean the quest for Enlightenment, all that rot?"

"Yes. All that rot. The reason Guan Yin came to you in the first place."

"That's the official view," Shiro said. "It's not the truth."

"You couldn't be more wrong."

"You talk like you know, but you don't. Why are you here, Jin? And I know it's not because I'm here; I'm not that deluded."

"I came to pay my respects to Joyce's life."

"That's Jin Hannigan talking. Guan Yin wouldn't need to. Guan Yin wouldn't walk out on Joyce's murderer. You can't be her, Jin. You try so very hard, but you can't."

Jin didn't say anything. More people were approaching the casket and she stepped aside but, before she did so, Jin reached out and briefly touched Joyce's hard cold hand.

Gotta go, luv. Gotta do what I should have done for you. Forgive me, whoever you are now.

"Follow me, Shiro," Jin said.

"The service is about to start. You're not staying?"

"I've done what I needed to do here. Time for the next item on the agenda. That would be you."

Shiro frowned but he fell into step beside her. Jin walked out of the chapel and turned left. The first stones of Medias Municipal Cemetery came into view after they'd walked no more than fifty yards from the driveway to the funeral home. Jin came to the first gate that was open and walked in. Up on one of the low rolling hills she could see the green canopy that marked the grave waiting for Joyce's body. Not Joyce herself, of course. Jin knew she wasn't there, had known it since day one. Life went on, even when the physical body didn't. She would go on, after a fashion, no matter what happened today. She tried to keep that in mind even though she knew what stakes she was playing for. If she made too many mistakes she could deprive the world of Guan Yin. How long would the sentences in hell be then?

"Jin, where are you going?"

"Up on the hill. Are you coming?"

Shiro hesitated. "What are you up to?"

"Only one way for you to find out. Or are you too afraid to come out of the shadows?"

"I never intended to stay a shadow, Jin. That's not what I wanted and it never was. I'm looking forward to the day I can give up shadows forever."

"Then this is your lucky day."

He shook his head. "I don't know what you're planning, but I know you think you're going to trick me, Jin. That's not wise."

"Yeah, well I never claimed to be wise, no matter what people say about my divine form. I just know we can't go on. You're a mortal in love with Guan Yin, and she's never going to feel about you the way you feel about her. That's chapter and verse, Shiro, and somewhere in that besotted brain of yours you know it. Otherwise you'd never have created the golden cord for me to follow."

"You don't understand about that."

"Do you?" Jin asked, and was rewarded with a slight blush from Shiro.

"I'm human, believe it or not. I have lapses and, even after all this time, I have doubts. They pass. They always do. I refuse Enlightenment, so you'll never get rid of me that way."

Jin reached the hilltop. There were a few graves about, and a few large old oak trees. Jin stopped and turned back to look as Shiro walked up beside her. "What makes you think I want to get rid of you?"

He shook his head ruefully. "Oh, Jin... Do you take me for a total fool? Of course you do, just as she did."

"You speak as if we were different people."

"I know you're not, Jin. You are my love. And yet... Guan Yin would never walk away from someone in need, the way you walked away from Lucius Masters. You are Guan Yin, I don't dispute that. But you're human, too. Same as I am. Do you know how long I waited for you to be human again?"

Jin took a breath. "You knew Guan Yin would incorporate in mortal form? Why?"

"Because she knew it was the only way she could be with me. All I had to do was wait long enough."

"You really think that's true? That the Goddess of Mercy, in essence, put a multitude of suffering people on hold and incarnated as a limited, frail human being for the sole purpose of falling in love with you?"

Shiro reddened. "Is that really so hard to believe?"

"It didn't work the first time, remember? I do, thanks to you. You do love Guan Yin," Jin said. "I know that. I thought it might be something else at first, but I was wrong. I'm human now. I get to be wrong now and then. Yet you never seem to stop. You didn't take the hint when Guan Yin's servants came to kill you?"

"Don't mock me," Shiro said. "I was there, remember? I know now that was a mistake. You never sent them."

Jin felt the first tug. "Wrong again, but just so you know -- Guan Yin does love you. I do think she sent me here to prove that love to you."

"Oh? How?"

"Simple: you think I'm here as a human being so I can fall in love with you. That would indeed be the human thing to do. Reckless. Impulsive. But it's not the only thing that fits that description."

"What are you talking about?"

"I'm talking about human patience, which is not limitless. I'm talking about being tired of your crap, Shiro. Lung Nu, Shan Cai, come to Guan Yin now."

In a flash of light, Lung Nu and Shan Cai appeared. There was nothing of either Ling nor Frank about them now. They were in full divine glory, with Lung Nu in her shining dragon form and Shan Cai holding a trident of light. They floated about two feet off the ground, looking down on their mistress.

"What do you wish of us, Immanent One?"

"Just this," Jin said, pointing at Shiro, "Kill him."

CHAPTER 27

Jin could almost imagine the scene pictured in a Japanese wood block print: here was Shan Cai and Lung Nu in their full glory facing down some shadowy monster, destroying him with the power of their righteousness. There was the monster, snarling defiance, his visage horrible, his eyes fierce even though he must know he was doomed. And there was Guan Yin...

Well, there was Jin, in her black dress, pearls, and sensible shoes. That, she realized, was where the tableau broke apart, and no artist was going to render this scene if confined to the truth. Jin just hoped the illusion would hold for a little while.

Is it...?

Yes. Jin felt the touch of the golden cord. The shock and betrayal on Shiro's face was almost painful to see, but Jin did not flinch. All Shan Cai and Lung Nu had to do was distract Shiro long enough. Jin stepped forward.

One touch and your sorry ass belongs to me...

Shiro laughed as the cord snapped. Jin stopped, looking for the cord that should have connected her to Shiro, that *had* connected her to Shiro just moments before. There was nothing but a frayed, unraveling remnant that vanished while she looked at it.

Both Shan Cai and Lung Nu were poised to strike, but Shiro ignored them.

"Never play poker with me, Jin; you don't know how to bluff. It was a noble effort, and quite clever, I do admit -- turning love into hate is easier than most people think, and that's so much easier to deal with than love, isn't it? Is what I offer you really so terrible?"

Jin sighed. "I could ask you the same thing, Shiro. You have a chance to move beyond this fixation. Let me help you."

Shiro looked like he was about to burst into laughter once more. "Oh, Jin, did you think it was going to be that easy? That all you had to do was connect with me and send me back to one hell or another? Did you really not know?"

Shan Cai and Lung Nu had reluctantly abandoned all pretense of attacking and were looking back at her for guidance. For the moment Jin ignored them too. "Not know what?"

"How many times you've already sent me back, Jin."

"Guan Yin freed you before? But... your memories! You had a blank slate! How could this have happened again?"

He shook his head, looking disgusted. "Guan Yin, I love you. Don't you understand what that means, even after all these centuries? No matter how many times I forget, no matter how many times I drink at the Terrace of Oblivion, sooner or later I find your image in whatever hell I'm sent to and it starts again. Then I use Emma-O's gift and I *leave,* and I always find you again, Guan Yin. There's no where you can go that I cannot follow, sooner or later. While Emma-O's gift makes my task easer, the simple truth is that *Hell does not work on me*!"

"Immanent One," Shan Cai began, but Jin held up a hand.

"Shan Cai, is he telling me the truth?"

"I really think -- " Lung Nu began, but Jin cut her off, too.

"Answer me, Shan Cai."

Shan Cai looked trapped, and finally admitted defeat. He nodded. "Yes, Immanent One. Shiro speaks truly."

"Then why do you fear my demon form, Shiro? And don't try to tell me you don't. I'm not blind."

Shiro shrugged. "Because I don't exactly *enjoy* being ripped apart, my love. It hurts. Plus it's one more delay. I think my patience may be infinite, but a thousand years or more is still a long time."

Now Jin understood why Guan Yin hadn't just killed Shiro. To return him to the Wheel of Death and Rebirth. She'd already tried that and it didn't work.

"Shan Cai, Lung Nu, thank you both for your service to me. I do appreciate all that you've tried to do and I apologize for not being as good at being Guan Yin as perhaps I should. You may go now," she said.

Shan Cai and Lung Nu shook off their divine forms and stood beside Jin as Frank and Ling once more. "Immanent One, what do you intend to do?" Frank asked.

"That's between me and Shiro," Jin said. "I'm sorry, but that's the way it has to be."

Frank started to protest, but Ling put her hand on his shoulder. He turned to look at her and Ling shook her head. "We must go." Ling turned to Jin and smiled a little sadly. "Goodbye, Guan Shi Yin."

Ling opened a doorway and pulled a confused-looking Frank through behind her as if she was leading a small child. Jin watched them go.

I think Ling understands, Jin thought, *I just hope that I do.*

Shiro was looking at her with the light of love in his eyes. "Have you finally decided to come to me, my love? Can it be?"

Shiro took a step forward but Jin took one back. Then she turned her back on him and started walking down the hill.

Shiro frowned. "Where are you going?"

Jin didn't break stride. "Does that matter? I cannot escape you, remember? You've been my shadow for over a thousand years. That's your choice and obviously I can't make you choose differently. So follow me for just a little longer, shadow."

"You're mocking me."

She shrugged. "Does that matter, if you've won?"

"If you do not love me I have won nothing!"

"When did I say I didn't love you?" Jin asked reasonably.

Shiro hurried to catch up with her quickly. "I'm not a fool, Jin. Guan Yin loves everyone; that's not what I meant and you know it! I want you to love *me*... and only me."

Jin nodded, sadly. "Shiro, once I wondered if I did love you. I was afraid I might. Then I shared the memory of a girl who had been in love, truly in love. Thanks to you I've also shared the memory of that other incarnation of Guan Yin, the one who married you all those years ago. She did love you, but only because it was what you needed at the time. I do not. I will not."

"You will. That's why you became human again, Jin. Not to search for a 'solution' that does not exist. With all due respect, what makes you think you can overcome my love where the divine Guan Yin failed?"

"But she did not fail, Shiro. She found the solution."

"What solution?"

"Me," Jin said quietly.

Shiro smiled with great good humor. "Oh, she hints at mysteries and things beyond mortal ken, and her nature may be divine, but right here and now she's just a mortal woman, no more or less."

Jin smiled. "Which is exactly the point. I am Guan Yin. I am also Jin Lee Hannigan, daughter to the lately departed Margaret Kathleen Hannigan. And it's Jin Hannigan who's going to settle your hash. You said I can't bluff, Shiro. You're right. Am I bluffing now?"

Shiro started to say something, but apparently reconsidered and kept silent. Jin set a brisk pace along the shoulder of the road, despite her uncomfortable shoes and sore foot. There were no really tall buildings in Medias, but it was still possible to make out the downtown area in the haze of distance. Shiro followed her in silence for some time, but after about a mile he spoke again.

"Jin, that outfit of yours isn't really made for hiking," Shiro said finally.

True enough. The dress was a little long and her shoes, if not exactly spikes, did have a three-inch heel that she wasn't really used to. "No," she said, cheerfully. "You're right about that."

"So why don't you just summon your servants to open a doorway to wherever it is you wish to go?"

"They're not my servants now. Weren't you listening?"

Shiro just stared at her for a moment as they walked, and Jin barely managed not to smile. "Jin, Shan Cai and Lung Nu may not be my favorite people, Enlightened or otherwise, but they *are* the servants of Guan Yin. They chose that role for themselves, and you accepted them ages ago."

Jin smiled. "Changing my mind goes with the territory. Isn't that what you're counting on?"

Shiro raised an eyebrow. "You're up to something."

"You're absolutely right," Jin said. "Keep following me and I'll show you what it is."

"If you're thinking of killing yourself so that you can return to divine form, I'd advise against it. Suicide is an error and invites karma."

"Since you want me in my addled human form, of course you would say that. You'd say anything to win me."

Shiro blushed again, but he did not back down. "It's true I love Guan Yin, but I have love great enough for a woman and the goddess within her. Your human form or your divine form, they're all the same to me."

Jin sighed. "You think so? Then you really are an idiot."

"Don't bother goading me, Jin. Are you actually going to try another of your silly traps? If that's what this is about we can stop here."

She shook her head. "No traps, no tricks, just a rather straightforward transaction. But I suspect there are legalities involved, so I'll probably need witnesses. That's where you come in."

"Witnesses? Don't tell me you're planning to marry me again?"

Jin smiled grimly. "Keep that sense of humor, Shiro. You're going to need it."

The silence was longer this time. Shiro looked intently thoughtful and Jin smiles again, though she was careful to look away from Shiro when she did so. The road stretched on and she kept up her pace. Jin finally passed the street leading to her house. Her feet hurt and she was perspiring, but she did not stop.

"Jin, tell me where you're going."

"I'm going to find Teacher... Emma-O, as you know him better. The King of Hell."

"Why?"

"Because I need witnesses for what I'm about to do. I told you that."

"Why do you need the King of the First Hell? Being a witness is not such a complicated matter, regardless of what you have in mind. Anyone would do."

"Not for this. Maybe I should ask him to send for Madame Meng, too," Jin said, thoughtfully.

After a while they passed the gate to Resolution Park, and Jin glanced inside, but saw no one. For a moment she actually considered asking Shiro to go check the men's room, but a glance from her Third Eye told her what she already suspected -- Teacher was not there. Jin sighed and kept walking. By the time she reached Pepper Street she was limping. She headed gamely toward the alley leading to the Gateway to All the Hells. Shiro, after a moment's hesitation, followed her in.

"What are the odds Teacher is at the Gateway? It'd beat walking all the way to the First Hell."

"Jin, tell me why we're here," Shiro said. "Whatever you're planning, it's a waste of time."

"If you're so sure of that, then there's no risk, is there?" Jin replied.

"I will always be where you are, go where you need to go," Shiro said. "That is destiny."

"Bullshit. Suppose I told you to stay away from me?

"But why? I will not interfere with your work, I promise."

Jin held up her wrist. "Careful, Shiro. Pain of any kind is what calls Guan Yin. Put your wounded pride on ice and answer me. I told you where we're going."

"You haven't told me *why*, though. Why are we going to the Gateway? What do you need witnesses for?"

"Answer my question, and I'll answer yours, Shiro. Promise."

"I... I won't stay away. I..." He didn't finish, but Jin just nodded.

"And that is the truth. You *can't*. You say I can never be free from you, but I think it's as much the other way around."

Shiro nodded, looking miserable. "I've never wanted to be a problem for you, Guan Shi Yin, then or now. If you don't believe anything else I've told you, please believe that."

She smiled then. "I do believe you, Shiro. Not that it changes anything. I'm Guan Yin. I have to free you from hell. That's what I do."

"But I told you -- "

"That you have the keys to all the hells? Wrong. You don't have the key to the one you're in *now*, the one you carry with you always. The one that looks just like me. So. I promised to tell you my plan. I'm about to do that, too."

They reached the doorway on the opposite side of the corridor and Jin walked right through with Shiro close behind. Down by the statue of Guan Yin and her servants, Teacher and Madame Meng were waiting for them. Jin wasn't really surprised. She'd called them, even though she wasn't quite sure how. One more aspect of being Guan Yin that she didn't understand, but she was grateful, and only partly because her feet hurt. She kicked off her shoes and let her bare toes sink into the sand covering the floor of the Gateway to All the Hells.

"In fact," Jin went on to Shiro, "let's go meet our old friends and I can tell you all at once."

Shiro put a hand on her shoulder. It was a firm grip, and the memories came flooding back, deeper and more intently than that first day. She steeled herself and let them come. She did not flinch this time when the vision took her through their wedding night in her previous mortal incarnation and through the years they had spent together as man and wife. She finally saw past the shadow this time, to what Shiro had been before and what he remained now -- a good man, like so many other good men down through the centuries whose only and greatest sin was that he could not let go.

"Please, Jin. Tell me now."

"I'm going to renounce my oath as a Bodhisattva. I'm no longer going to be Guan Yin."

Shiro took his hand off her shoulder. "Does this mean...? " he began, hopefully, but Jin had learned all too well that mercy and kindness were not the same thing. She crushed his hope like she would a biting fly.

"What were you thinking, Shiro? That, freed from my duties, you and I would set up housekeeping? Well, say that we do. What happens after?"

Shiro frowned. "We would be happy. I...I would be happy."

"As always, you're not thinking this through, Shiro. You may be outside the Cycle at present but as Jin Hannigan I most certainly am not. I will grow old, and I will die."

"And I will mourn you, my love, but you will be reborn, and wherever you go, I will find you."

Jin shook her head. "Try again, Shiro. The human avatar of Guan Yin may have accumulated some karmic debts to pay, but Guan Yin herself, your *true* love, is an Enlightened Being and renouncing her oath does not change that. She will pass into the Divine Flame or Transcendence or whatever you want to call it. Not that what you call it matters -- it is the one place that, by *your own choice*, you cannot follow her. Ever."

Shiro finally understood. His knees were actually shaking. "You won't. You wouldn't!"

"Watch me."

Shiro jumped in front of her and put his hands on both shoulders, holding her back. "I won't let you!"

Over Shiro's shoulder Jin saw Teacher running forward but she held up a hand to stop him and he obeyed, though with obvious reluctance. Jin looked into Shiro's eyes and faced the pain she saw there. She knew what that pain might make him do. She wondered if he knew as much.

"How are you going to stop me, Shiro?" In an instant she was in full demon form, and the grip he'd held on her shoulder was now transferred to her robes somewhere around the height of her belly button.

Shiro held his ground. "I'll... I just will! I'm not afraid of you!"

"Yes, you are, and it's not because of my demon form." Jin reverted to human shape and put a hand on his arm. "Shall I tell you why, Shiro? You're afraid of me because you know the only way you can stop me now is to kill me. Are you willing to do that, you who love me so much?" She already saw the answer in his eyes, but she waited to hear it from him.

"You would be reborn..."

She shrugged. "Which is rather beside the point. Kill me if that's the best you can do, and you go directly into the Avici Hell, which is the one place *I* can't reach *you* and those keys you received from Teacher are useless. Either way, we're separated for eternity. Deal with it."

He just looked at her for several seconds with an awful sadness. "You would deprive the world of Guan Yin just to spite me? Could you really be so cruel?"

"You call me cruel? Sooner or later your 'love' will chain me to the Wheel of Death and Rebirth and what is Guan Yin then? You want me for *yourself*, Shiro, and the world be damned. Well, if the world can't have Guan Yin, neither can you! I'll make sure of it here and now."

"You don't mean that..." Shiro began, but it was a lie and they both knew it.

Jin slapped him hard across the face. "Shiro, my love, I will do whatever it takes. Do you understand me? *Whatever it takes*. First I married you, then I hid from you. Right now I would flay the skin from your back six days a week and have a barbeque with the rest on Sunday if that would get through to you! Now either kill me or let me go. Those are your only options."

Shiro held his grip for several long seconds, but when he finally did release her he was smiling a grim smile. "You're wrong."

"How so?"

"First of all, Jin, you make a damn poor Guan Yin. I told you that before and it's the truth. After all, you abandoned that poor man in prison just because of some misguided sense of revenge. The Guan Yin I know would never have done that!"

Jin shrugged. "Maybe I'm not the Guan Yin you know. That doesn't mean I'm wrong."

"But you are wrong. I do have another option."

"Now *you're* bluffing," Jin said, though she prayed to whoever might be listening that he wasn't.

He grinned, and threw Jin's own words back at her. "Watch me."

Shiro walked straight up to Teacher, still standing some distance away.

"King of the First Hell, I release you of your promise made to me so long ago and I submit myself to your will and judgment." He nodded toward both Madame Meng and Jin. "I accept whatever you decide, and will bear it as long as necessary. So let these worthies bear witness. So let it be."

Teacher just stared at him for several long seconds. Then he finally sighed. "All right, Shiro. Let's go back to hell, shall we? And, may I say, it's about damn time."

EPILOGUE

"Do you have any idea what you almost did?"

Jin was seated on the dais of the statue of Guan Yin having tea with Madame Meng when Teacher came stomping back into the Gateway to All the Hells. Jin continued to sip her tea.

"Yes," she said, calmly. "I almost deprived the world of Guan Yin."

Teacher shook with barely controlled fury. "I cannot believe you would be so reckless! And for what? One man? No one is worth that!"

Jin thought of the girl called Azuki who was also Guan Yin. Probably, Jin thought, even more Guan Yin than she herself was. "Teacher, everyone is worth that," she said, "or no one is worth anything. That's the choice."

For a few long moments Teacher Johnson looked like someone who had just had a bucket of cold water dumped over his head. There was nothing but shock and surprise on his face. Then he started to laugh. Jin and Madame Meng continued to drink their tea while he pulled himself together. Teacher shook his head, looking chagrined. "And they call *me* 'Teacher.'" He leaned forward, studying Jin carefully. "Is it you, Guan Shi Yin? Do you remember yourself now?"

"I remember nothing beyond this one life, but I was always Guan Shi Yin."

Teacher sighed. "Pity. I would have liked to have known the real plan."

Now Madame Meng glanced toward heaven and sighed. "This *was* the real plan. Honestly, Emma-O -- I thought you'd have worked that out by now."

Teacher frowned. "This? This hap-hazard, stumbling sort of dumb luck ploy?!"

Jin cut in. "Teacher, what did you expect? Omens? Portents? A host of demons in full battle gear? The destruction of worlds? If I'd thought any of the above would have worked, I'd have arranged more of a show."

"That's not what I meant!"

"Wasn't it? Besides, if Shiro in his blindness and hurt had killed me, in cosmic terms that barely rates a 'so what?' That would have been the end of the avatar known as Jin Hannigan, unfortunately for me, but certainly not of Guan Yin herself."

Teacher shook his head. "I know that. Better, if Shiro had killed you he would have been banished to the Avici hell and Guan Yin would have been immediately returned to her normal divine state, and I score that 'win-win.' I assumed the plan was to provoke Shiro into doing just that. I didn't expect you to threaten to renounce your bodhisattvahood!"

Jin laughed. "Threaten, Teacher? I was *going to do it*, as you damn well know. Besides, the Avici Hell would only have buried the problem," she said. "Not ended it. Either way, if Guan Yin planned for me to die then technically she planned on committing suicide. Beyond the pale for a Bodhisattva, yes?"

Madame Meng spoke up. "Not exactly. I believe that is another reason Guan Yin drank from my fountain: with no memory or understanding of the danger she had placed herself in, you'd be hard pressed to assert that she had committed suicide. Say rather that she knew it was a risk, but that's all."

Jin nodded, slowly. "I can see that. Suicide wasn't even the greatest risk. Guan Yin would never renounce her oath as a Bodhisattva, but Jin Hannigan? She would. Shiro had seen me bluff before. He knew I wasn't bluffing this time, or it wouldn't have worked. That's why Guan Yin That Was couldn't tell me what to do. I had to figure it out on my own."

"Speaking of whom, do you want to know what I did with Shiro?" Teacher asked.

Jin shook her head. "No need. I have a feeling I'm going to see him soon enough...not that he'll remember me this time. Hell's going to work for him now."

"Sooner or later he will remember."

Jin smiled a wan smile. "Doesn't matter. He still loves me, but now he won't leave any hell until he's actually ready to leave. And I won't come to him one moment before. This part is over. Another has just begun."

"Smart girl," Teacher said. "What now?"

"As for myself," Madame Meng said, rising. "Pleasant as this has been, I have work to do."

Jin put her empty cup back on the tray, which a moment later had vanished along with Madame Meng. "I think that's probably true of all of us."

"Jin, you've done what you were put here to do. There's no need to stay in your human form. Personally I plan to abandon mine quite soon."

"And I'll mourn you, since it's the human thing to do. And that's what I am. It's not a 'form.' Teacher, this is *me*, right here, right now. Besides, I still have at least one more thing that I need to do as Jin Hannigan and not as Guan Yin. After that, feel free to convince me. But I warn you: I'm stubborn."

He smiled. "Suit yourself, but I guess you always do."

Teacher took his own separate way out of the Gateway to All the Hells. Jin remained alone seated on the dais.

Well, not quite alone.

"How did you know?" she asked. She glanced up at the serene golden face far above her. "Girl, I'm talking to you."

SO I ASSUMED. COULD YOU BE MORE SPECIFIC?

"How did you know I'd figure it out?"

WHAT DO YOU THINK YOU'VE 'FIGURED OUT,' JIN?

"Don't play coy with me. Not now. This was your plan, wasn't it? That I would confront Shiro, despite your warnings?"

YOU SAID IT YOURSELF, LUV -- YOUR CONFRONTATION WITH SHIRO WAS INEVITABLE, AND THERE WERE ONLY TWO POSSIBLE RESULTS. I THINK YOU MADE THE BETTER CHOICE, FOR WHAT THAT'S WORTH. HOW DID I KNOW? ARE YOU SO SURE I DID?

"No. That's why I want to hear it from you," Jin said grimly.

I AM YOU, JIN. HOW COULD I NOT KNOW WHAT I WOULD DO TO REDEEM SHIRO, OR ANYONE ELSE, GIVEN THE CHANCE? There was a pause, then: SOMEONE'S CALLING YOU.

"I know. And if you're really me, you know who and why. Two more questions before I go: Why Medias? And you knew my mother, once upon a time, and not as a client. What was she to you?"

IN ANSWER TO BOTH YOUR QUESTIONS: SHE WAS MY MOTHER, TOO. ONCE UPON A TIME.

Jin just shook her head. "Damn, I *am* an idiot."

EXCEPT WHEN YOU'RE NOT. YOU'VE GOT WORK TO DO, JIN. SHAN CAI AND LUNG NU ARE WAITING FOR YOU.

"I released them."

YOU CAN'T, OR AT LEAST NOT FOR LONG. LIKE IT OR LUMP IT, THEY COME WITH THE JOB. LATER, LUV.

In an hour's time Jin stepped through a portal into a jail cell where a man was awaiting a sentencing at once far worse and far better than he ever suspected or, deep down, believed he deserved.

"Hello, Lucius," Jin said.

He looked up, startled. "Jin? Jin Hannigan? Is that you?"

She smiled a little wistfully at him. "Yes, Lucius, it's me... more or less."

"How -- how did you get in here?"

"Never mind that. The important thing is: how do you get out?"

"I don't understand."

Jin nodded. "You sure as hell don't. Not yet, anyway. So, Lucius--you got a minute? We need to talk."

ABOUT THE AUTHOR

Richard Parks has been writing and publishing fantasy and science fiction longer than he cares to remember…or probably can remember. His work has appeared in *Asimov's SF*, *Realms of Fantasy*, *Lady Churchill's Rosebud Wristlet*, and several "Year's Best" anthologies. His first collection, **The Ogre's Wife**, was a World Fantasy Award Finalist in 2002 and he's also been a nominee for the Mythopoeic Award for Adult Literature. He blogs at "Den of Ego and Iniquity Annex #3", also known as: www.richard-parks.com

Personal Note: With or without a traditional publisher (I've gone both ways), it's hard for any writer to develop a readership in these days of fractured genres. If you enjoyed ATGOH, I would appreciate it if you would consider reviewing the book at Amazon, B&N, or the venue of your choice. Word of mouth and reader endorsements are simply the best advertising there is.

Made in the USA
Columbia, SC
09 January 2020

86582453R00170